THE MARATHON

WATCH

"ROSS"

SECOND EDITION

Larry. Las

D1502149

DEDICATION

To all the men of the USS *William M. Wood* DD-715 and to Captains Barker, Tsantes, and Castano—three of the finest captains it has been my honor to serve.

On his way to the US Embassy in Athens where he was stationed as naval attaché, Captain Tsantes and his driver were gunned down by a terrorist on a motorcycle in 1988.

Larry Laswell

ACKNOWLEDGMENTS

To Carol, whose interest, assistance, and support rekindled the fire I needed to finish *The Marathon Watch*.

Special thanks to Lindsay and my friends at Vistage.

PROLOGUE

In the early 1970's, the world lived under the threat of nuclear annihilation. The United States and Russia had thousands of nuclear-tipped missiles aimed at each other, and Cold War tensions grew greater every day. With no effective defense against a nuclear attack, Pentagon strategists created a doctrine of deterrence they called MAD (Mutual Assured Destruction).

A limited nuclear exchange of two to three dozen nuclear warheads was the only nuclear war scenario one could contemplate. Either national leaders would use restraint, or the human race would go extinct. War strategists believed that a limited nuclear exchange would devolve into a protracted naval war of attrition.

During this period, the compass of military doctrine was swinging towards today's high-tech military. The Pentagon had several high-tech weapons on the drawing board: Aegis for the Navy, stealth technology for the Air Force, and the M1A1 Abrams tank for the Army. The budgets for these systems were both historic and enormous.

Against this backdrop, the highly unpopular Viet Nam war raged on. Without any clear objectives or progress in the war, the American people had lost faith in their military. The My Lai Massacre, the napalm bombing of Trảng Bàng, and the Kent State Massacre fueled massive anti-war street demonstrations.

Congressmen and senators walked a political tight rope to show support for a strong military on the right, and support for anti-war sentiment on the left. Pentagon bashing became the political game *du jour* on Capitol Hill.

1

BREAKDOWN

August 1971, The Aegean Sea off the coast of Greece
Operation Marathon: Day 399

Ross hated August north of the equator. The hot, humid August days made engine room conditions almost unbearable. The USS *Farnley*'s engine room ran hotter than most others, and today, August served up its hottest day yet.

Seated on a battered wooden bench, Master Chief Machinist Mate Ross kept an eye on his throttlemen. Stucky and Burns both jerked their throttle valve open another eighth turn. That was the third time in the last past five minutes, but their speed held steady. Things weren't adding up.

Ross scanned the twenty-odd gauges mounted on the white enameled board above the throttlemen's heads. Steam pressure held at six hundred pounds, temperature at six-eighty, and vacuum at twenty-nine inches. The readings seemed okay. *I must be getting paranoid,* he thought.

Out of habit, Ross checked the gauge board again. This time he didn't see the gauges; instead, he took in the entire board. A year ago, the white enameled steel board had glistened; now it was covered in grease and grime. The board disgraced him. He told himself he didn't care. It was impossible to maintain his self-esteem aboard this bucket. It wasn't worth the effort.

Ross bent forward to rest his elbows on his knees and think. He hated the *Farnley* and wished he could forget the last year of his life. Except for dreaming about the day he would leave this ship, his present assignment held no hope and no pleasant memories.

Why the navy decided to shaft the *Farnley*, her crew, and him was a mystery. It wasn't fair; that wasn't part of the deal. He was tired and wanted to get off the *Farnley* and out of the navy. He just needed to survive eleven more months without screwing up.

Do your time, retire, and escape.

Ross' mind wandered, but the feeling that something was wrong pulled him back. He twirled his screwdriver in his fingers to give him something to do. Dozens of problems worth worrying about could cause

2

an increase in steam demand.

Why should I care? This isn't my engine room, and it isn't my ship.

Elmo, a cockroach and engine room mascot, scurried across the deck plates toward the bench, providing Ross a welcome diversion. On any other ship, Elmo would be a problem but not on the *Farnley*. Ross told himself he didn't care and shook his head to convince himself.

Hundreds of roaches infested the engine room and thousands infested the ship, but everyone knew Elmo. The crew envied his gift for not caring and for not being bothered by anything. Like all cockroaches, Elmo was the quintessential survivor, so the crew accepted him as a fellow shipmate and honored him. After painting a single red chevron on his back, they gave him the honorary rank of petty officer third class.

In a sharp movement, Stucky spun his throttle open an additional half turn.

"Stucky, what's your speed?" Ross yelled over the noise.

Stucky checked his shaft tachometer and turned his head to see Ross. "One hundred ten revolutions. Making turns for ten knots."

"You been holding steady?"

"Absolutely, Chief."

"Then why do you keep opening the throttle?"

Stucky shrugged. "Don't know. Didn't think it was worth worrying about."

Ross hated the words *not worth*. Most everything on the *Farnley* was not worth doing or worth worrying about or worth the effort. Every time he said those words to himself, a piece of him died, but it wasn't worth the fight; he couldn't win.

Burns jerked his throttle open a quarter turn. Something's wrong, he thought. You always tell your men, "Always stay alert down here. Your life and your shipmates' lives depend on it. The machinery can eat you alive. The high-voltage wiring can fry you, and six-hundred-pound steam'll cook you dead in seconds."

Pay attention.

Ross scanned the gauge board again. The condenser vacuum was falling. The problem centered on the condenser. Ross thought he could make out a high-pitched sound barely audible over the noise, but he couldn't be sure. He strained to pick the sound out of the cacophony. It eluded him. Perhaps it was something he felt, or he might have been imagining it. Nothing was ordinary on the *Farnley*. The engine room was full of sick equipment making unnatural noises.

The sound Ross heard came back a bit louder. The tormented scream was familiar, and his ears picked the sound out of the chaotic racket. What was it? Screaming in agony, a bearing sang its high-pitched song

3

of death. The hair on the back of his neck stood up, and the shock wave of adrenaline blasted through his body. The main condensate pump was about to seize.

With only one of four pumps operational, the situation was critical. If the pump failed, a wall of water would back into the steam turbines. When solid water hit the high-speed turbine blades, the result would be explosive. The resulting hail of hot metal shards would tear a human body to bits. For anyone aft of the gauge board, death would be horrific and instantaneous.

Ross bolted from his position and slid down the ladder to the lower level. His feet hit the lower catwalk deck plates with a metallic bang. Heads turned.

He yelled, "Clear the lower level! Everyone forward! Now!"

Dropped tools rattled into the bilge as firemen clattered across the web of catwalks. Ross kept moving. He flung himself over the railing and dropped the last four feet into the bilge. His feet splashed in the half inch of black, oily water. He was right; the high-pitched sound he heard was coming from the condensate pump.

Despite his forty-seven years, Ross vaulted over the catwalk guardrail and ran up the ladder to the main level. On the main level, he pushed through the excited firemen, reached for the bridge intercom, and yelled, "Bridge, Main Control! Request all-stop. We've got a problem down here with the condensate pump."

The reply was immediate. "Main Control, this is the captain. Negative on the all-stop. If you have a problem down there, fix it."

Shit, why is the captain always on the bridge? Ross thought for a second and pressed the send button again.

"Captain, this is Ross. If we lose the pump, we lose power and probably damage the pump. We need time. I told you this might happen with only one pump."

"Chief, if you have a problem, fix it. You're not stopping my ship in the middle of the ocean so you can baby one of your pumps. We're going to continue making turns on both screws. Those are my orders. Do you understand?"

"I can't stop the inevitable. Christ, Captain! You could kill somebody down here."

"Chief, it's not inevitable for someone who knows what he's doing. I'm tired of your insubordination and won't take any more. You have your orders. Make them so."

A year earlier, Ross would have bristled at those words. He wanted to now, but his pride failed him. It was no use arguing with an ass like Captain Javert.

What's the use? It's his ship, not mine. Eleven more months. Survive. Follow orders.

Ross hit the send button again. "Aye, aye, Captain."

To the six firemen huddled behind the gauge board, Ross said, "All of ya, out of here. Get me a cup of coffee or something, but get back quick when the lights go out."

Ross turned his attention to the gauges as the six men scrambled up the ladder like terrified plebes. Stucky, still at his throttle, wiped his sweaty hands on his tattered dungarees. "What now, Chief?" he asked.

"Stay on your toes."

The expression on Stucky's freckled face told Ross he hadn't answered the question. Without looking, Ross knew the eyes of the four remaining men were asking the same question. "You're safe forward of the gauge board," he yelled so everyone would hear.

Ross thought about warning Fireman Canterbury and his boiler room crew. With only fourteen months aboard the *Farnley*, Canterbury was the senior man on the boiler team. Ross cursed to himself. By normal standards, it takes four years' experience to run a boiler crew. Damn this ship! Ross knew what was going to happen. No danger there.

Ross stepped onto the wooden bench and stretched to reach the wheel on the main steam stop valve. His hands slipped on the warm, oily metal of the thirty-inch valve wheel. He wiped his hands on his trousers and tried again. This time, his purchase held. With a hand on each side of the valve wheel, Ross stood spread-eagled. He listened and waited.

The scream of the bearing became clearly audible. Ross braced himself to close the valve to shut off the flow of steam. The bone-chilling screech from the pump peaked. Ross tugged at the valve wheel. It gave a few inches, then jammed.

The pump's scream rose to a crescendo and abruptly ended as the pump seized. The turbines' whine turned into a growing deep, ominous growl. Within seconds, the turbines would explode. "All-stop! Close the throttles," Ross screamed as loud as he could.

The growl of the turbines held steady for a second, then died away as the panic-stricken throttlemen closed their valves.

Ross pursed his lips as the dial on the steam pressure gauge inched toward the danger zone. The boiler room crew wasn't paying attention.

§

In the boiler room, the boilers continued to produce steam with nowhere to go. The boiler room crew, standing in glazed-eyed boredom, didn't notice. Within seconds, the boiler pressure rose to almost seven hundred pounds and forced the safety valves open.

The explosive venting of steam through the stacks blocked out all other sensations. The sound possessed the boiler room. Canterbury's organs shook, his stomach quaked, and his lungs tingled from the vibration. Scarcely aware of the warm, moist burst of urine on his leg, Canterbury yanked the boiler's emergency kill switch. He was the fourth of six men up the escape ladder.

§

Deprived of steam, the electric generators spun to a stop, and the ship went dark. In Main Control, Ross waited for the battle lanterns to click on. Deprived of electricity, the *Farnley*'s motors, blowers, and other equipment went silent. Only the distant lapping sound of the ocean and an occasional echo from a drop of water falling into the bilge could be heard. A wave of angry despair washed the energy from his body.

This wasn't the deal. It wasn't the way his navy worked. He wanted to be able to do his job, to teach and mentor his crew. He wanted his pride and sense of accomplishment back. The heartbreaking silence shamed Ross.

Stucky turned toward Ross. "What happened, Chief?"

With a tired, fluid movement, Ross retrieved his screwdriver and turned toward the freckle-faced sailor. "Son, we've just done got *Farnley*ed. Again."

§

Minutes earlier, perched in his captain's chair, Commander Alan Javert carefully released the intercom's send button with his left toe, then froze in position as he listened to Ross' reply of "Aye, aye, Captain." He worried that the bridge crew would notice his awkward movement. He hated his Ichabod Crane body because it made it difficult to look and move like other ships' captains. Careful to make his movements deliberate but graceful, he withdrew his foot from the intercom and settled back into his chair to study the horizon.

Despite his effort, the movement still felt awkward. It was impossible to make his long, skinny legs move with the sure grace of an athlete. He told himself his body wasn't his fault and focused his thoughts on what to do next. He didn't know what to do. Mentally he panicked. What could he do? What should he do? Why was the world against him?

Javert couldn't tolerate challenges to his authority. He was the captain. He had to be decisive; that's what captains were. He couldn't fall behind schedule and let the world know he couldn't get the job done. Fearful the bridge crew would see through him, he kept his outward appearance calm as if he'd accepted Chief Ross' "Aye, aye, Captain" as a *fait accompli.*

The knot in Javert's stomach hardened into a painful, tight ball of muscle, and dizziness swept over him. Fearful he would fall from the chair, he clenched the arms with both hands. He riveted his eyes on the horizon and hoped its stability would give him equilibrium. He fidgeted and tried to compose himself. Composure was another captainly trait he tried to imitate.

The *Farnley*'s problems weren't his fault. He was a good captain with the experience and qualifications for command. His real problem was the incompetent group of disloyal officers and men the navy had given him. Other captains wouldn't put up with the derelicts he'd been given. He'd done the right thing by putting Ross in his place, but that didn't fix the pump. He had to do something. Other captains would. If he didn't do something quickly, the crew would know he didn't know what to do.

Anxiously, Javert turned to look across the gray, shadowy bridge to find Biron, the conning officer. All he could see was shadows. Half panic-stricken, he started to get out of his chair until he spotted the brown smudge of a khaki uniform in the distance. Standing on the far bridge wing, Biron leaned on the rail and calmly watched the sea. Reassured of Biron's location, Javert cleared his throat and settled back into his chair. What have I done wrong? he wondered.

When Javert had taken command of the *Farnley*, he'd forgotten about the cliquish nature of a destroyer crew like the *Farnley*'s or the *Renshaw*'s, where he'd been the gunnery officer during the Korean War. At OCS, they told him that the unique culture aboard a ship was almost tribal. He remembered how the crew revered the captain, loved him, respected him, feared him, and would die for him. At the time, he'd assumed crews always treated their captains that way because captains demanded it. Now he understood he had had it backwards; the crew demanded it of the captain. The captain had to come up to the crew's standards.

Javert tried to be likable, and failing at that, he tried to earn their respect by being commanding. That wasn't working either. Javert suspected the men had lost respect for him. He could see it in their looks, and he heard it in Ross' voice. They no longer followed his orders willingly or paid attention to his wishes. He'd done everything he thought other captains would do. Still, it wasn't enough.

The abrupt roar of escaping steam rent the quiet evening air. At first, Javert thought a CO2 fire extinguisher had discharged, but the sound was far too loud.

The status board keeper went rigid. "Sir, aft lookout reports lifting safeties."

Biron, already back on the bridge, shouted, "Very well!" as he headed for the intercom. Passing the helmsman, he yelled, "All-stop. Rudder amidships."

The roaring sound of escaping steam stopped as suddenly as it had begun. As Biron reached for the intercom, relays clicked, and in unison, red indicator lights dimmed, then blinked out. The ship went silent, lifeless, dead in the water.

Javert, self-conscious about his awkward body, resisted the urge to stand. Carefully controlling his voice, he turned to Biron and said, "Find out what happened and get it fixed. Get the emergency diesel started so we have power. I won't allow us to fall behind schedule."

Without power, the intercom was useless. Biron removed the sound-powered telephone handset from its cradle and turned his back to Javert. "Bridge, Main Control. What's your status?"

Javert squinted at the darkness as the aft bridge door opened and a man entered. Javert recognized the boxerlike silhouette as that of Lieutenant Commander Meyers, the *Farnley*'s executive officer. Many people mistook Meyers for a marine due to his thick neck and muscular upper body. Even in silhouette, he was hard to miss. Meyers hurried toward Javert and Biron. "What happened?" Meyers asked.

Biron lifted his head slightly. "Dropped the load. Diesel generator is coming online. Condensate pump, I think."

Biron lowered his head, directing his attention to the phone. "Bridge, aye." He looked around Meyers to locate Sweeney, the boatswain's mate of the watch. "Sweeney, tell the lookouts to be sharp. We don't have radar, and our running lights are out."

Placing the phone in its cradle, Biron leaned back against the wood sill so he could speak to both men. "Dropped the load. The emergency generator . . ." he paused as the distant, hesitant popping rumble of the diesel steadied out, ". . . is online. We should be back on steam in five. Ross says it'll take fifteen to assess the damage. We seized a bearing in the number two condensate pump."

A few indicator lights beamed back to life. The muted bell of the engine order telegraph clinked, and the lee helmsman called out in a subdued, almost apologetic, voice, "Sir, engine room answers all-stop."

Biron didn't speak but nodded his acknowledgment to the lee helmsman. Meyers shook his head in disgust.

Javert dropped from his chair and stepped directly in front of Meyers, forcing Biron out of the way. With his shoulders hunched and neck thrust forward, Javert squinted down at Meyers. "XO, this is unsat. It's your job to see that these things don't happen. Brief me when you find out how long repairs will take. Once we get the problem fixed, I want to know how you're going to keep us on schedule. I'll be in my cabin. Do you understand?"

Meyers' voice was businesslike. "Yes sir. And you'll have the breakdown message in a few minutes."

"No! XO, we've been over this before about breakdown reports. I told you, they're only required if we can't keep our schedule. We don't know that yet, so no report."

"Captain—"

Javert ignored Meyers' plea and stormed off the bridge, yelling, "I'll be in my cabin, XO. You have your orders. Make them so."

UNDER WAY

USS *Farnley*, Chesapeake Bay, May 1970
Operation Marathon: Day 1

Fifteen months earlier, Ross had finished his morning ritual by making his bunk. This was a moment of passage for Ross, a time of sweet beginning when one's next step led inescapably to a known and bittersweet ending. It was a step he was happy to take because the navy had lived up to its end of the bargain, as would Ross. It was just part of the deal.

After almost three decades at sea, this was his last, his sunset cruise, and the *Farnley* would be the last in his long list of great ships. At times like these, the navy allowed men to pick their final duty station, and for Ross, the decision was easy since the *Farnley* was the last of the Able-class destroyers.

Satisfied his bunk would pass inspection, he snatched the screwdriver from his pillow and bounded up the ladder through the forward deck hatch. On deck, the early morning fog mingled with the soulful call from the foghorn at St. Charles and the soft, reassuring splash of the bow wake. The moist, fog-laden air penetrated his thin khaki shirt and chilled him. He welcomed the sensation.

Ross bit his lip and pondered the thought that this would be the last time he would hear the St. Charles foghorn, but like so many other channel mornings he had known, it felt right.

Even on deck he could hear and feel the individual sounds of every piece of machinery. The ship's sounds were her symphony with the bass rumble of blowers, the timpani of the air ducts feeding hungry boiler fires, the high-pitched whine of the turbine, and the reassuring tenor voice of the reduction gears. Each ship made her own music, but the sounds of the *Farnley* confirmed her heritage. Ross' career had come full circle. The *Able* had been his first ship, and now the *Farnley* would be his last. His career was ending the way he had hoped.

Ross made his way aft, stepped into the engine room hatch, and slid down the ladder to the platform. His men, hard at work, didn't notice his arrival, so he headed for the coffeepot, then his white wooden bench. Despite the recent overhaul, he still heard a tick here and a rattle there. They weren't ready for white enameled bilges yet, but he had a good crew eager to learn, and he would teach them all he could. That was also part of the deal. His life would be a joy, and his last two years at sea a pleasure.

A new man, Fireman Apprentice Stucky, watched the port throttleman. This was Stucky's first day in the engine room, and in a few days, he would stand his first throttle watch. The freckle-faced kid was wide-eyed in wonderment. Ross knew what Stucky was going through. Even loafing along at fifteen knots, the *Farnley*'s engine room would be awesome to Stucky. Ross remembered how cavernous the *Able*'s engine room seemed his first time at sea. At full power, the rolling thunder of her seventy-thousand-horsepower engines frightened and humbled him. He still recalled the exhilaration of his first throttle watch and the heady sensation of power. The ship's nervous energy seemed limitless as if she were chafing at her mechanical harness, begging to be free. The *Farnley* was as good as the *Able*, both proud thoroughbreds.

Ross envied Stucky; his adventure was just beginning. Ross set his coffee cup down on the white enameled bench and smiled to himself. "Stucky, what's our speed?"

Ross' address startled Stucky, and he turned away from the gauge board to face the chief. "Me?"

"Yes. What's our speed?" Ross said.

"Fifteen knots."

"What's our top end?" Ross continued.

"Someone said thirty-six knots. Right?"

"Half-right. Our design speed is forty, but right now thirty-six sounds right. We're going to fix that 'cause the last four knots separate the men from the boys."

Satisfied Stucky's education was on track, Ross set his coffee cup on his bench, pointed to an open toolbox next to him, and said, "Stucky, come here, son. This box has your name on it."

"That's not mine, Chief, honest," Stucky replied.

"I just said it's yours," Ross began, "and I want to know what your toolbox is doing lying open in the middle of my deck."

Ross raised his eyebrows at Stucky as if waiting for a reply, then continued softly. "This is an engine room and not a garage. We keep toolboxes closed and stowed. And look here." Ross pulled a large wrench dripping with oil from the top of the box and handed it to Stucky. "That, son, is unsat. If you needed to use it in an emergency, you'd never get a good grip on it. Dirty tools make for dirty sailors, and dirty sailors make for dirty, dangerous engine rooms. Keep your tools clean. Understand?"

Stucky nodded yes, but his face betrayed his confusion. Ross continued, "Now, you're new, so I'm going to cut you some slack. After your watch, clean the tools until they're cleaner than the mess deck trays; then bring them to me and I'll tell you if they're good enough to stow. From now on, you own it. If the other men don't treat your tools right, you got the right to raise hell with them, 'cause if you don't, I'll raise holy hell with you. Never leave your toolbox in the middle of my deck where someone could trip over it. It's dangerous, and it makes my engine room look bad."

"But I didn't do anything," Stucky pleaded.

"No excuses. Someone's gotta be responsible, and you're it. That's the deal."

ASSESSMENT

August 1971, The Aegean Sea off the coast of Greece
Operation Marathon: Day 399

After leaving the bridge, Javert descended the ladder to the second level and stormed through the door to his cabin. He raised his hands to protect his eyes from the harsh shaft of light emanating from the battle lantern and searched the black shadows for his chair. After retrieving the chair, he sat and stared at the two framed photographs on his desk. Javert picked up the picture of his wife, Gloria, and his two children.

Why? Why must they always challenge me?

"Don't worry. I can't—I won't—let this opportunity go by," he had reassured her.

How have things gotten to this point? he wondered. Eighteen months ago he had thought his naval career was over and the navy he'd trusted and served for twenty years without question had betrayed him. The navy had not given him a command, and a successful shipboard command was a requirement for promotion. The rules were simple, unforgiving, and absolute. Passed over for promotion three times, if he wasn't promoted next year, retirement would be mandatory.

Javert needed to succeed as captain on the *Farnley*. She was his first command and his last chance. He couldn't understand the navy's reluctance to give him a command. With a few exceptions, his fitness reports were satisfactory. The only bad marks on his record came from his first tour at sea as gunnery officer. Javert guessed that was the reason they wouldn't let him on the bridge of the *Enterprise*.

He'd been angry with the navy. It wasn't his fault his assignments kept him away from sea duty. He deserved a chance. The navy owed it to him, and finally, albeit late in his career, the navy had rewarded his dedication by giving him command of a ship. When he took command of the *Farnley*, she was a good ship despite her age. Considering all the newer, sleeker ships, she wasn't much, but he was thankful because she was his only hope to stay in the navy.

Javert smiled to himself as his gaze drifted to the picture of him and

13

Admiral Eickhoff at his change-of-command ceremony. The day he took command of the *Farnley* was the happiest and proudest day of his life. He remembered how confident he was, but his confidence was quickly shaken. He realized command-at-sea was different from his previous assignments. The impregnable cocoon of naval tradition, rules, and regulations in which he found security and absolute stability unraveled. Nothing added up anymore. The system he loved so much stopped working.

The overhead fluorescent light buzzed, flickered, then came on. Javert was proud of the picture. A fleet commander normally wouldn't attend a change-of-command ceremony. It was a special day for him, but now he had a job to do. His mandate was to follow his orders, meet his commitments, and earn his promotion.

Other captains never argued or reasoned with their men. There were some honest differences, one professional to another, but nothing like what he contended with on the *Farnley*. On other ships, the men responded to their captains and fulfilled their every wish. Javert had done everything they did. He'd been just as assertive, bold, and daring. The navy wouldn't have given him command if he couldn't handle it. By elimination, his problems were with his officers.

Javert had tried to be their friend. He did everything right, but ungrateful officers such as Meyers betrayed him by defying his authority, and men like Ross followed their lead. The crew looked up to Meyers and Biron, not him. The crew followed them; they were suborners of his authority. *I need to reassert myself and take control away from them. That will be the best for the ship and the navy. Those are my fundamental orders.*

§

After Javert stormed off the bridge, Meyers turned to Biron and sensed they had the same unspeakable thoughts. There was nothing to say, so with his eyes, he warned Biron to remain silent. Biron sighed, hung his head, and walked away.

Javert's ranting shamed and appalled Meyers, but now there were more immediate problems, yet he was helpless until Ross got the generators and boiler back online.

The shadowy figures of the bridge watch stood at their posts like mute, lifeless mannequins, and the unnatural silence and absence of movement on the normally busy bridge unnerved Meyers. He wanted to make something happen, to do something.

"Any idea why we lost the boiler?" he asked Biron.

Biron, while cleaning the circular lenses on his glasses, shrugged.

"Don't ask me. I guess someone had their thumb up his butt. In any event, you don't want to know."

The response only heightened Meyers' frustration. He understood its meaning. Detestable as it was, it was the standard answer to every problem. How he hated those words, "You don't want to know." Every day, those words echoed in his head, reminding him he was unable to reverse the situation. He wanted to put it out of his mind and tried to focus his thoughts on manageable problems.

The red lights blinked, and the static hiss of the radios returned, signaling restoration of normal ship's power. Resigned to his next task, Meyers shrugged. "That's my cue. I'll be back after I talk to the captain."

Meyers left the bridge, descended the two levels to the main passageway, and headed aft. He didn't look forward to meeting with Ross or Javert, both immovable personalities. Ross was another of his nagging problems. He hated to see such a good man go to waste, but he'd been unable to pull him out of his shell. Ross, besieged as he was, had remained agreeable until a few months ago. Since then, Ross had become increasingly recalcitrant and taciturn. Considering the supply problems, the inability to get experienced men, and the captain, he didn't blame Ross, but he could never tell him that.

Meyers wished the world were simpler so he could say what he really thought. He couldn't. The unpopular orders from an unapproachable captain were his problem. As executive officer, his job was to take the heat, be the captain's lightning rod.

As Meyers walked down the passageway lit by dim red lights, he felt the scratchy crunch of grit under his shoes. In the soft red light, the passageway with its beige bulkheads and deck appeared immersed in a glowing bloody-cream-colored mist. Like rough blackened scabs, lint, dust, and dirt adhered to the deck.

Meyers couldn't decide whether the sight made him mad, sad, or guilty. He'd never seen a ship get run down like this before, and technically he felt the ship's filthy condition was his fault. He tried but wondered if the shortage of officers, the supply problems, the equipment breakdowns, and the low morale were his way of rationalizing his failure. Then there was Javert, who blocked every move he made to enforce discipline. Javert was the biggest problem.

Every time Meyers tried to assert himself, Javert went ballistic. Somehow Javert's twisted mind concluded that Meyers' attempts to do his job were disguised attempts to undermine the captain's authority. Was Javert a rationalization also? Problems, problems. He could handle any one of them alone. No one man could handle all of them at the same time.

15

You're doing your best. Don't get down on yourself. Just keep trying.

Meyers stepped out of the passageway, grabbed a nearby pipe for support, and stepped onto the vertical ladder leading to the engine room. As soon as his body was below the hatch, he felt the shift from the relatively cool evening air to the oppressive heat of the engine room with its steamy smell of hot metal.

Meyers located Ross, who was seated with his legs hanging over the edge of a catwalk, supervising four firemen at work in the bilge. Ross ignored Meyers' approach and kept slapping the handle of his screwdriver into the palm of his left hand.

"What's your status, Chief?"

"Three hundred and thirty-two days and a wake-up, then I'm outta here."

Meyers couldn't tell if Ross was trying to be funny, conversational, or sarcastic, so he decided to ignore the comment. "The pump, Chief, not you."

"Oh well, I guess we seized a bearing. We'll know soon as we get the housing off."

"Can you fix it?"

"If that's what you want me to do and if I got the parts, maybe."

"How long?"

"Don't know. Like I said, we gotta get the housing off first. Sometimes the shaft'll snap like a twig when a bearing seizes. If it's a clean break, we're lucky, but sometimes it gets all twisted up like a spring and it's a bitch to get out. Gotta wait and see."

"Chief, you're not helping the situation. We gotta get moving again. What are my options?"

"Well, if the captain had let us stop for a few minutes, we could have avoided this little fiasco, but—"

"Chief!" Meyers warned.

Ross pointed to a pump with his screwdriver and said, "We're bolting number four back together. It could be ready in twenty minutes." Ross pointed his screwdriver at another pump and continued, "Or we can tear that one down and see if it can be fixed. What do you want me to do?"

Perspiration was beading on Meyers' brow, and sweat was running down his back. Ross' deliberate obstructionism was angering Meyers, so he decided to wait Ross out and make him speak next.

A fireman handed Ross a shiny machined steel rod about eighteen inches long with a blackened donut-shaped ring at one end. Ross grabbed the hot shaft by the rags the fireman wrapped around it and examined it before holding it up for Meyers to see.

"Tell the captain he got lucky. The bearing's burnt to a crisp, but he didn't break anything else."

Meyers felt Ross was pushing, trying to find out how far the immunity of thirty years' service, two Purple Hearts, and the Navy Cross for heroism would extend. Irritated, Meyers said, "The captain is not part of this discussion. How long before we can get under way?"

Ross handed the shaft back to the sailor, and with an affected, tired shrug said, "Thirty minutes. Want me to fix the other one?"

"Yes, I'll tell the bridge you can answer bells at"—Meyers checked his watch—"twenty-two hundred hours." Meyers paused a minute. "Do you have another bearing?"

"Not a new one," Ross began, giving Meyers a silly grin, "but I'll ask the tooth fairy to put one under my pillow tonight." Collectively, the firemen in the bilge turned away to hide their snickers.

Ross had pushed too far. "Chief, I want to talk to you over here in private," Meyers said, motioning to the end of the catwalk. Ross shrugged and followed.

"I won't have this!" Meyers began in a low, sharp voice. "I know there are problems down here, but we all are in the same situation. Under the circumstances, you've done better than I could imagine, but if you don't stop soldiering on me and don't stop trying to be a wiseass, I'll put you in hack till you get out. Neither of us wants that."

Ross hung his head and examined his screwdriver as if it held some profound answer. After several seconds, he raised his head and trained his gray eyes on Meyers.

"Sorry, XO. I get so damned pissed about this. We can't get this, and we can't get that. I ask you to expedite repair parts, and I know you try, but nothing ever happens. What the hell's the use? Seriously, XO, this ain't my navy anymore, not the one I know. I just want to do my time and get out, but I'm not sure I'll live long enough. Do you realize the captain could've killed someone down here?"

"What?"

"You didn't know, did you?" Ross pointed into the bilge where the men were working and said, "This didn't happen suddenly. We knew it was coming, and I asked the bridge to stop, but the captain said no. Things got downright hairy. Tell the captain if it hadn't been for Stucky and Burns, the turbines would've come apart, and the shrapnel would still be ricocheting around down here. If that happened, you'd be counting body bags, not pumps."

Meyers' heart was pounding, and the heat built in his face again. He wasn't angry with Ross or Javert or anybody. He was angry with something that lacked identity or shape, and that only added to his anger. There was no adversary to attack, no specific problem to solve. He could

17

identify his enemy only as a shapeless, anonymous, insensitive something.

Meyers wanted to respond but couldn't. Anything he said would be wrong, so without a word, he turned and walked toward the ladder.

Ross walked back to his men, who had been watching. "What's 'a matter with him?" one asked in an accusatory voice.

"Stow it!" Ross yelled. "The XO's got the hardest job on the ship. He's caught between the devil and the deep blue sea."

§

Meyers needed time to calm down before he spoke with Javert. He considered himself a good judge of character and believed the navy would never give a man like Javert a command—or so he'd thought.

Meyers understood commanders took risks and gambled the lives of their men in critical situations. The life of every man was important to Meyers. He accepted the risk taking within limits. But Javert was risking lives merely to be on time for a gunnery exercise. It was senseless, and he couldn't comprehend the twisted logic. He wondered if he was missing something but concluded no worthwhile captain would risk life needlessly. It was another example of Javert's unsuitability for command.

Javert's actions frustrated him, but losing his temper in front of the captain would only do more damage. Meyers tried to redirect his anger by reminding himself that, in the final analysis, Javert wasn't the real problem. It was the navy that had given him a command, then promptly went dumb, deaf, blind, and stark raving crazy.

Knocking on Javert's door, Meyers called out, "Captain," and entered.

"Enter," Javert said in a deep, raspy voice while blinking the sleepiness from his eyes.

"We'll be back under way at twenty-two hundred hours, about fifteen minutes from now. Ross is bringing pump four online. Pump two will take some time to fix."

"Why wasn't another pump running?" Javert asked, propping up his body and crossing his arms across his chest.

The question surprised Meyers. They had gone over this yesterday before leaving Elefsis. Meyers assumed Javert was still disoriented from his nap. "It was torn down for repairs, Captain, and we're just getting it back together. Remember his status report when we got under way from Elefsis?"

"What about tomorrow?"

"No problem, Captain. We'll be about ten miles from where we wanted to be, but we'll be well within the firing area. I gave Biron the new course and updated the night orders."

"Good. Thank you," Javert said, lying back down.

At sea, captains, even Javert, were lucky to get three hours' sleep a day and catnapped anytime they could to survive. Meyers hated to intrude on Javert's sleep, but he persisted. "There is another item, Captain," he said, handing Javert the breakdown message.

Javert recognized it and sat up. "XO, we've been over this dozens of times, and you know I won't release this. I told you that on the bridge. My job and your job is to get the job done with as little muss and fuss as possible and not bother my superiors with your problems. When will you learn, XO?"

Meyers was uncomfortable standing over Javert, so he squatted before answering. "Captain, the regulations are clear. We've got lots of problems here, and we both know that. You don't want to bitch to squadron or fleet, and I understand that, but this is one polite way to tell them we're having problems. They can help, but first we need to tell them our status."

"You're no different from the last engineering officer." Javert yelled, getting to his feet. "He kept fighting with me over regulations because, like you, he didn't understand every regulation was written for a good reason and must be obeyed. He kept pestering me about supply problems. Then he demanded . . . demanded that I shake up the supply system and get him the parts he wanted. Other engineering officers get the job done, but he couldn't. That's what he was trying to cover up. That's why I threw him off my ship, and if you aren't careful, you'll be next."

Meyers had feared Javert would take off on another of his tirades and was prepared for it. He needed to maintain his composure. Taking a deep breath, he said, "Captain, I'm not trying to quote regulations to you. It's a matter of interpretation, but my responsibilities are clear."

Glaring at Meyers, Javert crossed his arms and yelled to drown out Meyers' voice. "XO, if and when you get your own ship, you can interpret the regulations your way. Until then, you're on my ship, and I won't allow you to question my authority. Do you understand?"

The growing truculence in Javert's voice made it difficult for Meyers to control his own. "Captain, I'm not questioning your authority. Consider the facts. We're just limping along and—"

"getting the job done!" Javert interjected.

Meyers lowered his head for a second, trying to summon some inner strength. "And most of our equipment is inoperable or barely working. The ship is getting dangerous, and our responsibility is to prevent that."

"Mister Meyers, our responsibility is to meet our operational commitments, period!" Javert said, waving his arms for emphasis. "Nowhere does it say we'll be excused because there are a few little problems. All the other ships are in the same navy, and they get along fine because they have excellent loyal officers . . . and . . . and I'm tired of your weak sister behavior, your whining, your disloyalty, and the way you keep trying to undermine my authority and make me look bad. As I said before, if and when you get your own ship, you will understand that every little problem you report is a mark against you because, as a captain, your job is to handle those problems and not—I repeat, not— trouble your superiors with them."

Familiar with Javert's tactic of diverting the discussion, Meyers ignored the insults. He needed to get Javert back to the central issue.

"Captain, this isn't bothering our superiors," Meyers pleaded.

"The hell it isn't, mister." Javert screamed. "You don't even understand the basics. The navy's rubric is clear. An officer follows orders, never admits it can't be done, never questions, never bitches, and never, never challenges the authority or competence of his superiors. All you do is bitch, bitch, bitch about supply. We have a good supply system. If there are problems, there is a good reason. An officer would never add to the problems of his superiors by creating a fuss. Other ships manage with the same supply system, and it's our job to manage the *Farnley*."

Meyers couldn't take it any longer. He wasn't bitching at Javert. Javert didn't realize what real bitching sounded like. Meyers was the one everyone on the crew was bitching at. He was the one who was taking the heat.

"Captain, I resent your saying I bitch about problems or that I'm disloyal. I'm not," Meyers said.

"The hell you're not, the way you're always trying to coddle the crew."

"I don't coddle the crew. Every time I try to enforce discipline, you stop me. Look at the facts, Captain. That's all I ask. Take the supply situation, for instance. I've seen the supply system lose a ship for a few weeks after they deployed to a different operating area, but never for fifteen months. Captain, something is wrong, and they might not even realize it. It can't hurt to ask."

"Don't you follow up on requisitions and try to expedite?"

"Damned well I do."

"Then you've asked! You should have faith in the navy like I do. Supply is doing its best, and we're getting the same treatment as every other ship."

"That's not true, Captain. I spoke to the XO on another—"

"You what?!" Javert screamed.

"Captain, I was—"

"trying to subvert me at every turn."

"Captain, I'm trying to help. Damn it, Captain, can't you see that?"

"Mister Meyers, all I see is you yelling and cursing at your captain. Your behavior borders on mutiny, and I could bring you up on charges for that. This conversation is over! Get out now!"

Meyers didn't think he was being mutinous, but with his frustration-fueled rage building, he was afraid he would cross the line and enter that no-man's-land. He was out of options. He quickly left, slid down the ladder to the main deck level, and stepped into the wardroom.

Roaches, small black spots in the red lighting, darted for shelter as Meyers entered. Everywhere he looked, he saw the evidence of his failure to keep the *Farnley* functioning as a naval vessel. If this was the officers' quarters, what type of hellhole must the men be living in?

Meyers knew the answer to his own question. He toured the ship every day. It was his daily exercise in frustration. As executive officer, the cleanliness of the ship was his responsibility, but normally he would have the authority to get the job done. Javert withheld all authority to enforce discipline and order, so every day, Meyers tried to make the men care. Failing that, there was little he could do without disobeying a direct order from Javert.

He could hear Javert now: "Reports of increased disciplinary problems only show superiors a captain isn't doing his job. Good captains don't have disciplinary problems." For once he was right, Meyers thought. Good captains don't have disciplinary problems. They handle the crew with a velvet glove, but inside the glove is a fist of steel.

In a rage, Meyers threw the steel desk chair out of the way as he entered his stateroom. The chair banged against the steel bulkhead, but the momentary act of violence did little to drain his frustration. He turned toward the sawdust-filled seabag hung from a pipe near his shower stall.

As Meyers looked at it, a voice inside his head screamed the litany of his frustrations. *I'm responsible for the condition of this ship, this floating rust heap. I can't get paint. I can't get parts. But that's okay 'cause they won't give me men who would know what to do with new parts if I had them. I asked for a man with five years' experience, and what do they do? They send me five men with one year's experience. I have half the officers I need. Will they give me more? No! But that's okay. Meyers can handle it. But in case we missed something, let's give 'em a shithead for a captain like Javert!*

The voice kept screaming and screaming. The more Meyers stared at the seabag, the louder the voice became. With a scream, Meyers threw an overhand jab at the bag. His fist landed on the shiny round spot in its midsection, which was worn smooth from months of punishment. The off-angle blow sent spears of pain shooting into his shoulder socket.

Swinging away from the first blow, the bag retreated from the assault. Meyers pursued it. The coarse twill of the bag grabbed, tearing at the skin of his hands. The pain only served to increase his rage. The voice was still there, but it wasn't getting louder. He growled and screamed at the bag with every blow, pummeling the bag with all his strength. His arms became leaden. He screamed louder to drown out the voice. The harder he punched, the quieter the voice became. Gasping for breath, he tried to punch faster. His hands began to bleed, but the voice wouldn't die. Exhaustion reached down to claim his legs. With his knees too weak to stand, he collapsed onto the built-in Naugahyde couch. The voice was gone.

Meyers lay there for several minutes before the world began to return. The unmistakable hum of the engines and the slow rise and fall of the bow told him the ship was under way. He held his hands up and looked at the gelatinous blood collected around the gouged skin under his Annapolis class ring. His hands hurt, and the dried blood on his knuckles cracked as he spread his fingers to remove his ring. He rubbed his thumb across the ring's large blue stone. The ring was the symbol of Annapolis, and Annapolis was the symbol of the navy's officer corps. It stood for greatness—for duty, honor, country and all the laws and traditions he learned there.

The first thing Meyers had learned at Annapolis was that the navy demands more of its officers than mere technical excellence. A captain of a naval vessel was in a position unlike any other military commander. Alone on the ocean, a ship can't retreat, can't dig in, and can't take cover, and the captain can't get on the telephone to ask for advice. Whether the adversary is a declared enemy, a terrorist, a two-bit dictator trying to make a name for himself, or the sea itself, a captain must face the challenge alone, armed only with his experience, skill, and courage.

With such responsibility comes authority commensurate with the task. For centuries, a captain's power over the life and safety of his men has been unlimited. Captains must be men of character, compassion, and conviction, and men not corrupted by absolute power.

Belligerent nations harass warships, so captains must be men who would stare down a hostile foe. A defeated captain who would strike his colors pays with the lives of his men, so captains must be men who would chuckle at adversity and wouldn't be afraid to look the devil in the eye. In this century alone, storms have claimed dozens of ships, so captains must be men whose whispers could be heard above a shrieking gale.

Meyers' teachers had taught him that it took more than study and hard work to earn the singular title of captain. The navy looks for leaders, for those few who stand a little taller, who walk a little differently, and whose voices exude contagious confidence. From the millions of officers who come and go each century, perhaps a few thousand are granted the sacred trust and honored with the title of Captain. These few special men who become captains, as singular as their office, stand before God as masters of their vessels. Their unrelenting responsibilities are enormous, their authority absolute. For those who would dare challenge these singular men, for those who would challenge the sacred trust, there is a singular word—Mutineer.

Meyers felt the navy had made a tragic mistake by giving Javert command of the *Farnley* and had thrust Javert into a situation he wasn't equipped to handle. In a way, Meyers felt sorry for Javert, but he grieved for the *Farnley* and her crew.

Meyers put the ring down on his desk and, as he'd done every night for the past nine months, began making his daily diary entry. In it, he recorded everything he could remember about the day—the funny, the sad, the mundane, the exciting, the inane, and the inept actions of a man unfit for command.

It was past midnight when Meyers fell asleep, exhausted. His dreams were of the men it had been his honor to serve, those few singular men the navy had honored with the singular title—Captain.

Larry Laswell

BASTARDS

June 1971, Bay of Naples, Italy
Operation Marathon: Day 339

Two months earlier, Stucky sat cross-legged on the *Farnley*'s fantail, and used his pocketknife to pick at the bleeding rust that followed a deck weld seam. The old, black, rough nonskid paint yielded easily to his knife as dime-sized flecks cracked free to reveal shiny silver-white metal. Stucky picked a few chips from the frayed cuff of his dungarees and carefully brushed them over the side.

A year ago, Fireman Stucky's life bristled with excitement and every day had its discovery. He had liked the navy and he had wanted to make it a career. Now, looking across the bay from the *Farnley*'s fantail toward the high riprap sea wall and the dingy harbor front of Naples, he daydreamed to help fight off the boredom.

From where he sat, Stucky couldn't see much of Naples. The sea wall, and a picket of black rust stained masts that jutted above it, stood like barriers between him and the jumble of dirty low masonry buildings lining the harbor front. Only the masts of the tender *Puget Sound* and the destroyers nestled to her side were clean, proud and purposeful.

Everything had changed in the past year. Time had transformed the once mysterious port cities from places of adventure to empty places of alternative imprisonment. Except places like Cannes or Monte Carlo, all harbors struck Stucky as places of dirty decaying despair.

For some unfathomable reason, even Naples, the dirtiest of them all, had eschewed the *Farnley*. Denied her rightful place in the destroyer nest, the *Farnley* lay at anchor in the bay; outcast, shunned.

Things like that only seemed bad if you cared and Stucky didn't give a shit. He didn't have to. Even Chief Ross had quit caring months ago, and who could blame him. The navy had transferred all his experienced men, wouldn't give him any repair parts, then gave the *Farnley* a shit-head for a captain. The XO cared, but he couldn't do anything, and it was anyone's guess if the captain cared. Normally, crap, like the *Farnley*, floats, but on the *Farnley*, it just settled to the bottom and stayed there.

24

He still had thirty minutes to kill until liberty call. His first stop, as always, would be Momma Sita's bar just up from the landing. Stucky liked Momma Sita. She cared. She greeted every sailor with a wide happy smile; the kind that made you believe she remembered you; the kind that made you afraid she would sweep you into a big bear hug of affection. She was cook, bartender, and waitress all rolled into one. Jabbering constantly in her broken English to everyone and to no one in particular, she darted from table to table, her gray print dress and white apron swishing at the terrazzo floor. When she moved, only her jet black hair, combed back tight into a bun, remained motionless.

Momma Sita was mistress of all she surveyed. Her scolding of those who forgot their manners came in a loud clear voice made sharper by the bareness of the beige stucco walls. On his first trip to Naples, Stucky fell victim to her full rage by simply asking directions to the Gut. With one fist shaking, Momma Sita snatched the bar rag from her shoulder and snapped it in his face. Under a barrage of her broken English, spitting Italian venom, and the snapping bar rag, Stucky retreated into the street. Momma Sita had thrown him out. Good boys who want to make something of themselves don't go to the seedy, sinful Gut. Momma Sita had her standards; she cared.

Stucky didn't care. Tonight he would go to the Gut. Maybe he'd get drunk with Sweeney and Portalatin and wander from bar to bar through the canyon-like maze of narrow, dirty, cobblestone alleys until he found himself a whore. Tomorrow would be like any other day and he'd feel bored, empty and unfulfilled. They would put to sea, and no one would work any harder than necessary to get by. After enough tomorrows had passed, he'd get out of the navy for good. Then what? Probably get a job as a mechanic, or something. He'd worry about that then. Right now he didn't care. His life was simple. No one cared. They didn't expect anything of him, and he certainly didn't want to disappoint the bastards.

ADMIRALS

August 1971, The Pentagon
Operation Marathon: Day 403

It didn't surprise Captain Patrick "Terror" O'Toole to learn that Admiral Durham would be late for their four o'clock meeting, but it bothered him when the aide insisted he wait in the admiral's office. O'Toole disliked special treatment, but when the aide said Durham insisted, O'Toole relented, yet it still bothered him. Only three or four men in the world rated being shown into the office of the chief of naval operations unescorted. O'Toole was certain he wasn't one of them.

Even though he disliked the special treatment, O'Toole welcomed the chance to be alone with the glass-encased model of the USS *Constitution* along the far wall. Maybe if he were given enough time to study it, his obsession with it would ebb. Perhaps it was the ship, *Old Ironsides*, not the model that fascinated him. Or maybe it was the heritage and traditions she embodied.

O'Toole approached the model and squatted to be eye level with it and caught his reflection in the spotless glass case. A lifetime of exposure to wind, sun, and sea had left his skin sunburnt and had turned his once-friendly face into a hardened leathery mask.

O'Toole didn't like his appearance or the way the elements faded and dried his once-flaming red hair. Rather than fight it, he managed to turn his appearance into an asset. His old sea dog face, scarred deeply with experience, intimidated most everyone and garnered him instant credibility and respect. He used his appearance and gravelly voice as mere tools of his trade. For the same reason, he carried his barrel-chested, six-foot body mainmast straight.

O'Toole enjoyed examining every part of the model—its rigging, hull, deck, rails, and masts. The care, patience, and attention to detail that went into its construction were phenomenal; even the knots around the belaying pins were correct. He had never met the model-maker, but they had much in common and would be best friends. The craftsman had built a fitting tribute to a great ship that, with her crew, had helped build a nation.

O'Toole would gladly give up his pension to command a ship like her. Looking at the model, he felt the exhilaration of wind, sea, and bounding deck as a westerly wind filled her sails and stretched her creaking rigging taut against the braces. Her victories reminded a nation of its identity. She was a great ship for strong men of courage and skill. The courageous acts of her crew had inspired generations of seamen and admirals alike.

With a sigh, O'Toole stood and surveyed the small, almost bare office and the massive mahogany desk that dominated it. Everyone called the desk the "Mighty Mo," a pun on the battleship *Missouri*'s World War II nickname. The desk, which sat forward of a spray of flags, was Durham's favorite possession. "Mighty Mo," as O'Toole had heard Durham joke about it, "was not quite as big, almost as strong, certainly as heavy, and positively as grand as any battleship." O'Toole shook his head at the thought. Nothing could ever be as grand as a battleship.

Like most things ashore, the feel of the office, the hushed whoosh of cool filtered air, the thick deep-blue carpet, the silence, and the dead rock-solid deck filled O'Toole with uneasiness. This wasn't his element; it lacked the sting of life and its immediate reality. Still, O'Toole accepted it as a necessary evil because the chief of naval operations couldn't command the fleet from the deck of a ship. He understood its purpose and accepted the facts. Durham understood also and had removed all the posh furniture and fixtures the day he took over. The result was an admirable compromise between political reality and fundamental values.

The desk, like the rest of the office, was worthy of the commander of the world's most powerful fleet. The office contained little more than the desk, a few chairs, the flags, and navy memorabilia. O'Toole sensed most visitors were unable to distinguish between the man and his office: both elegantly quiet, spartan, forthright, commanding.

He appreciated the office's quiet nobility, its understated feeling of overwhelming tradition, and the way it would awe and humble even the most ambitious men. O'Toole supposed such things were necessary in a town such as Washington. Still, he preferred salt in his eyes, a steel deck, and a dirty coffee mug.

Since their years at the academy, O'Toole and Durham had steered different courses. By choice, O'Toole was still a captain and would have it no other way. By acclaim, Durham was now the chief of naval operations. Durham had once confided in him that he wished they could trade places.

Under the circumstances, that was understandable, but O'Toole knew he didn't possess the skills or patience needed to deal with the political machine in Washington. Durham possessed those skills, but sometimes it took more than skill to kill projects such as Operation Marathon.

Operation Marathon was the brainchild of Admiral Eickhoff. O'Toole had tracked Eickhoff's meteoric rise from lackluster lieutenant commander to admiral with disgust. It was a classic case of Washington at its worst.

Eickhoff had parlayed three liaison positions to political leaders into a key position on the White House staff. He'd spent the last five years either on Capitol Hill or in the White House.

Each assignment came with an unearned promotion paid for with political IOUs. Clearly, Eickhoff had collected many friends and markers on Capitol Hill. That grated on O'Toole, but his dislike for Eickhoff was more basic. Eickhoff's hubris was exceeded only by his lack of scruples. Operation Marathon was but one example.

All Washington witch hunts hide behind the facade of high ideals. In the case of Eickhoff's Operation Marathon, it was fleet readiness. Eickhoff wanted to prove the newer high-technology ships would break down in a protracted naval war. To accomplish this, he would subject a group of ships to wartime conditions to determine their long-term reliability.

From what O'Toole knew of Eickhoff, fleet readiness was the least of the admiral's concerns. The war scenario drawn by Eickhoff was unrealistic; any commander worth his salt knew battles were won by men, not ships. O'Toole would rather sail into battle with a good crew on a rusty barge than the grandest battleship with a lousy crew.

Durham had briefed O'Toole on Operation Marathon the day after he took over as CNO. Eickhoff had had his senator friends apply pressure on the Pentagon to conduct the Marathon experiment. Durham had had no choice; he would conduct Operation Marathon or his replacement would. Stuck with it, Durham was doing the best he could.

Eickhoff put together a flawed plan with a heavy political slant that placed six test ships under his command. Only because of his political backing, Eickhoff almost pushed the project through before Durham took over.

Eickhoff's staffing levels were so low, exhaustion would overwhelm the crews within weeks. The supply situation was even worse. Eickhoff's original plan denied the Operation Marathon ships all repair parts. This was unsafe. Men would die under those conditions.

O'Toole helped Durham restructure Operation Marathon to feed the political beast while preventing fatal accidents. Supply compiled a master list of repair parts and supplies each ship required. Any requisition for those parts from an Operation Marathon ship would be flagged. The supply system would deliver on only about one-third of those requisitions.

Despite his dislike for Operation Marathon, O'Toole admired the way Durham had restructured it. With heavy security, Durham was running the operation as a valid blind test capable of yielding useful information. Dispersing the ships around the globe prevented potential adversaries from capitalizing on a weakened Operation Marathon ship.

O'Toole heard the door open and turned to see his friend enter. Despite his fifty-seven years, Admiral Durham retained the trim, muscular build of his youth. The only concessions to age were the sun-etched crow's feet behind his steady deep-blue eyes and a few streaks of silver in his black hair.

§

"Sorry I'm late, Pat. When did you get back?" Durham said, waving O'Toole to one of the simple teak armchairs in front of his desk.

"Oh-three-hundred this morning. I hopped a cargo flight back from Pearl," O'Toole said.

Durham shook his head and chuckled to himself. O'Toole would never change. He was a senior officer on special assignment for the CNO. He could have arranged a VIP flight home, but he would rather bounce around in a cargo net with enlisted men and junior officers. Durham's mind returned to the subject of the meeting: Operation Marathon and the latest test ship to drop out, the USS *Wilhelm*.

"How's the *Wilhelm* doing?"

"Great! Her crew is a pack of wiry junkyard dogs. Two months ago, she was ready for the scrap heap; now she's damned near in yard condition. Admiral Kurtis said he thought Dedek, the *Wilhelm*'s CO, was going to tear his head off when he told him about Operation Marathon. He was one pee-ohed SOB," O'Toole said.

"Don't say as I blame him. It's dirty pool we can't tell the captains what we are doing to their ships. Well, it will all be over on January first; eighteen months is the Marathon limit." Durham paused before asking, "Is he calmed down now?"

"Hell, he's okay, but I don't think you could ever call that man calm." From the response, Durham sensed O'Toole liked Dedek.

"Tell me what you found out, Pat."

O'Toole briefed Durham on the particulars, and when he was done, Durham asked, "Any recommendations?"

"Ron, I'm sorry, but I don't like this little experiment," O'Toole began. "It's the biggest load of whale dung to wash ashore on the

Potomac. It's not right to screw with the men like this. I told you before; someone is going to get killed before it's over."

Durham took no offense at O'Toole's reply. O'Toole was an old tin-can man with more destroyer experience than any other man in the navy, and his opinion was universally respected. O'Toole was just being O'Toole, speaking his truth in a forthright, unambiguous way. He would have used the same words had he been speaking to the secretary of defense, the president, or God Almighty. O'Toole was not known for his subtlety, but he was known for always getting his message across. It was why he had asked for O'Toole's help on Operation Marathon.

O'Toole was right but forgot the political realities. Durham closed his eyes for a second before responding. "There are three issues here, Pat. First, the battle readiness of the fleet concerns me, and say what you might about Eickhoff, we have to grant him one point: currently, there isn't any data telling us what will happen in a protracted naval war. If our ships are unreliable, thousands of men could die. The data we're collecting is valuable.

"Second, if we scuttle Operation Marathon, the political hacks on Capitol Hill will have a field day. Our appropriations will get cut back so far, we won't be able to buy coffee.

"Third, given the first two issues, how do we keep this operation safe so no one gets hurt or killed?"

"The biggest problem is safety," O'Toole began. "The supply system withholds almost seventy percent of supply part requisitions. The problem is they can't distinguish between a repair part, a light bulb, and a fire pump. Thank God they know what toilet paper is. The five remaining ships need a safety inspection. Safety items must get through."

The recommendation made sense to Durham, but he needed to find a way to do it without violating Operation Marathon security. He was about to respond but felt O'Toole wanted to say something else.

O'Toole, shaking his head, said, "You're in a box on this one, but understand, we're flirting with disaster. I hope I'm wrong."

"It's worth the risk," Durham said, hoping he was right.

"It's your decision, Ron, and I respect that. I'm sorry I couldn't come up with an alternative for you. Anyhow, it's all in my report," O'Toole said, sliding a small three-ring binder across the desk toward Durham, ending the discussion.

Durham bit his lip. He and O'Toole's wife were the only ones who knew of O'Toole's Mujatto vow. Nevertheless, he would try. "Pat, are you sure I can't get you to take an admiral's star?"

O'Toole, startled by the question, stood up and swiveled his head around the office before shaking it.

"No way," he said, patting Durham's desk. "Whatever I command will be cutting blue water, not beached on a blue carpet like yours. I prefer the honesty of a good nor'wester and the genuine feel of a bucking bridge deck."

O'Toole was right. He would never survive behind a desk. Despite the lack of recognition, O'Toole was happy with what he was doing, and Durham was certain "Terror" O'Toole did it better than any man alive. Durham envied him.

"You're a stubborn old Irishman, O'Toole," Durham said with a chuckle, and after a second of thought, added, "Pat, keep your bags packed. If this thing goes sour on me, I'm going to need your help."

"Don't worry, Ron. You move me around so much, I keep one bag packed just to stay in clean skivvies."

"Thanks," Durham said.

O'Toole winked at Durham and headed for the door. The door clicked shut, and Durham drafted a message and gave it to an aide with instructions to send it immediately. With that done, Durham picked up the phone to call Commander Beetham, the senior communications watch officer and an expert on the navy's elaborate communication system.

Beetham listened, and when Durham finished outlining what he wanted, Beetham replied, "Putting a complete communications watch on a couple of ships is easy, but doing it without attracting attention isn't. Give me some time to figure it out."

"Thanks. I know you'll do your best," Durham said, putting the phone back in the cradle.

§

In the dark Mediterranean night, the USS *America*, the Sixth Fleet flagship, steamed southward off the coast of Sardinia. On the *America*'s flag bridge, Admiral Eickhoff and Lieutenant Pew watched the dazzling light display of nighttime flight operations.

Eickhoff loved the sight. The lights were like Christmas in motion. Washed in a dim red glow, men with green and red wands led aircraft on their sinuous journey through a maze of other small lights. With their brilliant multicolored strobes slashing at the darkness, aircraft rolled into launch position. In a burst of golden-white light, their engines illuminated the flight deck, and the jets climbed into the sky until their lights were but a twinkle against the blackness.

"Beautiful, isn't it?" Eickhoff said to Pew.

Pew didn't answer but nodded his agreement.

Eickhoff smiled. That was one reason he liked Pew. He knew when to keep his mouth shut, which was most of the time. The son of some politician, Pew wasn't a career officer, but he understood the importance of patriotic veterans on Election Day. He was an ambitious man crafting his résumé far from the politically troubled shores of Viet Nam.

By Eickhoff's assessment, Pew, whose only liability was his appearance, knew how to play the game and appreciated the value of information. Eickhoff understood Pew and had briefed him on Operation Marathon before stationing him in Naples as Sixth Fleet liaison officer.

Information valuable to those who knew how to use it flowed through the NATO base at Naples. Another reason Eickhoff liked Pew was his uncanny ability to piece together vast mosaics of information from random and unconnected fragments.

"Would you like some coffee, Admiral?" Pew asked.

Eickhoff nodded and turned to pinpoint the lights of the screening destroyers. Eickhoff needed to find out where he stood with Operation Marathon. In some respects, Operation Marathon was working better than expected. In other respects, he had lost control of Operation Marathon due to O'Toole and Durham's interference. Their interference was an unforeseeable event and one Eickhoff didn't like. He never liked leaving his future to chance.

Eickhoff recognized the potential of the report Senator Carmichael had given him. One thing led to another, and after he submitted his article to the *Naval Review*, Operation Marathon took on a life of its own. So far, the results were beneficial. Durham, true to plan, gave him command of the Sixth Fleet so he would be involved in the operation. It was the least Durham could do after he had reorganized the entire operation at the last minute.

He owed it to me.

The *Farnley* was now Eickhoff's responsibility.

Eickhoff turned to Pew. "I need comprehensive intelligence on the other Operation Marathon ships. Do you have any ideas?"

Handing a mug of coffee to Eickhoff, Pew responded, "No. Durham shut down all information on the other ships. I protested, but they told me it was the way Durham wanted it. Each admiral was forced to decide when to withdraw his ship from Operation Marathon. He didn't want anybody to be influenced by the condition of the other ships."

"We need to find a way," Eickhoff said.

"I'll go back to Washington and ask around."

"Without some cover story, it would be too obvious," Eickhoff began while shaking his head. "There is no way Durham would release the names or locations of the other Operation Marathon ships. The first problem is ascertaining their identity and location."

Pew puckered the lips on his narrow, tapered face and said, "Maybe our approach is incorrect, our assumptions fallacious. If you tell me what concerns you, we might be able to find a solution."

Thinking, Eickhoff studied Pew, who had all the features of an effeminate weasel. *Let me have men about me who are fat, Marcus Antonius. Yond Cassius has a lean and hungry look. He thinks too much. Such men are dangerous.* Eickhoff decided not to mention the message Durham had sent him, but there was no harm in outlining what Pew had already figured out.

"Operation Marathon is operationally complex. Durham may have structured its command and control aspects so it'll fail and pull me down with it," Eickhoff began. "The *Farnley*, the last of the World War II ships, is the control ship, and that's why Durham gave command of her. All the other ships will be measured against her, so every move I make will come under scrutiny. If I'm too lenient on her, they'll criticize the results and invalidate the experiment. If Operation Marathon doesn't prove my point or if the results are invalidated, all my effort will be wasted. I must know the status of the other ships before I make any more decisions about the *Farnley*."

Pew waited until the crackling roar of a launching phantom jet faded away. "I don't see it that way. Your handling of Operation Marathon is masterful. Durham had no choice but to modify Operation Marathon's structure. He's in control now, so if a problem arises, it's his fault, but if it succeeds, you can take the credit. As for the other matter, Durham wouldn't try to rig the operation or pull you down. He's too scrupulous."

Taking a sip of his coffee, Eickhoff peered at Pew over the top of his mug. "Go on," he said.

"You are being as relentless and demanding on the *Farnley* as the guidelines permit. You're immune from criticism, but you can criticize the other admirals for being too lenient on their ships. That only makes your position stronger if someone wants to debate the results. You can't lose."

Eickhoff chose not to tell Pew about Javert, the *Farnley*'s commanding officer. Javert was his wild card in this game. No other admiral would pick such a weak man to command his ship. If the *Farnley* dropped out, he would blame it on Javert. Eickhoff would get bruised for a minor error in judgment, but it wouldn't affect Marathon. He wondered if Pew had figured that out. "What about Javert?" Eickhoff asked.

Pew's face told him the question was unnerving. Rendering an opinion on a senior officer was always dangerous. "His selection still adheres to the guidelines," Pew said as if exploring the idea for the first time. "I doubt the other Operation Marathon admirals selected a captain with so little sea experience, so that makes Javert a plus for you. Because of the information blackout, your only reasonable course is to keep bearing down on the *Farnley*. If you relent, the results will be open to question."

Eickhoff was right. Pew's intelligence made him even more dangerous. "What if she isn't the last to drop out?" Eickhoff asked.

"You can demonstrate you were harder on the *Farnley* than the other admirals were on their ships. Her early demise will be understandable, and you'll be justified in questioning any conclusion contrary to your theory. If Operation Marathon proves you right, the sky's the limit. Even in the worst-case scenario, Operation Marathon is worth at least one more star to you."

A staff aide poked his head through the bridge door and shouted, "Admiral, time for your staff meeting."

Eickhoff nodded. Pew was a dilemma. He needed an aide with a soft moral compass, but every bit of information he gave Pew was damning. He would need to promise Pew a huge reward to buy his loyalty. Eickhoff guessed Pew would do well in political life after he left the navy.

"This is all interesting, but I need sound intelligence on the other ships. I don't care how you get it," Eichkoff said.

§

Aboard the USS *America*, Admiral Eickhoff's staff meeting ended. Seated in the spacious public section of his quarters that doubled as a dining and conference room, Eickhoff played with his coffee cup while the last of his staff filed out. The message from Durham made concentration difficult.

The information blackout Durham had imposed on Operation Marathon presented more problems than expected. Operation Marathon was entering a new and dangerous phase. Eickhoff was sure it was the endgame, and with his next few moves, he would either win big or lose it all. His original plan for Operation Marathon was without risk, but Durham's restructured version increased the risk to Eickhoff.

There was one thing for sure—the *Farnley* was still running. Eickhoff had read Durham's message a dozen times in a vain attempt to glean additional information. The message simply directed the Operation Marathon admirals to inspect their ships for safety and report to the CNO.

Durham's attention to this detail nagged at Eickhoff. Why safety? That was part of the Operation Marathon study and should be left alone.

Durham was weak and didn't understand that Congress wanted Operation Marathon to succeed so he could replace Durham and reshape the navy. The stakes were high enough that an injured sailor or two would be insignificant unless the press found out.

What troubled Eickhoff was that there was no way of knowing where he stood, but he tried to reason his way through the puzzle. By his predictions, the *Farnley* should be the only operational ship left. However, if that were true, his point was made and the operation would be terminated. Obviously, his prediction was wrong, and that spelled danger.

Was Durham looking for more information? But what was it? If only he knew the status of the other ships, he would know what to report to Durham about safety matters aboard the *Farnley*.

If his report was too critical, Durham might pull the *Farnley* out of the operation. If his report was too positive when compared with the other reports, Durham would question his thoroughness. Either outcome was unacceptable; the stakes were far too high. Eickhoff needed answers before drafting his report. Pew's information, if he found out anything, would come too late.

After the last of the officers filed out and their footsteps on the steel passageway had subsided, the quarters became silent. The invisible marine guard in the passageway pulled the door shut with a metallic click, and Eickhoff dragged two thick computer reports and a binder across the oak table. He flipped through detailed equipment maintenance reports and found nothing unexplainable. The only thing of note was that the *Farnley* was overdue for regular hull cleaning and a new coat of paint.

Next, Eickhoff turned to his fleet readiness report. He turned to the page containing the *Farnley*'s summary and was elated to find her rating was 87.3 percent, a mere 5.5 percent below the fleet average. This was far better than he had imagined, and he was sure it was better than other Operation Marathon ships. All systems were operational, and none were limited in capability. The *Farnley* was holding together well and better than expected.

Eickhoff visualized how he would defend himself against his detractors. To draw his conclusions into doubt, they would quibble over details. He would point out, details aside, that he was harder on the *Farnley* than any other Operation Marathon admiral and had given the ship the least experienced captain. With what the *Farnley* had been through, if she was operational at the end of the operation, his point was proven. No one could argue that, hardship for hardship, the new high-technology ships held up better than the *Farnley*.

Building from a base of power, Eickhoff would point out how hard he had fought for Operation Marathon and how he alone was the risk taker. They would question his sincerity and motives. He would explain, once he read the Armed Services Committee nuclear war report, that he was the only one who had the courage and vision to challenge the status quo.

They would demand the source of his data. The information was available to anyone who wanted it, but he would point out he was the only one with the vision and insight to put it together. They would be jealous of his political power, and they would grumble about his promotion.

Eickhoff's detractors didn't understand that the political and populist winds were changing. Of all the potential replacements for Durham, Eickhoff knew he and he alone possessed the political sense to make the necessary changes to doctrine, ships, procurement, and, most of all, leadership. Leaders like Durham were too traditional, too cautious, too analytical. They lacked political savvy, stood on principle, and were anachronisms in modern times. Men like Durham were incapable of making the radical changes demanded by the American people. The high stakes justified Eickhoff's treatment of the *Farnley*. Someday, students would study his handling of Operation Marathon, and teachers would praise his courageous acts.

Eickhoff was satisfied. When Operation Marathon ended, he would be in a position of strength. He would convince Congress the hopeful thinking of the current Pentagon leadership was a recipe for disaster. He would become the architect of tomorrow's navy.

Eickhoff forgot his coffee and the thick report labeled *Past-due Parts Requisitions* and headed toward his desk and the large stack of message traffic waiting for his attention. He frowned at the stack and tried to understand why the navy expected admirals to handle such menial drudgery. He would delegate it to a staff aide in the morning. The message announcing his visit to the *Farnley* in Naples would also wait until morning.

TSUSHIMA-KAIKYO

July 1971, Tsushima-Kaikyo, Eastern Channel
Operation Marathon: Day 374

A month earlier, the aircraft carrier USS *Kennedy* and her battle group were four hours out of Sasebo, Japan, steaming northeastward through the brooding gray, choppy waters of the Korea Strait. The day was unremarkable in every respect; even the low gray clouds rolling seaward over the headlands of Tsushima posed no threat.

From his flag bridge, Admiral Kappel watched the screening destroyers intently, particularly the *Kuntz*. She sat dead in the water. Even at five miles, the two black balls hanging from her yardarm, the international breakdown signal, were visible.

When the exercise started, Kappel guessed she wouldn't last much longer. He had the message to the CNO already drafted. All he needed to do was take it out of his pocket and send it. Then this whole stupid affair would be over.

"Admiral, you won't believe this. We just received a FLASH breakdown report from the Can't-do-*Kuntz*."

It was one of his staff aides, and the derogatory name-calling struck a tender nerve. "It's the USS *Kuntz*," Kappel began and then asked, "Anyone hurt?"

"No," the aide replied, still reading the message.

"What's her status?" Kappel asked, relieved.

Looking up from the five-page message, the aide replied, "What's so amazing, Admiral, is that she reports estimated time-to-repair as four weeks. The message lists all the parts they need for repair. They had to have had this message ready before they broke down."

Kappel cracked a small smile, "They probably did. It's called, 'Even when you are getting your ass kicked, make sure you do it in a smart military manner.'"

Confused, the aide asked, "How could they have known how, when, and where they were going to break down?"

Kappel knew but chose to ignore the question. "Assign a ship to tow her back to Sasebo and send an escort with her. All of the repair parts she needs are in a warehouse there." Reaching into his shirt pocket, he handed the message to the aide. "Send this and a copy of all message traffic to the CNO."

"Two ships for a tow? The chief of naval operations? Her parts are in a warehouse?" asked the confused officer.

"Yes. I'll explain later," Kappel replied, dismissing the aide.

"Aye, aye, Admiral," the officer said, turning to leave.

Kappel reached into his pocket and retrieved two marble-sized brass bearings. He rolled them in his hand for a second and then jerked around to call after the officer. "Another thing. Her crew doesn't deserve this humiliation. Have the other ships give her men, parts, anything she needs. If they can patch the problem so she can steam back into port under her own power, do it. I'd like to see her steam into Sasebo with her head high."

Kappel was sad he had lost the *Kuntz*, but he was glad it was over. He had prepared for this moment and knew what he had to do next. If only he could figure out a way to tell the *Kuntz*'s captain about Operation Marathon. Resigned to his duty, Kappel lifted the phone from its cradle to call flight operations. He would be waiting on the pier when the *Kuntz* arrived in Sasebo. He owed her crew that much, and much more.

RETURNING HOME

August 1971, Norfolk Navy Base
Operation Marathon: Day 404

The clock on his dashboard read five a.m. when O'Toole drove through the main gate at the Norfolk naval base and headed toward the pier six parking lot. O'Toole had been stationed on the West Coast for almost a year, and the number of new patches added to the road surface surprised him. The base's ancient sewer system teetered on the verge of collapse, but he had no idea it was this bad.

In the early dawn light, O'Toole stepped out of his gray Chevy Impala, brushed back his red hair, and placed his uniform cap squarely on his head. With a smile, he inhaled a deep breath of air through his nostrils and savored the aroma of the sea air, marine growth, and fuel oil. It invigorated him, and he briskly headed to the pier and the *Wainwright*'s berth.

On the pier, O'Toole found himself alone except for a single sailor walking twenty paces ahead. The sounds of the pier, the airy whine of blowers, and the sounds of the ships' powerful machinery were familiar to him and put him at ease. Quickening his step, he kept his eyes trained forward, resisting the urge to look at the three-deep nest of sleek gray destroyers on each side of him. There would be time for looking later. For now, he was content just to feel their presence and smell the mixed aromas of ships and sea. He was home again.

In less than a week, O'Toole would take command of Destroyer Squadron Twenty-Three. He had never counted the number of squadrons he'd commanded but was sure it had been three in the last two years alone. For other commodores, a tour lasted two years, but for O'Toole, it spanned only six months because that was the length of his unofficial postgraduate curriculum in military seamanship. He knew dozens of admirals owed their stars to the training he gave them. Still, he refused promotion. He saw no incongruity in this and thought of himself as a simple teacher, and the subjects he taught best were leadership and the art of command at sea.

Larry Laswell

Destroyers, the navy's answer to the foot soldier, were O'Toole's home. He could see it no other way. When the admirals ordered the fleet to stand in harm's way, destroyers would take the point and carry the battle. The first flashes of battle in predawn twilight would come from the muzzles of destroyers and the last flashes from destroyers pursuing a shattered enemy or covering the fleet's retreat.

O'Toole's experience included both outcomes, and he knew the prerequisites to victory were the skill, steel, and audacity of command. Defeat, which had no prerequisites, was measured in the blood of fine young men.

O'Toole studied the sailor walking down the pier. The man carried a large sealed manila envelope clamped under his right arm, a heavy seabag on his left shoulder, and a medium-sized suitcase in his right hand. O'Toole liked the cut of his jib. His rolling gait with its broad beam would serve him well in a blow. O'Toole didn't have to guess; his morning companion was a seasoned tin-can man.

The man struggled under the heavy load, so O'Toole jogged several paces to catch up with him. As O'Toole came abreast of the man, the manila envelope slipped from its position and fell to the concrete.

"Let me help you," O'Toole said, picking up the envelope and snatching the suitcase from the man's hand.

Relieved, the sailor started to say thank you until he realized his Good Samaritan was a flag officer. They made eye contact, and O'Toole took a quick step forward to indicate a salute was neither expected nor necessary. The early-morning hour absolved them both of formality. This was just a matter of one tin-can man helping another.

"Where're you headed, sailor?" O'Toole asked.

Startled and a bit surprised to have a flag officer carrying his suitcase, the sailor replied, "Good morning, sir, and thank you for the help. I'm headed for the *Wainwright*. Commodore O'Toole?"

The man knew him, but O'Toole's infallible memory for names failed him. "I'm sorry, but I don't remember your name. Who are you, sailor?" O'Toole asked.

"Electrician's Mate Second Class Maholic, sir. DESRON Eight, San Diego, last year."

O'Toole smiled. "Now I remember. Come on. I'm headed for the *Wainwright* myself. After next week, she'll be my flagship."

Both men began walking again, and after a few seconds, a devilish grin spread across Maholic's face. "Excuse me, Commodore, but are they expecting you?"

"Of course not," O'Toole said, returning the grin. "Do you think I get up this early for the hell of it?"

40

Maholic replied immediately. "Commodore, would you mind if I wait on the pier until you get aboard?"

O'Toole permitted himself one last chuckle. "Not at all; just promise you won't tell on me."

Larry Laswell

STRAITS OF MESSINA

August 1971, Straits of Messina
Operation Marathon: Day 407

Protected from the hot evening sun by the bridge house shadow, Lieutenant Steve Biron relaxed on the bridge wing, gazing at the headlands of Italy and Sicily rising peacefully above a cerulean sea. The shadow was as welcome as cool grass in the moist shade of a maple. After the futile gunnery exercises and the exhausting pace of the six days past, the evening was a just reward, like a sleepy Sunday afternoon in a tree-lined park.

Older than most would guess, Biron had recently turned thirty, although his boyish features, blond hair, and blue eyes made most people miss his age by a good five years. His circular steel-rimmed glasses added to his youthful appearance and identified him incorrectly as a member of the sixties generation. Javert had told him, "Get rid of those damned hippie glasses." Biron didn't think it a problem, so he kept them.

"Hey, I hear Sixth Fleet is coming for a visit while we're in Naples."

Biron glanced to his right to see Petty Officer Sweeney standing next to him mirroring his pose against the bridge railing. Sweeney, the pudgy Okie, lacked appreciation for the solitude of a bridge wing. Whenever his duties permitted, Sweeney kept close station to the bridge officer so he could snatch any morsel of new information. Biron liked Sweeney, the natural nerve center of the ship's unofficial rumor mill. Sweeney proudly told newcomers, "'Round here, I'm the scuttlebutt king."

"That's the word. Admiral Eickhoff is coming for a visit," Biron answered matter-of-factly.

"How come?"

"Don't know."

"Why the gunnery exercise, Mister Biron?"

Another fishing expedition, Biron thought. Biron didn't mind Sweeney's questions, and in fact he found Sweeney's nonstop information-mongering an amusing diversion. Sweeney's nimble mind could connect two unrelated facts in a heartbeat. He could produce three

42

opinions on anything and an angle on everything. Guessing what tangent Sweeney would take next was an endless challenge.

"Don't know. What's the skinny?" Biron asked.

"Me, I don't know nothin'. Nobody tells me anything," Sweeney said innocently. "I thought you'd know what the exercise was all about."

Biron smiled. A quest it was, and an intriguing one at that. He didn't have an answer for Sweeney but decided to throw him an unrelated fact. Perhaps something would sprout. "Ever been to 'Nam?"

"Why?"

"Well, that's what we did there. We ran in a circle providing gunfire support in the day and rearming at night."

"That was different. You were doing something. This was practice. It doesn't take twenty hours of firing to teach the mount crews what to do."

"Don't know what to tell you, Sweeney," Biron said.

Of all the natural structures Biron knew, the Strait of Messina was his favorite. Some presence far mightier than man possessed the fjordlike strait. His memories of the strait remained as unchanged by time as the sea itself, its weather always the same as it was today: the air quiet, heavy, and somber; the waters forever a dark, brooding slate gray; while the currents, perpetually shifting on the smooth, oil like surface, etched the surface with eddies, rips, and whirlpools. It was a place worthy of the gods and the songs of Homer. Something mystical possessed this place.

"What'cha lookin' at, sir?"

Sweeney's question brought him back to reality, but Homer lingered in his mind. "This is an ancient land, Sweeney. It's a land of gods and monsters."

"Monsters?"

Biron was accustomed to Sweeney's appetite for mythology and sea lore. "To the ancients, the strait was home to twin monsters, Scylla and Charybdis," Biron began. "Do you know who the Sirens were?"

"A bunch of gorgeous broads who suckered sailors in by singing to them, right?"

Biron had never thought of comparing the Sirens to waterfront B-girls before.

Sweeney continued, "Charybdis? I think I heard that name in some monster movie once."

"That's a different monster," Biron said.

A voice from inside the bridge house announced, "Sir, it's twenty hundred hours. Range to point alpha is three-thousand-five-hundred yards."

Time to go to work. Biron acknowledged the quartermaster's report and turned to Sweeney. "Set the navigation watch."

Only vaguely aware of Sweeney's voice blaring over the topside speakers, Biron gazed at the calm sea and the majestic headlands. The sight tugged at him, and he realized how much he loved the sea, her beauty, her myths, her poetry, her fury, her tranquility.

There wasn't time for this; he needed to do his job. He jerked his body away from the bridge railing and stepped into the bridge house. Within minutes, the bridge overflowed with sailors, and the bosun posted extra lookouts. In bored, monotonous voices, men called out bearings, and the status board keeper tracked every surface contact. A safety observer, Ensign Hayes, took station behind Seaman Portalatin, the navigation detail helmsman.

With the navigation detail assembled, Biron walked to the center of the bridge and forward of the helm where there was room to move and give him an unrestricted view of both bows. Biron blocked out the commotion around him and was only remotely aware of the presence of Javert and Meyers. He concentrated on the only three things that mattered: the sea, his ship, and his helmsman, Portalatin.

Portalatin, the best helmsman he knew, possessed both the gift and the natural physique for the job. He was tall with broad, muscular shoulders, and his arms seemed to hang almost to his knees. Everyone on the crew called Portalatin Kong.

Biron's voice rose above the din, and he spoke with a slow, fluid cadence. "Right standard rudder, come to new course zero-three-zero."

"Right standard rudder. Aye, sir," Portalatin replied, echoing Biron's cadence.

Biron listened to the sound of the wheel as it spun slowly under Portalatin's hand. The turn would be a slow, graceful arc, just as he had requested.

The constant drone of contact and bearing reports continued. Biron didn't need the reports, but he checked each against what he could see and filed the information away. He was proud of his ability to con a ship by eye, the way sailors had done it for centuries before gyrocompasses and radar.

Everything was as it should be. Biron relaxed. The coastal traffic was light, and he had a few minutes until his next turn. It would be his easiest transit yet.

Meyers walked over to Biron, chuckling. "Have you heard the latest?" Meyers asked.

Biron shook his head no before Meyers continued. "The reason Admiral Eickhoff is visiting us in Naples is to give us new orders. The word is the navy is pulling us out of the Med next month and sending us to Viet Nam for gunfire support."

Biron wanted to change the subject but couldn't figure out how. "No kidding," he replied weakly.

"Yeah, it's all over the ship. I heard it coming up here."

Biron feigned a smile. "Too bad. I like the Med. I'll sure miss the scenery."

Meyers nodded toward Sicily. "It's beautiful, isn't it?"

Relieved, Biron turned toward the high southern shore and tried to formulate a response. Beautiful didn't cover it. The power and character of the massive granite cliffs spoke of strength in words unspeakable. The strait was as irrepressible and ageless as the gnarled trees that clung to every crag, as irrepressible as its people. The strait was nobility.

"Yeah, but the word doesn't seem to capture it," Biron began as he adjusted his wire-rimmed glasses. "Until you see this, you can't understand why this land gave birth to the indomitable legions of Rome. It inspired Fronto and Marcus Aurelius in their pursuit of Stoic philosophy and reason, and why the centurions and generals of Rome believed in death before dishonor. The Caesars, Rome, her legions, are all products of this land. Even today, the Sicilian Mafioso clings to the death-before-dishonor ethic. The land is harsh and unforgiving. One couldn't expect less of its people."

Meyers shook his head and grinned. "Biron, where do you get all that stuff?"

Meyers' expression told him he had gone far beyond the simple answer expected. It embarrassed him, and he attempted to recover. "I majored in history and literature."

"That's a strange mix. Why history and literature?" Meyers asked.

The question struck Biron as strange. "Sounds natural to me. You find the greatest literature in history, and the best history in literature," Biron said, wondering if he answered the question.

Meyers chuckled and slapped Biron on the back. "Well spoken, Sir Biron; I thought of this place as plain pretty."

Meyers' teasing didn't bother him; it was all in good fun. With a sheepish grin, Biron ended the conversation by raising his binoculars to get a closer view of the ferry.

"Sir, distance to point Bravo, one-thousand-five-hundred yards."

"Sir, nearest shoal water one thousand yards off the starboard bow. Sixty yards right of track."

"New skunk *Lima* on collision course. Bearing zero-one-zero, constant bearing decreasing range."

Biron's eyes were on it. The ferry leaving Villa San Giovanni for Messina would not be a threat. Wait two minutes, come right to about zero-six-zero to pass astern of her, then swing hard left to stay clear of the shoals, an easy and safe maneuver. He guessed the ferry would follow the normal pattern and increase speed, which made his maneuver easier and any other course of action perilous.

§

Javert, seated in his chair, listened to Biron's and Meyers' small talk. It annoyed him. "Pay attention, Mister Biron. You have a ferry on a collision course."

"Aye, Captain," Biron said.

Meyers left Biron's side and took a position between Biron and Javert.

Familiar with the strait, Javert felt Biron ignored the strait's salient qualities. Its sharp, craggy channel and stone bottom wouldn't ground ships; it would tear their bottoms out. The strait's unyielding stone cliffs made it absolute and unforgiving.

"Sir, range to skunk *Lima* one-thousand yards."

"Very well," Biron replied, acknowledging the report.

Javert wondered what hold Biron had on the men. He was always in control and calm, commanding, and confident. The men admired him and recognized him as a fine conning officer. Javert's eyes scanned the enlisted men on the bridge. They were a dirty, slovenly, uneducated, and unmotivated herd of sheep, yet Biron held some special power over them.

Doesn't the crew understand I outrank him? Don't they know I'm the captain?

The questions, unanswered, echoed through Javert's mind. His teachers had been right; the society of the sea is tribal. Leaders gained power through strength and gall. In his experience, no officer ever mustered the courage to challenge the authority of the captains he had known, all bold and daring men.

Javert feared he had let the challenge to his authority go unanswered too often. Oh yes, he would chastise his officers for challenging him, but it didn't help. To prove his superiority, he needed to show he was stronger, bolder, and wiser. That was what the crew waited for. If he could show up Biron, the men would follow him. They were sheep. It was tribal.

"Sir, range to skunk *Lima* nine-hundred yards. Still on collision course."

Javert tried to guess what Biron would do. He would do the safe thing, the cowardly thing, and pass astern of the ferry. He would turn right toward the shoal water. A bolder act would be . . .

"Sir, range to skunk *Lima* eight-hundred yards. Sir, navigation recommends new course zero-six-five to avoid."

A small smile crossed Biron's face. "Right standard rudder. Come right to new course zero-six-five."

"Belay that order," Javert called out in a strong, clear voice. Portalatin froze. His eyes jerked between Javert and Biron. Poised, his right hand hovered motionless above the wheel.

§

Shocked, Meyers spun to confront Javert. Javert had entered the gray area between law and tradition. The law held Biron, the conning officer, responsible for the ship's safety. As captain, tradition held that Javert had just relieved Biron of all responsibility by countermanding his order. If anything went wrong, the law would punish one, tradition the other.

Meyers understood Biron's dilemma. His only options were to follow orders and endanger the ship or disobey a direct order. Even if Biron disobeyed, Meyers wondered if he could regain control of the bridge crew in time. Anyone who followed Biron's orders risked court-martial along with Biron. The safety of the ship was his first responsibility. Biron needed to lead; he needed to ignore Javert's order.

"That course will take you closer to the shoals. Come to fifteen knots and come left ten degrees, Mister Biron."

"Captain, no," Biron said.

"I said do it now, Mister Biron. Make it so!" Javert yelled back.

"Sir, range to skunk *Lima* seven-hundred yards. Still on collision course."

Biron looked dumbstruck.

"Captain, there is room. We should turn sharply to signal our intentions. It is the safest maneuver," Meyers said to Javert.

"Sir, navigation recommends course zero-seven-zero to avoid skunk *Lima*. Still on collision course."

"Mister Biron, I gave you a direct order. Do it now," Javert yelled.

"Three-hundred yards to extremis skunk *Lima*."

"No, Biron," Meyers screamed, raising his hand toward Portalatin like a traffic cop. "Captain, that's a dangerous maneuver. Let Biron handle the ship."

"XO, I won't have you challenging me on the bridge like this. Do you understand? Mister Biron, you have your orders. Make them so!" Javert was yelling, his voice shrill.

"Sir, range to skunk *Lima* six-hundred yards. Zero-eight-zero to avoid. Two-hundred yards to extremis, skunk *Lima*."

Biron still didn't respond. For the safety of the ship, Meyers needed to end this and snap Biron out of his apparent daze. He stepped between

Javert and Biron and turned his back to Javert. In a firm voice that would brook no delay or second thoughts, he said, "Bring us about, Mr. Biron."

"Right hard rudder." Biron's voice was like a thunderclap.

"No," Javert screamed.

Portalatin's huge shoulders drove his hand in a slashing movement across the top of the wheel.

Oblivious to Biron's last command, Javert jumped to his feet, grabbed Meyers' arm, and spun him around. In a rage, Javert yelled, "I won't have you or any other officer questioning my authority. Do you understand? We would have been safe doing it my way."

"You're wrong, Captain," Meyers replied before catching his balance as the ship heeled sharply to starboard. The insanity of the situation appalled Meyers—a captain ordering his ship into a collision and an executive officer yelling and arguing with his captain in front of the crew.

Javert turned his rage on Biron. "Mister Biron, when I give you an order, I expect you to follow it. Do you understand, mister?" Biron ignored Javert and kept his eyes on the ferry as it passed down the port side a mere hundred yards away.

They avoided collision by less than twenty seconds, a time far too short for two large vessels. Meyers' temper flared at Javert's attack on Biron.

"Captain, do you see the puff of smoke behind the ferry?" Meyers began. "The ferry increased speed. If Biron had followed your order, we would be colliding with them right now."

Javert made no attempt to look. "Mister Meyers, I won't permit this insubordination. I won't allow you to challenge my authority. Off my bridge now."

Meyers welcomed those words. He'd done his job. The ship was out of danger. Meyers pushed his way past Biron and stormed off the bridge.

Descending the ladders to the main level, Meyers wondered if he'd crossed the line.

That's a stupid question. You did on several accounts.

Now his hell would be over, and the hell for the crew of the *Farnley* would soon be over. He had made the right decision no matter what happened now, or, he wondered, was there something else he might have done?

Meyers passed through the wardroom and stepped over the low combing to enter his small stateroom. The four-foot-long seabag hanging from its pipe swung with the roll of the ship. The rough green twill in the bag's midsection was worn smooth. The round, smooth spot stared at him, trying to tell him something.

Slowly, the message came to him. It wasn't over. He'd crossed the line, but it didn't matter. Javert wouldn't bring charges. Meyers could hear Javert's standard answer: "Reports of increased disciplinary problems only show superiors that a captain isn't doing his job. Good captains don't have disciplinary problems." Javert would find some way to deny what had happened on the bridge.

Meyers jabbed at the sea bag inquisitively. It swung away from the mild blow. The voice inside Meyers' head called out, *The captain knows he needs me; he can't shit-can me.* Meyers threw a left hook into the bag. The bag wobbled end for end and swung away. *I can't resign or force the issue. I have a responsibility to the crew.* The rage swelled up again. Meyers threw a right jab, and pain shot through his shoulder from the impact. *I can't do my job.* He braced himself. *I can't win.* He swung with his left. *I can't quit.* He stepped into the bag, driving his right fist deep into the bag's midsection.

I can't even get fired. I'm trapped!

The impact of each swing forced air from Meyers' lungs, making a grunting sound. He increased the speed of his blows. His blows become rapid, and his grunts became a continuous scream.

Just a few more days. When the admiral visits, he'll see. It'll be over soon. The captain will deny everything. He will continue as he always has.

§

About midnight, Meyers put his pen down and stared at the open page in his diary. While making his entry for the day, he searched for an avenue of escape and found none.

This was the second time in the last few days Javert had almost killed someone. Meyers had to do something, but what? He could continue to fight Javert, or he could bring him down. Technically, both were mutiny, the former private, the latter public.

At Annapolis, like all midshipmen, Meyers had learned about mutiny, and its causes, mechanisms, and inevitable outcomes. The written laws concerning mutiny were few and simple, but mutiny wasn't just a simple legal infraction. It was the unwritten law of the sea, the unwritten code of the navy that bothered Meyers most.

These laws were not written in ink on mortal paper; they were written in the blood of generations, tested by adversity, and presented as a gift of wisdom to the each new generation. As Meyers studied the handful of mutinies in naval history, the voice of generations was clear, their expectations high, and their standards unwavering. The gravest sin and ultimate travesty, mutiny was the coward's way out.

Tradition demanded that the conclusions were inescapable; mutiny was never justified. In the modern navy, mutiny was bloodless. Officers determined to bring a captain down wrote innocent letters, made innocuous statements to the chaplain, or told humorous stories to officers from other ships. Ultimately, the navy investigated, relieved the captain, and punished the mutineers. Even keeping a private log of a captain's irrational behavior was mutinous. The judges would see the log as a preplanned defense to a mutinous act; that proved premeditation.

Meyers' teachers had taught him the responsibilities of an officer, especially a ship's executive officer. He held a responsibility to protect the ship from a mad or incompetent captain, but he also had a responsibility to follow the captain with his full loyalty and obedience. Anything else was mutiny. The fact that the responsibilities were in conflict made no difference. It was up to the officer to resolve the conflict without impinging on the unlimited authority of the captain. All his teachers had been impeccable officers, and Meyers felt cheated; they never needed to apply the canons they taught.

Until now, Meyers thought his teachers had taught him well. Over his years at sea, the theology of tradition had withstood the test of experience. All his captains had been exceptional men whose mastery of their office wasn't just exceptional; it was pervasive. He'd seen captains calm a frightened bridge crew with a word, a wink, or a beguiling smile. If these men had anything, they could make men believe in themselves and in the impossible.

Out of the thousands of captains in every century, perhaps three dozen could be called mistakes. He'd also learned the navy rarely made mistakes. Perhaps a dozen would fall through the cracks and another dozen would keep their commands, but the navy would end their careers. The navy would relieve the remainder, but only a few of these would be brought down by mutinous officers. In every case, it was the executive officer who held the ship together despite the captain or who led the mutiny against him. Neither situation was good, but mutinous ships always paid the higher price.

No two cases were the same, and the *Farnley* followed the pattern. Meyers didn't know what to do about Javert. Javert wasn't a man gone insane or intoxicated by unbridled power. These would be easy to deal with, but his judgment of Javert was more a matter of opinion. Javert didn't have the experience, the emotional stability, or the native ability to lead or command.

"Excuse me. XO?"

Biron stood in the doorway. Meyers closed the diary and threw it into the lower-right desk drawer.

cruiser's eight-inchers."

Ross brought himself up short as memories of the boiler explosion flooded his mind. *How did I get out?* he asked himself. He reached up and rubbed the burn scar on his neck. The gap in his memory still troubled him. He remembered something about screams, heat, and pain. He didn't want to remember the rest. After the explosion, the next thing he could recall was a shipmate pulling him through the oily water toward a life raft. Somehow his mind retained a picture of Chief Barnes standing on the burning deck of the *Able*, but it was an unconnected fragment. It was the last time he saw Chief Barnes.

Why did I live while so many others died?

The group around Ross lowered their eyes and waited for him to resume. The man in the shadows swallowed and lowered his head. Behind Ross' wooden bench, Elmo found a cookie crumb and danced around it, waving his antennae with glee.

Ross shook off the memories and started again. "After we got hit, we took out two Jap destroyers."

"How?"

"I don't remember much. I was pretty well out of it, but from what the other guys told me, well, we had this crazy gunnery officer. Don't remember his name, but he was a fiery red-headed Irishman who was always raising hell about something. Well, this crazy Irishman has his gunnery crews stack ammo on the deck like cordwood. The Japs must have written us off 'cause this one Jap destroyer comes flying past us at point-blank range. We opened fire and hit her magazine, and she went down like a rock. Guess the Japs couldn't figure out what happened 'cause we opened fire on the other destroyer and got that one, too. Then this crazy Irishman starts shooting at the cruiser. The man was nuts. They said he'd have gotten the cruiser, but the gun mounts started flooding. The *Able* never struck her colors. She never gave up."

"Like us?" Stucky asked.

"We haven't given up. We just gotta be careful about which battles we pick," Ross said.

"When I came aboard a year ago, stuff worked, not like she is now," Stucky said.

"Yeah," Ross began. "I came aboard before you, and we had a damn good engine room, almost as good as the *Able*'s. Then the navy went crazy, transferred most of the senior petty officers, and the supply system lost our address. You can fix stuff with baling wire and chewing gum only for so long. If we could get half of the parts we asked for, this would be a pretty good engine room."

"So, Chief, what happened?"

"Hell if I know. This isn't the way things are supposed to be. It's not part of the deal, and this ain't my navy anymore. In eleven more months, I'll have my thirty years in, and I can retire."

§

An officer stepped from the shadows by the starboard escape ladder. Ross didn't recognize him, but the glint of silver on his collar told Ross he was a lieutenant junior grade. As the man stepped into the light, his face mesmerized Ross. He appeared Oriental with short, black hair that framed a young, friendly face. His eyes were clear, lively, and the blackest he'd ever seen. The man appeared to be smiling, but Ross sensed he wasn't; it just looked that way. The man's circular face made Ross think of a sticker with a smiley face printed in black ink. Ross shook the image off and took in the rest of the man. He was short; Ross had seen taller bollards.

The men scrambled to their feet, but Ross remained seated until the officer spoke. "You must be Chief Ross. I'm Mister Lee, the new engineering officer."

Ross stood, stuffed the screwdriver into his hip pocket, and extended his hand. He couldn't keep his eyes off Lee's face. He didn't know if it was the eyes or the smile, but then again, the entire face was a smile; even his eyes were smiling.

"Glad to meet you, Mister Lee."

Ross thought there was a change in Lee's perpetual grin and felt that he was now smiling on purpose. Lee's eyes twinkled intelligence. That bothered Ross. Young officers were always hard to break in, and the smarter they were, the harder the job became. Even the best officers had a lot to learn, and Ross had lost his appetite for teaching. He had no desire to break in another kid—not here, not now. "Well, welcome aboard," Ross said, only to be polite.

Lee turned to the gauge board and swept his eyes around the engine room. "This is complicated, Chief." Lee walked over to the railing behind Ross' bench and pointed toward the lower level. "What's that?" he asked.

Ross tried to figure out what Lee was looking at. "What's what?"

"That," Lee said, pointing to Elmo dancing around a crumb. "First roach I ever saw with paint on its back."

Ross smiled. "That's Petty Officer Third Class Elmo Cockroach. He's the engine room mascot."

Lee's silence surprised Ross. Lee's eyes probed Ross, and their steady penetration made the chief uncomfortable.

Lee turned to face the gauge board. The other men had vanished.

Ross couldn't take his eyes off Lee. Lee looked like a wide-eyed kid who had discovered his first caterpillar. Ross had seen this before and knew this kid was going to be a real pain.

"Are you busy now, Chief?" Lee asked.

"No, why?"

"Would you mind giving me a quick tour?"

Ross minded. "It's late. We can do that tomorrow. You need some time to rest and get bunked down."

"Already done, and I'm wide awake. My body still thinks it's afternoon. Chief, I'd appreciate a quick tour."

Ross guessed this wouldn't end until Lee got his tour. Resigned, Ross replied, "Well, okay." He knew it; the kid was going to be a pain. He would wear Lee out, break him in quickly, and teach him what the *Farnley* was all about.

"Let's start right here," Ross said. "This here's your gauge board. You have two vacuum and two steam gauges. One of your steam gauges is broken. Been waiting for parts for six months."

"All the gauges are PSIG, not absolute, right?" Lee asked.

The question surprised Ross. Lee had done his homework. "That's right. None of these gauges is absolute. Under the gauge board, you got your four throttle valves, two for each engine. The big one's the ahead throttle; the small one's the astern throttle."

"Why do you keep saying 'your,' Chief?"

The question came sooner than Ross expected. "Well, you're the new engineering officer, aren't you?"

Lee nodded.

"Then all this is yours. You own it and—" Ross was cut short by the same penetrating gaze he'd seen before. Lee's eyes lost their sparkle, but the crazy grin across his face remained. Ross couldn't pin it down. Lee wasn't judging him, but his eyes embarrassed Ross.

For the next two hours, Ross led Lee through the engine room and the two boiler rooms, pointing out equipment and introducing Lee to the men. Lee's curiosity surprised Ross. Lee was interested in everything and wanted to know something about everything. When Ross tried to bypass a section, Lee would veer down a catwalk, pointing and asking questions.

Ross couldn't do anything about Lee's curiosity, so he settled into the routine. At every opportunity, Ross began his explanation, "That's your . . . and it's broken . . . been waiting for parts for . . ." He hoped Lee would get the idea.

Lee listened, but the words had no visible effect. Ross tested Lee by stopping in places that would force the young engineering officer to stand in the steam plumes from the *Farnley*'s numerous steam leaks. Lee, drenched in sweat, didn't react. Instead, he kept asking questions, lots of good questions.

As the tour ended, Ross said with relief, "That's it, Mister Lee. You've seen everything."

"You must have good men, Chief," Lee said while mopping sweat from his forehead with the back of his hand. "This place is like Dante's Inferno."

Ross smiled at the greasy black streak Lee had spread across his brow. Puzzled, Lee held up his greasy hands. "And the Black Hole of Calcutta," he added.

Ross glanced at the clock. It was past ten. "Yes, sir, Mister Lee, and it's all your'n."

"Funny, Chief, it looks like a hole full of shit to me," Lee replied.

Ross' head jerked around to meet Lee's gaze. Lee had hit a long-dormant nerve, and the anger that exploded in his gut surprised Ross. Ross glared deep into Lee's firm but tranquil eyes. There was no malice or judgment there. He wasn't being cute or threatening. Lee's happy-looking face unnerved Ross, but neither man broke eye contact. Ross tried to stare Lee down but gave up. Lee's black, piercing eyes showed only honest interest. Lee wasn't trying to compete. He's just stating the obvious truth in a rather blunt way, Ross decided. Nothing to get upset about.

Lee broke the silence. "Chief, do the men always wear their oldest uniforms down here?"

Lee's questions no longer surprised Ross. "No, for some of them, what you saw was their newest uniforms. There's only one place in the Med to get uniforms, and that's here in Naples. Here we are, and the captain canceled liberty," Ross replied, letting the anger drain out with his words.

Lee's face brightened. "So that's why all the long faces."

Ross thought about that statement for a second. Sooner or later, he needed to make his position clear to Lee, and now was as good a time as any. "That's only the tip of the iceberg. It's the *Farnley*. They're like everyone else here, including you. We're all serving out our sentences, doing our time." Ross waited for a reaction. None came.

"What about the haircuts?"

"No ship's barber," Ross snapped back at his unflappable enigma.

"It's late now, but could you spend some time with me tomorrow and fill me in on the supply problems?"

"Sure," Ross said, surprising himself by his answer.

"One more question, Chief. Did you show me all the known steam leaks?"

Ross blushed a little. "Not all of them."

"You can show me the rest tomorrow."

"Can't. The rest only show up when we're using the engines." Ross couldn't believe he was almost laughing. Lee was one savvy kid.

Lee's eyes gleamed, and Ross guessed he was smiling again. "Well, once we get under way, you can show them to me. Good night, and thanks for your time." Lee headed for the ladder.

Ross, fingering the screwdriver in his hip pocket, waited for Lee to climb the ladder. A greasy sailor stepped around the boiler casing and asked, "Who was that, Chief?"

"That's the new engineering officer. His name's Lee," Ross answered.

"Does he always look so happy?"

"Don't know, but a shit-eatin' grin seems normal for him."

"He gives you the feeling he's always up to something. Couldn't play poker with him; it'd drive me nuts."

"You're telling me," Ross said.

"Is he going to be trouble, Chief?"

"Yeah, at least until the *Farnley* breaks him. So far, she's broken everybody."

"Will he break?"

Ross' eyes darted around for a second in thought. "Don't know."

Ross couldn't decide if he liked Lee. Something deep inside him hated the new engineering officer. He didn't understand his hateful and irrational feelings. Lee appeared eager, bright, intelligent, and likable. Ross wanted to do his time and get out. Lee was a man who cared.

§

In Norfolk, Virginia, O'Toole sat on a small raised platform set beneath a white canvas awning on the *Wainwright*'s fantail. This change-of-command ceremony had produced the usual splitting headache. The only thing he liked less than a change-of-command ceremony was a splitting headache. He wondered if there was a connection.

O'Toole took in the formation of the assembled officers and senior petty officers of DESRON 23. Over the past week, he'd climbed through every hole in each of the six ships of the squadron, ostensibly to check material conditions. His real purpose was to meet the men, and he had spoken with most of those assembled on the fantail.

O'Toole thought the situation a little ridiculous. The *Wainwright*'s fantail wasn't large enough for the hundred-plus men it held, and the result was more like an organized mob scene than a formation. O'Toole remembered how it had been for him when, as junior officer, he had to attend similar ceremonies. He still thought these ceremonies were chickenshit.

The men, in their dress white uniforms, stood at attention in the blistering sun and pretended to listen with interest to the words of Commodore Fosner, who was speaking from the bunting-draped podium. Fosner was droning on about what an honor it was for him to have been their commodore for the past two years. O'Toole had heard it all before, but out of respect for the men and Fosner, he did his best to pay attention.

When Commodore Fosner completed his address, O'Toole stepped to the podium and, with a salute, completed the ritual of relieving Fosner as commodore. With the ceremony done, Fosner walked away, and O'Toole stepped to the podium. He didn't speak because first impressions were important.

In the past few seconds, their relationship had changed but not in the way the men expected. They were now his students, and he would become their teacher. By their expressions, O'Toole could tell his reputation had preceded him. They expected him to rant about equipment, maintenance, tarnished brass, and poorly shined shoes. Instead, he would teach the officers to think, be resourceful, and lead. He would use his Irish temperament and gravel-pit voice to deliver each crafted lesson.

O'Toole understood only too well what most of the men were too young to know. In combat, the enemy is the greatest teacher. The lessons, written in the blood of young men, teach the officers to lead, gamble, dare, and not only think, but also do the impossible. O'Toole would give the officers the sum total of his battle experience so perhaps fewer young men would have to make the ultimate sacrifice.

O'Toole had learned from experience and years of scholarly research that all decisive naval battles were fought close to shore over sea-lane choke points or strategic land masses. Those battles were won by those with the greatest skill in green-water tactics and by those who could make the night their own, a storm their friend, shoal water their home, and tight channels their lair. The men of his new squadron were blue-water sailors, and he would change that.

O'Toole would be their enemy. He would do the unexpected and challenge them until they understood that the word *impossible* was a self-imposed limit. Pride, teamwork, and ingenuity would mold them into an enviable battle-ready unit. He would do nothing. They would do it all themselves, and the spit and polish would take care of itself. When that happened, they would meet his standards of excellence. Then and only then would he call them adequate. At that moment of his surrender, he would rejoice with them in their victory.

It was easy for O'Toole to evaluate these men. They were not only good; they were the best he'd ever seen. Inside, his nerves bristled. He was unsure he was good enough to be their teacher.

He forced himself to concentrate so his outward appearance would be right. He imagined himself a stone statue, cold, hard, and ever serene. His appearance, like his gravelly voice, were tools of his trade.

O'Toole glared at the captains of the six squadron ships standing in front of the podium. It was time for their first lesson: the enemy is unpredictable.

O'Toole stooped to reach the microphone and spoke in a low voice that sounded like a threatening growl. "I don't understand why you're standing here in your dress uniforms. In exactly"—O'Toole paused to check his watch—"three hours and eighteen minutes, this squadron will sortie for a three-day training cruise. Captains, I expect your sea readiness reports within the hour."

O'Toole didn't wait to examine the wide eyes and the stunned, mouth-agape stares of the men. The process had begun again. This was his home. Finished, he turned, strolled off the podium, and headed for his quarters. He didn't walk too fast. He could hear the commotion on the fantail and the buzz of a hundred voices filled with disbelief.

"He can't do that. It's impossible. It takes six hours to prepare a ship for sea."

You mean it used to take six hours.

O'Toole smiled to himself. They could do it in less than ten minutes. They hadn't learned that yet, but one lesson at a time.

O'Toole was almost off the fantail when someone called his name. It never failed. It was time for lesson number two. He turned to face the six squadron captains chasing him. "Yes?" he asked.

"Commodore, it takes six hours to get a ship ready for sea. There's no way we can be ready in three." It was John Flannery, the newest and most junior skipper in the squadron. O'Toole liked that Flannery had something on his mind and was saying it. Flannery wasn't going to take a backseat to anyone.

"Oh, why is that?" O'Toole asked.

"BUSHIPS regulations require a six-hour gradual heating of the boilers."

O'Toole scratched his head, pretending to be perplexed. "We certainly wouldn't want to violate any regulations, would we? Guess we should play it safe. Guess we should run this squadron by the book, right?"

All nodded agreement.

"Tell me, Captain Flannery," O'Toole began, "how important is training for a peacetime navy?"

"Very important. It's one of our primary missions."

"Why?" O'Toole probed.

"To prepare for war," Flannery answered.

"Why?" O'Toole repeated in the same soft voice.

Flannery didn't answer.

O'Toole let the growl in his voice start from his stomach and work its way up. "I'll tell you why. It's so men like you and I don't lose ships and good men because we made stupid mistakes or played it safe. It's so we don't have to write letters home to bereaved mothers. We're under way in three hours." O'Toole checked his watch. "And twelve minutes."

O'Toole started to leave, but Flannery persisted. "What about the BUSHIPS regulations?"

"Regulations written by a bean-counting desk jockey who never had to stand a ship in harm's way or face muzzle-to-muzzle combat. Regulations guaranteed to produce the longest boiler life. The only lives I'm concerned about are those of your crews. I used my judgment and just suspended the regulations. If you live by the book, your enemy will bury you with it.

"In war, you would push your ship and men to their bitter limits. You and your men don't know your real limits because of a bunch of landlocked, cost-conscious GS-13s who wrote some idiotic regulations. By the time you learned the limits, good men would be dead. That's wholly inadequate. You'll learn those limits now.

"Do any of you know the safe limits are for boiler warm-up?" O'Toole asked the group.

No one chose to answer.

"You're all inadequate as captains," O'Toole began, lowering his voice to a bare whisper. "You should know that. The lives of your crew depend on it. Read the BUSHIPS tech manuals. Do any of you know the safety factor built into the BUSHIPS numbers?"

Silence.

O'Toole continued, "Does anyone know the safety factor built into the boiler design limits?"

Silence.

"Get your manuals. Read them. Talk to your chiefs. When you deliver your readiness reports in an hour, I expect each of you to have the answers. You'd better be able to tell me what the minimum safe boiler warm-up time is and what the absolute minimum is in an emergency. We're under way in three hours."

O'Toole studied the eyes of each of the six men. As expected, he had silenced their protests, but there was no fear or intimidation in their eyes. That was good. He did see surprise and would fix that as well as the stunned confusion. They were good men, and they were thinking. Never again would they accept the status quo without challenge. They would be under way on schedule. It was going to be a good day.

Smiling at the group, O'Toole said, "There's another purpose to all of this. Audacity, audacity, forever audacity. To that end, my first rule of tactics is never be where the enemy expects you to be. It seems the expectation is that we'll be here in four hours, so we'll be somewhere else. I'll see you in an hour." He turned and resumed his casual journey.

VISITS

August 1971, Bay of Naples
Operation Marathon: Day 409

Meyers, dressed in his tropical white uniform, stared at the blank beige wall over his desk. He had dressed almost an hour earlier, and his body begged him for motion as though an imaginary force were pulling on his arms and legs. He wanted desperately to do something, but his thoughts rendered him immobile. Admiral Eickhoff was due any minute; the only thing to do was wait.

Even if Eickhoff came aboard oblivious to the situation, it wouldn't take him more than five minutes to tell there were serious problems. Then what would Eickhoff do? Investigate? Relieve Javert?

Meyers couldn't make himself believe Eickhoff wasn't suspicious about the *Farnley*. In all his years at sea, Meyers learned not to be deceived by an admiral's detached, distant air. Admirals were a shrewd, perceptive lot.

If Eickhoff understood what was going on, he wouldn't walk softly. He would be decisive and relieve Javert. It would be over quickly and quietly. Conceivably, Eickhoff had ordered the *Farnley* to anchor out. Perhaps he had privately communicated with Javert and told him to cancel liberty.

Meyers wondered what entry he would make in his diary tonight. Usually, the navy makes an effort to rehabilitate a captain and give him a chance to turn the ship around under close supervision. In this case, it wouldn't make much difference. Javert didn't possess the experience or personality to command even under the best of circumstances, and Eickhoff had to know that. Eickhoff would see the ship had deteriorated to the point the ship was in dangerous condition. Had someone on board been writing letters home? Had the word gotten back to the admiral?

Meyers felt relieved by the sound of approaching footsteps. Soon the speculation would be over, and he would have answers to his questions.

"Sir, the admiral's barge has left the *America*."

"Have you told the captain?" Meyers asked, looking up at the young sailor.

"Yes sir. He said to meet him on the quarterdeck."

As Meyers approached the quarterdeck, the captain was waiting, pacing up and down. Javert's lanky frame only made his nervousness appear awkward and foolish.

Once Eickhoff was aboard, Javert took the lead, heading up the port side toward the wardroom. Javert and Eickhoff, walking side by side, engaged in small talk.

As they walked forward, Meyers stopped listening. Instead, he wondered if Eickhoff had noticed the gritty deck, the rusty bulkhead, the frayed and rotted fire hose, the shaggy haircuts, or the yellow hue of the crew's frayed white uniforms. The cheerful small talk continued even as they walked across a spot on deck where the paint was worn through to bare metal. Eickhoff gave no indication there was anything that concerned him. Meyers' mind raced to make sense of Eickhoff's lighthearted behavior. This wasn't what he had expected.

The small talk continued while they seated themselves in the wardroom and nervous stewards served coffee. After the stewards left, Javert turned to Eickhoff. "Well, Admiral, what brings you to the *Farnley?*"

Eickhoff smiled. "I like to visit ships under my command every so often."

Eickhoff's tone and artificial smile set off an alarm in Meyers' head. He realized all his thinking had been wild, hopeful rationalization. Eickhoff wasn't going to do a thing. Meyers' temper began to flare. Liar! he cursed to himself.

"And frankly," Eickhoff continued, glancing over at Meyers, "I wanted to visit the *Farnley*. She's the last World War II destroyer left. Did you know the navy is going to scrap her after this cruise?"

Javert shook his head with just the right amount of sorrow spread across his face.

Meyers' thoughts shut out the conversation again. He managed to quell his anger, and the warmth in his face subsided. He hoped Eickhoff and Javert didn't notice the inevitable redness in his face. None of what was happening made sense. Eickhoff was lying through his teeth, or he was a blithering idiot, or both.

"Well, tell me, how are things going on the *Farnley?*"

Eickhoff's words brought Meyers' mind back into the conversation.

"Not too bad, Admiral." Javert and Eickhoff were smiling.

Meyers had had enough. He was going to flush Eickhoff out. "Well, Admiral," Meyers interjected, "there are some supply problems, and—"

Javert cut him off. "Nothing to worry about, Admiral. The usual supply snafus. Most of it is the type of stuff legends are made of, like the time the supply system delivered a semi-trailer-load of toilet paper to a submarine."

Both men laughed, but now Eickhoff was deliberately avoiding eye contact with Meyers. *What the hell is going on?* Meyers thought.

"Well, there's one small detail I need to talk to you about. I could have done it formally, but since I was coming over anyway, I thought I would talk to you about it," Eickhoff said.

"What's that?" Javert asked.

"We got a formal complaint from a ferryboat pilot down at Messina. The complaint said the *Farnley* tried to cut him off, and you almost collided."

Javert fidgeted a bit, then smiled. "I'm not surprised he filed a complaint. He was probably trying to save his job. You know how those Italian pilots are. We were going to pass safely ahead of the ferry when he increased speed. We did what was needed, Admiral. We came hard on the rudder and passed astern of him. It was the only reasonable thing to do."

"I thought it would be something along those lines," Eickhoff said. "We can't win this game with Italy being a NATO ally and all, so we'll make a polite apology. I'll take care of it."

"Thank you, Admiral," Javert said.

Javert's side glance toward him was to ensure the subject was closed. The gesture was awkward and ill disguised. Eickhoff must have noticed it. Meyers couldn't believe what was happening. Eickhoff had bought Javert's obvious lie, and the two men were chatting like old buddies at a class reunion.

"Let's get back to the purpose of my visit," Eickhoff said, glancing at Meyers. "Captain, could you give me a tour of this antique of yours? It'll probably be my last chance to see a grand old ship like this."

Javert jumped to his feet, and instead of answering Eickhoff directly, he turned to Meyers. "Mister Meyers, inform the quarterdeck the admiral and I will be taking a tour. You wait for us there."

Meyers walked to the quarterdeck, and as he waited, he reran the facts in his mind. Admirals were never as dumb as Eickhoff appeared. The *Farnley* was a dangerous wreck, and Eickhoff had to be blind not to see it. No one, especially an admiral, would call the *Farnley* a grand old ship. Admirals don't visit ships to take a walk and get a cup of coffee. Something was wrong. Nothing added up.

After Eickhoff left, Javert was all smiles. Without saying a word to anybody, he headed to his cabin, arms swinging wildly. The bounce in his step caused his legs to swing curiously outward like a waddling duck.

Meyers returned to his stateroom to change into his khaki uniform. He reviewed everything he knew and tried to reconcile it with Eickhoff's visit. It didn't make sense. His navy wouldn't let this continue. In his navy, admirals were smart and got to the point. They certainly weren't like Eickhoff. Why was the navy trying to protect Javert and screw the *Farnley?*

Eickhoff had killed his last ray of hope. There was no way out short of giving up. The thought of giving up was as repulsive as all-out mutiny. He couldn't quit because he would be letting the crew down, but he couldn't stand the frustration of fighting it. This wasn't his navy anymore.

A burning warmth filled Meyers' face, and he glared at the seabag hanging serenely from the pipe. The shiny smooth spot in its midsection stared back like some cyclopean apparition, waiting, beckoning to him. He charged the seabag, throwing his full weight into a single blow he hoped would blind the apparition. The seabag wobbled and swung away, apparently unhurt.

Tears flooded Meyers' eyes. He chased the retreating bag, punishing it with his fists. "Damn you!" he screamed.

§

Eickhoff hurried back to his quarters aboard the *America* and told his yeoman to track down the *Farnley*'s maintenance and supply reports. After the yeoman left, Eickhoff pulled the binder containing the fleet readiness reports from his desk drawer. Not waiting to sit, he turned to the *Farnley*'s page. The report was less than two days old and gave the *Farnley* an 85.7 rating, a mere seven points below the fleet average.

Eickhoff examined the report and sank into his chair. Operation Marathon was slipping away. The condition of the *Farnley* appalled him. He no longer needed the report, but it confirmed what he already knew. The bastard Javert was lying on his readiness reports. The report was a complete fabrication. Equipment tagged as inoperable was listed as operational or only marginally impaired.

The screwup at Messina had been Javert's doing. The way Meyers looked at him, any kid four weeks out of OCS wouldn't be dumb enough to cut across the bow of an Italian ferryboat.

The yeoman returned and walked toward Eickhoff, carrying two large computer binders.

"Is Pew back yet?" Eickhoff yelled at the man.

The yeoman froze and replied haltingly, "I think so."

"What the hell's he doing? Get him in here now," Eickhoff screamed. The yeoman turned and started toward the door before Eickhoff stopped him. "Leave the damned reports, nitwit."

The yeoman hurried to the desk, dropped the reports, and left.

When Pew stepped into his quarters, Eickhoff confirmed his worst fears. The condition of the *Farnley* was worse than he had guessed. The parts requisition backlog report showed critical parts for every major system had been on order for months.

He was in no mood for pleasantries. "What did you learn in Washington?"

Pew started to sit but changed his mind. "Not much, and what I did find out wasn't good."

"Out with it," Eickhoff urged.

"There were seven Operation Marathon ships. The *Farnley* and four others are still running. One is operating out of Pearl, probably under Admiral Barker. I drew a blank on the others."

"Damn," Eickhoff cursed, throwing the printout to the deck. It was worse than Pew was thinking. Barker, a vocal opponent, had almost prevented the publication of his article in the *Naval Review*. Barker would do anything to prove him wrong. "How reliable is your information?" Eickhoff asked, calmer now.

Pew sat cautiously in the chair before replying, "It's reliable. Well, John Stevens owed me a big favor, and—"

Eickhoff waved off Pew's explanation but remained silent.

After a second, Pew asked, "You seem worried, Admiral. Is something wrong?"

"The *Farnley* is a disaster. I don't know how she can keep going."

Eickhoff pulled himself up short. He was telling Pew too much. With what he had observed, he had grounds to pull the *Farnley* out of Marathon, but it was too early. He couldn't do it with four other ships still running.

"What are you going to do?" Pew asked.

"I don't know." Eickhoff's voice was almost a whisper.

"If you pull her out of the operation, all will be lost. If you help her or lighten up on her, others will be able to question your conclusions. The same would happen if you replaced Javert. It's all or nothing. Your promotion depends on it," Pew said.

Eickhoff started to reply but stopped himself. He was in a pickle, and the suppressed smirk on Pew's face said he was enjoying it. He didn't want to be beholden to Pew or give him any more information he could cash in on later.

"That will be all, Pew. Have a nice weekend," Eickhoff said, dismissing the lieutenant.

By the time the door closed behind Pew, Eickhoff had made up his mind. Pew was right. He was past the point of no return. If he pulled the *Farnley* out of Marathon, he would never be able to prove his point. He was right about the reliability of the newer ships. They would never hold up in a protracted naval war, and the country would be left defenseless. The low technology ships like the *Farnley* would be more reliable and less expensive. That was what was important. Marathon must prove his point. Marathon would last only another four months. He needed to keep the *Farnley* running, and he couldn't give her any special treatment.

Special treatment wouldn't help. Javert was an idiot and more incompetent than he could have imagined. Javert was weak, and that was the reason he had put Meyers, a strong, competent officer, aboard as the executive officer. But it appeared Meyers was ineffective. For that, the only explanation was, again, Javert.

The state of the *Farnley* could be blamed only on Javert. Javert was no longer a minor error in judgment on his part; he was a disaster. Now that Eickhoff had toured the *Farnley*, he had lost plausible deniability regarding the ship's condition. He was right about the high-tech ships. Marathon was too important. He must keep things quiet and keep the *Farnley* running regardless of the risk.

Operation Marathon had to work, had to prove him right, had to discredit Durham, O'Toole, and the rest of the Pentagon brass. After they were discredited, to whom would Congress turn to lead the new navy? Who else but the visionary admiral behind Operation Marathon? They would turn to him, and he would have the power, prestige, and position he deserved.

Durham's safety concerns only showed how weak and undeserving he was of such high office. Military leaders can't be frightened by a little blood. The safety of a few enlisted men was insignificant when compared to reshaping the navy's senior ranks.

As an admiral, Eickhoff was responsible for thousands of men. He told himself such men were exempt from the safety concerns of a few when so much was at stake, and the stakes were getting higher every day.

Eickhoff couldn't pull the *Farnley* out of Operation Marathon. It would look bad, and there would be no way for him to justify his conclusions. If he relieved Javert, people would ask why. Ultimately, they would ask why he had picked such an unfit man for command in the first place. This would destroy his credibility. Without the *Farnley*, Operation Marathon gave him no political leverage. Without leverage, promotion was gone.

Eickhoff considered the repercussions if he was caught lying to Durham. Not a problem; Durham isn't that smart, he thought. Eickhoff pulled a message form from a desk drawer and began drafting a message.

§

```
BTEKEUT RKELTTHETD 0018-8-EIEIEI-EKTHESSB.
ZNYEEEEE
R 14 1316Z AUG 71
FM   COMSIXTHFLT
TO   CNO
REF      A⦿ OPERATION MARATHON
         B⦿ YOUR 05 2012Z AUG 71

SUBJ  SITREP//N05823//
BT
CLASS  SECRET

AS PER REF B. PERSONALLY INSPECTED FARNLEY THIS DATE. FARNLEY
CONDITION DETERIORATED AS EXPECTED AND PREDICTED BY REF A. ONLY ONE
MINOR SAFETY ITEM IDENTIFIED RELATING TO CONDITION OF FIRE HOSE.
SUPPLY DIRECTED THIS DATE TO RELEASE MATERIAL TO CORRECT SAME NAMED
DEFICIENCY. DETAILED CONVERSATIONS C.O. AND X.O. FARNLEY INDICATE
NO OTHER OUTSTANDING SAFETY CONCERNS.

BT
N0833
NNNN
```

§

Twice that afternoon, Lee located Meyers and asked him if he had some time to talk. Both times, Meyers knew what Lee wanted and asked him to wait until later. The issue wasn't critical, and Meyers didn't have the answers Lee would want. That knowledge frustrated Meyers and made his temper flare. It would be better to wait.

At dinner, Lee brought a cardboard box with him and set it in the corner. After dinner, Meyers left the table and headed for his stateroom. He just sat at his desk when Lee appeared in his doorway, holding his cardboard box under one arm. "Excuse me, XO, but I only need five minutes."

Meyers couldn't put it off any longer, and he would be forced to admit to Lee he was helpless. Meyers faced his frustration and coming humiliation and turned toward Lee. "What is it?"

"I don't know what happened before I got here, and I don't know how much pull Chief Ross has," Lee said.

Meyers guessed Lee had rehearsed the speech. He might as well let him get if off his chest.

"Our supply status is a disaster. We're barely operational. I've only been on board a day, but by a quick tabulation, one hundred percent of our engineering equipment is impaired in some way, and over fifty percent is inoperable."

Lee reached into his box, produced a sheaf of papers, and handed it to Meyers. "There are three problems, XO. First, we need repair parts. I brought copies of our overdue supply requisitions." Meyers didn't move. Lee continued, "Something is seriously wrong with supply. Less than a third of the stuff we order gets through. That's the most important problem.

"Second, with the status of the equipment and our inexperienced crew, the engine room is dangerous. My average man has less than two years' experience. According to my staffing charts, the average should be over five years."

Lee paused, so Meyers prompted, "And the third problem?"

"The men, sir; they're exhausted. We're at sea so much, every time we get into a port, the crew needs to work four times as hard and long to keep the equipment running. It's not right, XO. They need some slack."

"Anything else, Lee?"

"There are other problems, but they're manageable."

"Like what?"

"Morale. All the men are in a ditch from Chief Ross on down."

A pep talk would do no good. What Lee needed most was the unvarnished truth.

"I'm impressed with your grasp of your situation," Meyers began. "I know about this stuff, but you've only been here a day, and there is a bit more to learn. Take heart, Lee; you're not alone. We have two radars. One hasn't worked for three months, and the other can barely reach out ten miles. Our sonar is so sick, the only way we could find a submarine is to run into it. Half the stuff in the laundry is busted. The reefers can't keep stuff frozen anymore. The cook's upset because his mixer's broken."

"What's the problem, XO?" Lee asked.

"First and foremost, it's supply. We can't get the stuff we need. I'll follow up on your supply requisitions, but no promises."

Lee seemed happy with the reply. Meyers was growing to like Lee. His eyes sparkled devilishness. Maybe he and Lee could help each other. Meyers thought for a second. He needed to choose his words carefully.

"All I can tell you, Lee," Meyers said, "is to be creative. They're your men, and you're responsible for morale. It's your engine room, and you're responsible for it. You have a free hand to solve the problems. Just don't do something dumb or in direct violation of orders."

Lee seemed perplexed. He needed time to think it out.

"Thank you, Lee," Meyers said, dismissing him.

Once Lee was gone, Meyers picked up the sheaf of papers from his desk and pitched them into his in basket, then opened his lower-right desk drawer, pulled out the diary, and threw it into the trash can. He didn't need it anymore because Lee was going to be an effective ally. The battle for the *Farnley* was starting anew.

§

It was just after eight when the messenger told Ross that Lee wanted to see him. Ross was familiar with the unpredictable behavior of junior officers. He had to live with it, and considering the current conditions on the *Farnley*, this wouldn't be too irritating by comparison.

Ross walked back to Lee's stateroom and entered unannounced.

Lee was lying in the lower bunk, reading a navy tech manual. A stack of manuals sat on the floor next to his bunk. Before Ross could say anything, Lee lifted his head. "Chief, thanks for coming."

Ross shook his head at the sight of the manuals and Lee's cheerful face. "What are you so happy about? Are there some jokes in them I missed?"

Lee's eyes twinkled at Ross. "If I were happy, I wouldn't be reading these books. But then, I'd read them anyway."

Ross tried to figure out what Lee was talking about and decided it was some kind of joke. Ross wasn't in the mood for mirth. "What did you want to see me about, sir?"

"Bad news, I'm afraid, Chief. First, tell the men there will be a seabag inspection as soon as we get under way. Set up the time when you can make sure all the men will be available. Tell them I expect every man to have a complete set of clean, serviceable uniforms."

Ross began to object, but Lee's black eyes were so steady and clear, the chief felt Lee knew what he was going to say. Ross remained silent.

"The other bad news is that I've ordered special work details for all our men." Lee pulled two sheets of paper from the bunk beside him and handed them to Ross.

Both orders were identical, one for each of the next two days.

"You want me to lead a work detail to the navy supply depot on the NATO base to scrounge around for repair parts? It doesn't take half our men to do that, and it doesn't take ten hours a day for two days. It'll take about five minutes. I've tried before, and they wouldn't give me the time of day."

"What's across the street from the supply depot?" Lee asked casually.

Ross thought for a second, then squinted at Lee. "The navy uniform shop."

"What's next door to the uniform shop?"

"The enlisted club," Ross said, smiling.

"That's why I want you to lead both work parties. The men have been pent up for a while, and I wouldn't want them to get into any trouble like getting caught drinking while on an official work detail."

Ross grinned and tried to detect a smile or smirk on Lee's face, but he couldn't tell. Lee, with his sparkling eyes, probably looked the same way happy, sad, or angry. Ross turned serious. "Mister Lee, I know what you're trying to do. If the captain finds out about this, you're in big trouble."

"I don't understand. I expect you to turn that supply depot upside down looking for anything we need. Our parts are somewhere. I think they got lost in the inventory at the depot."

Ross understood this game well. "I'll do my best, but no promises."

"Thanks. That's all I can ask. Don't forget the seabag inspection. I'm going to be tough."

Ross got up to leave and, halfway to the door, turned to Lee. "I'll make sure no one is caught drinking while on duty."

Lee returned to his book, and Ross headed forward to the chief's quarters. Things had happened quickly with Lee, and Ross wondered what his real motives were. He still hadn't figured him out. Lee always looked the same—happy. He could always see the wheels spinning tirelessly behind Lee's black eyes, but it was impossible to tell what the man was thinking. The seabag inspection was a dirty trick, and the men were going to hate it. Maybe Lee was trying to bribe the men into looking good with his fake work party or trying to make points with Javert or Meyers.

Ross decided it didn't matter. In a few more weeks, Lee would learn his efforts wouldn't make any difference. Meanwhile, Ross resolved to enjoy the fresh breeze while it lasted. It never lasted long on the *Farnley*.

§

It was almost ten p.m. Commander Beetham's boxy office made Admiral Durham feel tired, but this was important. He didn't want to snub Beetham's efforts by putting it off until tomorrow. Beetham had done an excellent job and used the bureaucracy to trick the bureaucracy. By tapping into the navy's computerized message routing system, he had put the equivalent of a phone tap on every Operation Marathon ship.

"What we did was put a tag routing on each ship," Beetham explained. "The tag routing is only in the computer system and never appears on the messages. Anytime a ship's name appears in the routing, the message is automatically sent down to the tag routing."

Beetham smiled. "In this case, the message is copied to CINCGLOBNAVCOMCORFORFLOT."

Durham almost laughed. The fictitious command name was so absurd—Commander-in-Chief Global Naval Communications Coordination for Forces Afloat—no one would question the routing. The average sailor would conclude that anything that stupid had to be official.

Beetham continued, "We receive the messages here, and I have briefed three officers trained in intelligence analysis on how to screen the message traffic. We'll know where they are and what they're doing, and we'll have a pretty good idea of what's happening aboard the Operation Marathon ships. If anything significant happens, you'll know about it."

Durham was pleased. "Any significant developments relating to safety, I want to know about them immediately," Durham began. "You'll need some phone numbers, access to my private message network, and a way to track my movements."

"Don't worry. We have all that stuff."

Behind Beetham's deadpan response was a little bravado. He was playing with Durham because both men knew "all that stuff" was highly classified.

Durham raised an eyebrow and asked a silent question. Beetham tried to conceal his pleasure that Durham had noticed. "Well, you told me to set this thing up, so I did."

"A good job it is," Durham said, getting up to leave. "Just remind me never to ask you to do a favor for the president."

"Service with a smile," Beetham said, still deadpan. "If anything major happens, you'll know about it in seconds."

PLACING BETS

August 1971, Bay of Naples
Operation Marathon: Day 414

Ross gulped down the last quarter cup of tepid coffee. He'd been up all night coaxing the *Farnley*'s engineering plant back to life, and the coffee did little to dispel the puffy, tired feeling. Other than that, this day was just another day, one less day until retirement. It didn't even matter they were leaving Naples for ten straight days at sea. Ross looked at the brown stains in his coffee mug and thought about getting another cup. He decided against it. It was almost breakfast, and the plant still wasn't ready for sea.

Ross retrieved his clipboard and walked to the main platform railing. He yelled, "Ya got the main circ pump online yet?"

A voice from under the starboard turbine answered, "Almost." Ross guessed it was Stucky.

"Almost," Ross muttered to himself. Everything on the *Farnley* was either almost working or almost broken. Ross watched as three firemen and Lee made their way from under the starboard turbine and joined Stucky on the catwalk. The group exchanged words before Stucky gave a thumbs-up to Ross and headed for the ladder.

He'd lost track of Lee, but he should've guessed Lee was with the men working on the pump. Lee had his nose into everything. He wasn't getting in the way, but his habit of watching everything and helping the men got on his nerves. He'd told Lee to leave the men alone, but Lee had ignored the warning.

Now the men were bitching; bitching about everything. At first, it was about having to buy uniforms; then it was about the seabag inspection. Next they'd be bitching about the chow. He'd been afraid Lee would get the men's hopes up by setting expectations too high, like the uniforms. Now his black gang was the envy of the entire crew with their new, clean uniforms, and they were strutting around as if they were important. Until Lee showed up, the men hadn't bitched about anything for months.

Ross looked at his checklist. Satisfied, he called to Stucky, "Open the

75

main steam stop valve."

This was almost the last step and one of many Ross worried about because the valve had become unpredictable. As he looked at it, it wasn't any wonder. The main steam line, wrapped in dirty gray insulation, jutted out from the forward bulkhead almost eight feet above the platform. After five feet, the insulation bulged to cover the main body of the valve.

The insulation was different from the rest, ratty and black with blackened, oil-soaked plaster powder bleeding through the torn asbestos fabric wrapping. The cast-iron valve wheel, devoid of paint, was black from the dirt hiding in pores of the metal casting. Only a greasy coat of oil protected the wheel from rust. Ross felt the valve would be at home on a derelict or a tramp steamer but not on a US man-of-war.

Stucky mounted the wooden bench, stretched to reach the valve wheel, and twisted his entire body trying to open the valve. His hands slipped on the oily valve wheel, and his extended body denied him the leverage required. He readjusted his body and grasped the wheel with a clean rag. In one all-or-nothing attempt, he yanked at the valve wheel and wound up jerking his body completely off the bench. Still hanging onto the valve wheel, Stucky let go and dropped to the deck.

"What now, Chief?" Lee asked.

Ross didn't need this. He turned to confront Lee. "We open the valve," Ross said as caustically as he could, then yelled to the men standing on the platform, "Just don't stand there. Give him a hand."

Two men jumped onto the bench with Stucky, carefully positioned themselves, and tried again in vain. Lee was staring at Ross, but he ignored the young officer. Soon a man found a pipe and wedged it between the spokes of the valve wheel. Stucky gave the pipe a jerk. The valve cracked open with a snap of rusty metal breaking loose, and steam hissed into the main piping. The *Farnley* was slowly catching up with him. He would never make it to retirement. Dejected, Ross turned and leaned on the railing.

"You did a hell of a job getting that second boiler online."

Ross recognized Lee's voice. The statement sounded patronizing and angered him. To Lee he said, "Bull! It was kids' stuff, the type of stuff I learned as a recruit."

"On the *Able*?"

Ross tightened his grip on the rail with his bony hands until his knuckles turned white. He hadn't known how far Lee's nosiness had extended. Ross glared at Lee. "Where'd you learn that?"

"She was a good ship, wasn't she?"

Ross forgot his previous question. "Sure wasn't anything like this bucket."

"How's that? The *Able* was the same class ship."

"Stuff worked." Ross turned his back on Lee and walked toward his bench.

Lee followed, and after Ross sat down, he asked, "So?"

Ross looked away from Lee. "So what? If we could get supply parts, I could make this a good engine room, at least as good as it was when I came on board, which was pretty damn good. That's if you and the captain leave me alone."

"I don't think so, Chief," Lee said.

Ross had hoped the truculence in his voice would register, but Lee either ignored it or failed to notice. Ross looked directly at Lee's grinning face and sparkling eyes. The kid was playing some kind of game, but Ross couldn't guess what or why.

"What do you mean by that?" Ross asked.

"I heard you bragged about rebuilding the main steam valve on the *Able* and that you could spin it with one finger."

"Who told you that?"

"Sounds like an awfully tall sea story to me. Even if you had the parts, I don't think it could be done. Three or four fingers, maybe, but not one finger."

Ross had had all of Lee he could take. Maybe this was a chance to teach the young officer something and put him in his place. Ross stood and looked directly into Lee's black eyes.

"Mister Lee, I know you're an officer, but you've got a lot to learn about the navy and especially about this ship. I resent your implication that I was lying. What I said was true. You get the stuff required to overhaul that valve," Ross pointed to the main steam valve, "and I'll prove it to you. If you can't get the parts, you leave me alone. Okay?"

Lee glanced up at the valve, then looked into Ross' eyes.

"That valve is over thirty years old. You're taking on one hell of a job, but I'd settle for three fingers."

"One finger," Ross snapped. "Deal? You get the parts or you leave me alone."

Lee shrugged. "It's a deal."

Ross smiled at his victory. The seals and parts required to overhaul the valve had been back-ordered for months. Lee didn't stand a chance.

"Good. Now I can finish my tour in peace and quiet," Ross replied.

Lee continued to look into Ross' eyes as if he were expecting something more.

"Is there something else, Mister Lee?" Ross asked.

"No. I just wondered if there was anything I could do now."

It was as if the previous conversation had never taken place. Ross couldn't figure this kid out.

"Yeah, get some chow so I can get this bucket to sea."

Lee's black eyes sparkled as if they'd just made some marvelous discovery.

"Sounds like a good idea." Lee turned and walked away.

Ross frowned. He thought he'd actually seen Lee smile, but he wasn't sure.

§

All through breakfast, Meyers deflected questions from the other officers about Eickhoff's visit. He didn't have any answers that made sense, and Eickhoff's apparent pleasure with the *Farnley* troubled him. Was Javert lying about what Eickhoff had said, or was Eickhoff lying? Meyers knew he was missing a major piece of the puzzle. Everything about the *Farnley* seemed insane, but he knew somewhere there was a logical explanation.

Lee had just finished his breakfast and was getting ready to leave when Meyers asked, "Could I see you in my cabin for a few minutes, Lee?"

After Lee took a seat on the couch in Meyers' stateroom, Meyers said, "I noticed some of your men this morning. They look good considering the work details you had them on in Naples."

Lee fidgeted, confirming Meyers' suspicion. "I didn't do anything," Lee replied, then changed the subject.

"What is the problem with supply? I've never seen anything like this."

Lee had asked the sixty-four-thousand-dollar question, and Meyers didn't know the answer. "Don't know. It just seems that any requisition with our name on it gets circular-filed by the supply system. I've talked with other ships, and they order the same part on the same day as we do, but they get forty-eight-hour service. I can't figure it out. It's funny, though, because sometimes we put the wrong part number down, something for a piece of equipment we're not supposed to have, and we get it right away."

"Other ships don't have the same problem?" Lee asked.

"No."

Lee's face lit up, and his body language told Meyers he had something he urgently wanted to do.

"Is that all, XO?"

"Yeah."

"Thanks, XO. You gave me an idea."

§

In the engine room, Stucky didn't have a chance to ask Chief Ross what to do. Ross had seen the order.

"All the way! Open the throttles all the way! Jam 'em open, son! Quick!" Ross screamed. For a fraction of a second, Ross' mind snapped into a state of *déjà vu*. *"Jam 'em open, son!"* It was a peripheral thought that flashed into his mind, glanced off his conscious thought, then disappeared. He tried to pursue the thought, but it was gone.

Ross knew Biron was the bridge officer, and Biron was one of the best. He wouldn't make a mistake like this. An officer had two ways to tell the engine room an order was an emergency bell. Biron had used both; a sequence of flank–stop–flank, and asking for more power than was available. The emphasis was unmistakable. Biron told the engine room crew the ship was in serious danger, and he needed every ounce of power the *Farnley* had, even if it risked equipment and personnel.

§

The lee helmsman's erratic behavior attracted Ensign Hayes' attention. After a few seconds, he noticed the engine room had not responded to the full engine order. Knowing something was wrong, Hayes took a deep breath and yelled as loud as he could, "Engine room does not answer; indicating all ahead flank."

§

With the wind, Biron hadn't heard what Hayes had said, but knew Hayes would only speak in an emergency. Biron's head snapped around, and when he saw the engine order telegraph, he immediately understood.

§

In the boiler room, Canterbury had seen the order on his small repeater and wondered if Ross would answer the flank bell. He only wondered for a second; steam pressure began to plummet. Canterbury jammed the fuel valve wide open, and another member of the boiler team slammed the air dampers open. That's all there is. I hope it's enough, Canterbury thought.

§

It took several seconds for Biron to collect his thoughts. Meyers had charged at the captain yelling, but Javert pushed the lee helmsman out of the way and guarded the engine order telegraph. The bridge was in total confusion.

Biron turned his attention to the oiler. The *Farnley* was accelerating now and pulling ahead. If they lost power alongside the oiler, all he would be able to do was pray.

§

In horror, Canterbury watched the steam pressure fall and along with it the boiler water level. Pressure fell past five hundred pounds. The vicious cycle had begun. The engines consumed every ounce of steam generated. The pressure dropped. The lower the pressure, the faster the water boiled. The faster the water boiled, the faster the water needed to be replaced. The pumps would never be able to keep up.

§

Ross leapt from his bench and stood directly behind his throttlemen, one outstretched hand on the shoulder of each. A timer ticked in his head. He knew about how much time he had. Watching the pressure gauge, he kept repeating to his throttlemen, "Steady . . . Steady . . . Steady."

§

Canterbury watched the water level drop past the red line indicating the minimum safe operating level. He prayed. Pressure stabilized at four hundred pounds.

§

The timer went off in Ross' head. "Half throttle! Now, quick." he shouted.

§

Canterbury had stopped breathing when the water level completely disappeared from the sight glass. He knew boilers don't melt down under these conditions; they exploded. He couldn't hold his breath any longer. He jammed the valve closed and took a deep breath. The boilers' torchlike flames vanished. Defeated, Canterbury lowered his head and waited for the lights to go out.

§

Biron heard the hollow pop emanate from the stacks. Relays clicked, and the *Farnley* fell silent.

The sight before him seemed unreal, unimaginable, thousands of tons of steel hurtling through the sea, slowly, inevitably being drawn together. If they collided, it would be no contest. The *Farnley*'s thirty-five-hundred-ton mass was no match for the *Severn*'s mass of twenty-five-thousand tons moving at sixteen feet per second.

The suction between the ships tugged at *Farnley*'s stern, pulling it slowly, inextricably toward the oiler. Without power, Biron had no rudder to compensate.

"Sound the collision alarm," he yelled. The high-pitched, pulsating klaxon sounded, and shouting men ran to safety.

Biron took a deep breath and wanted to close his eyes, but he couldn't. It was going to be close. The ships were almost even now, and the *Farnley*'s stern continued its slow swing toward the oiler.

Miraculously, the *Farnley*'s stern swung past the oiler's stern with less than five feet of clearance. Biron ran across the bridge to the opposite wing and sighed in relief when he saw the guard destroyer behind him heeling heavy into a turn to avoid collision. They had made it. Drained, he braced himself against the bridge rail.

"Biron!"

It was Meyers. Biron pivoted and looked back through the bridge house. The oiler seemed closer now. He had thought they were safe, but the bow was now caught in the suction and was swinging menacingly toward the oiler.

On the port bridge wing, Meyers was screaming at the refueling crew on the open torpedo deck just forward of the bridge. "Clear the deck! Clear the deck!"

All Biron could see was the gray mass of the oiler's side as he ran to the port bridge wing. Just as he reached the door, Meyers threw Sweeney through the door. Sweeney and Biron collided full chest but caught each other. Charging like a fullback, Meyers drove a shoulder into Sweeney's back, pushing both men well into the bridge.

Biron fell backward. Meyers' and Sweeney's combined weight crashed onto his chest. In pain, Biron screamed as the weight crushed the air from his lungs.

For a second there was silence, then the impact. Its immediate effect surprised Biron. There was no loud crash, but it felt and sounded as if they had run head-on into a wall of water at ninety miles an hour. He bounced on the deck, and Meyers and Sweeney were thrown clear.

Metal started tearing, groaning, screaming. Biron saw the port life raft cage crush, break free, and cartwheel like a toy, dropping mangled onto the port bridge wing.

Still gasping for air, he pulled himself up to the bridge windows to check the bow. The deck was clear, but the bow was scraping down the oiler's side.

There was a loud bang. At first he thought it was a gunshot, but then there was another. He couldn't tell what had caused it. The oiler's stern pulled ahead of the *Farnley*'s bridge with another loud bang.

Biron looked down toward the noise. The steel cable that made up the *Farnley*'s main deck rail had snagged on a piece of equipment on the oiler. As the oiler continued forward, the snagged cable ripped stanchion after stanchion from the deck with loud bangs.

The oiler was ahead of them now, trailing the cable with bent stanchions twirling in the air. The last stanchion broke loose. The cable, with its bitter end attached to the most forward part of the bow, snapped taut with an ominous twang.

The bow jerked slightly before the cable snapped. Biron didn't have time to duck. The cable, with stations dangling from it, snapped and shot back toward the *Farnley*. There was a loud bang; then it was over.

"Sound general quarters."

Biron turned. It was Meyers giving orders and helping bridge crewmen to their feet. "Tell engineering I want a damage control report now."

Their eyes met. Meyers seemed remarkably calm. Stopping to wipe some blood from his forehead, Meyers said, "Biron, I'll take the bridge. You get below and check for casualties and damage on the main deck."

Without thought, Biron bolted from the bridge and descended to the torpedo deck. It was littered with debris. He worked his way forward until he saw an officer lying face down on the deck forward of the refueling station. It was Lee.

§

The captain of the *America* had heard *Severn*'s terse message crackle over the radio circuit. The collision could be serious or just a brush. Logically, he had two choices; wait for a status report or respond. There was no decision to make. Injured men would need help; men could be in the sea. Seconds counted.

He snatched the phone set to Flight Operations from its cradle and began issuing orders. "Vector three SAR helos to *Severn* now. Spot a P2 on the catapult for possible medevac. Clear all flight patterns. We're coming about now."

§

In the engine room, the general quarters klaxon echoed through the darkness. Ross got to his feet and quickly surveyed the main platform. He could account for four men. He ran to the railing overlooking the lower level and shouted the roll call of his watch into the darkness below. As he shouted the names over the general quarters klaxon, the *déjà vu* he had experienced earlier returned. He shook it off and continued shouting names into the darkness. After each name, the darkness echoed an "Okay." Satisfied no one was hurt, he turned his energy to restarting the boiler.

§

The captain of the *America* sat serenely in his chair and, without giving any outward sign, monitored the dozen simultaneous events taking place on the bridge. Aircraft were cleared from their landing pattern, equipment re-spotted on deck, new course and speed computed, and screening destroyers notified of the change. He hadn't had to give an order; the bridge watch had heard *Severn*'s call, and everyone knew what needed to be done.

The *America*'s captain knew there were two powerful forces motivating his crew. The sea was cruel, full of vicious surprises and instant death. All sailors were comrades pitted against a common foe, and to refuse assistance was unthinkable. It hadn't changed since man had invented the sail.

The second force was more powerful and difficult to understand. Somewhere deep in the American psyche was something special that produced fighting men who would risk all to save the life of a single comrade. It defied logic and military doctrine. Time and again, it produced the greatest acts of heroism in military annals, as the helicopter rescues of downed pilots in Viet Nam would attest. Unable to explain their acts, the heroes in these rescues dismissed their heroism with the same casual words, "Just doing my job."

The *America*'s captain watched as his crew did their job. Signals flashed and radio circuits, crowded with voices, rapidly converted the battle group to a search-and-rescue force. It barely dawned on the *America*'s captain that he had by default taken control of Admiral Eickhoff's forces. Eickhoff obviously agreed.

The *America*'s conning officer shouted, "Left full rudder. All ahead flank."

It had taken less than forty-five seconds to convert the battle group from the business of war to that of rescue. Seven thousand men and billions in hardware were now devoted to that single purpose that wouldn't change until all hands were accounted for. Steel Henge could wait. It all seemed natural, the way things should be.

§

Biron made his way through the twisted mass of metal pipes and light metal on the torpedo deck, and scrambled to Lee's side. He saw no blood, so he pulled at Lee's shoulder. "Lee," he called.

Trembling, Lee rolled over, his eyes wide, dazed, his face white and solemn. Lee looked up. Biron followed Lee's eyes to the stanchion buried halfway into the bulkhead just a foot above Lee's head.

"You okay?" Biron asked.

"Yeah," Lee said, still trying to regain his composure. "I came back out to make sure the deck was clear, then we hit, and my escape path was blocked."

§

Admiral Eickhoff had taken an extended lunch to read the Washington Post and get caught up on the political analysis and speculation coming out of Washington. As usual, he left orders not to be disturbed, which explained his surprise when a staff aide entered.

"Admiral, the *Farnley* just collided with the *Severn*."

"What?"

§

The light seemed to be the only constant, the only absolute naked truth left in Javert's life. The sun's rays burned bright, stark, and harsh through the jagged hole in the forward bulkhead of his cabin. The light flowed down the length of the stanchion that protruded almost to his desk, then cascaded daggers of white light across the floor.

Javert tried to regain control of his trembling body. His emotions whipsawed from anger, to embarrassment, to shame, to fear, to panic, to humiliation, and back to anger again.

His mind churned. *What have you done? You could have killed someone. What's wrong with you? Why can't you command? You can't blame the officers; you did this yourself. Ross didn't sabotage you. He had no way of knowing. He would have thought Biron had given the command.*

Twenty years in the navy. Your first command. Your last chance for promotion. Are you worthy of a promotion? Are you worthy of command? God forgive me! I could have killed someone! I have to do better. The navy is my life; I can't give up. I can't quit the navy. I was trying too hard. I made a serious mistake. Captains aren't allowed to make mistakes. Captains aren't allowed to fail. You're a failure. The harder you try, the worse you fail and the bigger the mistakes become.

The chaos of voices on deck had subsided. The *Farnley* was silent, but other sounds continued. Helos were overhead, and a ship was hailing them by bullhorn close to starboard. These were the sounds of the Sixth Fleet, the voice and arm of Admiral Eickhoff. Javert wondered if he would lose his ship. His promotion? His career?

Javert fumbled in the darkness for the picture of Admiral Eickhoff and him when he took command of the *Farnley*. It wasn't on his desk. He pulled the desk drawer open and rummaged in the pool of blackness. He pulled some loose papers and pens from the drawer, then grabbed at the biggest object. He held his service 45 semiautomatic pistol in his left hand while his right hand probed. It found the picture, and he placed it on the desk. Javert dropped the gun into the drawer and banged it closed.

Javert looked at the picture and remembered how confident and proud he'd been that day. This was his ship, his chance at promotion, his only chance to stay in the navy. It was all slipping away. Eickhoff would punish him, as his father had so many years before.

Tears filled Captain Javert's eyes and blocked out the light. Spasm after spasm racked his body. He fell to the floor, pulled his knees to his chest, and wept.

DAMAGE CONTROL

August 1971, Mediterranean Sea south of Crete
Operation Marathon: Day 420

Damn, I wish he'd get back, Eickhoff cursed to himself. Everything hangs by a thin thread. Operation Marathon and my future may well be lost. Eickhoff couldn't believe the tightening downward spiral of events. Every step took him deeper, and now he had to trust Pew to save his skin.

Trust Pew? Never!

But it was the only way out.

Eickhoff knew Pew was a double-edged sword, and the very traits that made him valuable also made him dangerous. Eickhoff never gave Pew more information than he needed and always kept him on a short leash. Now Pew was the cornerstone in Eickhoff's damage control operation because he had no other choice.

If he had helo'd another officer to the *Farnley* to investigate, he would never have been able to contain the damage, and his mistake of giving Javert a command and his lie to Durham would be exposed. He had to make the incident seem minor. He couldn't go personally. Admirals wouldn't get involved in minor incidents. That only left Pew, a minor lieutenant for a minor incident. It seemed to fit, but now Pew knew too much. *Damn!*

Eickhoff's only public involvement had been the simple bland message to the *Severn* and *Farnley* that all reports about the incident would be coordinated and filed through his command. In the message, he also set up Pew's visit and set some rules for the investigation. Such things were normal and considered almost administrative, and wouldn't raise any eyebrows.

Eickhoff had read the preliminary report from the *Severn* and *Farnley*. The *Severn*, merely a spectator to the incident, was no problem. Apparently, neither ship suffered structural damage, and no one was injured nor killed.

The thought made Eickhoff shudder. It was like a ghostly echo of

O'Toole's voice a year earlier when they had argued over Operation Marathon. "This operation of yours is a disaster. Pray no one gets injured or killed."

Eickhoff reconsidered his cavalier attitude over safety. Serious injury or death would have made the incident major, something he would never be able to cover up. Safety wasn't important in itself, but his cover behind Operation Marathon was.

Eickhoff knew his mistake. Javert was too weak, too inexperienced, and he was the only flaw in his Operation Marathon. Eickhoff wanted to relieve Javert, but relieving a captain would be a high-visibility act. Remove him and everyone would start asking questions. They'll look at the *Farnley* and Javert's record, and the conclusions would be inescapable. Eickhoff had made a grievous error in judgment, then covered it up at Messina and in the Naples inspection. He knew it could end his career and Operation Marathon. Eickhoff needed political leverage. He needed the *Farnley*, and he needed to keep Javert out of the way. Operation Marathon was important, and he was in too deep to back out. It was all or nothing.

If he kept Javert, heaven only knew what would happen. The man's an idiot. He had to be neutralized but kept in place until Operation Marathon was over. After Operation Marathon, who cares?

Pew presented a different problem. Pew knew too much. If he pulled this assignment off, he would hold a big marker that he would certainly cash in for everything it was worth.

Eickhoff had to be rid of Pew, but how? Buy his silence with a choice assignment? Send him to an insignificant remote post? Or destroy him with bad fitness reports and fabricated disciplinary problems? That was the only way out. Any other way would leave Pew's credibility intact. Destroy him and his attacks would look self-serving and vindictive.

§

Pew slipped out of the horse collar when his feet hit the *Farnley*'s deck. This was the third time in three hours he'd been lowered onto the deck of a ship from a Sea Stallion helicopter and the second time he'd been lowered to the *Farnley*. Meyers met him on the fantail and headed forward, leading Pew to the captain's cabin.

As they walked forward, neither man spoke. There wasn't much to say. He'd already debriefed Meyers, and if Pew guessed right, everyone except Javert knew about the blown fuse because Javert had sequestered himself in his cabin and had barely spoken a word with Meyers.

The fuse was a one-in-a-million quirk that happened at precisely the wrong second. The odds of it happening were astronomical. Javert's meddling started the chain of events, but it was an accident nonetheless. The fuse would make it simple to keep the collision quiet and keep men higher up from asking questions. If Javert didn't know about the fuse, it would be easy to keep Operation Marathon going.

So far, everything had worked out well indeed. This was a play in three acts, and now only the final decisive act remained. First, Pew had toured the *Farnley*. She had taken a heavy hit, but things looked worse than they really were. Other than huge scrapes down the port side, the damage was minimal, a davit, two life raft tubs, a dozen deck stanchions, and three gear lockers. Injuries were limited to a few cuts and bruises.

Next he debriefed Ross, Biron, and Meyers individually. Ross was the plum, the crown jewel of the day, the man who would make the plan work. Ross blamed himself, claiming that the fuse shouldn't have mattered since it was his error in judgment on when to cut power that caused the real problem. It was fortunate he'd started with Ross.

After receiving written statements from the three, he shuttled to the *Severn* to inspect the damage and debrief the captain. The *Severn*'s captain was naturally upset. Someone had scratched his ship, but really, that was all that had happened. A few gallons of haze-gray paint and all evidence of the incident would disappear.

Technically, the visit to the *Severn* wasn't necessary, but Eickhoff insisted he make Javert sweat as long as possible. It was why Eickhoff's message to the *Farnley* instructed the officers not to discuss the incident among themselves until the investigation was complete. That also increased Javert's isolation. Pew was learning quite a bit from Eickhoff. The man was good at this.

The key ingredient to Eickhoff's plan was a letter Eickhoff had drafted just in case it was needed. Eickhoff was going to owe him for this, but no matter what happened, Pew knew he could cash in on Operation Marathon.

Meyers knocked on the captain's door, introduced Javert to Pew, then left. This was the first time Pew had met Javert, and the captain struck him as almost comical. Javert was obviously nervous, and when Meyers left, he snapped to attention. His tall, skinny body and drawn face made his exaggerated attempt to stand at attention look ridiculous. Pew knew he was in a position of control.

Pew looked at Javert for several seconds to increase Javert's discomfort, then, motioning toward the couch, said, "Please, Captain, have a seat." Pew sat in the desk chair.

"Captain, I'm afraid we have a little problem," Pew began while leaning back in Javert's chair, "but with your help, we can work it out."

"I'm . . . sorry. It's all my . . ." Javert stammered, but Pew cut him off.

"We're all sorry about what happened, but this whole thing is a minor incident. An accident, actually, but we'll get to that."

Javert bolted from his seat to retrieve some papers he had on his desk, which he handed to Pew. "It's all right here in my report."

"Sit down, Captain, and please relax. Everything will be okay," Pew said. Once he had Javert's attention again, Pew slowly tore Javert's report in quarters and threw it into the wastebasket. It seemed to have the desired effect; Javert looked petrified.

Pew reached into a manila envelope and retrieved a single piece of paper. "Captain, we don't need your report. We all know what happened. We also know what really happened at Messina."

The last statement was a gamble on Pew's part, but Javert blanched and took a deep breath. Confident, Pew continued, "I'm going to make you a proposition, and just so you know, I have the authority to do so, Admiral Eickhoff has written you a short note. Please read it."

Javert took the paper from Pew with his trembling hands and studied it for a moment. Looking up at Pew, he asked, "I'm not going to lose my ship?"

"No."

"I'll get my promotion?"

"Of course. That is, if you cooperate. You do want your promotion, don't you?"

Javert's response was more of a plea than a statement. "Yes."

"Good, because if you don't cooperate, not only will you lose your ship . . . " Pew paused for a second to take a deep, soulful breath, then continued, "But we don't have to go into those unpleasantries."

"What do you want me to do?" Javert asked.

"First, I need that letter back," Pew said. When the letter was safely back in the manila envelope, Pew continued, "Just so you know what the score is, Captain, Admiral Eickhoff handpicked you for this assignment. He felt you would do a good job despite your lack of deck training. Now, I can't go into detail because this matter is highly classified, but you and the *Farnley* are part of an important operation that's being personally supervised by the CNO."

"Admiral Durham?" Javert's face flooded with awe.

"That's right. Before I go on, you must understand that this entire conversation is Top Secret. That's the CNO's classification, not mine. Admiral Eickhoff and I are taking a risk telling this much. You must never repeat a word of this. It's national security."

"I understand," Javert said.

"Good. Here's what you're going to do. You won't release a report on this incident. We'll release one for you under your name. The report will essentially sweep this matter under the rug, just as we did at Messina. Whatever it says, you will agree to. Next, you'll never again interfere with the navigation of this ship. It's imperative for the success of the CNO's operation that you leave the ship handling to your officers."

"Is one of them part of the operation?" Javert asked.

"I'm sorry, Captain, but I can't answer that. Everything on Durham's operation is strictly need to know. I can't confirm nor deny anything related to the operation." Pew loved that touch. He couldn't have set it up better if he had planned it.

"We need you to continue as captain, handle administrative matters, hang out on the bridge, do whatever you like, but don't interfere with your officers. Is that clear?"

"Yes, I understand. I have my orders," Javert began. "Don't issue a report. Agree with the report Admiral Eickhoff sends. Don't interfere with the officers, and this meeting never happened."

Pew looked quizzically at Javert for a second. Javert looked like a man emotionally drained and defeated, but there was steel in his voice that seemed out of place with the rest of the image. He wondered where that came from. Pew knew many navy captains, and Javert was no captain. Considering Javert's behavior so far, he'd concluded Javert was a nutcase.

Pushing ahead, Pew replied, "Exactly, Captain, those are your orders. Follow them and everything will work out just fine."

With a flourish, Pew stood. "That concludes our meeting. Would you do me a favor by calling the bridge and have them retrieve my helicopter, and have your XO meet me on the fantail?" Pew shook hands with Javert, who was smiling.

"Thank you, Captain, I'll find my own way aft."

Pew met Meyers on the fantail and briefed Meyers on his findings. Several contributing factors had led to the accident; Ross' miscalculation, Javert's interference, and Biron's yelling had contributed to the accident, but a blown fuse was the root cause. No one would be reprimanded; it was a simple act of God.

Pew directed the conversation to small talk until the Sea Stallion approached. He had one loose end to tie up for Eickhoff, and he didn't want to deliver his message and leave time for questions. Meyers was too professional not to ask questions given the chance.

"Just a few more things before I go," Pew said, hoping he wasn't having to shout too loud to be heard over the helicopter's beating rotors.

"This is difficult for me. After all, I'm only a lieutenant, but Admiral Eickhoff had me deliver a personal letter to your captain. He told me to assure you that he's aware of the problems you've had with the captain. I don't know what was in the letter, but Admiral Eickhoff assures you Javert will be a new man starting tomorrow. Also, and I can't speak for the admiral on this one, but I suspect he'll give you some downtime, maybe even release the *Farnley* early from Steel Henge. He knows how much time you've spent at sea."

Pew timed it just right, and as he finished, he had to hurry to get into his life jacket and helmet for the pickup. Meyers didn't have time to say a word.

§

Ross wiped the sweat from his face with his orange shop rag. Things were almost back to normal except they were still limping along on one boiler.

He had put the incident out of his mind. Technically, he'd screwed up by keeping the power on too long. It didn't matter. He would do the same thing again, and he wasn't the real problem; it was the navy and the *Farnley*. Maybe his written report would get him transferred, or maybe he'd get discharged early. Ross didn't care either way, but one thing bothered him.

His own words haunted him. *"Jam 'em open, son!" Why did I say that?*

He walked to his bench, sat down, and buried his face in his hands. He blocked out the engine room noise, summoned the earlier feeling of *déjà vu*, and searched for an elusive thought in the black corners of his memory. *"Jam 'em open!"*

Ross caught a thread, then another. Slowly, he began to reweave the tattered tapestry of thirty-year-old memories, and when he was done, he was back aboard the *Able* again.

"Jam 'em open, son! Jam the valves wide open! Lift safeties if you have to, but keep the valves jammed open!"

Chief Barnes' words crackled through Ross' sound-powered headset. His hand, clenched around the boiler fuel control valve, was turning numb. He kept trying to push the valve past the stop.

The *Able*, at full power, charged ahead. The rumble of the blowers and the thunder of the fires blocked out all other sound and reverberated through his body, numbing his consciousness. The fifteen men in the boiler room with Ross were silent. Communication was impossible in the pandemonium. Ross didn't look at them, but he knew they were there with their faces blanched, eyes drawn wide and tight. He could feel them as sure as he could feel the oppressive heat from the boilers.

It was impossible to hear the bark of *Able*'s six five-inch guns, but the ship shuddered from their constant sharp reports. He imagined he heard the pummeling sound of the sixteen 40 mm and 20 mm guns, but he knew he couldn't. The horrific sounds of battle had swallowed even the thunder of guns.

Ross flexed his knees to keep from being bounced off the catwalk by the bucking deck.

The ship swayed ferociously, heeling with each frenzied evasive turn. All Ross could do was hang on. He couldn't move, hear, or think. Every nerve in his body tingled, screamed, and trembled in terror. Every inch of the *Able*, every fiber of her being screamed angry rage at an enemy Ross couldn't see.

The *Able* lurched, slid sideways, and heeled sharply to port, throwing Ross against the bulkhead. He tumbled over the railing and fell into the bilge. Over the sound of a distant explosion and the din of the boiler room he heard inch-thick metal plates pop like the top of a tin can. The *Able* righted herself and screamed onward through the seas.

Driven by instinct, driven by a will to live, Ross pulled himself to the catwalk, grabbed the valve handle, and pushed. His knuckles glowed white through streaks of smeared blood.

He wished he knew what was going on. He wished there were windows so he could see. The boiler room was closing in around him. He longed for the open air topside. He wished he could stand in the hell raging above him. The boiler room encased him, trapped him, and closed in on him like a giant crypt. He wished he could escape. He wouldn't and couldn't let his shipmates down. Their lives, their survival, depended on the *Able*. She in turn depended on each of them, collectively and individually.

Barnes' words echoed in his ears, *"Jam 'em open, son! Jam 'em open, son!"* He pushed harder, hoping it would be enough.

The *Able* snapped upward, knocking Ross off his feet and driving his knees mercilessly into the grillwork of the catwalk surface. He felt pain in his ears and was aware of a thunderous explosion. He tried to regain his feet, but his knees were weak, and he couldn't straighten his legs. The forward bulkhead was buckled, and water gushed through its torn seams. Fountains of water and oil spewed from shattered pipes. The boiler still roared with life. *Survive. "Jam 'em open, son!"*

Ross didn't know what to do, but knew he couldn't let his shipmates down. Using his arms, Ross pulled himself to his feet, grabbed the valve handle, and pushed.

The *Able* convulsed.

A wall of blinding light and searing heat snatched Ross from the catwalk, throwing him backward and upward against the side of the ship.

A sharp pain shot through the back of his skull. He was falling. The steam's hot, moist grip of death engulfed him as he fell through its lethal cloud. Gratefully, he fell facedown into the cool water of the Pacific surging into the bilge. He lifted his head and heard the agonizing screams of souls; his friends.

Gotta get back to my station. Gotta jam 'em open.

He tried to move, but his arms and legs wouldn't respond. His world dimmed. He was floating into a vortex that spun him downward into a welcome world of silence, silence without screams of agony from dying shipmates, a peaceful blackness, a blackness without fire.

"Chief, Chief."

Ross looked up to see Stucky's freckled face. Ross shook his memories off with a shiver. "What is it, son?" Ross asked.

"Number two boiler is online. Should I tell the bridge we can make twenty knots now?"

Ross wiped the clammy sweat from his face with the orange shop rag and said, "No, not yet. I'll take care of it."

§

"Well?" Eickhoff asked, standing behind his paper-cluttered desk. His question was direct and without perfunctory hellos.

Pew could see Eickhoff was perspiring slightly and acting as if he'd consumed several pots of coffee.

"It's all taken care of, Admiral," Pew said nonchalantly before adding, "It went just like you said it would, but there are a few details you should know."

"Like what?" Eickhoff asked, sitting down.

Pew enjoyed this and wanted to string it out as long as possible. "Rather than jumping around, let me start from the top."

Eickhoff nodded reluctantly before Pew continued. "It was as we expected. Javert caused the entire incident by overriding the conning officer's orders."

"We can't put that in a report. They'll make me replace him, and when they start looking at Javert, they'll finish with me."

Pew let Eickhoff finish. "Don't worry, your letter took care of Javert. The rest we can take care of."

Pew paused for a second, then said, "Admiral, I don't know if this is important, but I think something is wrong with Javert, like he has a screw loose or something. The man just didn't seem right."

"Stress, probably," Eickhoff replied, dismissing the comment.

"Next," Pew resumed, "the *Farnley* took a pretty good smack, and underwater hull damage is a distinct possibility. The interior inspection showed nothing, but she needs to be dry-docked for a complete check."

Eickhoff was seething. "Putting her in dry dock is as bad as relieving Javert."

"We have two things that save us," Pew said slowly. "First, there were extenuating circumstances. Specifically, a fuse blew, and the chief responsible of the engine room claims the loss of power was caused by an error in judgment on his part. Between the two, we put together a report that makes it look like an unfortunate accident."

"Are you proposing we hang the chief?" Eickhoff said incredulously.

Pew expected that reaction. Hanging something like this on a chief petty officer would be tricky and dangerous unless the evidence was irrefutable.

"Not at all," Pew began. "His record is strong and impeccable. No one would ever question his judgment, but he said it and put it in writing. Our report will be factual and point to the chief's statement. However, in the conclusion section, we'll dismiss the idea that the chief could have made a mistake. After we list his experience, no one will question absolving the chief. That leads to only one final conclusion; the fuse caused the incident, and no one is to blame."

Eickhoff, staring out of a porthole, was calming down. "What about the hull inspection? Putting a ship into dry dock for a hull inspection makes it a major incident that will be investigated further by someone else."

Eickhoff went back to pacing the floor behind his desk. After a second, he said, "However, we're in luck. The deck repairs on the *Farnley* are yard level and will take three or four days at most. Nothing major, so we have an excuse to get her into a shipyard. The *Farnley* is overdue for hull cleaning and painting, which requires dry-docking. And what's part of every hull cleaning operation?"

"A hull inspection, done by the ship's crew, not nosy outsiders," Pew responded, playing along with Eickhoff.

"Precisely," Eickhoff said, grinning widely.

Until now, Pew hadn't figured out how to close the trap on Eickhoff, but a fabulous lie popped into his head.

"That leaves us with Operation Marathon. Putting the ship into the yard could endanger your strong position on the *Farnley* by making it look like you gave her some time off."

Eickhoff was back in his seat, smiling. "Do I detect a 'but' coming?"

"Yes," Pew said, wiping perspiration from his upper lip. "On the way up here, I stopped by my cabin to freshen up, and as luck would have it, I had received a letter from my source back in Washington. The letter contained some interesting information. The other Operation Marathon ships averaged only fifteen days at sea per month. The *Farnley* has averaged over twenty-one."

Eickhoff leaned back in his chair and placed his hands behind his head. "And let me guess," Eickhoff began, obviously buying the story about the letter. "I planned it that way to account for the hull cleaning. How could anyone fault me for advanced planning and my concern over ship maintenance?" Eickhoff's smile was absolutely radiant.

Pew smiled and made no attempt to respond. He wanted to see where Eickhoff would take the conversation next.

"What about Javert? Did you give him the letter?" Eickhoff asked finally.

"Yes, and it had the desired effect. We'll have no more problems with him."

"You didn't let him keep the letter, did you?"

Pew understood Eickhoff's concern since the letter contained statements that Eickhoff could never explain. It would end his career if it fell into the wrong hands. "I took it back, tore it up, and threw it overboard," Pew lied.

"Good!" Eickhoff said. "And what about the *Farnley*'s exec, Meyers? He's not going to take this lying down."

"Yes he will. As instructed, I implied that you had Javert under rehabilitation. With the change we should see in Javert, he'll believe it. Who knows? Operation Marathon may be over before the *Farnley* gets back to sea or Meyers suspects anything."

Pew and Eickhoff discussed the incident in detail and ironed out the final details. Nothing except the *Farnley*'s schedule would be altered, and Pew would coordinate arrangements to schedule dry-dock time for the *Farnley* at the Skaramanga shipyards near Elefsis.

When they were done, with a sigh Eickhoff said, "I guess that's it. Now all I need is your report as inspecting officer to file on the incident."

"Yes, sir," Pew said, giving Eickhoff a playful salute, then headed for his cabin.

He'd handled it skillfully, and now he couldn't lose. Eickhoff was in so deep, he could never back down on Operation Marathon. If Eickhoff came out on top, Pew had lots of hard evidence that would make blackmailing Eickhoff quite lucrative. If the roof caved in on Eickhoff, Pew would switch sides and become Eickhoff's chief prosecutor.

Pew already had the official report Eickhoff wanted mentally drafted. With its careful wording, Pew would look like the *Farnley*'s guardian angel, recommending downtime and yard time for the ship. By the time Eickhoff's court-martial was over, Pew would look like a saintly lieutenant fighting for the poor *Farnley* against a brutal and powerful admiral.

It was as Pew's father had told him years ago, "When you can't tell who's going to win, support both sides." How wise his father had been.

§

After Pew left, Meyers buried himself in the work of getting the *Farnley* shipshape again. The light metal framework of the lifeboat tubs was quickly cut up and jettisoned, and numerous pieces of jagged, sharp metal left clinging to the superstructure were removed. Makeshift stanchions were welded to the main deck and line strung between them.

The most worrisome problem to Meyers was the heavy scuff marks that ran the length of the port side. From what he could see above the waterline, huge patches of paint had been removed, and without a coat of covering paint, the salt environment would turn the *Farnley*'s side into a dark-red rusty scab within hours.

The corpsman, armed with disinfectant, bandages, and a hypo containing a tetanus booster, caught up with him just as the men had finished welding a temporary patch on the forward bulkhead to Javert's cabin where the flying stanchion had hit. Meyers, who had completely forgotten about the inch-long cut, still couldn't remember how he had gotten it.

He realized, also, that he'd forgotten about the captain, whom he'd not seen except for a few seconds when Pew was aboard. Meyers found him on the bridge in a strangely pleasant mood. Javert gave him a copy of the official report to read, and Meyers headed to his stateroom to clean up for dinner.

In his stateroom, Meyers read the four-page report carefully, but something kept gnawing at him as being out of place. The report downplayed Javert's interference with Biron to the point that it was only mentioned in passing. Excerpts from Ross' written statement were quoted heavily, especially those in which Ross took responsibility for the accident due to his error.

Meyers couldn't accept any conclusions that led to placing the blame on Ross, and the report concurred, absolving Ross of any responsibility. The report concluded that an unlikely fluke event, the blown fuse, was the ultimate cause.

Meyers, still uneasy about the report, read it again. He'd missed it the first time. The report was formatted as a *Farnley* outgoing message, but the codes at the top indicated the message had been received by the *Farnley* as a rebroadcast. Suspicious, he read the message a third time, alert for anything else out of place.

Meyers disagreed with the report in terms of detail and emphasis, but not on the conclusion. Tenaciously, he read the report again, and as he read the conclusion section, it hit him. The report was smoothly worded and crafted with skills he knew Javert didn't possess. This wasn't Javert's report.

Had Javert submitted the preliminary report to Eickhoff for final review and approval? he wondered. Meyers dismissed that line of reasoning because Javert didn't have access to Ross' written statement. That meant Eickhoff or Pew had drafted the report, but why?

Pew's comments on the fantail came back to him. "Javert will be a new man starting tomorrow." Without saying anything directly, Pew had made himself clear. Eickhoff was working to rehabilitate Javert as a captain. That didn't alter the facts. Javert was unfit for command, and Eickhoff had to know that. Meyers reasoned that an attempt at rehabilitation was expected as a matter of fair play. Eickhoff had to give Javert a chance.

The tragedy was that it took the collision to bring some positive action. More important, things would begin to get better, and in the meantime, Javert shouldn't be the problem he'd been in the past. Javert's pleasantness on the bridge indicated he'd gotten the message.

Meyers looked at the sea bag swaying gently from its pipe. There was a glimmer of hope. The navy was beginning to work the way it should. Maybe his fight wasn't as hopeless as he had thought.

Playfully, Meyers punched at the bag and started expanding his plans to square the ship away. Javert wouldn't interfere now, and if he did, it would only accelerate the inevitable. The exercise lifted his spirits until a thought of caution occurred to him. This all might be a lie. Eickhoff had lied to him before. Meyers screamed and drove his fist hard into the bag, trying to destroy such negative thinking.

BURIAL AT SEA

August 1971, Mediterranean Sea south of Crete
Operation Marathon: Day 420

In Lee's stateroom, Nat Hayes and two other junior officers, Ensigns Harold Devore and Don Beck, were trying to tell Lee something. "Don't get so upset. This crap happens all the time on the *Farnley*. If you let it get to you, it'll drive you nuts," Hayes said.

Lee was seated in his gray steel desk chair, looking up at Hayes' dour face. Hayes liked the upper bunk despite the cramped space caused by the air-conditioning unit. The unit hung from the overhead, leaving a bare eighteen-inch clearance between the bunk and the unit's drip pan. Hayes initially thought the lower bunk was better until his bunk mate in the upper berth got sea sick one night. Even though Lee outranked Hayes, Lee let him keep the upper bunk once Hayes promised never to get sea sick.

Lee turned to Beck and Devore, who were lounging on the green Naugahyde couch. "Is that the way you guys see it?" Lee asked.

Devore nodded while Beck replied for both of them. "You got it. This ship sucks, and there isn't a darn thing you can do about it. We're the oldest ship in the navy, and the navy doesn't care. So why should we?"

"I don't buy into that," Lee replied.

Nat Hayes lifted his head so he could see Lee and bumped his head on the air conditioner drip pan. "Ouch! Look, Lee, face it. The *Farnley* is the leper of the fleet. We're supposed to be assigned to DESRON 12, right? We haven't seen any DESRON 12 ships in over a year."

"There has to be an explanation. Maybe we don't know everything," Lee said.

"Tell ya what I know," Beck began. "Hayes is right. Not only are we the leper, we're an old leper who doesn't count. You talk about the supply problems. I've talked to some guys from other ships, and they can get anything they need. Face it, Lee, no one else cares, so why should you?"

"I can't accept this. We have to do something."

"Why?" Hayes asked.

"This ship is dangerous and it's way below par. Someone could have gotten killed today."

Hayes raised his head again, this time more carefully. "You're right. That's why survival is the name of the game here. Look, I was there, and I don't know what the official report will say, but believe me, it was all the captain's doing."

"Doesn't matter," Lee began. "We should've been able to answer a flank bell. End of discussion."

"Yeah, I bet," taunted Beck. "On a normal ship, the shit would hit the fan, but on the *Farnley*, it's like nothing ever happened. This is the normal routine around here. Lee, you've got to get this through your head. This is normal, and it's called survival. Don't let it get to you," Beck said.

"Cut him some slack. He hasn't been on board long enough to be *Farnley*-ized yet. He'll learn," Hayes told them.

"Learn what?" Lee asked.

"Are you dense? On the *Farnley,* you don't do a tour. You're like a convict serving time in prison. The way I got it figured, the *Farnley*'s some kind of mobile Devil's Island. There isn't anything you can do, and there's no escape."

"No," Lee said softly. "Look at you guys. You look like hell, just like the ship. You don't feel good about yourselves. You're a sorrowful lot. I haven't seen one honest smile since I got here. I haven't seen one person try to make one thing better."

"Ah! You finally got it. Three hundred and fifty guys on board this ship, and no one cares except you. Does that tell you anything? Lee, believe me," Hayes said, then laid his head back down on the pillow. "Don't try to be happy on this ship; it'll only make you sad."

"I think you guys are full of it," Lee said as he stood and looked at each one in turn. "I can't agree with a word you've said. It's worth the effort, and the first thing you should do is lighten up a bit and find something to smile about before you drown in your own self-pity. If I were you guys, I'd watch my backside." Lee turned and headed for the door.

"You'll be sorry. You'll get hurt or the captain will dump on you," Beck called after him.

Lee stopped and spun to face Beck. "I'd rather get punished for doing something than have to punish myself for the rest of my life for doing nothing." The edge on Lee's voice and his piercing stare maintained the silence until Lee was out of the room.

"Touchy, isn't he?" Beck said.

"Give him time, Beck. You were the same way once; we all were," Hayes said. After a second's pause he asked, "What did he mean by watch our backsides?"

"Beats me. I think the guy's nuts the way he's always grinning. Wonder what he looks like when he's mad," Beck said with a chuckle.

Hayes rolled over and looked down at Beck. "You weren't paying attention. You just saw him mad."

§

Lee left the stateroom, headed aft on the weather deck to where the railing was still intact, and rested his hands on the oiled steel cable running between stanchions. Sunset was a half hour away, and the low sun made Lee squint as he stood motionless. After a moment, he took several deep breaths and headed for the engine room.

Descending the ladder into the engine room, Lee slid down the brass rails and broke his free fall at the last second. His feet barely made a sound as they hit the deck.

Lee headed toward the gauge board where Ross and Stucky were talking. Elmo scurried across the deck, but when he saw Lee, he stopped, twitched his antenna, and retreated toward Ross' bench. Lee saw Elmo and blocked his retreat with his shoe. Elmo swerved to go around the obstacle, but Lee carefully placed the toe of his shoe against Elmo and, with a gentle kick, flung Elmo almost to where Ross was standing.

Stunned and on his back, Elmo's legs clawed at the air as he tried to regain an upright position. Lee walked around the struggling Elmo and addressed Ross. "Chief, could you get all the men not on watch to huddle up for a minute? I want to talk to them."

Ross looked closely at Lee. The sparkle was gone from his coal-black eyes, but his voice seemed normal enough. Without comment, Ross went to the railing and yelled to the men below. While the men assembled, Lee teased the frantic Elmo with the toe of his shoe. Lee silently watched Elmo and, for a second, ignored the assembled group. Then, to no one in particular, he asked, "What happened today when we lost power?"

Ross bristled. "That wasn't their fault. I talked to Sweeney. He told me what happened on the bridge. The captain started it, the fuse cinched it, and I was the one who blew it. The men did their job, and Canterbury ought to get a medal 'cause he took the boilers to the limit. In another three seconds, he would have melted the boilers down. They don't run too well without water in them, you know."

Lee ignored Ross' comment and looked at Stucky's freckled face. "What do you think?"

Stucky shrugged. "It happens all the time; no big deal. This is the

Farnley, you know."

Lee turned to the assembled group. "Do you all agree with Stucky?" The group shuffled and turned their eyes downward. No one chose to answer.

Ross didn't like the direction Lee's questions were leading. "Don't jerk our chain. We did our job. We're just trying to survive down here. It happened. I know you almost got killed, but I could say the same for the boiler crew, so you don't have the right to get high and mighty over this. It happened before, and it'll happen again. It's over, done, and forgotten. We got by; that's all that matters."

Lee's voice turned soft. "I know you all did everything possible under the circumstances today. From what I heard, I'm proud of the way you all hung in there. You're a good group of sailors."

Lee turned to Stucky and asked, "Someone told me you wanted to be a barber but joined the navy instead. Is that right?"

Stucky blushed and shuffled his feet a little. "Well, yeah, once. I practiced a little, but I never got too good."

"Do you want more practice?"

"What do you mean?" Stucky glanced toward his shipmates, his voice cautious.

"It looks to me like no one here has had a haircut in months. I'm appointing you our official barber," Lee said, turning toward Ross, who was wrinkling his forehead at Lee.

"Chief, first thing tomorrow, make up a schedule and see to it that every man gets a haircut. Put me first on the list."

Ross removed his cap and ran his hand across his bald scalp. This kid is going too far, Ross thought. He looked directly at Lee and said, "Mister Lee, you can't do that. Stucky doesn't know how to be a barber. It's not our fault we don't have a ship's barber."

"Chief, I'd like you to be the second one on the list," Lee interrupted.

Ross smiled weakly. "But I don't have any hair."

"You'll be second, Chief. You have a little left around the sides, and it's getting shaggy." Before Ross could answer, Lee started to turn away as he spoke. "That's all I wanted."

Lee continued to pivot on his left toe as his right foot swung toward the ladder.

One of the men yelled, "Mister Lee! Watch out! Elmo!"

Lee was startled. His head swung back toward the voice, and his right foot swayed slightly to the left in response to the head movement. With his body twisted, Lee's foot fell to the deck.

Elmo died instantly.

For what seemed an eternity, Lee stood motionless. The eyes of the group left Lee's surprised face and followed his torso down to the right shoe. Slowly, Lee lifted his right foot and bent down. He gently picked Elmo's body up with his fingertips and placed it in the palm of his hand. Lee turned back to the group, holding his hand so all could see Elmo's crushed body. Lee looked at the group. "I'm sorry," he said in a soft, airy, commiserative voice.

No one spoke. The group slowly broke up as each man headed off in silence until only Ross and Stucky were left. Ross squinted a bit at Lee and tried to decipher what he saw behind the grin. There was something deep, black, and ominous in Lee's eyes. Lee looked directly at Ross and said, "Chief, I want all your men who are not on watch mustered on the fantail in five minutes."

"Why?" Ross asked, still probing with his eyes.

"I'll tell you then." Lee turned and headed for the ladder.

§

When Lee walked onto the fantail, Ross and his men were milling about in an unorganized group. Lee looked serious and was carefully carrying a brown Masonite clipboard. A small American flag like those given to children on the Fourth of July was taped to it. Under the flag was a walnut-sized bulge. Ross looked inquisitively at the clipboard, but Lee offered no explanation.

"Have the men form up, Chief, facing outboard."

Ross scratched the back of his neck and shrugged before complying. The sun had almost set, and the sky was aglow with gold and orange tones. The men stood casually in formation, shuffling their feet, their heads turning to one side or looking down, trying to hide their smiles and snickers.

Lee stepped in front of the men and, holding the clipboard in his right hand, rested it on top of the railing stanchion. When he spoke, his solemn voice was strong but low, and its edge cut through the sound of the sea and the wake.

"Men, I thought it would be appropriate for us to say good-bye to our fellow shipmate, Petty Officer Third Class Elmo Cockroach, and commit his memory to the deep," Lee began.

The furtive shuffling and head movement of the men increased, but penetrating the half-darkness, Lee's eyes stabbed at each man, forcing them to return his gaze.

Lee continued, "It's only fitting that Elmo be buried at sea since he lived his entire life aboard this ship, and, sadly, they became inseparable.

"What can we say about Elmo as we say good-bye to him? What do we know about him? He was a shipmate and a diversion from the boredom of the sea. He wasn't a fighter. Elmo was nonjudgmental. He neither looked up nor down on anyone. He had no ideals, no heroes, and no enemies to strengthen him. Elmo was neither coward nor hero. All he wanted to do was get by, to survive.

"Elmo was Elmo, nothing more, nothing less. Elmo's only single accomplishment was that he accomplished nothing."

Lee paused and scanned each face in the silent formation. Ross had watched his men grow quiet and had tried to catch Lee's eye. Lee ignored him.

Lee took a deep breath and resumed. "Elmo was a cockroach, and like all cockroaches, he was a survivor. Strangely, we identified with him."

Lee stopped abruptly and fixed his gaze on Ross. The fading sunlight and shadows somehow made Lee's clear black eyes appear hard as steel. Ross lowered his head to look at his shoes, but Lee's eyes and the eyes of his men bit at him. When he raised his eyes to return Lee's gaze, Lee continued.

"Elmo wasn't an able seaman."

It was as if the other men had disappeared. Two men, Ross and Lee, eyes locked, unflinching, faced each other. Lee lowered his voice as if talking only to Ross.

"His legacy is that he left no legacy, and that's not part of the deal. The real tragedy is, Elmo died a survivor."

Lee tipped the clipboard up, and a small white bundle slid down the board and fell into the sea.

"Dismiss the men, Chief." Lee walked away before Ross had a chance to react.

WOODEN SHIPS AND MEN OF STEEL

August 1971, Mediterranean Sea south of Crete
Operation Marathon: Day 420

It was just past ten that night when Ross poked his head around the corner of Lee's quarters. Lee, lying in his bunk, looked up over the clipboard propped on his knees. "Mister Lee, I saw your light on. I hoped you were still up. Do you have a minute?"

"Sure. Come on in. What do you want, Chief?"

Fifteen years earlier when he put on his chief's stripes, Ross had accepted this responsibility. Without being asked or told, he knew it was his responsibility to help train young officers. This wasn't Ross' first avuncular visit, and he had hoped he could avoid this one, but he couldn't.

"Mister Lee, I want to help you. We have to work together. Can I speak openly?"

Lee nodded.

"That stunt you pulled earlier this evening. What the hell was that all about?"

Lee's eyes sparked back at Ross. "I was burying a fallen shipmate. It's your fantasy, Chief, not mine. What was Elmo all about?"

Ross screwed his face in thought. "Mister Lee, I know what you're trying to do. Don't do it. You'll only hurt the men and yourself."

"What about you? Will you get hurt?"

"That doesn't matter. I can ride things out. Don't screw up your career."

"What do you mean?"

Ross looked into Lee's eyes again, trying to figure out what Lee meant by the question. All he saw was honest curiosity.

"The *Farnley* is the *Farnley*. She's an old ship, and under the best circumstances, we'd have to hold her together with baling wire. The navy has written her off."

"What has that got to do with getting hurt?" Lee asked.

"You're just going to get the men all excited, and when you can't

110

support them, they'll get more discouraged than they are now. Don't do that to them, please."

"Are you worried about the men, Chief?"

Ross' pulse quickened. "Of course I am. Most of them are just kids, but they're good kids. Some really grew up today when we lost power. It takes guts to do what they did today."

"I know they're good men, Chief, but don't you think they deserve better?"

"Don't patronize me. Damn right they deserve better! But the navy doesn't care and won't give us the support we need. Don't raise their hopes, then let 'em down. They're good men; don't poison them against the navy forever."

"The navy isn't poisoning them; you are."

"What?" Ross yelled. "I'm not doing a damn thing to them."

"Or for them. That's my point."

Ross buried his face in his hands. The kid just didn't understand. Ross raised his head to look at Lee. "It's not my fault because there isn't a darn thing we, you, or I can do. I tried. No matter which way you turn, the navy stops you."

"Chief, the situation today wasn't good. I'm not going to let that happen in my engine room. I won't give up. That's the deal."

Ross half rose from the couch. "Your engine room?"

"You said it was mine the first time we met. Remember?"

Ross' mind was reeling. "Well, there's nothing you can do to keep it from happening again."

"The men can fix the engine room. They don't need parts; they need your example."

"Come off the crap, Mister Lee. Just lay it on the table. What do you want from me?"

"All I want is for you to do your job."

"I am," Ross yelled

"Are you?" Lee's voice was calm.

Ross was tiring of this game and was having difficulty controlling his anger. "If you're so god-awful smart, what do you think we should do?"

"We're going to make an honest effort."

"That's what I've been trying to tell you! It's not worth the effort. There's nothing you can do; you can't win!"

Ross was confused and angry; he had to get away to be by himself. Ross threw up his hands and stood. "Mister Lee, I don't know what I have to do to get through to you. Just leave me alone."

Lee remained seated, looking up at Ross, still smiling, eyes clear and firm. It was as if the conversation had no effect on him.

Ross stormed out of the room, and when he reached the chief's quarters, he didn't undress but lay down in his bunk fully clothed on his stomach. He tried to concentrate on something that would take his mind away from the day's events.

He put Lee out of his mind and tried to imagine what it would be like to be out of the navy. Those thoughts only brought him sadness and melancholy. He turned his thoughts to happier times and the *Able*. His mouth had turned dry and he swallowed, trying to moisten his mouth. He swallowed wrong, and it made him cough as the ship rolled awkwardly to port, and Ross drifted across time and became the young man again in the *Able*'s boiler room.

His chest heaved spasmodically. Chief Barnes' words echoed through his head. *"Jam 'em open, son!"* He was calm and languid, his body floating gently on the breast of a cool, peaceful cloud. The coolness caressed his face and chest. He felt a paralyzing burning pain down his neck and back; the pain was far away as if the pain wasn't his but someone else's.

The choking paroxysm in his chest returned, and, wrenching his head away from the coolness of the cloud, he spat the foul taste of phlegm, blood, oil, and seawater from his mouth.

With rasping heaves, he sucked in the oven-hot air. His arm, floating limp in the water, hooked itself around an object he could sense but not feel and steadied him against the awkward sloshing movement. He opened his eyes to the darkness, but he couldn't see anything. He opened his eyes again to make sure. The blackness was total. He tried to move, but his limbs didn't respond. The world lurched, sending a wave across the water in the bilge, and he felt himself pivot on his arm and roll slowly onto his back.

Where am I? Where am I? He twisted his face in concentration and tried to focus his feeble senses on the blackness. Voices. No voices. Moans. Someone was moaning. *The Able. I'm on the Able.* He could hear a roar. A continuous roar like a boiler but different. Heat. Searing heat. *Fire. I'm being cooked alive.*

Unable to move, Ross knew he was dying. He closed his eyes and accepted death with calm, quiet anticipation. He reached out to embrace it and begged it to take him before the fire reached him. Floating peacefully, he waited as eternity swirled around him, lovingly wrapping him in welcome silence and darkness.

With a start, Ross jumped out of his bunk gasping for air, his heart thumping heavily in his chest. He looked around and saw that he was in his compartment on the *Farnley*. Ross sat back down on his bunk and tried to calm himself. He wasn't sure if he'd been remembering or if he'd been dreaming; it was so vivid.

Ross climbed back into his bunk. He didn't try to sleep. He couldn't.

§

After his midwatch, Biron went to his stateroom to catch up on paperwork and reports. When his work was done, it was too late to go to bed; reveille was less than thirty minutes away. The sea was calm and the weather nice so he headed to the fo'c'scle for some quiet time.

Once on the fo'c'scle, he sat, as he always did at times like this, on the anchor windlass. Biron ignored the chilling sensation as the heavy, cold morning dew on the windlass soaked his trousers. He wanted time to think and watch the sunrise. He had less than six months to go before his hitch was up, and he didn't know what to do.

He knew he had a brilliant career ahead of him, and he loved . . . loved what? The navy? The sea? The ships? He loved his wife, Ann, and his daughter, Sarah. When he thought of them, his heart ached. He hated the separations, and he grieved over the time he had lost with them.

Biron knew what his options were and knew exactly how the navy would deal with him. The navy would give him his new orders and a choice; accept the orders or leave the navy. The orders would be the naval equivalent of a bribe, a good billet at a good duty station, probably with early promotion to lieutenant commander thrown in to sweeten the deal. He wanted, and had promised Ann, to make up his mind before the orders arrived lest he be seduced.

Was that the real issue, or was it Sarah, his daughter? He'd missed her first tooth, her first step, and so many other things. What of her? What had she missed? What responsibilities and obligations had he failed to fulfill? What special moments had he missed?

He had marveled at Sarah's nimble child's mind and the way she could connect ideas that seemed childish at first but upon reflection were almost profound. Recently he had taken Ann and Sarah to Sounion for a picnic lunch. The talk had turned to the navy, and a new word for Sarah popped up, *warship*. She connected war with killing and death, then after a few questions climbed into his lap and hugged him.

"Promise me you won't ever do anything that would kill people. Please, Daddy?" she pleaded.

"I promise."

"Promise me you won't get hurt or killed."

"It's okay sweetheart. I promise."

"Promise, Daddy?"

"I promise," he had assured her.

It was a precious moment and one he would treasure. How many treasures had he lost?

Biron's thoughts were interrupted by the sound of footsteps and a shadowy figure as it emerged from the forward deck hatch. In the soft glow of the morning light, he recognized Ross, tired and haggard. Ross saw Biron and walked forward to join him.

"Good morning, Chief. Up a little early, aren't you?" Biron said.

"What about you? As for me, I couldn't sleep," Ross replied, seating himself on the moist deck.

"Why not?"

"It's Mister Lee. I'm worried about him."

Biron looked at Ross carefully. "You know, Chief, you look like hell. Are you all right?"

"Yeah, I'm just worried and a little mixed up right now. Maybe you can help. We've both been in the navy for a while, and we're both due to get out soon."

"Haven't made up my mind yet, Chief," Biron corrected.

"Well, anyway, maybe you could talk to Lee before he gets himself into trouble. I tried last night but couldn't get through to him."

"What's the problem?"

"Lee thinks he can get everything fixed just like that," Ross snapped his fingers for emphasis. "Only one of two things can come of it. Either he's going to take a fall, or he's going to destroy the morale of the crew. Probably both. He's just going the wrong way with this. And now with the crew talking about him, he's already made a fool of himself."

"I wouldn't be too sure about that," Biron said. "Tell me. What do you think is the right way?"

"Don't fight it. Roll with the seas."

Biron looked at Ross for a long moment, then turned toward the brightening sky that was now a crescent of brilliant white above the horizon. As if speaking to himself, he began:

> *Her decks, once red with heroes' blood,*
> *Where knelt the vanquished foe,*
> *When winds were hurrying o'er the flood,*
> *And waves were white below,*
> *No more shall feel the victor's tread*
> *Or know the conquered knee—*
> *The harpies of the shore shall pluck*
> *The eagle of the sea!*

Ross listened intently to Biron's soft voice, and when Biron paused,

he asked, "What's that from?"
Biron ignored Ross' question and continued:

Oh, better that her shattered hulk
Should sink beneath the wave;
Her thunders shook the ocean deep,
And there should be her grave;
Nail to the mast her holy flag,
Set every threadbare sail,
And give her to the god of storms,
The lightning and the gale!

Biron turned to Ross and said, "That's from Oliver Wendell Holmes' poem 'Old Ironsides.' Do you know why he wrote it?"
"No, but what does this have to do with Mister Lee?"
"Nothing and everything. Holmes wrote that poem in the early eighteen hundreds when the navy decided to scrap the USS *Constitution*. The resulting public outcry forced the navy to keep her and ultimately turn her into a national memorial. Why do you think that happened?"
Ross thought the question trivial and shrugged. "She was a great ship."
"Not exactly. A mountain, a tree, a bridge, a building, a flower, or a hull is a thing. Things can be beautiful, ugly, awe-inspiring, simple, but they can't be great. Greatness springs only from strength and courage; only from the soul and spirit of man. The men who served on Old Ironsides made her great, and their greatness is our inheritance from them.
"Old Ironsides is a symbol of greatness. She inspired a nation to greatness. Her destruction would have destroyed her legacy."
Biron fell silent for a minute, then looked at Ross, his face sad. "The thing that always troubled me was that the admirals didn't understand that, but the common man did."
"Understand what?" Ross asked.
Biron took a deep breath and tried to find a way to explain something he'd never said in words. "Each generation gives its wisdom to the next. That's their gift. But with the gift comes the responsibility to keep it, cherish it, care for it, add to it, make it better, then give it to the next generation.
"It's like the watch," Biron continued, pointing to the bridge. "Each watch turns over its knowledge to the next. Watches proceed in an endless, unbroken chain from officer to officer across generations. Each watch carries with it the accumulated knowledge and wisdom of those

who went before and the duty to stand the watch well. The watch I just left is as connected to Old Ironsides as the watch I'll stand ten years from now."

Ross looked confused. "But this is the *Farnley*, not Old Ironsides. We're an old, broken-down ship, and if she ever had any glory days, they're far behind her."

"Doesn't matter. It's our watch now, and that's why I won't ask Lee to back off. He knows what he's doing."

"What's he doing?" Ross asked.

Biron pursed his lips, then began, "Your last station was the shipyards, right?"

"Yeah, so what?"

"You're a certified navy shipyard inspector, correct?" Biron asked.

"Yeah, so?"

"I would think that a man of your experience and credentials could figure something out. Anyway, I've got to get going. I've got a lot of things to do before chow," Biron said, getting up to leave.

"But what do you think he's trying to do?" Ross asked.

Biron stopped and looked down at Ross. "Emerson said, 'Tis man's perdition to be safe, when for the truth he ought to die.' Think about it, Chief. Emerson knew something about greatness."

ASHORE

August 1971, 2 Miles off the west coast of Greece
Operation Marathon: Day 423

Even though it was just after six in the morning, sailors lined the
Farnley's rail straining for the first sight of the brilliant Glyfada beaches,
which to Mediterranean sailors are the outer beacon on the approach to
Athens. The mixed sand and marble dust beaches, bleached by the
scorching Hellenic sun since the dawn of time and washed by the pristine
cerulean waters of the Saronic Gulf, appeared to luminesce a brilliant
white despite the long morning shadows of the resort hotels and rocky
inland hills.

Charged with quiet excitement and anticipation, the crew watched as
they passed the airport, Kalamaki, Faliron Delta and the inland city of
Athens crowned by the Parthenon poised high above the Athenian plain.
After forty-three days away, they would soon be home.

As they entered the channel between Salamis Island and the ancient
port of Piraeus, the deck hands readying the mooring lines paused to
admire the picturesque cruise ships, ferries, and wooden fishing boats
huddled in the harbor's natural basin.

The *Farnley* steamed northward, entering the murky waters of Elefsis
Bay. Once abreast of the Skaramanga Shipyard she came thirty degrees
to port, setting her head on port of Elefsis.

The late August sun in Greece was relentless and the ever present
stony terrain its anvil. The knot of pier spectators, of incomplete families,
was dressed in breezy light colored clothing that was their Grecian
Sunday best. All the children jumped, ran, and continued to vent their
excited energy. The women had stopped talking and each turned toward
the sea, straining their eyes to find their man, their sailor returned from
the sea.

Soon the *Farnley* was secure alongside the pier. The in-port watch
was set and all of the off-duty married men collected their loved ones
and headed home. Ross did not go ashore.

§

Ross finished lunch and headed directly to the engine room; he had a noisy fuel pump that needed tending. When he arrived, the engine room was as cool and quiet as Ross thought an office would be. No steam hissed and no machinery hummed, but the engine room buzzed with activity. Hushed voices echoed from the bowels, catwalks rattled quietly under unhurried footsteps, tools clinked. The sound and peaceful mood of a sleeping ship were special to Ross as if it were a mystical undersea temple of steel.

Ross went directly to the lower level and found that Stucky had already started on the pump, so Ross sat on the catwalk, cleaned his screwdriver with his shop rag, and watched.

For the first time in months, he felt good, really good, because he'd accomplished something. Since the night Elmo died, Ross had done a lot of thinking. Part of it was because of Lee, part because of what Biron had said, and part because for some reason, the *Able* had been haunting him.

What would Barnes have done? Ross kept asking himself. No matter how many times Ross asked the question, he came up with the same answer. He could hear Barnes bellowing, "That's the deal," to add emphasis to every lesson, but these were different times, different ships, different navies. Chief Barnes' old bromides didn't cut it anymore.

Ross had also decided he hadn't given Lee enough credit, and saw no problem letting Lee do little things like uniforms, morale, and cleanliness. It wouldn't make much difference so long as Lee didn't get expectations set too high, but at least the men would have something to keep their minds off their other problems.

Earlier, when they had tied up at the pier, the Greek pier workers had connected the *Farnley* to the shore electrical power, but had refused to connect the steam lines that would provide steam for hot water and heat for the cook's large steam kettles. Without the steam line, Ross would have to keep the boilers and his engineering plant running. The pier workers insisted that they only had orders to hook up the electricity. Without the appropriate paperwork, there was no way they would connect the steam.

Normally, such incidents were taken to the captain, who would threaten the pier workers as only a captain could, with death by slow dismemberment or some other equally unpleasant event, and the matter would be quickly resolved.

This had happened before because the *Farnley* never had authorization to hook up to shore steam. The screwup had to be administrative because the only real problem was the piece of paper the dock workers had didn't have a small X in the right box. Ross knew that going to Javert wouldn't produce the desired effect, so, in the past, he'd resigned himself to the situation.

As Ross had walked back to the ship from the shack the dockworkers used for an office, he experienced an almost perverse pleasure in his anger at the workers and their damned piece of paper. By the time he had reached the brow, Ross had worked himself into a fighting frenzy. He wasn't gonna take this shit anymore.

Ross headed forward, spoke with the gunner's mates, and got dressed in his ribbon-covered dress-blue uniform with its left sleeve blanketed in gold hash marks and insignia. Ross almost tore the door off the hinges when he stormed into the pier workers' little plywood shack and demanded to know who was in charge.

The three men in the shack were dressed alike, black dirty slacks and semi-dirty Greek white shirts that resembled short smocks. The fat one continued to munch on some bread, the one with the butch haircut scratched the black stubble on his head, and the short one stood and said, "I speak English. Can I help you?"

Ross' entrance hadn't had the effect he desired, but he was determined to see it through. "Who's in charge?" Ross demanded.

"The supervisor," Shorty said.

"Which of you's the supervisor?" Ross yelled, trying to sound fierce.

"He left to go to town. Should be back in an hour."

Ross had learned that, to a Greek, an hour is the same as tomorrow, and tomorrow is the same as next week. He had to find a way to speed up the timetable. "It doesn't matter. You have ten minutes to connect the steam lines. Do you understand?" Ross shouted.

"Yes, but you do not understand. The work order says no steam," the short one said, pointing to the work order, "and without authorization, we'll get in trouble. You have to wait for the supervisor." Shorty finished by translating for his friends, who nodded in agreement.

Ross snatched the work order, marked an X in the appropriate box, and signed across the face, "Fleet Admiral J. A. Ross, Esquire." Handing the paper back, he said, "You now have your authorization and nine minutes to connect the steam."

The short one didn't look at the paper but handed it to the fat one, who handed it to the one with the butch haircut, who put it on the desk.

"I am sorry, but without permission, we'll get in trouble," the short one said apologetically.

"Very well," Ross bellowed, "but tomorrow you'll have no job, because you'll have no boilers to tend." Suddenly all three men knew how to speak English, or at least they seemed to understand. He now had their undivided attention. Ross pushed on. "My captain is upset that he doesn't have steam, and my captain is a crazy man. Do you understand crazy?" Ross said, making a circular motion with his finger next to his ear. They all nodded.

"He ordered me to blow up the generators and this shack if he doesn't have steam in eight minutes. It doesn't make any difference to me; it's up to you."

Ross stormed out and tried to tear the door off the hinge on the way, but it held. Forty feet down the pier, he stopped and turned toward the shack. The three men were jabbering in Greek and looking out the window at him, obviously discussing who the real crazy man was.

Ross raised his right hand, and the forward gun mount came to life with a deep *whoooop* from its motors as they started. The pier workers heard it but didn't know what to make of it until the gun mount's heavy gear trains let out a threatening growl, and the mount rumbled around and jerked to a stop. Next, the high-precision gears meshed and sang their ominous tune as the two five-inch barrels lowered and took dead aim on the workers, their shack, and their steam generators. The three men prudently vacated the shack and started to approach Ross.

As sun glinted off the teeth like rifling at the tip of the muzzles, Ross shouted, "You have five minutes."

The men decided to take a wait-and-see approach, so Ross lowered his right arm to hold it horizontal with the ground. From inside the mount, machinery clanked. The Greeks looked quizzical as the hydraulic hoist hissed, lifting shell and powder to the mount. They understood the hoist's hiss when the brass loading trays clacked down into position. Shell and powder dropped into the tray with a metallic thud. What followed was the unmistakable sound of shells being rammed and breach blocks banging shut into the locked position.

The short one reconsidered and made a decision for the group. "No, no, we hook up steam now," he said as the three men ran past Ross toward the *Farnley*.

Within minutes, the *Farnley* was connected to the steam generators, and the forward gun mount had returned to its normal benign position. For the first time in eleven months, the *Farnley*'s engineering plant was shut down. In a cold iron status, maintenance and repair was now safer and easier.

Afterwards, Ross had changed back into his work uniform and returned to the engine room. He had been surprised to find his entire crew smiling, laughing, and working. The way they looked at him, smiling with admiration, had made him proud. He'd beaten the system. He had forgotten how good it felt.

Ross knew his theatrics and the work of his crew were only symbolic gestures. They didn't have any parts, but they would try to overhaul, clean, and oil what equipment they could. Some of it had been running continuously without rest or maintenance for months. It wasn't much and it wasn't going to help, but it was something.

"Chief? Chief?"

Lee's voice retrieved Ross from his private world of thought. Ross' eyes were drawn to Lee's grinning face, and he barely noticed the oil-stained cardboard box he was carrying.

"Mister Lee," Ross said, "I thought you'd have hit the beach, this being your first time in beautiful Elefsis."

"Too much to do. No place to go," Lee replied, taking a seat next to Ross. More cheerfully, Lee added, "What's doing with the pump?"

"Been rattling like hell. Sounds like a dryer full of loose nuts and bolts. We're tearing her down to see what the problem is. Probably can't do anything, but at least we'll know where we stand."

Ross and Lee watched in silence as Stucky meticulously dismantled the pump. Ross' eyes spotted something.

"Hold it, son," Ross shouted as he jumped into the bilge.

Ross examined several parts, fitted them back together, and played with the assembly again.

"Here's the problem," Ross said to Stucky. "See how the bearing rattles around in the housing? The bearing has to fit tight." Ross demonstrated as Stucky nodded.

"Fixable?" Lee asked.

Stucky and Ross turned to look at Lee. Stucky's freckles were half covered with streaks of grease.

Ross spoke, "The bearing and shaft look okay, but the bearing housing's shot. We don't have another one."

"What are the options, Chief?" Lee asked.

"T'ain't none, Mister Lee. We clean her up, put her back together, and hope for the best."

"Let me see the housing, Chief."

Ross handed Lee the two machined parts that bolted together to hold the bearing. Lee examined them for a second, then asked, "Anything special about the steel?"

Ross frowned, trying to figure out what Lee was asking. "No. It's just standard steel. Why?"

Lee turned the parts over in his hands several times before replying, "I don't know; they just seem like cheap parts."

"Hell, there isn't anything to them. Just two blocks of steel, a couple of holes drilled through them, and some simple machining. Some company probably sells them to the navy for a hundred bucks apiece, though."

"What do you mean by simple machining?" Lee asked.

"That type of machining is simple. Any high school kid could do it after a month of shop classes."

"Can you make another set in the machine shop?" Lee asked.

The question put Ross on guard. Ross formulated his answer carefully. "Sure, but that's against regulations. We're not allowed to manufacture our own parts."

Lee's black eyes opened wide and sparkled. "Then why did the navy put a machine shop on board?"

"Look, Mister Lee, to say the navy won't like it would be putting it mildly."

Lee started to giggle. "What would the navy say about what you did this morning on the pier?"

"That was different. It was . . . How did you find out about that?" Ross asked. Stucky smiled, almost laughing at the defensiveness in Ross' voice.

Lee raised his hand to cut Ross short. "Tell you what, Chief, you make the parts you need to fix your noisy dryer down there, and I'll sign the log authorizing the work. That makes it legal."

"It's a Fuel—Transfer—Pump," Ross snapped back, then realized how stupid his words must have sounded. Ross turned dead serious and spoke to Lee in the most pedantic voice he could muster.

"Your signing the log will make it legal for me to do the work, but it doesn't make it legal for you. The navy will nail your hide to the gauge board like a trophy.

"Will the new part be safe?" Lee asked.

Damn. Why does this kid keep asking questions when he should be listening? Ross thought. Then, to answer Lee's question he said, "Of course, it's just a simple housing."

"Do it, Chief. Make the part," Lee began, "and until further notice, any part you need, you make it if you can. Don't worry about me, Chief, I can take care of myself. You just worry about the equipment."

Ross knew Lee had just put him in a box. The box protected everybody except Lee. Ross didn't like to see anyone go out on a limb like that, but there was nothing he could do except appeal to logic. "Mister Lee, I've got to tell you this is against regulations."

"I'll also make an entry into the log explaining that you objected and explained the regulations to me," Lee said, grinning at Ross.

Shit. I can't win with this kid. Every time I open my mouth, I just make things worse. Quit while you're ahead, dummy.

"Quit while you're ahead, Chief. You're going to need your energy for another project I have for you," Lee said.

Ross stood dumbfounded by the apparent echo for several seconds. Ross was afraid to ask, but he knew he had to. "What project?"

Lee tapped the cardboard box sitting on the catwalk. "I think this contains all of the parts you need to overhaul the main steam valve. One finger; remember?"

"Where did you get them?" Ross asked in astonishment.

"You don't want to know."

"You're unorthodox. Do you know that?" Ross said.

"No, Chief, I'm a methodist."

"I wasn't talking about religion," Ross said, annoyed.

"Neither was I," Lee replied.

Ross tried to recover, to find an escape. Ross countered, "You know, when we overhaul the valve, we have to replace all of the steam flange studs. It'll take thirty-two of them, and I only have four left."

"You have thirty-six now." Lee beamed from ear to ear. "There are thirty-two in the box."

Ross noticed his screwdriver lying on the catwalk next to Lee. Impulsively, he reached out and rescued it. When it was safely in his hip pocket, Ross grabbed the box and tore it open to examine the contents.

As Ross rummaged through the box, Lee got up and said, "I know you're busy, so I had better leave you alone."

Ross couldn't believe it. The box contained everything he needed and then some. He looked up expecting to see Lee, but he was gone.

Stucky had been watching the exchange like an enthralled spectator at Wimbledon. Ross was clearly at a loss for words, so Stucky broke the silence. "What'ya got there, Chief?"

Ross paused for a second, then said slowly, "Son, I think I done just got had by a pro."

"What's in the box?" Stucky persisted

"Shut up, sonny, and get your butt to work on the main steam valve while I try to remember how to use a boring machine."

§

In the late evening hours, the surf on the public beach at Santa Cruz was all but gone. Michael Milford Morrison was lonely. His friends had left the beach earlier, but he wanted to stay behind. It was getting dark, and Morrison had just taken a ride.

The ride was groady, the wave soft and sloshy. Even the surf had gone home. The surf, the fun, the excitement had died slowly over the summer since high school graduation. He thought it was going to be better than this.

Laying the board on the sand, Morrison threw a towel over his bare shoulders and stared at the Pacific. For the first time in his life, he felt alone. Sure, he had his parents and younger brother, but now even they were different. His father always ragged at him about everything, calling him a bum and yelling at him to make something of himself. His mother babied him and applied the same rules to him as she did to his younger brother. It wasn't fair.

His buddies had changed. They were different now, and they knew it. Slowly, the group was falling apart, with some going off to college and others taking jobs. All had developed other interests, and it was getting difficult to get them together for some fun. The only bond they shared was rapidly disintegrating.

Morrison pulled his legs in and rested his chin on his knees. The sun had just disappeared below the horizon, and the two-foot waves looked like gray shadows under the crimson sky. Santa Cruz wasn't exciting anymore. The adventure of childhood was gone. He knew it was time for him, but he wondered what one did to become a man.

Morrison had never been more than four hundred miles from home. He closed his eyes to visualize what the world was like where the sun was headed. With its girls and neon signs, Tokyo would be exciting. In Rome, there were ruins to explore. There was a world far more colorful and exciting than Santa Cruz waiting to be discovered.

The world was unlike Santa Cruz; it was full of adventure. Exotic places waited for him, like those in the movies and in *National Geographic*. They were all there for him to see and explore, but they all lay across the sea. Morrison swiped a tangle of his long brown hair from his shoulder, picked up his surfboard, and headed toward the parking lot. He knew what to do, and he would tell no one, especially not his parents. Tomorrow would be a big day.

§

Since the ship had arrived at Elefsis two days ago, Biron's world was in turmoil. Schedules had been changed at the last minute, and he had a thousand details that had to be taken care of on short notice. They had expected to be sent to Skaramanga for minor repairs, but unexplainably, the schedule was changed to include hull painting. However, before the ship could be dry-docked, all ordinance had to be unloaded at the NATO pier at Sudha Bay.

Then the supply system had made the most colossal blunder he'd ever seen. At first, he went looking for Meyers so he could vent, but when he couldn't find him, he returned to the fantail. As luck would have it, Meyers and Ross were standing on the fantail watching the work party load provisions from the pier.

"XO, do you know what the navy sent me in place of the gray paint I had ordered?"

"No," Meyers said. His grin betrayed his lie.

"Well," Biron began.

"Did you hear about the maple syrup?" Meyers interrupted.

"Hell, that's not maple syrup; that's my paint."

Meyers looked at the pile of shiny, square metal tins stacked on the aft part of the fantail and asked, "What the hell were you going to do with six-hundred gallons of gray paint?"

"I only ordered a hundred gallons," Biron began, "but that was six months ago. When it didn't come in, I reordered it the first of the next month. I've been doing that for six months. Now the great navy supply eagle gets diarrhea and delivers all six-hundred gallons at one time, but instead of paint, I get maple syrup. The only similarity is that they both come in five-gallon containers. What the hell am I going to do with one hundred and twenty tins of maple syrup?"

Meyers seemed unimpressed and was having trouble not laughing. Ross was looking at the small mountain of maple syrup on the fantail, enjoying Biron's predicament.

"Have you talked to the cooks?" Meyers asked.

"They told me to stuff it. They don't have room for it, and it seems like that's about a three-year supply of syrup."

"Sounds like a good idea because you can't leave it on the pier. Find a place to stuff it," Meyers said.

"Where?" Biron shouted in exasperation.

"I don't know. I didn't order six-hundred gallons of anything," Meyers said, waving his hands in front of him as if trying to ward off a curse. Ross started to walk away, but Meyers reached out and put a hand on Ross' shoulder.

"Chief, we have a sticky situation here. The engine room is the only space big enough to store all of that . . . whatever it is. Have the work detail help you get it stowed."

"What? You can't be serious, XO," Ross pleaded. "I can't have that stuff in my engine room. Why, it'll take hours just to get the stuff down there."

Meyers began to walk away, so Ross changed tactics. "Come on, XO, I have enough troubles of my own."

"So do we all, Chief. It'll only be temporary," Meyers said.

"I've heard that before," Ross said, storming off in a huff.

"What problems is he talking about, XO?" asked Biron.

"Oh, the usual. He got about ten percent of what he'd ordered, but he expected that. What really has him peeved is that he ordered some machinery-gray paint."

"Did he get syrup?" Biron asked, allowing himself to smile.

"No, he got medical white enamel. Lee changed the order."

"Medical white?"

"Yeah, the stuff they use on hospital ships for the surgical rooms," Meyers said.

"Did you tell Ross what Lee did?"

"Why should I?"

"What does Lee want with white enamel?" Biron asked.

"Beats me. Lee said the supply system seemed to be out of regular paints, so he was going to start ordering different types and colors until he found one they had. He started with medical white and hit the jackpot on the first try."

TO SUDHA BAY

September 1971, Elefsis Pier
Operation Marathon: Day 428

The *Farnley* had been held at the Elefsis pier for five days to accommodate the dry dock schedule at Skaramanga. They were finally preparing to get under way for Sudha Bay to offload their munitions.

The sound of the single motor running in the engine room was lost in the deck-vibrating rumble that emanated from the boiler room. Ross did more than listen to the sound. The air was lifeless, unaffected, and the vibrations felt frothy and lacking intensity, depth, and power. She wasn't the awakening giant Ross had known.

He and his crew had been up since midnight warming up the boilers and preparing the plant for sea. The men, excited, were attacking their work with an energy and purpose Ross had not seen for almost a year. He knew what it was all about, but he felt it'd be best if he didn't make a big deal out of it. So despite wanting to, he never looked up at the valve in the main steam line. It looked so out of place amid the jumble of dirty piping crowding the overhead.

The main steam line, wrapped in dusty gray insulation, entered the engine room high along the forward bulkhead. After five feet, the insulation changed abruptly to a shiny white bulge around the main steam stop valve.

Its fresh new insulation gleamed in tribute to its three coats of white gloss enamel. The valve appeared factitious in the grayness of the *Farnley*'s engine room. It looked like an apparition, a mirage, that couldn't belong on the *Farnley*.

Trying not to draw more attention to the valve, Ross paced the main platform with his checklist. He tended to business and directed the men as they clambered over the maze of pipes, checking settings and opening or closing valves. Ross had seen that his men were not as restrained as he was. Grinning in anticipation, they regularly snuck a glance at the overhead.

Not all of the excitement was over the valve. Lee had done more to

127

lift the spirits of the crew than anybody, and Ross wasn't totally immune. Lee insisted that he be directly involved in preparing the plant for sea, and Lee had put on quite a show. Ross thought Lee would reconsider when he almost got his eyebrows singed off lighting the boiler, but his enthusiasm and wide-eyed grin never faded.

Ross told Lee to follow Stucky on his errands, and Stucky was milking this rare opportunity to have an officer do all of the dirty work for all it was worth. Stucky's uniform was spotless, but Lee's was covered with grease and drenched in at least four types of oil. Although anyone could tell Stucky was making the work harder and dirtier than necessary, Lee apparently relished it and had become dirtier than any officer Ross had ever seen.

The men had taken a liking to Lee, whose intelligent, smiling face seemed impervious to dirt and grease. Initially, Ross guessed that Lee's silly perpetual grin was contagious, but now he knew it was more than that. The men, talking and smiling, had become animated and reacted purposefully to commands, carrying them out without instruction or coaching. They were beginning to care, and Lee was the spark plug.

Ross had seen and felt this before and remembered the pride he'd felt on the *Able*. That valve was his victory. This valve was not. It belonged to the crew and to Lee. Ross was lonely and frustrated. He'd only been a spectator. Ross cursed himself for not doing more.

He pocketed his screwdriver and walked to the starboard escape ladder that opened directly onto the weather deck. Over the noise, he could hear the distant sound of water beating against the steel deck above as the boatswain's mates hosed down the deck.

Unexpectedly, water started pouring into the escape hatch over Ross' head, drenching him. He jumped to one side and looked up at the sparkling spray of water cascading through the open hatch. Accustomed to the dim light of the engine room, Ross was blinded by the bright circular window of the hatch open directly to the clear morning sky. "Who the hell left the hatch open?" Ross yelled.

Lee, Stucky, and the others on the main platform laughed as Ross danced out of the way, shaking his arms in a vain attempt to shed the water. Ross glowered back at them, and they all swallowed their smiles except for Lee. One of the free men from the lower level quickly came to the rescue and scaled the ladder to close the hatch.

With water still pouring in, the man's body was partially eclipsed. The bright sunlight and the water splashed and sparkled off his head and shoulders. Ross had seen this image before, and the feeling of *déjà vu* returned.

Ross returned to his bench and tried to remember. Slowly the darkened windows to his memories opened. *"Jam 'em open, son."*

Where was he? His friends were dead. He was dying; the boiler room a charnel vault, the *Able* his tomb, and then he heard the clang of metal, the squeak of heavy hinges, then a voice. Ross floated serenely. He smiled and opened his eyes to see the face of God. Everything about him was blackness, but in the distance, he saw a round, bright light, and in its center was the face of Chief Barnes. Behind the face raged a fire of brilliant red and orange dancing flames. The heat. *Am I alive? Oh God, the heat. I'm going to burn. Hell. Is this hell? Oh God, no!*

Ross tried to move, but he couldn't. He closed his eyes and waited.

"Son. Son. Ross, is that you?"

Ross opened his eyes and looked into the light.

"Hey, he's still alive."

Barnes' face was joined by another. Ross lay helpless, watching the valkyrian drama unfold.

"Forget it, Chief, we need more help. I can't handle this fire hose alone."

"I'm going after him. He's one of mine."

"You can't do it, Chief."

"Got to. That's the deal. They never let me down, I never let them down. I ain't quittin' now. That's the deal."

A third face appeared in the light, a blackened face with hair the color of the flames that framed it.

"We got the hose, Chief. We'll cover you with fog. Let's go."

The light diffused and sparkled, and shadows moved in it and the shadows shimmered and the light was eclipsed. The heat closed in around him.

The heat; tongues of flame reached out for him. The light was dim. It sparkled, and shadows moved in it. It didn't matter; the fires of hell were about to consume him. He longed for the light.

Cold. A cold mist caressed him. The heat was gone. The mist, like a blizzard of flying ice crystals, pricked his skin. He wanted to shiver; he couldn't. From the mist emerged a face. It was Chief Barnes.

"Son. Ross. Dammit, son. Stay awake. We're getting you out of here. Hang on."

His head jerked back. His brain felt too small for his skull. Barnes snatched him from the cool water. The cold, icy mist was everywhere. He was upside down, bouncing, Barnes' shoulder in his gut. He wanted to vomit; he couldn't. His body quaked trying to shiver, but it couldn't. He felt safe; Barnes wouldn't let him die. Tired, he closed his eyes.

"Stay awake, son. Fight it. You're a fighter. You'll be all right, just stay awake. Keep trying. You gotta try to survive. Stay awake."

Ross opened his eyes and looked into the reddened face of Chief Barnes. He realized he was on deck, and Barnes was holding him up by a life jacket. He tried to speak, but his lips barely moved. He tried again and heard a weak, distant voice that he knew was his. "Sorry, Chief. I tried."

"I know you did, son. You did good. You did your part, but now you have a new job. Stay awake. You have to keep trying to survive. Promise me you'll stay awake. Don't let me down," Barnes yelled while shaking Ross.

"I try, Chief," Ross replied.

Barnes took the screwdriver from his hip pocket and stuffed it inside his shirt under the life vest.

"Here's my screwdriver. Take care of it for me," Barnes said urgently.

"Yes. Screwdriver, take care."

"I know you will, son. You're a good sailor. I want it back. You have to stay awake to do that."

The world spun around Ross, voices shouted. Fire and smoke were everywhere. He felt his body shake. Barnes was still shaking him. Barnes was holding him up by the collar of a life jacket, shaking him. "Stay awake, son. You're gonna make it. Someone will pick you up."

Ross tried to focus, but Barnes was gone. The world tumbled. He saw the sky, the sea, the side of the *Able*, then Chief Barnes standing there watching him. The blue Pacific had surrounded him. The life jacket had popped him to the surface. There was floating debris, and someone was swimming toward him. *Stay awake. Survive. I won't let you down. I got your screwdriver, Chief.*

Sitting on his bench, still dripping wet, Ross could still feel the Pacific swirling around him. He looked up at the valve and remembered how proud he'd been as a young sailor on the *Able*. Barnes had given him pride, a pride that had lasted almost thirty years.

Ross yelled to Stucky, "Open the main steam stop."

Stucky jumped onto the bench, ceremoniously extended his index finger, then slowly raised his hand, hooking the finger on the valve wheel spoke. With his single finger, he spun the valve open.

Cheers and screams drowned out the sound of steam rushing into the engine room's labyrinth of steam pipes. Stucky's freckled face glowed, and Ross recognized the look in Stucky's eyes. He was looking at himself thirty years ago.

Stucky jumped from the bench and ran to the railing overlooking the lower level, raised his right arm in a "we're number one" gesture, then spun his arm in a sweeping circular motion and yelled, "Wind her up."

Ross felt confused, and he looked at Lee. For the first time he could remember, it was clear Lee wasn't smiling. Ross took the screwdriver from his hip pocket and held it. In his hands it felt weightless but in his heart . . . *Here's my screwdriver. Take care of it for me . . .Yes. Screwdriver, take care.*

Tears welled up in his eyes.

"Chief?" It was Stucky.

Ross wiped the tears out of his eyes and turned toward Stucky. "Son, do you know you have water all over your grimy, scuzzy, filthy deck?" Ross said, pointing to the puddle under the hatch.

Stucky squinted at Ross in mock confusion and asked, "My deck?"

"I didn't stutter, did I? It's your deck, and it's making my engine room look bad. Why, it looks like a marine's latrine. If it isn't a sparkly clean by dinner chow, you'll be cleaning bilges with a toothbrush for the rest of your tour."

Burns, the port throttleman, began to laugh. Ross swung around and blasted him next. "What the hell you laughing about, son?"

Burns tried to straighten up, but it was too late. Ross continued, "Your evaporators look like crap and work even worse. They even make my engine room look worse than Stucky's deck. You own 'em. Fix 'em."

Burns looked to Stucky for moral support, but Stucky was standing at attention by his throttle. "But I don't know anything about evaporators," Burns pleaded.

"That's no excuse. They're yours now. Learn what you have to and I'll teach you the rest, but they're your responsibility. That's the deal."

"But—"

"But, but, but, but what? Do I look like a billy goat? How would you like to drain the bilge with a soda straw?"

"Aye, Chief." Burns, legs trembling, turned back to the gauge board and gave Stucky one fleeting, desperate glance, which Stucky didn't return. Stucky's eyes were glued to the vacuum gauge.

Cautiously, Stucky turned his head toward Ross and said softly, "Chief, we've got vacuum."

Ross turned away and marched over to the intercom. He flipped the switch labeled *Bridge* and depressed the send button. "Bridge, main control. This is Ross. I'm ready for sea."

§

Biron looked at his watch.

"That's the first time I can remember Ross being right on schedule," Biron said to Javert.

The on-time report from Ross wasn't lost on Javert, who was seated in his captain's chair, observing the bridge crew. He leaned back and propped his feet on the wooden sill under the bridge windows. Eickhoff's instructions to be supportive, handle administrative manners, and not interfere with ship navigation had been right. Eickhoff was a wise man.

During their stay in Elefsis, he'd kept to his cabin and not interfered with the operation of the ship. He performed his duties diligently, signing papers, filling out reports, welcoming new men, and bidding farewell to those being transferred. He relished the work and submerged himself in it.

It troubled him that no one came to him for decisions or advice, but he was getting along splendidly with Meyers, who seemed to have everything under control.

Still, Javert felt awkward in his new role. It didn't feel right. A captain should command, direct, be decisive, all things Eickhoff's letter had warned him against. All in all, he'd enjoyed the stay in Elefsis and left his officers alone, except on a few occasions when he sought them out to make helpful suggestions.

Rather than be confrontational with Biron while he was getting the ship under way, he had tried to be helpful, and it seemed to work. This was the first time he could remember they were getting under way almost on time. No arguments had broken out, and Meyers hadn't challenged him. How could Meyers challenge me? Javert thought. I'm doing what any good captain would do by being helpful and showing faith and confidence in my officers. It is as easy as that. No more confrontations. I'll let my officers run the ship, and I'll stay aloof. Even though it doesn't feel right, those are my orders.

NIGHT OPS

September 1971, En Route to Sudha Bay
Operation Marathon: Day 429

It was just after midnight when Biron heard the metallic clicks of the bridge door and recognized Lee's short silhouette. Lee was uncharacteristically late, and the remainder of the bridge watch already had been relieved. It would still take Lee several minutes to check navigation, tactical, engineering status, weather reports, and the night orders, so Biron walked to the bridge wing to bid farewell to the beautiful night.

The hot, humid day had followed the sun westward, leaving a cool midnight breeze. The sky, God's special gift to the sailor, was free of city lights and urban pollution. Placed on display, all of creation was set on the night's canopy of blue-black velvet adorned with the glistening diamond dust of billions of lesser stars and the sparkling one-point diamonds of the major stars.

A deep golden harvest moon hung low on the eastern horizon. Its glow cut a pewter path from moon to ship across shifting liquid swells rolling forward to meet the *Farnley*'s bow. The bow, rocking gently, rose, then floated gently down to embrace the next swell.

On the bridge, men spoke in soft airy voices and the engines' soft drone and the radio's static hiss were whispers in the night. The men, with limbs recently deprived of warmth and slumber, moved about slowly in the low red lights that bathed their faces in ghostly red and black shadows.

Standing on the bridge wing on nights like this, he opened his senses as he seemed to glide effortlessly across the sea; the sensation of speed was phenomenal. It was like a magic carpet ride.

Biron also knew these nights to be dangerous. The sensation of solitude and closeness to God overwhelmed man's logical mental apparatus, and the thoughts and conclusions reached required reexamination in the harsh light of day.

"I'm ready to relieve you. Sorry I was late."

Biron turned casually and had difficulty seeing Lee standing in the moon's black shadow from the bridge house. Biron and Lee then began the traditional ritual of changing the watch, a ritual perfected over generations in response to tragedies or near tragedies. Its point was simple; clean cut transfer of authority and control with no confusion.

The men exchanged salutes. Biron called out in a clear voice, "This is Mister Biron. Mister Lee has the deck and the con."

Lee's reply was immediate and as clear. "This is Mister Lee. I have the deck and the con."

Next, replies came from the quartermaster, helmsman, and lee helmsman. "Aye, the log shows Mister Lee has the deck and the con."

"Helm aye, my head is one-seven-zero true, one-six-seven magnetic."

"Lee helm aye, all ahead two-thirds. Making turns for twelve knots."

With the ritual complete, Lee moved deeper into the shadows, nestling himself in the corner closest to the bridge house. Lee waited placidly until Biron had completed his log entries and left the bridge, then he entered the bridge house and took a position directly in front of the helmsman.

"Right standard rudder, come to new course two-six-zero," Lee whispered.

All heads turned. Surprised, the helmsman lifted his eyes from the compass and, with a shrug, threw the wheel over in an obedient but puzzled movement. "Right standard rudder, Aye, sir?" he queried back.

The bow of the *Farnley* slowly swung to the west and headed into the trough. As it turned, each new swell caused the ship to roll a bit more. "Steady on new course two-six-zero," the helmsman said.

"Very well," Lee replied.

Lee divided his attention between the compass and the gauge, which measured the ship's roll. The last roll had been five degrees, but once the ship began rolling, the motion would feed on itself, up to a point. The next roll was seven degrees and the one after that twelve.

"Okay," Lee said. "That should do it. Right standard rudder. Come to new course one-seven-zero."

§

Sandwiched between his mattress and the air-conditioning drip pan, Ensign Nat Hayes lay on his back, sound asleep. The upper bunk, barely thirty inches wide, provided enough room for Hayes and his constant sleeping companion, a small rubber purse-sized pouch that held an inflatable life jacket.

The gentle rise and fall of the bow that had lulled him to sleep earlier began to change. At first, it was only a gentle right-to-left roll. The next roll was slightly more severe. Hayes scrunched himself diagonally across his bunk and wedged himself between the boxlike sides.

The rolling motion increased, but Hayes, securely wedged into his bunk, slept on, his breathing deep and regular. The rolling motion built. At the height of the biggest roll yet, a mini-tidal wave sloshed over the edge of the air-conditioning drip pan and cascaded downward. The first few drops to hit Hayes' face brought him abruptly out of his sleep.

"Arghaspewt!" Hayes screamed, lurching upward, forcing his face fully into the waterfall.

Instinct took over. His arms hooked the strap on the life jacket pouch, and he leapt from his bunk into the darkness in the hope the deck would be where it should. He landed on one foot and was about to gain his balance when the ship rolled the other way spilling Hayes across the room, over a steel chair, and forcefully parking him face down in the corner with his cheek pressed firmly against a cool five-gallon tin of maple syrup.

Glug.

With his heart pounding and his sleep-disoriented mind racing, Hayes snapped to his feet and ran from the room screaming, "Abandon ship! She's going turtle! Abandon ship! We're going over! Abandon ship!"

Bursting through the doorway into the small passageway connecting the officers' staterooms, Hayes, as he had mentally rehearsed many times, executed the right turn toward the exit with amazing speed and agility. His rehearsals, however, didn't account for obstacles such as Biron, who had heard him coming and took Hayes and his life jacket down with a textbook perfect tackle.

"Hayes. Get a hold of yourself. What's the matter?" Biron yelled, shaking Hayes.

"Huh? What a . . ." Hayes replied, then stopped to measure the slow, gentle roll of the ship. There was clearly no danger.

With Hayes under control, Biron let go and got to his feet. As he did, he looked at his wet uniform, then back down at Hayes. "You're soaking wet. What happened?"

Hayes, now on his feet, was trying to answer that exact question. "I don't know."

Lights flicked on, and sleepy officers staggered into the passageway. Hayes, not wanting to face the disgruntled faces, walked back into his stateroom, hit the light switch, and looked at his soaked bunk, then at the air-conditioning drip pan.

Hayes turned to the knot of officers peering over his shoulder. "I'm sorry. It looks like the air conditioner backed up and doused me with water."

Hayes walked across the room, righted the steel chair, and positioned it next to his bunk. He climbed onto it and began to inspect the drip pan by reaching between it and the cooling coils. His hand hit something by the drainpipe. He dislodged it and, to his surprise, pulled a small cork into view.

"What the hell?" Hayes cursed as he turned toward his fellow officers. "Who's the wiseass who stopped up the drain line?"

Biron, having a hard time controlling his laughter, managed enough strength to say, "I don't know, but look," as he pointed to a piece of paper pinned to the foot of Hayes' bunk.

Hayes retrieved the typewritten note. It read, "You've been had by the Phantom Corker."

§

Commander Kahn, captain of the fleet oiler *Cuyahoga*, concentrated on the pitch and roll of his ship. The bow fell sluggishly into a swell, throwing white froth into the rainy black night. With the weight of a full load of oil, she was riding well, but he would be happy when the refueling was over, O'Toole or no O'Toole, despite the loss of ballast.

Two years ago, as a destroyer captain in O'Toole's squadron, Kahn had refueled on a night as dark and nasty as this. Wistfully, he recalled how terrifying and educating the experience had been, and how O'Toole had haunted the exercise like a ghost.

Two years ago, he'd assumed, as did everyone else, that O'Toole was on one of the squadron ships and that he'd opportunistically ordered refueling to continue despite the bad weather just to be ornery.

The effect had been long lasting, and he refused to believe he could ever forget the refueling or any of the numerous nail-biting expeditions O'Toole dreamt up.

Kahn reached into his pocket and pulled out two marble-sized brass bearings and rolled them in his hand. With a smile, he recalled the night O'Toole had made them refuel like this. O'Toole seemed everywhere, seeing things no one else could see. It seemed he could even read your thoughts. Until now, he never knew how O'Toole had done it. O'Toole had waited for the bad weather. He'd been through the drill so many times, he'd seen every mistake possible. He wasn't on a squadron ship; he was on the oiler, and he was using the radar.

He turned to O'Toole and asked, "Are you ready, Commodore?"

O'Toole looked up from the radar screen. "Not yet. Let's give them a few more minutes."

O'Toole was acting as a safety observer for the exercise. The radar gave him a bird's-eye view of proceedings. "Do they know where you are?" Kahn asked.

O'Toole smiled. "No, and if you ever give away my secret, I'll have you keelhauled."

"How good are they?"

"Damned good and getting better every day. I'd say they're almost adequate, but don't quote me on that."

§

Two-hundred-fifty yards astern of the *Cuyahoga*, John Flannery, captain of the *Wainwright*, braced himself as the bow rose to meet an oncoming but invisible swell. Flannery strained his eyes trying to see something, anything, through the rain-spattered bridge windows. It was useless. The weather was foul and the night the blackest he'd ever seen. All he could see through the bridge windows was blackness and the reflection of the tiny red lights that dimly illuminated the bridge.

Flannery had been in the navy twenty-one years and captain of the *Wainwright* for two months. No matter how he looked at the situation, he knew his training hadn't prepared him for this. O'Toole seemed to be able to order bad weather for exercises. Tonight O'Toole wanted the impossible. This wasn't O'Toole's normal impossible, like navigating a fog-choked channel without radar or merely refueling during a nighttime storm without radio communications. O'Toole had already made them do those things. Now he really wanted the impossible; refuel without radar, without operational use of the radio, and without navigation lights in a storm on the darkest night he could order up.

Flannery, knowing the oiler was somewhere in the darkness a few hundred yards ahead, tried to control his nerves and shed the clammy feeling. Flannery couldn't believe this was happening. With his conning officer and executive officer huddled at his side like close family members, he felt like a condemned man waiting for a last-minute reprieve from the governor. Flannery looked at the other men on the bridge. It only added to his despair; everyone looked like cast extras in a deathwatch scene from a nineteen-thirties movie.

A radio speaker crackled, "All stations in Tango Tango, this is Tango Tango. Play ball." O'Toole's voice was unmistakable despite the static.

The conning officer and the executive officer inched closer to Flannery. There would be no reprieve.

The conning officer asked, "What now?"

No one answered, but the executive officer raised a night vision scope to his eyes and scanned the darkness. Lowering the scope, he finally said, "Can't see a damned thing."

Almost dead ahead, a flickering white pinpoint of light appeared amidst the darkness. Squinting, the conning officer said, "It's the oiler, Captain. We're cleared to make our approach."

"Batter up." O'Toole crackled over the radio.

Turning toward the radio, Flannery cursed. "I'm not going to take this." He keyed the radio and spoke into the microphone, "Tango Tango, this is Bravo Juliet. Negative on the approach. We can't see the oiler."

The crackling radio response from O'Toole was immediate. "Steeeeerike one!"

Flannery tried to think of a response, but before he could, the radio clicked and O'Toole's voice boomed from the speaker. "Bravo Juliet, this is Tango Tango. It's all in the eyes. You can't see a thing from inside the bridge, so get your stern pieces off the bridge and onto the bridge wing. You're going to need every bit of night vision God gave you, so kill all the lights on the bridge except for the compass."

In unison, Flannery and his executive officer looked at each other, then, without breaking formation, zipped up their green foul weather jackets and followed the conning officer to the port bridge wing.

All of the bridge lights went out, and O'Toole's voice returned. "Now that you can see, close your interval to two-hundred yards like you were supposed to do in the first place. Then you'll be able to see the oiler."

The conning officer ordered a five-knot increase in speed, then asked Flannery in an airy voice, "How did he know?"

The ship slowly increased speed to fifteen knots, a speed that to Flannery seemed like ninety knots under the circumstances.

The executive officer raised the night vision scope and trained it on where he thought the oiler should be. In despair, he said, "Can't see a damned thing."

O'Toole's voice crackled over the radio. "Bravo Juliet, this is Tango Tango. Stow the night vision scope; it won't help a bit."

Silently the quartermaster stepped onto the bridge wing and took the scope from the executive officer, who handed it to him like a kid caught with his hand in the cookie jar. The executive officer turned and peered into the darkness astern and asked, "Where the hell is he?"

"Everywhere," Flannery said.

Flannery's nerves were about to snap. He was sweating so hard, he was as wet inside his foul weather jacket as he was outside from the driving rain. It seemed they had been closing on the oiler for hours. He looked at his young conning officer, whose tense drawn face showed the near terror they shared. It wasn't fair to put a young officer through this.

Flannery placed his hand on the conning officer's shoulder and tried to think of a gentle way to relieve him of the con. The radio crackled, "Bravo Juliet, this is Tango Tango. Remember, it is all in the eyes. You need a conning officer under thirty for this maneuver. Their night vision is thirty-seven percent better than a man of forty."

Flannery's head snapped around, and he looked carefully into the bridge house. It was a foolish, instinctive move. O'Toole wasn't there, and Flannery knew it.

"Shit," the conning offer began, "I can't believe this. What's the superlative of terror?"

"Terror-est," offered the executive officer.

"O'Toole," Flannery corrected.

"There." the conning officer called out. "There's the oiler, Captain. I can see her now."

Flannery's eyes followed the direction of the conning officer's extended arm, but Flannery couldn't see a thing. "Where?" he asked.

"There."

"I'll take your word for it," Flannery said, trying to keep his voice from breaking. "Better get your speed up. Wait, are we lined up?"

The conning officer ordered full speed, then replied, "I think so."

"You think so?" blurted Flannery. "I thought you said you could see her."

"Well, it's hard to tell in this rain. I can't believe we're doing this. Is this a bad dream? Am I going to wake up?"

Flannery now saw a gray smudge in the blackness off the port bow. Relieved, he replied to his conning officer's questions, "Yes. No."

With alarming speed, the gray smudge took the shape of the oiler's stern. They were closing fast, and both the conning officer and Flannery took a deep breath in preparation for a shouted engine command.

O'Toole's voice boomed through the radio static. "Bravo Juliet, this is Tango Tango. It's all in the eyes. Remember, everything looks twice as close as it really is under these conditions. Keep your speed until you see the whites of their eyes."

Exhaling, the conning officer asked Flannery, "How close is that?"

"A little closer."

After a second, the conning officer interjected, "Captain, I can see the white lettering of her hull number."

Flannery, who was now supporting his weight on the bridge railing, whispered, "Close enough."

The conning officer yelled, "All ahead two-thirds. Indicate turns for ten knots."

Slowly the *Wainwright*'s speed dropped, and she slid into position beside the oiler. Flannery held his breath. He couldn't believe what he was seeing. They were going to be a bit wide of the mark, but other than that, they were in perfect position. His knees still trembling, Flannery took a deep breath in relief and said, "Well, I'll be a . . . I don't believe it. That audacious SOB."

Flannery slapped the conning officer's back and with a big grin squealed, "We did it."

The bridge crew's cheer was cut short by the radio. "Bravo Juliet, this is Tango Tango. That approach was unsat. You started out of position. That made the approach wide and ninety seconds too long. If you had started in position, you would have been able to compensate. Then the approach might, I say again, might, have been adequate. Remember, two-hundred yards; it's all in the eyes."

Two-hundred yards astern of the *Wainwright,* a captain and his conning officer stood shoulder to shoulder on their dark, rain-swept bridge wing. The captain asked, "Can you see them?"

"I think so," replied the younger man.

"That's adequate, I think. Keep your eye on them."

SKARAMANGA

September 1971, Skaramanga Shipyard
Operation Marathon: Day 433

A few days later, the *Farnley* entered the dry dock at Skaramanga, and Chief Ross had some important papers Lee needed to sign. Lee was in his stateroom when Chief Ross and a Greek shipyard worker entered.

Ross gestured to the shipyard worker and said, "This is Mister Dananixous." Ross pronounced the name carefully, and when the worker didn't grimace too bad, he continued, "He is the dry dock's Number Two, and he needs an officer to sign the work order to connect sanitary drains, power, and steam."

Lee stepped forward and with a bigger than normal smile shook hands with the black-haired worker. "Glad to meet you, Mister Dana . . ."

"Danathaxus," the worker assisted.

"He speaks a little English, Mister Lee," Ross added.

"Good. Do you have a paper for me to sign?" Lee asked.

Danathaxus fumbled with the papers stuffed into his shirt pocket and retrieved a wrinkled piece of paper and handed it to Lee. As Lee unfolded the paper, his eyes widened. He looked back at the shipyard worker. "This is in Greek. What am I signing?"

Before the shipyard worker could respond, Ross said, "Don't worry, just sign it. If we don't get the sanitary drains hooked up, there's going to be a mutiny outside the crew's head."

Lee looked at Danathaxus and asked slowly, "This just authorizes . . . just says it is okay to hook up power and steam, right?"

"And crappers," Danathaxus added.

"Okay," Lee said, turning to his desk to sign the paper. When Lee tried to return the paper, Danathaxus wasn't paying attention. His eyes were glued on several shiny square tins lined up against the bulkhead. Each tin was clearly labeled in one-inch-high letters, *Maple Syrup*.

Absentmindedly, Danathaxus took the paper from Lee and asked, "Real maple syrup, sweet?"

Ross and Lee exchanged glances. As Lee walked over to the tins,

Ross looked into the worker's joyous black eyes and studied him. Lee tilted one tin back so he could read the fine print under the main label, then turning back to Danathaxus, said, "It's real. It says no artificial additives."

"Artificial?" Danathaxus asked.

"Good. Real," explained Ross.

The worker smiled broadly. "Cannot get in Greece. Very special. Very much costly. Very, very precious. It is a delicate."

"A delicacy?" asked Ross.

Danathaxus nodded. "Yes, delicacy. Maybe get little spoonful on Christmas," he said, demonstrating the size of the portion with his fingers.

"Do you want some?" Lee asked.

"Oh, yes." Danathaxus almost squealed with joy.

Ross grabbed the worker's arm and began leading the confused and dismayed man out of the room. "Come on, Mister Dananixous, we gotta talk business," Ross said brusquely.

"Hey, Chief," Lee objected.

"Sorry, Mister Lee. This is a shipyard. They fix ships like us for a living and have warehouses full of stuff we could use. What I have to talk about to Mister Dana . . . whatever . . . ain't fit for your young, tender ears. It's gonna get sticky."

Lee's eyes grinned and he asked, "What are you going to do?"

"You don't want to know, Mister Lee, but I promise you, it'll be the ultimate in naval justice."

And then Ross and the worker were gone.

§

Meyers welcomed the eight days in dry dock for more than just the new coat of paint the *Farnley* would receive. It would give the crew a break from their normal routine, but the heat was stifling. The September heat was summer's last hurrah, and by nine in the morning, the closed ship grew oppressively hot. The sandblasting was done, but the vents hadn't been reopened.

Meyers told the quarterdeck to pass the word to uncover all the vents and open all ship's doors to help fight off the heat, then began his morning rounds. Before he reached the personnel office, he was caught by a strange sight. To the side of the main passageway, a large, square bundle of rags was bouncing up and down on the open but small twenty-inch-diameter hatch to the engine room. The sight was so strange it took him a minute to figure out what was happening. Someone on the ladder below the hatch was trying to pull the large bundle of rags through the small opening.

"What's going on?" Meyers yelled at the bouncing bundle, hoping the man could hear him.

A voice, dampened by the intervening bundle of rags, yelled back in earnest irritation, "Don't just stand there, you asshole. Give me a hand."

Without hesitation, Meyers grabbed the bundle by the heavy twine and lifted. The other man was still pulling the other way, so Meyers jerked hard and yanked the bundle away from the hatch.

A surprised and embarrassed young sailor stood on the ladder looking up at Meyers. "I'm . . . I'm sorry, XO, I didn't know it was you, sir." the man said in a quavering voice.

"It's all right. What do you want me to do?" Meyers asked.

"Please help me get this through the hatch, sir. Chief Ross will be back any time now, and I have to hurry. I think if you push, and I pull, it'll go through."

Meyers put the bundle back on top of the hatch, put his foot on it, and began pushing. When the bundle was almost through, Meyers asked, "You haven't told me what you're doing."

"The chief gave me the bilge," the man answered as he gave the bundle a hefty tug.

"Gave you? The bilge?" Meyers asked, puzzled.

The bundle popped past the hatch combing, and the sailor neatly caught it with one hand as it swung down below his waist while he held to the ladder with his other hand. Sweating, the young sailor looked up at Meyers. "Yeah. I mean, yes, sir. The chief gave me the bilge and was fuming mad 'cause he said it made his engine room look bad."

"Are you cleaning the bilge?" Meyers asked, almost sure he understood.

"Naw, it's clean, but Stevens' fuel pump is leaking oil on my bilge. Gotta get it cleaned up before Ross sees it."

Meyers smiled. "I'll let you get back to your work."

"Thanks, XO, and if you see Stevens, tell him I want his butt."

Meyers had been in the navy long enough to know better than try to figure out chiefs and engineers. Ross was both, so he put it out of his mind. Still smiling to himself, Meyers started back down the passageway to resume his rounds.

After a few steps, he stopped and, for reasons unclear to him, turned and stepped out onto the main deck.

One thing that seemed right was the crew. For the *Farnley*, that was unnatural. He had felt the change a few days ago as he walked around the ship. Inexplicably, the atmosphere had changed. The men looked dirtier and more tired than normal, but they smiled and seemed happy despite the unbearable living conditions aboard a dry-docked ship.

Now he was making a point to observe the crew closely. The signs were unmistakable; the dirt was the reward of honest labor, the tired faces the product of honest effort. The smiles were simmering pride that transcended the abysmal circumstances. They seemed totally unconcerned about their environment.

Meyers could see it was more than just a group of individuals. They seemed almost conspiratorial. Their eyes flashed knowingly at each other, and they would raise their hand and, smiling, touch their hair as they passed. Every man had his hair cut in the same horrid style; regulation, but lopsided with gouges and nicks along the side.

A mysterious common language was developing. The words Meyers heard most often were "That's sweet" and "Wind her up." As he approached the fantail, he could see the constant procession of men carrying heavy bundles back and forth across the gangway to the dry dock. Even this had taken on the form of a mysterious ritual.

Some of the men returning to the ship would signal their return as they walked down the dry-dock wall. They raised their arm high above their head as if pointing to the sky, then swung their arm in a wide, sweeping circular motion. Meyers knew this wasn't an idle gesture because, invariably, a few men watching from the *Farnley*'s deck would rush, pushing and shoving, back into the interior of the ship or disappear down a hatch amid a flurry of snickers, giggles, and excited words.

Meyers had seen similar strains of contagious weirdness sweep through ships before and knew it to be a beneficial bug, one that he would never attempt to diagnose or eradicate. It was the type of thing that, no matter how hard he tried, he would never be able to make happen on purpose. Something good was happening, something Lee had probably started, and something that was best if he "didn't want to know."

§

Despite his apprehension, Michael Milford Morrison knew he was going to be all right. He was on his own, and now for the first time in his life, he felt like a man. The navy recruiter in Santa Cruz had been friendly, had shared some sea stories with him about Tokyo, Pearl Harbor, Saigon, and Subic Bay. He even took the time to tell him exactly what to do when his plane landed.

Today had been a big day for him, saying good-bye to his mother, father, and brother. Now entering the San Diego Airport, Morrison scrupulously followed the recruiter's instructions and had brought no luggage, only a small athletic bag containing a few toilet articles and a towel. The recruiter had told him it didn't matter what he wore, so Morrison, concerned he would meet a lot of new friends his own age, had dressed comfortably in shorts, a Hawaiian shirt, and sandals.

When he reached the main baggage claim area, he looked for the navy ground transportation liaison sign as the recruiter had instructed. He saw the small kiosk set in the center of a large open area with the sign above it. Inside the kiosk sat a beautiful smiling WAVE tending a phone and several clipboards.

Outside the kiosk, a man whom Morrison guessed was important paced patiently back and forth. The man was old, like his grandfather but maybe a little younger. His blue uniform, covered with a bewildering array of insignia, ribbons, and gold stripes, made him look really impressive.

Morrison walked directly up to the man and boldly stuck his hand out to introduce himself. "Excuse me. I'm Michael Morrison. The recruiter told me to check in with you."

The elder man turned and greeted Morrison with a big warm grin. "Morrison? Well, welcome to the navy. Would you follow me, please?"

The WAVE nodded to the older man and made a mark on one of her clipboards. As they walked through the terminal, the older man asked Morrison how his flight had been and engaged in small talk until they stepped outside, leaving the milling crowd of civilians in the terminal behind. The older man had led Morrison through a side door, which to Morrison seemed natural; navy men would be able to use shortcuts denied most travelers.

Outside, Morrison noticed they were in a small, sidewalk-rimmed parking lot. When they reached the curb, the older man turned on Morrison and in a stern, angry voice yelled, "OK, squirrel. You see the man down there by the bus? Report in to him. On the double, dweeb. That means now!"

Stunned by the sudden change in his new friend, Morrison stared at the man dumbstruck. The elder man had little patience. "I said now, slimeball."

Wounded, Morrison began to walk toward the gray navy bus. From behind him, the older man screamed, "I said now. That means on the double. Run!"

Morrison broke into a sprint, and by the time he was halfway to the bus, the other man had run to meet him. As they ran toward the bus together, the other man screamed in Morrison's face, "OK, squirrel. You're in the navy now. No more mama. Fall in with the others at attention. You'll see footprints painted on the concrete. Put your left foot in the left footprint and your right foot in the right footprint. Put your bag down next to your right foot and come to attention. When you're at attention, you will not twitch, you will not move, you will not blink, you will not scratch, you will not talk, you will not pass gas, you will not do anything, not even think, unless I tell you to. Do you understand, squirrel?"

Morrison did his best to comply with the barrage of instructions and replied, "Yeah."

"What? What did you say, loon lips?" screamed the man. "You mean, 'Yes Sir' don't you?"

"Yes, sir?" mumbled Morrison.

"I can't hear you, whale turd. What'd you say?"

"Yes, Sir!" Morrison bellowed.

Silence returned. Morrison didn't think boot camp was going to be like this. Maybe he'd made a mistake. The other man looked away for a second, then spun to glare at Morrison. "Did you say something, bubble brain?"

"No, Sir!"

Morrison tried not to think about it any more.

DIEGO GARCIA

October 1971, Fleet Anchorage, Diego Garcia, Indian Ocean
Operation Marathon: Day 474

Dotting the mirror smooth Indian Ocean just off the island of Diego Garcia, the aircraft carrier USS *Enterprise* and her resting pride of destroyers lay at anchor. Their high hurricane bows turned into the gentle breeze, the ships basked lazily in the brilliant noonday sun. On the Enterprise's flag bridge, Admiral Knutsen commander of the battle group waited for his visitor. An invigorating breeze swept in through the bridge doors and swirled inside the bridge. Knutsen soaked up the fresh air and looked across his carrier battle group. The breeze was as gentle, as calm and as clean as the Indian Ocean.

Still, Knutsen felt dirty and had felt that way for months. The pleasantness of the day only made him feel dirtier. After his visitor left, he would take a shower; maybe he would finally feel clean again. He looked across the calm sea toward the USS *Talbot*, one of the ships riding at anchor. The *Talbot* was impossible to miss; she was rusty, dirty and looked tired. He knew how she felt.

"Admiral, Captain Braunagel is here to see you."

Knutsen turned and nodded to Braunagel's marine escort who stepped back through the door leaving the two men alone.

Braunagel's appearance shocked Knutsen. It was worse than he thought. Six months ago, Braunagel had been a proud man, the ideal image of a naval commander. This wasn't the Braunagel he remembered. His hair was mussed, uniform dirty and disheveled. His eyes were deep shadows of endless nights of vexing questions unanswered.

"Welcome aboard," Knutsen began, hoping he sounded sociable. Knutsen motioned for Braunagel to join him on the bridge wing and continued, "I have some good news for you, Captain."

"Well, I'm always in the mood for some good news, Admiral." Braunagel said mustering a weak smile. "What is it?"

Knutsen looked into Braunagel's haggard face and spoke softly. "Captain, I have been watching the *Talbot*'s readiness reports."

147

Braunagel stiffened and his eyes turned hard.

Knutsen noticed the change, but continued in a soft conversational voice. "I need an honest answer to a question. And please don't take this wrong, but your ship is now ineffective as a fighting ship, isn't she?"

Braunagel came to attention and squarely faced Knutsen. He took a deep breath. "Admiral, I take full responsibility for the condition of my ship. I have a good crew from my exec all the way down to the cooks."

Braunagel's voice was steady, clear, and professional, but somber tones of resignation filled every word. Knutsen started to interrupt him, but his attention was drawn to the two marble-sized brass bearings in his pocket. They seemed to have grown heavier in the past few seconds. He let Braunagel continue.

"The condition of the ship is in no way a reflection on them. I am sure if we could get our backlog of supply parts they could have the ship back in shape in no time. I'm the captain, sir, the ship is my responsibility."

Knutsen smiled. Putting his hand on Braunagel's shoulder, he said. "And so is the crew. I think you answered my question. Captain, you must understand you've done a hell of a job, and the condition of the ship is not your fault, nor a reflection on the crew."

Knutsen continued despite the puzzled look spreading across Braunagel's face. "The good news is, most of the supplies you want are on board, and I'm sending experienced men aboard your ship to help. I'm also rotating your ship back to Subic Bay early for some much deserved time off."

"Admiral?"

"You don't understand, so it is time I tell you about Operation Marathon. It's a race against time your ship just finished."

WINDS OF NOVEMBER

November 1971, Elefsis Pier
Operation Marathon: Day 501

Two months after dry-docking, the *Farnley* was at the pier in Elefsis and would be getting under way Friday for Naples, so as he'd planned, Meyers left the ship early on Wednesday. He didn't go home but headed for the air force base south of Athens to visit a psychiatrist.

Meyers' visit wasn't for himself but for his ship and his captain. As Meyers spoke to the psychiatrist, he picked his words carefully so as not to identify Javert by name or position. Not knowing what was important and what was not, he told the psychiatrist everything that had transpired in the last eight weeks.

The crew had become a spirited, cohesive unit that had found a way to feed on adversity. In the last eight weeks, they had spent six at sea, and the supply situation hadn't gotten any better. However, the crew had seemed to find a way to manage.

Every attempt he made to find out how met with the same flippant response, "You don't want to know." It was the magic he'd seen taking root in Skaramanga. He knew it was good and also knew magic was delicate, so he never pressed the issue. Thankfully, breakdowns seemed to be a thing of the past, a welcome blessing as the stormy winter approached.

All their troubles weren't behind them. After they left Skaramanga, the old Captain Javert returned for a while. In a silly mix-up on the bridge, Javert was embarrassed by forgetting his own ship's call sign. It was a small slip that happened even to the best officers. Nonetheless, Javert, mortified by the mistake, had retreated to his cabin and spoke to almost no one for a week.

At first, Meyers tried to ignore it, but he couldn't. He tried to cajole the captain out of his shell, and when that failed, he took over, as any executive officer would do when the captain was ill.

Javert finally returned to the bridge, and they had argued over a small disciplinary matter. Instead of asserting himself or resorting to one of his typical rages, Javert retreated again to his cabin. When he visited Javert, what he saw was a pathetic, shriveled man huddled on his couch.

Meyers spent hours without success trying to figure out what demons haunted the man. He'd tried to get the captain to talk, but to his questions, his coaxing, his urging, Javert's replies always carried the same theme: "Go away. There are things that captains can't talk about. There are things captains must do on their own. It's a lonely job, but it's my duty. I must follow my orders."

The three-hour meeting with the psychiatrist provided little of the help, guidance, or insight Meyers had hoped for. The psychiatrist quickly saw through Meyers' ruse to protect Javert's identity and barraged Meyers with pointed, leading questions.

The last hour of the discussion kept going in circles, covering the same ground over and over. The conversation ended when the young doctor looked at Meyers and said, "I get the sense that you're confusing your problem by clouding it with emotions that are good but misplaced in this situation. From what you've told me, your captain may be psychotic, and you must do what you think is right. We can talk for hours more, but don't you think you know the answer already? Don't you think that, deep inside, you know you must take action to relieve your captain? It'll actually be for his own good."

Meyers never answered the doctor's question because he didn't totally agree. By the time he'd reached his home in Kiffissia, he knew he had to do something about Javert, but what? To do nothing would only hurt the ship and the man; to take action would help the ship but would destroy the man. Tonight, he would spend a peaceful evening at home with his wife and children. Tomorrow, with his mind clear, he would decide.

§

It was a typical night at the Anchor Bar; crowded and rowdy. Seated at a table near the center of the room, an irate Sweeney was trying to hold court. The *Sampson* had been in port for three days, and her crew had seized Sweeney's sanctuary as their evening base of operations. Nearly half of the seventy men crammed into the grimy little bar were from the *Sampson*.

"This pisses me off!" Sweeney yelled over the roar of voices and the sounds blaring from the jukebox.

"What do you mean?" Portalatin asked, squinting in a vain effort to make his eyes focus on Sweeney, who was sitting not three feet from him across the table.

"It's those cocky *Sampson*-ites. This is our turf, and they just move in and take over," Sweeney replied as he looked across the smoke-filled room.

Sweeney crushed a cigarette out on the hard terrazzo floor, fingered the steel band around the edge of the worn and faded Formica table, and took stock of the situation. An informal line of demarcation had developed, with the *Sampson* crew taking the back half of the bar, including Sweeney's favorite table.

Sweeney took a deep swallow from his bottle of beer and said to Portalatin, "Like I've been saying, the way I got it figured, something's up. The *Farnley* has taken a lot of crap but keeps on going. I tell you, the word is out that we ain't takin' no more shit offa nobody no more."

"You mean the captain?" Portalatin asked in disbelief.

"Naw. He couldn't navigate across a bathtub. It's higher up than that. The XO's in on it though. I mean, look at what Ross and Lee have done. They stopped putting up with it."

"So?" Portalatin asked.

"So look at the abuse we're taking. I'm telling you, we don't have to put up with this anymore, but it's gotta be an all-hands effort. Here we're letting those scuzzy *Sampson*-ites move in on our bar; then we let them take over the best tables and control the jukebox. Kong, I'm telling you, we ain't doing our part."

Portalatin emptied his beer before replying, "It's the only jukebox in Elefsis."

"That's exactly what I mean. It's not right," Sweeney began as he spotted Stucky weaving his way through the door. "Hey, Stucky. Over here. Get us another round, would ya?"

Stucky spotted Sweeney and smiled, then wove his way toward the black and white marble bar.

"So what can we do about it?" Portalatin asked, squinting into the mouth of his empty beer bottle.

"Don't know," Sweeney began as he stood, "but stand by for heavy rolls."

Sweeney steadied himself on the table, and toward the back half of the bar yelled, "Would you guys mind holding it down? Turn that jukebox down. Us respectable guys can't even hear ourselfs think."

Sweeney's shout silenced the crowd for a second as heads turned toward him. "Shove it." came the reply from the back of the bar near the jukebox.

Portalatin started to stand, but Sweeney put his hand on his shoulder. "Not yet, Kong," Sweeney said, dropping back into his wooden chair.

The loud clamor of voices returned as the *Sampson*'s crew resumed their partying. The men of the *Farnley* glanced over at Sweeney and started tucking their shirt tails in.

Stucky, who was more occupied with trying to hold the room steady than he was with navigation, misjudged the distance to Sweeney's table. He collided with the table at full speed, and only the table's heavy round metal base kept Stucky and the table upright. Oblivious to the empty bottles that rattled across the table before falling to the floor with a crash, Sweeney and Portalatin each grabbed a bottle from Stucky's hands.

Sweeney positioned a chair behind Stucky. "Drop anchor," Sweeney commanded.

Stucky dropped into the chair with an, "Aye, aye, cur," but was looking toward the door.

"What's the skinny on the guy stacked up by the door there?" he asked Sweeney.

Sweeney craned his neck to see what Stucky was talking about.

He said, "Oh, him. He's the *Sampson*-ite known as the ouzo warrior. He took a six-shot broadside salvo from an ouzo bottle and went down hard by the bow. They stacked him up there so he wouldn't be in the way. Shore Patrol'll haul his butt back on their next round."

"So what we gonna do?" Portalatin asked.

"About what?" Stucky asked.

"I don't know, but it won't take too long," Sweeney said.

"How long is too long?" Portalatin asked.

"For what?" Stucky asked.

"Don't know," Portalatin said with a shrug.

"I don't know," Sweeney said thoughtfully, "but I gotta visit the head."

Standing, Sweeney stuffed his loose shirttails under his belt and pulled in his copious belly. "I said hold it down back there." he screamed again.

No one seemed to notice, so he headed off through enemy territory toward the door to the left of the jukebox.

After Sweeney relieved himself, he reentered the bar and stopped next to the jukebox. He looked over the bar. It was going to be his kind of night. The bar was hopping, and things were getting extremely drunk.

When the jukebox paused for a breather between records, Sweeney surreptitiously reached behind the jukebox and turned the volume up. The next record came on just as he reached his table. The ear-splitting sound made all heads turn.

Indignantly, Sweeney turned toward the *Sampson* crew and yelled, "Hey, this is your last warning. I said hold it down."

A chorus of shouted support from the *Farnley*'s side of the room welled in agreement with Sweeney's words, and those who hadn't done so yet rolled up their sleeves.

A *Sampson* sailor staggered to the jukebox to turn the volume up higher, and another yelled, "Stow it, fatso."

Portalatin tried to get to his feet again, but Sweeney held him down. "Not yet, Kong."

"Yet what?" Stucky yelled, trying to be heard over the racket.

"Hold it down," someone near the door screamed.

"You don't want to know," Sweeney yelled back at Stucky.

A voice near the jukebox rose above the din. "Why don't you *Farnley* fatheads go back to your flivver or whatever it is you call that thing."

Portalatin looked at Sweeney.

"Not yet."

"Yet what?" Stucky screamed in exasperation.

"It's a ship whale turd." someone behind Sweeney yelled.

"That ain't a ship. It's so old, it ought to be called an ark. I heard your captain's named Noah," the voice by the jukebox returned.

"Please?" Portalatin pleaded with Sweeney.

"Not yet."

"Will someone tell me what's going on?" Stucky pleaded.

"Well, at least she's run by men, not fancy computers," yelled Sweeney.

"Is that why they call you the USS *Rustoleum*?" a man yelled, seated at the table opposite Sweeney's.

Stucky's head snapped around to locate the source of the last insult and, having located the smug grinning face, launched himself across the table with a shriek. "Oh, yeah."

Sweeney watched as the surprised *Sampson* sailor disappeared under his up-ended table and under Stucky and three other *Farnley* crewmen. Admiring his handiwork, Sweeney almost forgot to duck a body and several beer bottles that flew over his table. Safely behind the table, Sweeney shouted, "Incoming! Incoming! Counter battery! Counter battery!"

From under the table, Portalatin asked, "Now?"

"Now, Kong! General Quarters! General Quarters! Man your battle stations!" Sweeney yelled, climbing on top of his table.

Portalatin jumped to his feet and grabbed the nearest man he didn't recognize. The man took one look at Portalatin's huge upper body and chose not to use traditional tactics. Instead, he decided to deliver a kick to Portalatin's groin, which, to his surprise, stopped almost before it began. He looked down and saw Portalatin's huge hand holding his ankle. In shock, he looked back up at Portalatin, who was still standing straight.

"Kong, left hard rudder," Sweeney ordered from his tabletop command center.

"Left hard rudder, aye."

Out of the corner of his eye, the man saw a scythe like right hook hurtling toward his chin. He thought he would be safe, but he leaned back just to make sure. It didn't help. To his amazement, he didn't notice any pain when he crashed against the bar, but there was a tremendous ringing in his head, then the lights went out.

"Sweeney, what now?" a voice yelled.

Portalatin, holding half of a man's shirt in his large fist, neatly held a *Sampson*-ite suspended at arm's length with his feet kicking, trying to find the floor. Terrified, the man flailed wildly at Portalatin, giving the air between them a tremendous beating. Sweeney ducked another beer bottle and ordered, "Kong, rudder amidships."

Portalatin delivered a piston like right jab to the nose and watched the man's head wobble on its gimbals for a second, then fall forward.

"Drop anchor, Kong."

Portalatin let go of the man's shirt, and the man crumpled to the floor.

"Way to goooo . . . " Sweeney started to yell, but someone yanked his legs out from underneath him.

Sweeney fell to the tabletop and landed in a sitting position facing an angry-looking *Sampson*-ite holding both of Sweeney's ankles. Sweeney smiled, flipped his beer bottle into the attack position, but before he could deliver a shot across the bow, the man disappeared under a splintering crash of a barstool.

Grinning from ear to ear, Stucky handed Sweeney what seconds before had been a whole barstool leg and said, "Don't make 'em like they used to."

"Thanks, Stucky." Sweeney replied and turned to see the battle conditions behind him. It was an unfortunate mistake, and Sweeney knew better. He always told his men never turn your back to a storm. A wave of *Sampson*-ites crashed down on Sweeney and buried him.

The noise of shouts and crashing furniture woke the ouzo warrior who, from floor level, couldn't quite figure out what was going on. The ouzo warrior managed the perilous climb up the wall to regain his feet when the door opened, and two shore patrolmen entered. Portalatin stepped forward, took one punch at the ouzo warrior, and watched him go down hard by the stern. Ignoring the shore patrolmen, Portalatin waded back into the sea of bodies.

The two shore patrolmen stood motionless. One stared at the fallen ouzo warrior, the other looked at the churning mass of sailors busy destroying the bar.

"What the hell?" the first shore patrolmen said.
"You're telling me," replied his partner.
"Time for reinforcements."
"You got it. We're outa here," the first patrolman replied, slamming the door behind him.

§

Lonely, Meyers turned the collar up on his foul weather coat and huddled in closer to the bridge house, seeking refuge from the biting November wind blowing off Elefsis Bay. He wasn't sure how long he'd been standing there, but he'd watched the *Sampson* leave, and now he could see the *Raynor* entering the channel to claim the vacated berth. *Everything changes*, he told himself; *ships, men and the seasons*. And the November winds that brought the early gales marked a time of change from autumn's pleasantness to the angry slate-gray swells of icy winter storms.

Athens had turned prematurely cold this year. The damp, gusting wind was chilling, but Meyers didn't want the warmth and security of the ship's interior. He wanted to be alone with the stinging reality of the November winds. He'd promised himself to make a decision today and had delayed it long enough to handle the aftermath of the riot.

Called back to the ship just past midnight, he'd been up all night. The fight in the Anchor had evolved into a rolling riot that had spread to several bars and involved hundreds of sailors. Meyers, with the *Sampson*'s executive officer, met with police officials, promised to pay all damages, and obtained the release of dozens of drunken, battered men to the relief of the local police, who only had cell room for five people.

Secretly, Meyers was happy about the fight and the admirable way the *Farnley*'s crew had acquitted her honor with alacrity. Three months ago, the insults would have gone unanswered. He'd seen spirited fights like this many times before, and the pattern was always the same. Drunken sailors could destroy a bar in minutes but were extremely poor fighters. No one had been hurt. It was part of the magic that no officer would deliberately try to quash.

Today, however, he would have to deal with the magic. Last night's boisterous riot couldn't be officially ignored. He'd spent the night interviewing the men as the shore patrol dragged them back to the ship kicking and screaming. They were a battered and bruised lot, but each man answered his questions standing at attention with exaggerated erectness, chest thrust out and a trace of an insolent smile on his lips. He found it difficult to hide his own smile behind the facade of professional disdain. He knew each man expected to be punished and that, regardless of the punishment meted out, the men would consider it a small price to pay for the privilege of defending his ship's honor.

He'd already held a mass preliminary hearing for over half the crew. He found that none of the offenses were serious enough to go to the Captain for punishment. Instead, he'd lectured them, fined them for the damages, and restricted them to the ship for two days. Those punished immediately entered an elite fraternity envied by the rest of the crew. The magic wouldn't only survive, he would nurture it.

Afterwards, Meyers had sequestered himself on the bridge, deserted as it always was when the ship was at the pier, as a quiet place to think.

The November winds whipped Meyers' thinning brown hair and lashed at the *Raynor*'s signal flags as she slowly approached the pier across the gray, choppy waters of the bay. The *Raynor*, a proud, sparkling ship with modern lines, was the navy's newest ship, and this was her maiden voyage. Everything about her was new. Even the line handlers huddled against the merciless wind seemed to be wearing uniforms right out of the box. She was the type of ship he'd dreamt about as a midshipman so many years ago.

Midshipman Meyers had been an exuberant lad filled with innocence, excitement, wonder, and enthusiasm. In youth, the world was so simple. The navy had taught him the canons of duty, loyalty, and honor. They had seemed so right, so pure and perfect then. Not in his wildest imagination would that idealistic youth believe what the man was now contemplating.

He'd read the regulations over again, and every word dripped disdainful warnings and cautions to the reader. The venom of generations oozed between the lines, and he could almost hear the hateful shout, "Mutineer!"

For his part, Meyers knew he had no choice. Duty now was more important than loyalty or honor. His part would be simple. Next Wednesday in Naples, he would present himself to his next immediate superior, Commodore Stoner, make his case, and formally request the command review. The meeting would be polite, professional, and short. It would end Javert's career, and the loss of the *Farnley* would crush whatever dignity and pride Javert had left. Meyers' action would be recorded in his record without comment on the cause or the result of the command review. Promotion boards would see no honor in his disloyal act regardless of duty. His career would end as certainly as Javert's. The prescription was clear; mutineers were men who forgot their first duty was to uphold the canons of loyalty with honor.

Meyers pushed his hands deeper into the pockets, seeking a spot the cold November wind couldn't find, and watched the *Raynor*'s captain bring his ship to the pier. The *Raynor* was a beautiful, dashing ship light years removed from the *Farnley*. It was the type of ship Midshipman Meyers believed he would command one day; so much for the dreams of youth.

Meyers bade her farewell, put thoughts of Naples out of his mind, and stepped into the warm bridge house. He descended the stairs from the bridge level and stopped outside of the captain's cabin, knocked once, and entered. Javert, unshaven and unkempt, sat at his desk. He didn't acknowledge Meyers but stared at the pictures of his wife and the change-of-command ceremony he'd set at the edge of the desk.

"Captain, it is a beautiful day outside. You ought to get some time topside," Meyers said cheerfully.

Javert looked at him with hollow, vacuous eyes. Meyers turned serious. "Have you heard about the problem last night?"

"Yes," Javert began with a deep, mournful sigh. "Take care of it, will you, XO? I want to keep this quiet. The men should be severely dealt with for breaking the law. You take care of it. By the way, the cook was looking for you, said the coffeemaker was broke."

The loss of a coffeemaker could be devastating to the morale of the crew, but at the moment, it didn't seem important to Meyers. "I'll take care of everything, Captain." Meyers paused for a second before continuing, "Captain, are you feeling all right?"

Javert shrugged, and with a tired voice said, "I'll be all right. I'm just tired and feel washed out. It's the flu probably. It's probably this damn Greek weather."

"I'll send the corpsman in to see you," Meyers said.

"No, don't do that. I'm all right, really," Javert began. "Is there anything else you wanted to see me about?"

"Well, yes. The chiefs have asked me if we could leave at six instead of eight tomorrow morning. They want a few extra hours to run casualty drills. I think it's a good idea."

"Fine, whatever you want to do," Javert replied absentmindedly.

"Thank you, Captain," Meyers said. "Is there anything I can do for you? Anything you want to talk about?"

"No. Now, please leave me alone."

Meyers had one more moral bridge to cross. "Captain, as your executive officer, I have to tell you that I'm concerned about your health. I insist that you submit to a medical examination." As he waited for the captain to answer, he silently pleaded with him to agree.

Javert didn't. "I said I was okay, Mister Meyers. I won't have any more talk about my health. Is that clear?"

Meyers looked at his captain and wanted to say something; anything except "yes, sir." He had the same feeling before at funerals trying to pick the right words to say to the grief-stricken family members. Nothing appropriate came to mind, so he said good-bye and left the captain alone with his thoughts.

MIDNIGHT PARTIES

November 1971, Elfsis Pier
Operation Marathon: Day 503

Later that night, Lee relieved Ensign Nat Hayes of the quarterdeck watch just before midnight, and Hayes headed directly for his bunk. Preparations for getting under way for Naples had begun, and he could hear the deep rumble of the boilers. As he entered officers' quarters, he was surprised because there didn't seem to be anyone around.

After the Corker incident, Hayes had abandoned his upper bunk and had taken the fold-out bunk on the sofa as his. Not only was it closer to the deck, but it gave him a vantage point from which he could keep an eye on Lee across the room. Hayes undressed and released the catch to the back of the couch. With the squeak of springs and the metallic sound of metal sliding on metal, Hayes swung the back of the couch down to prepare his boxlike bed.

Suspiciously, Hayes looked around the compartment and noticed that Lee had done an excellent job of cleaning the room. Even the steel chairs were neatly stacked in the far corner. *It's too neat.*

Hayes had fallen into the habit of keeping the blanket and sheets half folded down. He inspected his bunk and ran his hands under the sheets. Carefully, he lifted the pillow. The coast was clear. Hayes took a single step and swatted the light switch, sending the small compartment into total darkness except for the shaft of light entering the door.

Hayes stepped back to the bed and sat down. As he sat, he felt the mattress sink as the steel springs strung between the sides of the metal bunk gave a little. He thought he felt a slight snag, then a release as the mattress sank, but he didn't have time to think about it. There was a loud pop under his bunk, followed immediately by a hissing sound.

Without warning, his mattress rose, lifting his feet clear of the deck. Hayes jumped up and turned around, but in the darkness, all he could see was that his mattress was rapidly disappearing behind a black somethingness. The hissing sound grew louder, and the black something began to close in on him. Hayes jumped for the light switch but was too

159

late. The blackness blocked his path and was pushing him back against the cabinets on the far side of the compartment.

The blackness was cool, and it grabbed at his skin. It was rubber. *It's a three-meter weather balloon. This isn't a three-meter compartment.*

Hayes, trying to escape under it, dove toward the shaft of light coming from the door. He didn't make it. It pinned him gently, but firmly to the deck. "Help! Help! Someone help!"

§

Barely thirty minutes later, a dozen men dressed in black with blackened faces and black stocking caps pulled down over their ears crouched low in the passageway. They had turned off all the lights, and in the darkness, it was almost impossible to see the large stainless steel double-tank coffeemaker pushed against the bulkhead. They listened intently as footsteps approached from the far end of the passageway.

A shadowy figure also dressed in black appeared and said, "Okay, the watch has changed, and they just finished their first round. We have an hour. Remember, teams three and four have everything aft of the stack. The last thing we want to do is start running into each other. What's that?" he asked, pointing to the coffeemaker.

From the darkness, a voice replied, "You don't want to know."

"You can't carry that thing across the pier. The metal will glow in the dark."

"Yeah, I know. We polished it up real good."

"Cover it with something!"

"Here, use my fart sack," another voice offered, and two men worked to drape the mattress cover over the coffeemaker.

"What the heck you doing with a fart sack?"

"Midnight supply shopping bag."

"Okay, remember, if you're caught, it is name, rank, and serial number only." The man paused as a wave of giggles swept the group. "Let's go."

With a squeak, the watertight door to the main deck swung open, and the men poured onto the dark deck, made their way over the side, and stealthfully worked their way through the cold night across the pier toward the *Raynor*.

The two men carrying the coffeemaker were the last to make it to the *Raynor*. They hoisted the machine to men already on deck, pulled themselves aboard, and disappeared through a door.

Less than two minutes later, they had located the mess deck and had set the old coffeemaker on the floor in front of the *Raynor*'s shiny new machine.

"Kill the frigging lights," one said, unrolling a cloth containing tools.

The other man scampered away and, when all the lights were off, returned and held the flashlight while the other man worked with the precision of a surgeon to separate the *Raynor* from her coffeemaker.

The final touch was switching the serial number plates pop-riveted to each coffeemaker. "That'll really mess with their minds," the head surgeon said with a smile.

When they removed the coffeemaker from its stand, the sound of sloshing liquid surprised the men. "Damn, it's still got coffee in it."

"What now?"

"Pour me a cup while I get the old one hooked up."

When the transplant was complete, they examined their handiwork. As a final touch, they poured the coffee from the new machine into the old one.

"Let's get out of here."

They collected their tools and carried the new machine off, pausing only long enough to turn the lights back on and place the dirty coffee cup on the scullery table.

In the *Raynor*'s engine room, a black-clad figure hid behind a large locker next to the escape ladder. The *Raynor*'s twelve-hundred-pound steam plant was operated by pneumatic computers and controlled from a glass-encased control booth set high against the forward bulkhead. The cold iron watch had been set, and the only other man in the engine room was in the control booth reading a comic book.

The shadowy figure crawled around to the front of the locker and slowly opened the doors, careful not to make any noise. At the bottom of the locker was a large locked tool chest, and a tug at its handles indicated it had to weigh at least a hundred pounds. A hemp line, uncoiling as it fell, dropped from the escape hatch and snapped taut, leaving its bitter end dancing inches above the deck.

The toolbox was first to make the trip to the main deck.

§

Later that day in Norfolk, VA, O'Toole heard the ship's bells chime twice; it was five p.m. He was exhausted. DESRON 23 was the best squadron he'd commanded, and the extra effort to stay ahead of them was wearing on him. *Being a dragon is hard work. First, you have to be ferocious, malevolent, and cunning so you can terrorize the villagers. Once you establish yourself as a dangerous and evil dragon, you have to let the dragon slayer kill you. There's no victory in slaying a friendly dragon.*

He rubbed his tired eyes, stuffed the Operation Marathon file into the

161

lower desk drawer, cleared his desk, and waited. Tonight he had another lesson to teach; a lesson that would allow him to leave his dragon suit behind. He looked forward to it and shook his head with a wry smile, knowing the men would never say "Terror O'Toole" quite the same way after tonight. It was important for the villagers to rally behind the dragon slayer. It was equally as important for all concerned to believe in the mortality of the dragon slayer and the dragon.

"Enter." O'Toole bellowed at the knock on his door.

Commander Flannery, captain of the *Wainwright*, stepped into the small stateroom. "It's seventeen hundred, Commodore. You said you wanted to see me."

This was Flannery's first command, and he'd only been in command for a few months. O'Toole thought highly of Flannery, who had done an extraordinary job under the circumstances. Learning to command a ship took time. The number of details and the fine nuances of dealing with the crew were endless. Flannery had the double burden of learning how to command while having to put up with what O'Toole knew to be a difficult curriculum.

So far, Flannery had done almost everything right, but O'Toole had noticed he was having difficulty keeping the hundreds of command details in perspective. The most important thing was he had forgotten that it was all right for a captain to be human. Tonight O'Toole would teach him how important it was for a captain to be mortal.

"Have a seat, Captain," O'Toole said, waving Flannery to a chair.

Flannery wasn't intimidated or frightened, but he looked wary, and O'Toole liked that. "Tell me, Captain," O'Toole began, "are you ready for sea tomorrow? Are you staying on board tonight?"

Flannery obviously thought these were trick questions, since in O'Toole's navy, there was only one answer. "Yes to both questions," Flannery replied.

"Good." O'Toole said, softening his voice. "Anyway, I wanted to talk to you about the uniform inspection yesterday."

Flannery immediately stiffened in his chair. "Commodore, with all due respect, I thought the men looked great. I felt you were a bit hard on them."

O'Toole had expected that response. "You don't need to defend your men," O'Toole said before dropping the bomb. "I didn't see a thing wrong with their uniforms."

"You didn't?" Flannery replied, dumbfounded.

Before Flannery could recover, O'Toole interjected, "Do you know your ship's readiness rating is the eighth highest in the navy, and that this squadron is rated the second highest in the navy?"

Puzzled, Flannery responded, "Yes."

"Have you told your men that?" O'Toole asked, but before Flannery could answer, O'Toole continued with a wave of his hand. "Anyway, back to the inspection. You probably think I was looking at the uniforms. If so, you missed something important; I was looking at their eyes."

Flannery shifted in his chair and frowned as if he was trying to recall any regulation about eyes that he might have missed. O'Toole saved Flannery from the embarrassing silence. "Their eyes told me they were afraid I would gig them for some uniform discrepancy. There was fear in their eyes."

Immediately Flannery replied, "Commodore, again with all due respect, I think that's only natural. Do you know what they call you?"

O'Toole smiled. "That's the point. They call me 'Terror O'Toole' on the *Vreeland,* too. When I inspected them, every man glanced at his captain first, stuck his chin out, and dared me to find something wrong. Their eyes were saying, 'Take your best shot, you SOB.' I could see it in their eyes. In the end, I grumbled and spit a little fire, but I gave them an adequate rating."

"I'm sorry, Commodore, I still don't know what you're getting at," Flannery said.

"I know," O'Toole began. "Tell you what. Let's go over to the officers' club and have a few drinks and talk this over."

"Commodore, I appreciate the offer, but we're getting under way tomorrow morning, and there's a thousand details, and—"

"And, believe it or not," O'Toole interrupted as he stood and headed for the door, "your ship will get along quite well without you for a few hours. Tell your executive officer you're going ashore."

Flannery chased O'Toole, who was already out the door, babbling something about his private stock of good Irish sipping whiskey.

§

After O'Toole and Flannery left the ship, the evening passed quietly until just before ten. Brightly illuminated in a blue-white light from the floodlights, the pier was almost deserted and, like the ship, was silent except for the constant hum of machinery. It was almost Taps.

With little to do, the quarterdeck watch, an officer, a bosun, and a messenger, casually chatted under the white canvas awning strung from the aft gun mount. The conversation was interrupted by singing on the pier. *"Too-ra-loo-ra loo-ra, Too-ra-loo-ra-li."*

"What the hell," exclaimed the quarterdeck officer as he turned to look down the pier. O'Toole and Flannery were staggering, arm in arm, down the pier.

163

The singing continued, *"Too-ra-loo-ra-loo-ra, Hush now don't you cry . . ."*

The bosun's mate of the watch screwed his white hat down tight on his head and chuckled. "Do you know who the loud out-of-key one is?"

Trying to control his laughter, the quarterdeck officer asked, "How can you tell the difference?"

Seeing that they now had an audience, the two officers turned up the gusto on their evening serenade. *"Too-ra-loo-ra-loo-ra, That's an Irish lul-la-byyyyyy."*

Carried by their forward momentum, the duo missed the end of the gangway and tried to execute a U-turn to come back to the foot of the brow. O'Toole turned left; Flannery turned right. With their arms locked, they both fell to the pavement, landing squarely on their stern sheets.

"Didn't I say right rudder?" the giggling O'Toole asked.

Regaining his feet, Flannery replied, "No, I distankly hear you think lef rubber."

With both men leaning on the brow railing, O'Toole looked at Flannery and said, "Right! Thafs what I thought I thought."

The bosun mate of the watch looked at his wristwatch and said to the quarterdeck officer, "Sir, it's ten."

Still enjoying the show, the quarterdeck officer replied, "Go ahead, I'll take care of this."

Flannery bowed and waved to O'Toole. "Senior ossifers first, Commode-adore."

O'Toole returned the bow and started across the gangway. When O'Toole's foot hit the deck of the *Wainwright*, his legs gave way, and he fell to the deck.

"Whoops!" Flannery was giggling.

The bosun mate keyed the microphone on the ship's public address system. The ship's speakers carried his solemn, controlled voice through the night air, "Taps, Taps. Lights out. Maintain silence about the decks. The smoking lamp is out in all berthing spaces. Now, Taps."

O'Toole raised his head and in a childish voice exclaimed, "Nighty night." He closed his eyes, and in less than a breath, his head was back down on the deck.

"Commodore, you can't go to sleep here," the quarterdeck officer pleaded.

O'Toole began to snore. Giving up on O'Toole, the quarterdeck officer looked up to find Flannery standing almost nose to nose with him.

"Guess whaf?" Flannery asked.

Flannery's breath made the quarterdeck officer recoil. The young officer smiled at his captain and said, "A . . . the Commodore tried to drink you under the table, but it looks like you won, Captain. Now, I think it's time you turn in."

"Right." Flannery exclaimed, then in a bewildered voice asked, "Where to turn in I?"

"Your quarters are up forward, Captain," the young officer replied.

Flannery executed a left face and started wobbling toward the stern. "Do you need some help?" prompted the young officer.

Flannery continued his aftward wobble. "Negative. Anyone who can out tip the Terror can turn hisself in."

"Excuse me, Captain," the young officer said while exchanging glances with the bosun, "but you're headed toward the blunty end of the ship. Forward, where your quarters are, is toward the pointy end."

Spinning on unsure feet, Flannery bellowed, "Who shipped my turn around?"

Flannery's spin had left him with a precarious list, and the bosun caught Flannery just before he would have capsized. Leading Flannery forward, the bosun said, "Don't worry, Skipper, we'll put it back the way it was by morning. Come on, I'll show you where we put your cabin."

When Flannery and the bosun were out of sight, the quarterdeck officer looked down at the snoring O'Toole. To the messenger he said, "I'll be damned. The skipper's a closet hell-raising SOB. Wonder if he did this to get even with the commodore for the uniform inspection. Wait until the crew hears about this."

O'Toole gurgled something, and the quarterdeck officer asked the messenger, "What was that?"

"Don't know. Sounded like he said something about . . .villagers?"

§

The next morning on the bridge of the *Farnley,* Biron was almost through his underway checklist. They would be under way for Naples in a few more minutes.

"Bridge, main control. This is Ross. Engineering's ready for sea," the bridge intercom blared.

Biron looked at his watch. It was five till six, and Ross was right on schedule.

Biron looked at the black clouds rolling in from the west. The forecast had been right; a big storm was brewing. He just hoped they would make it to the open sea before it hit.

The morning was a bit warmer than it had been the day before. The wind held the *Farnley* off the pier as she rocked in the choppy waters of the bay. Mirroring the day, Captain Javert, drawn and gray, sat sullen in his captain's chair.

The crew had been pulling together over the past several weeks, but this morning, something had happened. Maybe it had been the brawl. Despite a large black and purple bruise on his left eye, a smiling Portalatin anchored the other team members at their stations, and they stood equally battered but alert, proud, and erect.

The static hiss of the radios charged the air with electricity. The men were speaking in low, urgent, sharp tones, and every piece of equipment contributed its own electrified whir to the oneness of the sounds.

Biron let the excitement flow through him. He loved it. It was the way things were meant to be.

Biron stepped from the crowded bridge house to the bridge wing and joined Meyers, who, looking puzzled, was staring at the *Raynor*.

"What'cha looking at, XO?" Biron asked.

"The *Raynor*. She's a brand-new ship and probably has two of everything she needs, but look at her. Just on this side, she has two fire hoses missing, and the one aft fire hose is missing a nozzle. I didn't notice that yesterday. It just doesn't figure."

"Maybe they took them inside to clean them or something," Biron guessed.

"Come on," Meyers said with disgust. "They aren't old enough to be dirty. She's only been out of the yards for thirty days."

Biron returned to his mental checklist and, turning to one of the phone talkers, said, "Tell the signal bridge to hoist the call letters."

Biron and Meyers watched as two sets of four brand-new flags snapped to the top of *Farnley*'s port and starboard yardarms.

"Oh God." Meyers said. To Biron's surprise, Meyers ran up the ladder to the signal bridge and returned within seconds, yelling, "Execute an emergency departure drill. Get us the hell out of here. Now."

"Single up all lines. Rig in the brow," Biron yelled, a bit confused.

Immediately, the phone talker replied, "Brow is in. All lines are singled up, Sir."

The report confused Biron. They couldn't have completed those actions that quickly, but looking over the side, he could clearly see that the report was correct.

Biron, turning to Meyers, asked, "What's going on?"

"You don't want to know."

"Know what?" Biron persisted.

"We got new signal flags. None came through supply. I asked a signalman where he got them, and he said, 'You don't want to know.'"

Biron looked at Meyers, then at the *Raynor*. "Bring in all lines." Biron shouted. To Meyers he said, "The wind will blow us away from the pier; I won't have to twist out."

"I don't care if we have to take the highway. Get us the hell out of here," came Meyers' urgent reply.

"All lines in, Sir."

"All back one-third," Biron yelled.

"Make it two-thirds," urged Meyers.

"All back two-thirds," Biron yelled.

The rumble of the engines paused for a second to take a breath, then resumed with a loud roll sounding like distant thunder. The immediate acceleration made Biron happy to be at sea again, especially now since the spirit of fun and adventure had returned.

The top-side speakers of the *Raynor* came to life. "Now, reveille, reveille, reveille. All hands heave out and trice up. The smoking lamp is lit in all berthing spaces. Now, Reveille."

In unison, Meyers and Biron yelled, "All back flank!"

THE CONQUERED KNEE

December 1971, En Route to Naples, Italy
Operation Marathon: Day 505

A few hours later, Admiral Eickhoff went into a rage while reviewing his morning message traffic. Cursing, he kicked the gray metal wastebasket next to his desk, sending it flying across the cabin. It clanged against the chairs pulled around his conference table, fell to the floor, and rolled, making a hollow metallic sound. The steward ran into the room to see what had happened. "Get out. Leave me alone." Eickhoff shouted.

Javert couldn't leave well enough alone. The guy was a total incompetent; the only man in the world who had been told to do nothing and still had screwed it up. First came the message from the US Embassy and now the message from the *Raynor* putting a spotlight on the *Farnley*.

These events indicated his situation was not good because the crew of the *Farnley* still had some fighting spirit. Marathon assumed crew morale would be low, and that was part of the test. A spirited crew would do things contrary to Marathon's intent. Such actions on the part of the *Farnley*'s crew would call his Marathon results into question. The shipyard visit, Eickhoff knew, was the beginning of the trouble.

He couldn't allow anyone to look too closely at the *Farnley*, and that was the reason he kept the *Farnley* away from Commodore Stoner. If anyone looked too carefully at the *Farnley*, his lies would be uncovered, and his career would be over. He only needed six more weeks for Operation Marathon to end so he could clean things up quietly. He had to get the *Farnley* under control or all would be lost, including his promotion.

§

```
REKTHE REKEJELTTE 495763-EIEIEI-REKEHTEB.
KETEEEEE
R 18 1347Z NOV 71
FM    COMSIXTHFLT
TO    USS FARNLEY
SUBJ       DISCIPLINE
BT
CLASS  UNCLASS EFTO

1. US EMBASSY ATHENS REPORTS HOST COUNTRY LODGED
STATEMENT OF CONCERN REGARDING DISTURBANCE ELEFSIS
AND CONDUCT OF FARNLEY CREW NIGHT OF 13 NOV. SUCH
ACTIVITY UNACCEPTABLE AND WILL NOT BE TOLERATED.
SUCH BEHAVIOR IS UNMILITARY  DISCREDITS THE NAVY
AND WEAKENS ALREADY TENUOUS NATO ALLIANCE.

2. COMMANDING OFFICER RAYNOR REPORTS THEFT OF PAINT
FIREFIGHTING EQUIPMENT  SIGNAL FLAGS  AND TOOLS
WHILE BERTHED AT SECURE PIER ELEFSIS NIGHT OF 14
NOV. INVESTIGATION INTO TOTAL EXTENT OF LOSS STILL
UNDER WAY. DUE TO SECURE NATURE ELEFSIS PIER AND
FACT THAT FARNLEY ONLY OTHER SHIP PRESENT LEADS TO
UNEQUIVOCAL CONCLUSION THEFT PERPETRATED BY FARNLEY
CREW.

3. THIS COMMAND VIEWS ITEMS Φ1Φ AND Φ2Φ ABOVE MOST
GRIEVOUS AND A DISGRACE TO FARNLEY  HER OFFICERS
AND SIXTH FLEET. PREPARE RESPONSE ABOVE ITEMS
OUTLINING DISCIPLINARY ACTIONS TAKEN AND ACTION PLAN
FOR OFFICERS FARNLEY TO REGAIN CONTROL OF THEIR
COMMAND.

4. COMMANDING OFFICER FARNLEY UPON ARRIVAL NAPLES
REPORT PERSONALLY THIS COMMAND CONTENT OF REPORT
ITEM Φ3Φ WITH EXPLANATION OF UNMILITARY CONDUCT
FARNLEY CREW.

BT
N1Ø48
```

§

"What do your intel guys make of this?" Admiral Durham asked Beetham while setting the sheaf of messages down.

"They read it as good news," Beetham began. "First, the fight indicates strong morale, which under the circumstances is amazing. Second, the raid on the *Raynor* also indicates strong morale and solid teamwork that includes the whole crew. With the amount of stuff they filched, it had to be an all-hands effort. For heaven's sake, they even stole a huge coffeemaker and two sets of signal flags."

"And what would you do if you couldn't get parts or supplies from the supply system?" Durham asked, smiling.

"Improvise, which they did in a big way."

"What about Eickhoff's message to the *Farnley*? It seems a bit harsh. My assessment was the same as yours and the same Admiral Eickhoff should have reached."

Beetham shrugged. "We searched for past incidents like this to see how Eickhoff reacted but came up dry. We don't have a clue. All we can do is speculate."

"Speculate," Durham urged.

Beetham held up three fingers and ticked off his points as he spoke, "First, that's just his style; so the message means nothing. Second, he's trying to hold a tight rein on the *Farnley*, which is what he's supposed to do. Or third, and this is a variation on number two, he wants to talk with the *Farnley*'s captain so he can measure what's going on."

Those were essentially the same options Durham had come up with, and he knew they weren't right. Disappointed, he said, "Thanks for your help. Keep me posted."

§

The *Farnley* was heading for Naples and had just turned west into the teeth of a storm. A rogue swell hit and almost threw Javert out of his captain's chair. He'd been thinking and fingering the folded message form he had in his shirt pocket. He pushed hard against the wooden sill with his feet to jam himself deep into the back cushion. The storm and the growing unease in his stomach had chased him from his closed cabin to the bridge. There he could watch the steady horizon and perhaps quell his growing nausea.

He knew Biron was pretending to ignore him, so he pretended to ignore Biron. He knew Biron was trying to show how well he could command the ship. Javert was thinking to himself, Biron is trying to humiliate me in front of the crew. I know they're all watching me. I can't interfere. I have my orders. They know I'm a failure.

Javert ignored the bridge crew and Meyers, who was standing next to Biron, where the captain should be. *Meyers knows what he's doing. He has taken the Farnley away from me. He's not like the rest. He has made no attempt to hide the fact that he's watching me. He's daring me to try to take my ship back. They have all conspired against me. I don't blame them. I don't deserve to be a captain.*

Javert fingered the folded piece of paper in his khaki shirt pocket. *I've done everything I can. I've tried. I've worked harder at this than anything else in my life. Where have I gone wrong?* A tear swelled up in Javert's eye, and he raised his hand to wipe it away. He tried to understand why he'd failed as a captain. The navy wouldn't have given him the *Farnley* if he couldn't handle it. Captains never failed. It wasn't permitted. It was inexcusable.

Javert braced himself for the next swell and wondered where he'd gone wrong. *Earlier when I fought tenaciously to keep the officers in line, they fought back, and my ship went slowly downhill. How do the other captains manage? Why can they succeed? They were handpicked by a selection process that has been refined over hundreds of years. It was that process that picked me. How have I failed the navy and my ship?*

I tried. I even tried to be nice to my officers. They ignored me. The ship got better. Without me, the ship got better. Eickhoff was right, and you followed your orders. That's the only thing you did right. You were such a miserable failure. No captain was better than you.

What would you have done in this storm if things hadn't been fixed? The ship would have floundered and all hands lost. God. I almost killed someone before. Do your job and you kill people. Don't do anything and they're saved. You can't blame the navy. It doesn't make mistakes like this. You can't blame the officers; they saved the ship.

There's only one person responsible. There's only one person to blame. There's only one person who must admit defeat. There's only one man to be dishonored.

Javert slid out of his chair and began to make his way across the bridge toward the door. He felt old and awkward. He was careful not to make eye contact with any of the men. He was alone, and he wanted to keep it that way.

When he reached his cabin, he opened the drawer to his desk and laid the pictures of his wife and the change-of-command ceremony on the desktop. The ship pitched and they began to slide, so he caught them with one hand and with the other reached into the drawer and retrieved a roll of masking tape. With gentle care, he taped the framed pictures to the top of the desk.

He sat in the steel chair for several minutes, looking at the pictures. He looked at his wife and thought about the day her father told him the truth about his father's death. His father had been a war profiteer, and the authorities were going to arrest him. He would lose the bank, and his family would be disgraced. His father drove the car off the road at Robinson's Hollow, crashing through the guardrail and falling to his fiery death in the creek bed below. His father had committed suicide.

Gloria's father said it was because he didn't have the strength to face the consequences of his actions. Javert knew better. His father had saved them from disgrace and the dishonor of a public trial. His father was a man of honor.

Javert looked at Gloria's picture and wondered how he could face her again. He was disgraced. Not only was the *Farnley* going to be taken away from him, but he would be denied a promotion. He would have to leave the navy, the only life he knew. How could he live without it? How could she live with a total failure? She deserved better.

He opened the flap on the breast pocket and pulled a folded piece of paper from it. Slowly, he unfolded the paper and taped it to the desktop. It was the message from Admiral Eickhoff. He'd underlined the last paragraph. He read it aloud.

"This command views items (1) and (2) above most grievous and a disgrace to *Farnley* and Sixth Fleet. Prepare response above items outlining disciplinary actions taken and action plan for officers *Farnley* to regain control of their command."

Grievous, disgrace. He'd disgraced his command. He'd disgraced his superiors. He'd disgraced himself. He'd disgraced his family. He couldn't go to Naples. The sea, the military ethos, and honor prevented it. They were unforgiving. They wouldn't allow a man to admit defeat. He couldn't avoid the disgrace, but he could avoid the public humiliation. *Death before dishonor. I can't allow myself to further dishonor my name, my wife, my ship, my navy, my superiors. My wife, my ship, my navy will be better off without me.*

Javert couldn't hold back the tears flooding into his eyes; he let them roll down his cheek. Slowly, he slid from the chair, rested his arms and head on the desk, and knelt to pray.

§

```
REKETYT REKLWERJLY 375485-EIEIEI-REKEKESB.
ZEKEEEEE
R 19 0823Z NOV 71
FM    USS FARNLEY
TO    COMSIXTHFLT
      COMDESRON12

SUBJ  INCIDENT REPORT//N05849//
BT
CLASS CONFIDENTIAL

AT 0811Z CMDR ALLEN JAVERT USN  Ф495 54 5920Ф C.O.
USS FARNLEY TOOK OWN LIFE SINGLE ROUND THROUGH RIGHT
TEMPLE. WEAPON COLT  SEMIAUTOMATIC  45-CALIBER.
SERIAL NUMBER 3738395383. FULL REPORT TO FOLLOW.

LT. CMDR JOHN MEYERS  USN Ф793 73 0376Ф X.O.
FARNLEY SENIOR OFFICER AFLOAT.

EN ROUTE NEAREST NATO PORT SUDHA BAY. ETA 19 2130Z
NOV 71. AWAITING INSTRUCTIONS.

BT
N0597
```

§

```
REKEKTT RKKJKJEDKE 475364-EIEIEI-RKEKEESB.
ZZZEEEEE
R 19 0838Z NOV 71
FM    COMSIXTHFLT
TO         USS FARNLEY
INFO       COMDESRON12

SUBJ   INCIDENT REPORT//N05849//
BT
CLASS  CONFIDENTIAL

AWAIT REFUELING PIER SUDHA AIR FORCE MEDICAL TEAM.
TEAM TO TRANSPORT BODY CMDR JAVERT BY AIR ATHENS.

UPON COMPLETION REFUELING SUDHA  RETURN ELEFSIS
IMMEDIATE. NAPLES VISIT CANCELED.

COMSIXTHFLT IN ROUTE ELEFSIS TO CONVENE BOARD OF
INQUIRY DEATH CMDR JAVERT. FILE YOUR FULL
PRELIMINARY REPORT ONLY THIS COMMAND. REPEAT ONLY
THIS COMMAND NLT 20 1500Z NOV 71.

BT
N0853
NNNN
```

§

The first ring of the phone on Durham's nightstand woke him, but he let it ring a second time to be sure it was the secure phone, not the regular phone on his wife's side of the bed. Before the second ring was complete, he reached out and pulled the receiver to his ear. "Durham."

"Admiral, this is the duty officer. The captain of the *Farnley* is dead."

Durham sat up and rubbed the sleep from his face before asking, "How?"

"The report said suicide, sir. They're at sea and are heading to Sudha Bay to await orders. That's all we've got right now."

Durham took a deep breath. His sixth sense had tried to warn him, but he'd missed it. O'Toole had been right; someone got killed. Operation Marathon had put a lot of pressure on crews, but he never would have guessed it would lead to this. He was going to find out what happened.

"I'm coming in. Get everything together and see if you can find the personnel record for the *Farnley*'s XO, and find out where a Captain Patrick O'Toole is." Durham pinched the bridge of his nose in thought, then continued, "I think he's with DESRON 23 right now."

"Should I send your car, sir?" the duty officer asked.

Durham looked at the illuminated clock on the dresser. It was three-forty-five. "No, I'll drive in myself. Give me about forty minutes."

"Yes, sir." The phone clicked dead.

Durham mentally went through his morning schedule. There wasn't anything important until ten. What he had to do would only take a few hours, and he would return home for breakfast and to get into uniform. He put his hand on his wife's shoulder and, without turning over, she said, "I know. I heard."

He bent over, kissed her on the cheek, and whispered, "I'll be back in time for breakfast."

Thirty minutes later on I-95, Durham passed a truck and carefully steered his car into the right lane. Traffic was light, but the highway was covered with small patches of drifting snow, so Durham had held his speed down. When he passed the green and white exit sign for the Pentagon, wary of icy spots, he carefully eased his car off I-95 onto the Pentagon exit.

The truck behind him began blowing its horn. Durham looked over his left shoulder and watched the truck rumble past him. Unable to determine who the trucker was blowing his horn at, Durham looked forward again.

There were two lights directly in front of him, and it took almost a half second before the meaning of the two lights registered. He drove his foot hard into the brake pedal and swerved to the right. He hit the guardrail just as the drunk driver hit him broadside.

HARPIES OF THE SHORE

November 1971, Bethesda Naval Hospital
Operation Marathon: Day 507

Twenty-four hours later, Admiral Durham felt someone playing with his hand, and when he opened his eyes, he saw Nurse Scalzo, dressed in surgical garb, taking his pulse. He looked up at the shadowy ceiling, focused his eyes on the enameled plaster surface, and tried to understand the shadows from the dimples and irregularities in the surface. He'd been here a long time but couldn't remember why. He'd seen Nurse Scalzo before and knew her name but didn't know how. He remembered his wife being there, standing next to his bed, but couldn't remember when.

He looked at Nurse Scalzo and tried to speak, but all that came out was, "Akkk."

Nurse Scalzo smiled. "Welcome back, Admiral. You had us worried." Scalzo leaned forward and, putting a thumb on each eyelid, pulled painfully on his eyelashes and shined a small flashlight into his eyes. She smelled like antiseptic. Durham couldn't understand. He tried to speak again, but his mouth was so dry, all he did was make that awful noise again.

"Don't try to talk; we need our rest," Nurse Scalzo began. "You were in an accident. You have a bad gash on your head, a few broken ribs, a broken leg, and a bad cut on your arm, but we're going to have you shipshape in no time. You're in Bethesda Naval Hospital. We have to rest. Doctor's orders."

The pieces started to come together; he remembered the accident and understood what had happened, but he couldn't remember why. His mind told him it was important.

"I need you to cough," Nurse Scalzo ordered.

The tight binding tape around his chest made it difficult to move, and not knowing why, he complied and tried to cough. The attempt was feeble but caused sharp bolts of pain to shoot from his sternum.

"Good, can we do it again?" Nurse Scalzo asked while smiling her best all-knowing aren't-we-being-cheerful-today smile.

175

In disbelief, Durham shook his head no.

Still smiling, Nurse Scalzo commanded, "You must."

Durham coughed harder, hoping it would make Nurse Scalzo go away. His entire body winced and tensed up from the blast of pain.

"Good. I have to change the dressing on your arm now," Nurse Scalzo said, ripping a large bandage, and what felt like most of the skin, off his forearm. Durham winced again.

"Now that wasn't too bad, was it? It's better just to get it over with," Nurse Scalzo said with a smile.

Over with, Durham thought. *Operation Marathon.*

Nurse Scalzo decided to let him have his arm back and was turning to leave when Durham tried to speak, but all that came out was that awful sound again, "Akkkk."

"Don't try to talk. Be quiet."

"Akk. Akk."

"If you insist. Your mouth is dry. Here, let me give you some ice," Nurse Scalzo said, making a commotion with a water pitcher. The thought of a drink of water filled Durham with pleasant anticipation, but instead, Nurse Scalzo delivered a sliver of ice about half the size of a small vitamin pill to his lips. She was all heart.

"I have to see," Durham began weakly.

Nurse Scalzo smiled her all-knowing smile again and said, "It's okay, go right ahead. The catheter will take care of everything."

"No, SEEEE someone."

"Over my dead body. Doctor's orders. No visitors," she said, walking to the foot of the bed and grabbing his foot.

"Can we feel this?" she asked, jabbing a needle into the sole of his foot.

Durham jerked his foot away. The sudden movement brought back the stabbing pains in his chest.

"Excellent." Nurse Scalzo smiled again and was gone.

Durham remembered why he recognized Nurse Scalzo so well. He couldn't forget her. She looked and sounded like a bosun he knew once. His name was Scalzo also, and one night he'd single-handedly dispatched a squad of burly marines to the dispensary for making unkind comments about the nude tattoo of his girl on his forearm. He called her Sweet Pea. Although they might be related, Nurse Scalzo would never be confused with the gentle, affable bosun.

§

Eickhoff sat in the backseat of the black Chevrolet sedan the embassy had placed at his disposal. Knowing that it would be over in an hour, he relaxed and enjoyed the scenery as they made their way through the winding, crowded streets on the outskirts of Athens. The week since Javert's death had started in a panic, but now his plan was thought out and prepared. His only obstacles were Commodore Stoner and Meyers, but he could handle them. The *Farnley* unknowingly had fought back against Marathon, and he would quash her insurrection today.

Eickhoff felt no remorse over Javert's death. Remorse had no place in the heart of great military leaders. It was something the bleeding-heart admirals back in Washington didn't understand. All great military leaders, like himself, assumed power by climbing a mountain of dead and wounded. So far, casualties had been light, and Javert was an insignificant loss.

Eickhoff thought Javert's death ironic. If Javert hadn't blown his brains out, he wouldn't have had an excuse to inspect the *Farnley* and discover why her efficiency rating and morale had been climbing. As soon as he got word of Javert's death, he put together a fifteen-man inspection team to turn the *Farnley* inside out and tell him exactly what was going on. If the man who had almost destroyed Operation Marathon hadn't killed himself, Eickhoff would never have had the chance to save it. Perhaps Javert wasn't worthless after all; ironic.

It was important that the men on the *Farnley* be kept in the dark, and the investigation into Javert's death provided the perfect cover. Even adding two JAG officers to the inspection team, ostensibly to protect the rights of potential suspects and ensure that the investigation into Javert's death was conducted legally, went unquestioned.

Eickhoff was especially proud of that little added touch of intimidation. When they were told that the investigation would be far reaching and investigate the possibility of foul play, it frightened almost everyone except the officers. Terrified they might be implicated in some type of cover-up, they talked and talked and talked.

He quickly learned everything he needed to know, and the inspection team had been sent home yesterday. Today, in the presence of Commodore Stoner, he would present the findings of his investigation.

At the bottom of the hill, the car stopped at the coastal highway intersection. In the distance, the refineries at Aspropyrgos lined the shore of Elefsis Bay. Eickhoff turned to his left so he could see the Skaramanga shipyard where the most serious threat to Operation Marathon had begun.

The shipyard had given Lee and Ross a base of operations for their exploits that came dangerously close to tainting Operation Marathon and opening his conclusions to question. Hopefully, his inspection uncovered it in time, and things could be restored so no one could contest his

177

findings. He'd been tough on the *Farnley*, so his conclusions couldn't be questioned. Operation Marathon would succeed. Today he would neutralize Ross and Lee, then negate the damage they had done.

§

Commodore Stoner waited in the *Farnley*'s wardroom with Meyers and Lieutenant Pew. Stoner reached for one of the white coffee cups clustered around the coffee service and poured himself a cup. As he held the silver coffeepot, he nodded to Meyers, who had been staring into his empty coffee cup for several minutes. Meyers waved the offer off with a small movement of his hand.

Stoner knew how Meyers felt, and if he had a choice, he wouldn't be a party to what he guessed was going to happen. Stoner didn't have a choice; the *Farnley* was part of his squadron, and Eickhoff needed at least one other flag officer for his investigation.

Over the past few days, Eickhoff had rankled Stoner. When Eickhoff briefed him on Operation Marathon over a year ago, the operation had seemed a bit extreme, but he quashed his questions when Eickhoff told him it was Durham's pet project. Stoner knew Durham by reputation as a straight shooter and one who wouldn't mount something as extreme as the *Farnley*'s treatment without reason.

Now he wasn't sure he had the information straight. Over the last three days, he'd developed a healthy dislike for Eickhoff and Pew. Eickhoff had acted secretively during the entire investigation and withheld most of the inspection reports from him. Eickhoff hadn't even told him what the findings would be. He was part of the inquiry board in name only. This was Eickhoff's show from start to finish. Eickhoff was trying to hide something or protect someone, and it certainly wasn't Durham.

The last few days had made one thing clear to Stoner; the inquiry had little to do with Javert's death. By noon the first day, the entire investigation was centered on Lee. Javert had been all but forgotten. Eickhoff's agitation over what Lee had done went much further than technical legal matters.

Stoner interceded on Lee's behalf by reminding Eickhoff that what the *Farnley* had been through couldn't be considered normal by any stretch of the imagination. In his view, Lee had done exactly the right thing, regulations and Operation Marathon be damned.

§

Meyers had the opportunity to observe Eickhoff and Stoner carefully and reach some firsthand conclusions. As an admiral, Eickhoff had let

Meyers down. Eickhoff's single-minded pursuit of information to support his conclusions was the antithesis of what an admiral should be. Eickhoff wasn't to be trusted.

Stoner's behavior over the past few days was everything Meyers expected from a commodore. Stoner looked and acted so much like a commodore, he seemed born to the position.

The whole investigation had depressed Meyers, and trying to guess what Eickhoff would do had depressed him even more. He would gladly accept any finding Stoner reached without question, but Eickhoff was another issue.

Meyers was emotionally exhausted and was glad it would be over soon. The admiral would do his thing, and in a week or two, a new captain would show up, and life would go on. He didn't care what happened to him, but he was concerned about what had happened and would happen to the *Farnley*.

News of Javert's death had swept through the crew like a freezing wind that had reduced the magic he had seen to no more than scattered, bitter ashes. The heavy-handed witch hunt by Eickhoff's henchmen had dealt the death blow. Now every man looked sullen, gripped by drifting impregnable loneliness, and melancholy consternation darkened every expression.

When Eickhoff entered, Meyers, like the others, stood and waited until Eickhoff seated himself at the head of the table. Eickhoff flipped the flap that covered the top of his briefcase and retrieved a thick folder of papers.

He looked at each man and began, "I'll dispense with the formalities in this matter if that's agreeable to all those present."

No one moved, so he continued. "There are several matters that we must dispose of today. The first is the finding concerning the circumstances surrounding the death of Captain Javert."

Eickhoff opened the folder, turned over the first sheet of paper, and began reading from the typewritten page. "It is the finding of this board that, although the information is mixed, we can find no information positively linking the death of Captain Javert to an act of suicide."

What is this? Meyers asked himself. He looked at Commodore Stoner and saw the perplexed look on his face.

Eickhoff kept on reading. "Furthermore, we find no evidence of foul play and completely exonerate all crewmen of the *Farnley* of wrongdoing. Finally, then, this board rules the death of Captain Javert an accidental shooting."

Stoner almost came out of his seat. Meyers could see his face was red. "I object," Stoner began, trying to control the tremble in his voice. "The evidence indicates otherwise. The gunner's mate who cleaned the gun said that Javert never kept the clip in the gun."

Stoner took a deep breath and resumed in the same controlled voice. "The pictures and the message were taped to the desktop, and from the position of the body, it's highly likely the man was kneeling when shot. The only reasonable conclusion is that it was an act of suicide."

Seeing that Stoner was through, Eickhoff said, "However, the absence of a suicide note indicates otherwise."

"What about the message taped to the desk?" Stoner asked.

Eickhoff covered his mouth with one hand and thought for a second.

"It's in the best interest of the man and his family that we not leave a bad mark beside his name. We can't prove it was suicide, so there's no purpose in burdening his family with such a terrible accusation. It's the only honorable thing to do."

Stoner was about to speak again, but Eickhoff leaned back in his chair and cut him off. "The findings of this board are final."

The room fell silent as the two men stared at each other. Meyers watched the standoff intently. If Stoner couldn't carry the day, anything he could add wouldn't help. He'd prepared himself for almost any "finding," including this one. In a way, it did make sense on humanitarian grounds, but what had happened to the truth?

Eickhoff reached for a coffee cup, and while he poured himself a cup, he asked Meyers, "Are Mister Lee and Chief Ross standing by as I requested?"

Meyers had a sudden urge not to answer the question, but since it would do no good, he replied, "Yes, sir, they're waiting outside."

Eickhoff turned to the next sheet in his folder and looked up at Pew. "Would you please escort them in?"

Pew jumped up and returned with Lee and Ross, who came to attention at the far end of the table. Ross looked apprehensive. Lee's happy appearance hadn't diminished, but his eyes were silent and filled with concern.

"I don't know where to begin with you two," Eickhoff began in mock exhaustion. "I have a list here, three pages long, of navy regulations you two have broken."

Eickhoff fingered several of the sheets of paper in front of him. "You two have misappropriated government property. As best we can determine, that was almost six hundred gallons of, of all things, maple syrup. You have, against regulations, manufactured parts. You have, against regulations, procured parts and supplies from sources outside the navy supply system using maple syrup as currency, then you two went blithely ahead and used these parts in your engine room." Eickhoff looked up at the two men. "Is this correct?"

"Yes." Lee's voice was clear and unequivocal.

The warmth of the blood rushed to Meyers face. He couldn't believe what was happening. "May I speak, Admiral?" Meyers asked.

Eickhoff glared at Meyers. "No."

Meyers ignored the rebuke and continued, "I knew what was going on. I permitted it. If you're going to hang them, hang me first."

The comment brought immediate reactions. Lee's mouth dropped agape, Ross grinned, Stoner nodded, and Eickhoff yelled, "You'll be silent, Mister Meyers." He turned back to Lee and Ross. "Did you know your acts were against navy regulations?

Silence.

"Answer the question."

Ross tried to speak, but Lee cut him off. "Yes, I did."

"Admiral," Ross said.

Eickhoff cut him off. "You'll have your say in a minute, Chief." To Lee he said, "Mister Lee, I find only one thing admirable in your actions. You used the engineering log with impeccable grace. You meticulously documented every deviation from regulations and cited what was done and why. In addition, you logged every entry as a direct order to protect Chief Ross and your men from their illegal acts. In a way, I have to thank you, Mister Lee, because your entries were so thorough, you made our inspection easy. Tell me, Mister Lee, was this your idea or a conspiracy?"

"It was my duty," Lee replied.

Simultaneously, Ross said, "It was a conspiracy."

"Admiral, I object to your insinuations. These are two of the finest men I've had the honor to sail with," Meyers yelled.

"That will be all, Mister Meyers," Eickhoff yelled back, then in a normal voice continued, "Before these proceedings get out of hand, let me be clear on one matter. My findings are not open for discussion nor debate. They're final. No amount of arguing will change that. I understand that the past few days have been difficult for you, but don't make matters any worse than they are."

Stoner slowly rose to his feet and addressed Eickhoff. "Admiral, I insist that your final report indicate that I dissented in this finding."

Eickhoff didn't flinch.

Stoner continued, "Furthermore, I request that I be excused from the remainder of these proceedings." He pronounced proceedings with obvious disgust.

Eickhoff's face turned pale, but he gave no other outward sign of his reaction. "You're excused," he said casually.

181

Lieutenant Pew began to stand, and Stoner turned to Eickhoff and said, "Admiral, tell your puppy-dog bitch to sit. I can find my own way out."

Stoner, whose eyes had turned cold and calculating, was way out of line, and was asking for Eickhoff to come down on him hard. Meyers knew he was testing Eickhoff and deliberately trying to create an incident Eickhoff would avoid only if he had something to hide. Eickhoff ignored Stoner's insubordination.

On his way to the door, Stoner glanced at Meyers as if to say, *You saw it, too.*

Eickhoff cleared his voice and turned back to Ross. "Chief, I ought to have you drawn and quartered for what you've done. However, considering your service record, the fact that you have only a few more months left in the service, and that your superior worked so diligently to protect you legally, I'll let this pass, but you'll receive an official letter of reprimand that will be made part of your service record. Do you have anything you wish to add, Chief Ross?"

"Yeah, I mean yes, Admiral. Did your inspection team find one unsafe item? Just one?"

Eickhoff looked down at his papers. "You're excused, Chief."

"He's right, Admiral," Meyers said. "Did your inspection team evaluate what the safety of the engine room would have been if they hadn't done what they did?"

"Chief Ross, you're excused," Eickhoff insisted.

"I'd rather stay," Ross said defiantly.

"Excuse me, Admiral, but may I speak to Chief Ross privately outside for a minute?" Lee asked.

"Yes," Eickhoff said after a second.

Lee pushed Ross through the door. Meyers listened to the sound of the heated argument outside the door and wondered, *What other surprises does the admiral have up his sleeve?*

Lee returned alone and came to attention at the far end of the table. Eickhoff resumed as if the interruption had never taken place. "Mister Lee, I understand that you're single, live on the ship, and don't have an apartment here or anything. Is that correct?"

"Yes, Admiral." The concern in Lee's eyes intensified as if he were bracing for the fatal blow.

"Mister Lee, do you understand how serious the charges are against you?" Eickhoff asked.

"I wasn't aware that I was charged with anything."

Eickhoff looked at Lee carefully. "Mister Lee, this isn't funny. I could have you court-martialed for what you've done. However, I'm going to chalk this incident up to the misguided actions of a young, inexperienced, and overly exuberant officer. Nevertheless, I can't just ignore the situation and will place a letter of censure in your file."

"That's not fair, Admiral. That effectively kills any chance the man has at promotion or a career if he wants one," Meyers protested.

"Admiral?" Lee asked.

"Yes."

"With all due respect," Lee said slowly, "I request the court-martial."

Eickhoff blanched and visibly recoiled as if he'd been hit in the face. Good for you, Lee. Meyers thought. You got him.

Eickhoff cleared his throat while he pulled pensively at his ear with one hand, then in a slow, unctuous voice replied, "I was concerned you would say that and unduly hurt yourself, so I had my JAG officers research the matter. You have no choice in the matter, Mister Lee. You will take the letter of censure."

He's lying, Meyers thought. Out loud he said, "That's not right."

"Believe it, Mister Meyers," Eickhoff said, then turned back to Lee. "There's one other thing. I'm directing that you be transferred immediately. You're to be off this ship within an hour."

"Admiral." Meyers yelled.

Eickhoff raised his voice to be heard over Meyers. "Mister Pew, escort Mister Lee to his quarters, help him pack, and escort him off this ship. He's to report to the air base for transport to Naples, where he'll wait reassignment. Here are his travel orders." Eickhoff handed several sheets of paper to Pew.

Lee's eyes betrayed his bewilderment at what had happened, but his smile had returned. As he followed Pew out the door, Lee glanced soulfully over his shoulder at Meyers.

Meyers was aghast. He didn't know what to say or think. It was several seconds before he realized that Eickhoff was speaking to him. "Mister Meyers, I have good news for you."

"Huh?"

"Effective immediately, you're the commanding officer of the *Farnley*. Congratulations, Captain."

"What? Why? That's not regular. I don't understand."

"It's not necessary for you to understand. Let's just say that under the same circumstances in wartime, you would be appointed captain. So you have it. The *Farnley* is yours. You can move your things into the captain's cabin anytime you want."

"I can't. We don't have any paint to cover the blood," Meyers yelled angrily, then he realized Eickhoff didn't seem surprised at his statement. Meyers looked deep into Eickhoff's eyes and tried to figure out what he was hiding. To himself he said, *You know we don't have any paint, don't you? You bastard. You're trying to cover something up. You come in here, tear my crew apart, cut the commodore completely out of the loop, and now you try to buy my silence by giving me a command.*

"What? No promotion to commander to sweeten the deal?" Meyers said sarcastically.

"Don't push it, Mister Meyers. Be happy with what you got."

"I don't want it. You keep it," Meyers said.

Eickhoff got up and put his papers into his briefcase. Remembering something, he reached into the folder, retrieved two pieces of paper stapled together, and laid them face down on the table.

"You don't have any choice in the matter, Captain." The unctuous tone was back in Eickhoff's voice.

"I know this morning went by a bit quick for you and you need time to sort things out, so I'm going to leave you alone to do just that; but let me tell you in no uncertain terms, there's more at stake here than just what meets the eye. In my position, you would have done the same thing. Your official orders giving you command of the *Farnley* and some additional final orders I have for you are in the papers I left on the table. Good-bye, Captain." Eickhoff turned and left.

Meyers was still trying to absorb what had happened in the last thirty minutes. The navy had gone berserk. Stoner saw it and didn't want any part of it. *The admiral is hiding something. I know it. Stoner knows it and didn't like it. What's the bastard up to?*

§

Just as Eickhoff was wrapping things up on the *Farnley,* Seaman Apprentice Michael Milford Morrison jumped from the shore patrol pickup truck and screwed his white hat down tight over his short blond hair. Through the high chain-link gate, he could see the pier and two beautiful ships. He wondered which would be his.

Morrison easily snatched the ninety-pound sea bag from the truck bed and hoisted it to his muscular shoulder. He checked with the guard at the gate and asked which ship was the *Farnley.* He got a curious answer, "The old rusty one."

Morrison walked easily down the pier despite the heavy load perched on his shoulder. He didn't care about old, and he didn't care about rusty. He was just two weeks out of boot camp, and his life's dream was about to come true. He was going to put to sea on a man-of-war, a ship with guns, not one of those ugly, defenseless, slow-moving supply ships.

Morrison felt like a man and was proud that he'd put his bodybuilding surfer boy childhood behind him. He wished his high school buddies back at Santa Cruz could see him now. Surfing at Big Sur was exciting, but Morrison knew it would be nothing compared to what lay ahead. He was on his own now. Everything he owned was on his shoulder, and he was going to sea. The greatest adventure of his lifetime was about to begin.

He'd practiced the age-old ritual of boarding a ship—salute the Ensign then the Quarterdeck Officer, and request permission to come aboard—a hundred times in his head. He was still afraid he was going to screw it up and look like some kid just out of the sticks. He ran through it one more time, trying to visualize how he was going to add just the right amount of casual salty swagger to his motion and words.

He'd just stepped onto the brow when out of nowhere an admiral appeared and headed right for him. He was blocking the path of an admiral, and on the narrow brow, he couldn't escape. His right hand held his sea bag, so he couldn't salute. Panicked, Morrison dropped his sea bag and tried to step backward. He fell backward over his sea bag, sending his blue bell-bottomed trousers skyward. Lying on his back, he saluted and stammered, "Good morning, Admiral."

The unamused admiral returned the salute and replied, "Welcome to the fleet, sailor."

§

Meyers had said a quiet and somber farewell to Lee, then cloistered himself in his stateroom until midafternoon. Of all the things that had gone wrong, Meyers felt the worst about Lee and Ross. He felt responsible for letting them get into trouble. He felt he'd let them down by getting into a position where he couldn't protect them. The whole thing was his fault.

He spent most of the time lying on his couch, staring at the same spot on the ceiling. Inside, he felt like a broken jumble of parts, and he didn't have the strength to be angry at anything or anybody. A distant voice kept coming back deep inside his head, telling him that the bastard Eickhoff had killed Javert. It wasn't any use. He would never figure it out, just as he would never figure out why Eickhoff had shafted Lee and Ross.

Meyers found himself saying over and over that he didn't want command of the *Farnley* under these circumstances. Being given his first command, he knew that this should be the happiest day of his career, but instead, a lonely, hollow ache gnawed at him.

Meyers finally realized he was wallowing in self-pity, and the anger returned. He told himself that what happened wasn't important anymore. *The past is past. You'll go on. The Farnley will go on. Like it or not,*

185

you're a captain and have three hundred and fifty men depending on you. You're not important anymore; it's all about them. It's time to take care of your men and your job.

Slowly, the realization came to him. Eickhoff's actions were directed not just at two men. Either on purpose or accidentally, Eickhoff had assaulted the *Farnley* and the crew. The orders he left behind were the last nail in the coffin, and he wasn't going to take it lying down. He knew a way to fight Eickhoff and screw up his plan, no matter what it was.

Meyers walked through the wardroom and headed for the engine room. As he climbed down the ladder, he could hear the metallic *tink* of his feet on the rungs. The silence was sepulchral. There were no sounds in the engine room except for the echoes of his footsteps on the ladder. When he reached the bottom, he saw that Ross was seated on a shiny white enameled bench. On the deck plates in a semicircle around Ross, Stucky and several other men sat in the same general pose, shoulders rounded, head hung down, and their hands hanging limply in their laps.

None of them had turned to look at Meyers but sat unmoving as if listening to some silent dirge. Meyers started to walk over to them but felt unwanted, as though he were intruding into their private grief. Instead, he turned from the bereft group and walked to the railing to give himself time to think of something to say.

Meyers looked over the maze of pipes, turbines, and equipment for several minutes before he realized what he was looking at. Every pipe was the same color and had the same clean white sheen as Ross' bench. The overhead was the same as the pipes, as were the turbines and every other piece of equipment.

He looked down at the lower level and could see the clean, polished steel deck plates along the catwalks. A glance back across the main level deck toward Ross revealed the shining circular swirl marks left by a floor buffer on steel plate and confirmed what he had expected. Meyers turned and looked down into the lower level. The bilges were clean and dry, and despite the shadows, the white enamel sparkled. Meyers slowly turned a complete circle. Everywhere he looked, he saw white except for the valve wheels painted in green, blue, and red. The bulkheads; everything was white and immaculate.

Meyers had seen many engine rooms before, but none that came close to this. He knew Lee had done a good job, but this was exceptional even under the best circumstances.

Meyers took slow, careful, lingering steps toward Ross and his group. When he reached the outer edge of the circle, he stopped so he wouldn't enter it. He waited for someone to speak. No one did.

Softly, Meyers asked, "Do you know what happened?"

Ross turned his head slightly and glanced up at Meyers. "Yeah. I could smell it coming. I told him, I warned him this would happen, but he just wouldn't listen. I told him it wouldn't be worth the effort and that all he'd do is get himself and the men hurt."

Ross paused, then continued, "The least the admiral could have done was let us say good-bye to him. I warned him. I pleaded with him, but he wouldn't listen, then I got swept into it. It's my fault."

"Don't blame yourself, Chief. Lee was his own man, and he did what he felt he had to do. Lee had high standards, and he couldn't have lived with himself if he'd done any less," Meyers said.

Ross pulled the orange shop rag from his pocket and held it in his hands, inspecting it. "What next?"

"Under way tomorrow," Meyers replied.

"When we gonna get a new skipper?"

"I'm it, Chief," Meyers said. The question in Ross' eyes made him continue. "I'm not a temporary. It's my ship, just like any other command. There's no spot promotion with the job. That's it.

"I wish I could say congratulations," Ross began ruefully, "but I just don't have it in me right now. I know you busted your butt for this ship, and you'll be a good skipper."

"Thanks, Chief. I understand," Meyers said softly, then fell silent. After a moment, he had summoned the strength needed and took a deep breath. "There is something else you don't know about."

"Oh, you mean there's more?" Ross said sarcastically.

"Before the admiral left, he gave me written orders to remove all the parts in the engine room not approved by the navy."

Ross snapped to his feet and threw the shop rag down on the deck. "That'll take weeks." he shouted.

"I know," Meyers said.

"And when we're done, this ship won't be able to go anywhere because I don't have any other parts to replace them with."

"I know," Meyers' voice was soft.

"And you want me to do that?" Ross asked in angry disbelief.

He looked Ross square in the eye and said in a low, constant-level voice, "I just told you what the admiral ordered me, not you, to do. The engine room is your responsibility. You do what you have to do. I'll do what I have to do." Before Ross could respond, Meyers turned and walked away.

Ross watched Meyers disappear up the ladder. Stucky picked up the shop rag and held it up like an offering to Ross. Ignoring him, Ross walked over to the railing and looked at his engine room. He couldn't believe it. Why had Meyers looked at him that way? He wasn't going to disassemble this engine room, and he wasn't going to let Lee down. *What was it Biron had said? Harpies of the shore shall pluck the Eagle from the sea.*

Stucky stood, rag in hand, and started to walk over to Ross but stopped. Ross' face was red, and he was taking deeper and deeper breaths. With an explosive scream, Ross threw his screwdriver across the engine room. "Not on my ship."

Ross' scream echoed through the engine room as the screwdriver flew across the compartment, striking the aft bulkhead with a sharp bang. No one moved as they listened to the metallic clicks and rattles of the screwdriver fall into the bilge, then roll back and forth across its notched handle and slowly come to a rest. Silence returned.

OF DRAGONS

November 1971, Bethesda Naval Hospital
Operation Marathon: Day 513

Durham had waited for this day. Nurse Scalzo had finally let him out of solitary confinement and transferred him from ICU to a real room. It was a large private one on the upper floor of Bethesda Naval Hospital.

Durham wasn't disillusioned. He knew he was still in enemy hands and took in every detail of the room as they wheeled him in, especially the telephone beside the bed.

As they wheeled him past the dresser, he finally got to see himself in the mirror. He didn't think he looked too bad, but he felt the large bandage around his head made him look a little ridiculous.

The orderlies lifted him to his bed and attached his right leg to the wire and pulley apparatus. Nurse Tufly (her shiny black and white name badge said Lt. Tufly, RN), two-blocked the IV bottles on the pole and played with the tubes as the orderlies worked.

Nurse Tufly had to be a change for the better; she was young, beautiful, and smelled better than Scalzo. When the orderlies left, she started fussing with the sheets and began her standard prisoner indoctrination.

"Like I said, I'm Lieutenant Tufly, and I'll be in charge of your care while you're here. If we need anything, just push this button." She pointed to the call button pinned to his pillow, then continued, "We still aren't allowed visitors or phone calls, doctor's orders, but if we behave, the doctor will remove the IVs tomorrow and put us on a solid diet. We missed lunch, but we can give you some Jell-O for dinner. What flavor do we want, cherry or lime?"

Durham, Ronald R., Admiral USN, 432-34-5967, Durham thought, but out loud he said, "Cherry." He hated lime.

"Fine, do we need anything else?"

The *Farnley* had been on Durham's mind, and he had to get a message through to O'Toole. He'd planned this moment and knew his first objective was to test the enemy's defenses. "Yes, there is,

189

Lieutenant. I must see someone."

"No, we must not. Doctor's orders."

In all his years of service, Durham never once made an issue of his rank, but he was desperate. "Excuse me, Lieutenant, but do you know who I am?"

"Yes," Nurse Tufly replied petulantly, leaving the *so what?* implied but clearly understood.

"I have to see someone, and I'm ordering you to deliver a message for me."

"Now hear this. Misses Scalzo briefed me on you." Nurse Tufly put her hands on her hips and rustled her starched white uniform at him. "You may be top swabbie outside, but in here, you're patient third class. Follow orders or I'll bust you all the way down to bedpan."

"Yes, mum," Durham replied meekly.

"Good. Now, I have to go to the desk and call downstairs and have your phone disconnected so we won't get in trouble with the doctor."

Without another word, she made some notes on his medical chart, holstered her pen, slung her stethoscope over her neck, snapped the metal chart holder shut, and, cradling the clipboard in the crook of her arm, marched out the door. *God help me. She's captain of the third armored nurse's precision clipboard drill team.*

Durham listened as the sounds of the rustling uniform and the squeaky sneakers subsided down the hall. When he was confident the coast was clear, he started inching his way over to the phone. He knew he had to act fast. Calling a staff aide or even the marines would be useless. Tufly and Scalzo would cut them down before they got to the front door. He picked up the phone and dialed quickly. When a voice answered at the other end, he said, "Commander Beetham?"

§

Captain John Flannery sipped his coffee and listened to the other seven ship's captains gathered in the *Wainwright*'s wardroom. Most of the talk was speculation about what O'Toole was up to this time. Flannery didn't have to speculate. He knew even his wildest nightmares couldn't predict O'Toole's next move. Flannery looked at his watch. It was one minute until nine. Less than three hours ago, O'Toole had ordered them into Charleston, then said they would be back under way by six that afternoon, and now this unexpected meeting.

Highly unusual for anyone except O'Toole; all-in-all, it was shaping up to be a fairly typical day. Flannery reached for the coffeepot to refill his cup but withdrew his hand when O'Toole blew through the wardroom door.

"Be seated. We have work to do," O'Toole said before anyone had a chance to snap to attention. O'Toole tossed the armload of charts and navigation tools into the center of the table and headed for his chair.

"Golden Lance," O'Toole began, "you know the drill. We're the Red Force, the bad guys. We're supposed to be bent on blockading the Panama Canal. We have six destroyers, one oiler, two subs, and recon aircraft out of Pensacola. The good guys, Force Blue, are going to try to stop us. They have a sixteen-ship carrier battle group formed up around the *Forrestal*.

"Red Forces never win one of these exercises. We're the punching bag, and we're supposed to get creamed. That's not going to happen. To reach the Canal all we've got to do is take out the carrier battle group. I'm open for suggestions."

Flannery scratched his head. They were outnumbered three to one and outgunned at least twenty to one. *All we've got to do is take them out. Simple.* He'd been right on all accounts; it was shaping up to be a fairly typical day.

Borger, the *Foster*'s skipper, spoke up. "Commodore, as soon as the *Forrestal* gets her aircraft up, it's all over. It's not a matter of whether they find us; it's when; and when they do, it'll be like shooting fish in a barrel."

"When?" asked O'Toole.

"When what?" Borger replied.

"When will she get her air cover up?" O'Toole asked in a sing-song voice that made Borger recoil.

Flannery's mind was reeling at O'Toole's suggestion. He looked closely at O'Toole, trying to gain a hint as to what he was thinking. Nothing.

Months ago, he had lost his fear of O'Toole. The only thing that frightened him anymore was the thought of earning O'Toole's displeasure. Thankfully, that hadn't happened for over a month.

Now he would do anything to earn a single, solitary compliment from the man, but the best he'd been able to do was earn O'Toole's indifferent silence. It was the same with the rest of the squadron ships because no matter how hard someone tried, no matter how well someone did, the best outcome was not getting chewed out. It was simple. O'Toole had set some high standards, which Flannery had initially felt unattainable. Live up to O'Toole's standards and nothing happened; fall short and all hell broke loose. Flannery felt like a boy trying to earn the approval of a distant perfect father.

"Well," Flannery began, trying to buy time to think, "officially the exercise started an hour ago. *Forrestal* should be under way, and her flight wing will fly out from Pensacola after lunch. They gotta get their act together and refuel, probably tonight. They'll start flight operations tomorrow morning."

"Where?" O'Toole asked.

Borger's response was immediate. "She'll head west of Cuba and take up a defensive position north of the canal. It makes sense; carrier skippers hate green water, and there's plenty of blue water north of the canal for her to operate. To get to the canal, we'd have to go right through her."

Something wasn't right; a piece was missing. "Admiral Timmons is in command of Force Blue. What do we know about him?" Flannery asked, turning to O'Toole.

Flannery thought he saw O'Toole swallow a smile before he answered. "He was in one of my squadrons years back. He's no dummy. I taught him a thing or two."

O'Toole's words hit Flannery like the burst of popping white light from a flash bulb. *Taught.* He couldn't believe how dumb he'd been. O'Toole was always talking, always explaining, always challenging. He didn't chew ass in the normal sense. Make no mistake about it, if he came down on someone, they definitely knew what they had done wrong, but he always made sure they knew why and what to do next time, and why that would be better. O'Toole; father, coach, master, dreaded professor.

Flannery's startled look must have caught O'Toole's eye. Smiling, O'Toole raised one eyebrow toward Flannery and asked, "So?"

Addressed directly by O'Toole, Flannery flipped through his mental index of O'Tooleisms; *green water, choke points, audacity, take the battle to the enemy . . .*

"He won't do a damned thing we expect. He won't be where he's supposed to be," Flannery began. "He won't go west. He'll go east. He won't head for blue water. He'll head for the shallows. He won't defend anything; he's going to come out and get us."

"Where? When?" O'Toole asked.

Flannery shuffled through the charts and found one covering the eastern Gulf of Mexico and the Straits of Florida. "Here." Flannery said, pointing to the chart. "He'll stay just off Marquesas Keys. Cut east and break into the Atlantic. Tomorrow, just after dawn."

The implications of what he'd just said gelled in his mind. If that was what Admiral Timmons planned, it was a brilliant maneuver. "It's perfect." Flannery gasped. "As soon as he makes his turn, he'll have the wind on his bow to launch aircraft. Within an hour, he'll have a squadron of fighters headed north along the coast, and we're going to be headed south and right into his buzz saw. It would be an ambush on the high seas. We don't stand a chance."

"Unless . . . " O'Toole droned.

Again, Flannery's mind ticked through all of O'Toole's tactical bromides. They added up to the naval equivalent of judo or karate, which taught students to use an enemy's strength, weight, and aggressiveness against him. The conclusion was obvious.

"We take them out," Flannery replied, not believing what he'd just said or that he really meant it. He actually believed it. Everything suddenly made sense. It was simple.

"Where?"

Flannery looked at the chart. Marquesas Keys looked like an atoll, a circular ring of islands. The major island, crescent shaped, faced south. Off the points of the crescent, dozens of smaller islands completed the circle. Properly stationed, a motionless ship would be impossible to pick out of the radar clutter.

"Timmons' choke point is Marquesas Keys," Flannery began. "If we stay stationary, with all the radar clutter from the islands, they'd never see us, and he'd never expect it."

Suddenly everyone in the room was talking at once, except O'Toole, who seemed satisfied to sip at his coffee.

"Weather's supposed to be overcast, and there's no moon tonight. It'll be blacker than hell out."

"Water's too shallow. I've been in deeper swimming pools."

"Pool, hell. Look where the ten-fathom curve is. My bathtub is deeper than that."

"Forget it; that's six-hundred-seventy miles. Even if we used flank speed, we couldn't get there until . . ."

"Oh-three-thirty tomorrow morning, just in time to get into position."

"And then what? At that speed, we'd burn all of our fuel, and we'd be running on fumes."

"And riding mighty high in the water. When is high tide?"

"Oh-four-oh-six."

"That'll give us another four feet."

"To stay still, we'll have to keep station using our engines. Currents will be vicious."

"Guess what? We'll have to do it by eyeball in the dark. Remember, no radar."

"No lights."

"No radio."

"Shit, we've got to clear the Charleston channel in thirty minutes."

The room fell silent, and all faces turned to O'Toole. "Well?"

Flannery asked.

"Well," O'Toole drawled, "since this is a training exercise, I think Flannery should be made acting squadron commander."

His worst nightmare had just come true. "What?" Flannery blurted.

"What nothing," O'Toole snapped. "You're in command, Flannery, command."

Flannery turned to his fellow captains. "Emergency sortie. Ten minutes."

Within a second, the wardroom was empty except for Flannery and O'Toole. Flannery grabbed the telephone and spun the crank to ring the quarterdeck. At the first sound of a voice on the other end, he began speaking in a steady staccato.

"This is an emergency. Man the special sea and anchor detail. Rig in the brow now. Anyone ashore is going to stay that way. Have the department heads meet me on the bridge. Now. Emergency sortie in ten minutes."

Flannery dropped the phone to the table, darted for the door, then stopped. "I didn't even tell them who was calling."

O'Toole, who was studying the charts, looked up. "Don't worry, I think they know." O'Toole took a sip of his coffee, then added, "Have you looked at this chart? It's shallow around Marquesas Keys. Hell, it isn't even a puddle. This is going to get hairy."

O'Toole's comment sucked all the air out of Flannery's lungs. This was the second unexplained change in O'Toole's demeanor in five minutes. *What does it take to make this man happy?*

A combination of anger and frustration raised the hair on the back of Flannery's neck, and he lashed at O'Toole. "With all we've been through, we don't need a puddle. Give me heavy morning dew and I'll park this damn ship on your front lawn."

"Getting a bit audacious, are we?" O'Toole chuckled.

O'Toole was smiling. It was like a gnarled watchdog growling and wagging his tail at an intruder. No one ever knew which end to believe, but this dog never wagged his tail. Dumbfounded, Flannery looked at O'Toole. Only one word came to mind. "Balls!" he cursed and charged out the door.

§

The *Mississinewa*, heavily laden with oil, plodded northward toward Charleston to rendezvous with the ships of DESRON 23. Oblivious to the slow, graceful roll of the table caused by the following sea of five-foot swells, Captain Kornfeld, settled down to enjoy his dinner. The sound-powered phone mounted under the table interrupted him with its shrill call before he had a chance to get started. Kornfeld shrugged and retrieved the handset. "Captain," he said, hoping it wasn't something important.

"Captain, you better get up here. We just rendezvoused with DESRON 23." It was the conning officer.

Kornfeld knew better than to ask the obvious question. They weren't supposed to rendezvous for another eight hours. "Be right there."

When the *Mississinewa*'s captain stepped onto the bridge, it took him a second to absorb what he saw. It was DESRON 23 all right, in perfect column formation charging southward through the rolling seas. The sense of speed was sensational. Their hurricane bows exploded into the swells to launch great walls of white water that rose higher than their masts, hung motionless for a heartbeat, dissolved into glistening spray, and fell back into the sea. The lead ship was less than a thousand yards off the starboard bow. "What the hell?" Kornfeld blurted.

The conning officer turned and, seeing his captain, said, "As soon as I had visual on them, I challenged them and asked their intentions via flashing light. In reply, the *Wainwright* sent us three messages."

"And?"

"It was a single word in plain English; Tallyho," the conning officer said, making no effort to hide his bewilderment.

Kornfeld laughed.

The young officer frowned, obviously trying to figure out what was so funny.

Finally, *Mississinewa*'s captain asked, "The other two messages?"

"They were in standard code. The first ordered us to shut down all radar and radios and go to darkened ship. The second telling us to rendezvous with them tomorrow for refueling. The rendezvous point is . . ." The conning officer paused for effect. "Southwest of Key West, Florida."

Kornfeld wasn't surprised a bit. He smiled as he realized the hunter had become the hunted. To his conning officer, he said, "Just don't stand there; we're headed in the wrong way. Bring us about."

Kornfeld walked to the bridge wing and watched the column of destroyers racing for the southern horizon.

"Captain," the quartermaster called out, "to make the rendezvous, we have to make twenty knots."

"Very well," Kornfeld replied. Just before ordering twenty knots, he paused. The thought of his oiler crashing through these seas at flank speed intrigued him. He missed destroyers. Oilers never get to steam at flank speed. It would be a once-in-a-lifetime experience, and maybe he could get close enough to be in radio range to hear the play-by-play tomorrow morning. To the conning officer, he said, "Come to flank speed. Make turns for twenty-six knots."

The conning officer looked at the seas, then back at his captain, silently asking for confirmation. Kornfeld nodded. The conning officer complied, then asked, "Who is O'Toole?"

The *Mississinewa's* captain reached into his pocket to retrieve two marble-sized brass bearings. He rolled them in his hand for a second and said softly, "The fox we're chasing."

§

When the scratching sound woke Durham, he could still taste the lime Jell-O in his mouth. The sound was coming from a door opposite his bed that connected to the adjoining room. The door opened, and Commander Beetham peeked around the corner.

"It's clear," Durham whispered, propping himself up in bed.

Dressed in a white lab coat with a stethoscope draped around his neck, Beetham entered the room carrying a large, flat box of candy with a pretty little red ribbon on it.

"Did you bring the stuff?"

"Yes, sir, it's all right here." Beetham opened the candy box to reveal the files, pens, and message forms he'd asked for.

§

```
REKJET RCAEKEOKDY 847362-EIEIEI-RKEKLVBB.
ZCKEEEEE
R 26 1301Z NOV 71
FM    CNO
TO        COMSECONDFLT
          COMDESRON23 - CAPTAIN PATRICK O'TOOLE

SUBJ  FARNLEY/OPERATION MARATHON
BT
CLASS  CONFIDENTIAL

FOR COMSECONDFLT  DETACH IMMEDIATE CAPTAIN O'TOOLE
COMDESRON23. ORDERS TO FOLLOW.

FOR O'TOOLE  PROCEED ATHENS DEBRIEFING COMMODORE
STONER RE FARNLEY BEST SPEED. DEPART CONUS ANDREWS
AFB. CONTACT DUTY OFFICER ANDREWS FOR FILES AND
ADDITIONAL INSTRUCTIONS. ADVISE ASSISTANCE NEEDED
SOONEST. OFFICIAL ORDERS TO FOLLOW.

BT
N0821

NNNN
```

AND DRAGON SLAYERS

November 1971, Fifty miles north of the coast of Libya
Operation Marathon: Day 514

It had been seven days since Javert's death and two days since Eickhoff had thrown Lee off the ship. Ross was glad to be at sea; it would help him maintain his sanity. At sea, the long hours and monotonous routine would dull the senses and would make past events seem so long ago.

He had found time to think about Lee, something that filled him with sadness, and he wondered what would become of Lee. Besides, in his heart, he hadn't said good-bye. Lee had set some high standards, the highest of which demanded that Ross live up to his and the standards he'd learned from Chief Barnes. Ross would forever be thankful to Lee for that; he had his pride back. He knew Lee would survive and, if he guessed right, would find some way to come out on top, but still he missed him.

He'd also had time to think about Meyers and the orders Eickhoff left, and that was why Ross was standing at his small makeshift desk, little more than a flat piece of metal welded between two stanchions. Ross' memory was vivid; Meyers' words had finally sunk in. "I just told you what the admiral ordered me, not you, to do. You do what you have to do. I'll do what I have to do."

Meyers never ordered him to do anything; he was just giving him fair warning for what might happen. Meyers had done with Eickhoff's orders what he had to do; nothing. Ross was now doing what he had to do and was almost finished.

Ross had known what his crew had done with the engine room. The transformation had almost been miraculous. He now owned one of the finest engine rooms in the fleet, and his men owned the equipment in it. He owed it to Lee, the men, and Meyers never to let anything or anybody destroy the pride they had in their accomplishments.

He'd been writing for over an hour in the green bound engineering logbook, and his fingers were cramping from having to press so hard

197

with the cheap navy ballpoint pen. Ross had lost track, but he'd filled over ten consecutive pages with part numbers, descriptions, and locations. When he'd added the last part to the list, he finished his log entry with a single sentence.

ALL OF THE ABOVE LISTED PARTS HAVE BEEN FULLY INSPECTED BY JAMES A. ROSS MMCM USN, CERTIFIED SHIPYARD INSPECTOR C845952 FOR STRICT ADHERENCE TO MILSPEC STANDARDS AND ARE HEREBY CERTIFIED AS NAVY APPROVED PARTS.

BY AUTHORITY,

JAMES A. ROSS MMCM USN

§

Leaning on the bridge wing pelorus, John Flannery listened to the sounds of the dead, still night. All he could hear was the gentle purr of the ship's engines and the adrenaline-charged thump, thump, thump of his heart. It was buck fever, and every man aboard had it.

Motionless, silent, and dark, the *Wainwright* lay abreast a small island. Dead ahead lay an exposed reef, the *Forrestal,* and her fifteen screening destroyers. Secluded in the five-mile-long ring of islands to the east, the other squadron ships waited. To reduce their radar cross section and complicate visual identification, Flannery had ordered the ships to keep their bows pointed at the formation. They hadn't been detected, and he wondered if the small detail had helped.

Three hours ago, jubilation had swept the ship when the ELINT operators picked up the battle group's radars. When the first screening ship appeared off the point of the key, the crew fell as silent as the dead calm night and became as motionless as the satin mirrored sea. Now, only clipped, terse, tense, hissing whispers pierced the silence.

Flannery turned to see if O'Toole was moving. He wasn't; he was sitting motionless in the port bridge chair. O'Toole's behavior troubled Flannery. O'Toole hadn't moved from his chair or said a word for hours. The last conversation had been only a few words. "Flannery, as acting Commodore, let your exec handle the ship. You're not to interfere with him under any circumstances."

After that, O'Toole returned to his chair and sat staring stone-faced, straight ahead, trancelike. Flannery didn't like leaving the *Wainwright* to his exec. He wanted to be part of the bridge crew, to be part of the action. Not being at the helm was harder than he'd imagined. It was harder than letting a child go, but orders were orders.

O'Toole was a problem, and it was what O'Toole wasn't doing that was troublesome. Normally, O'Toole exhibited unlimited energy, especially verbal alacrity. O'Toole always occupied himself by sniping at mistakes or dispatching lessons wrapped inside his never-ending sea story homilies. Flannery knew that, despite O'Toole's inactivity, nothing, not even the smallest detail, had escaped his notice, yet not a word.

Flannery sighted the *Forrestal* with the pelorus; another two degrees and she would be dead in their sights. A hand fell softly on his shoulder, and Flannery turned.

"Is it time?" O'Toole's voice was so soft and the tone of his question so unintimidating, it startled Flannery.

"Are you okay, Commodore?" Flannery asked.

"Never better," O'Toole began in the same soft voice. "It's time; now watch."

Flannery, mesmerized by O'Toole's uncharacteristic tone, lost track of time. After a second, O'Toole glanced down at the pelorus. Flannery took the hint; the *Forrestal* was in position.

"One minute," Flannery called out.

Without another word, the *Wainwright*'s exec reached for the radio microphone and keyed it. The radio speaker gave out an almost imperceptible click. To some, it would have sounded like static; to the other ships, it was a signal. Simultaneously, the quartermaster clicked a stopwatch. The whisper "one minute" echoed and rippled through the ship. The exec handed the microphone to the exercise referee who would score the mock attack and turned toward the captain's weapons console.

The sound of the engines began to change from a gentle purr to a threatening growl. Softly, the conning officer gave an order. Slowly, without any forward motion, the ship began to pivot so they could use both the forward and aft missile launchers. Atop the bridge, the fire-control radar dish whined, spun, and stopped with a jerk, aimed directly at the *Forrestal*.

Oddly, Flannery felt like he was witnessing a ballet; a ballet never practiced, a ballet with three hundred dancers in perfect harmony. The feeling had been the same when he watched the crew maneuver the ship through the maze of shoals and reefs around the key, but he'd missed it. It was different, yet the same, as the chaos he'd seen when the emergency sortie order was given in Charleston. There was a steadfast purpose in what he saw, a perfected confidence in themselves and their shipmates. He'd learned a lesson he would never forget, a lesson he

would pass on to all who would listen.
He listened to the whispered voices.
"Fire control radar in standby."
"Fire control computer on."
"Launch sequencer on auto."
"Target selection to manual."
"Launch command to manual override."
"Forty seconds."
"Bearing to *Forrestal* loaded, two missiles."
"Bearing to second target one-seven-five."
"Aft battery clear."
"Weapons control to manual."
"Thirty seconds."
Across the ocean, a distant general quarters klaxon sounded. An alert lookout had spotted their silhouette. The whispers continued.
"Computers engaged."
"Roger, second target entered, two missiles."
"Engine room ready to answer all bells."
"Navigation radar ready."
"Course to clear the reef one-six-five."
"Bearing, target three, one-five-three."
"Roger, third target entered, two missiles."
"Fifteen seconds."
"Weapons ready."
"Fire control radar on, now."
"We have target acquisition."
"Five seconds."
"We have lock."
"Right hard rudder."
"Weapons free."
"Solution."
"Green board."
"Launch."
"Navigation radar on."
"All ahead flank."
Twelve red flares, two from each DESRON 23 ship, arched gracefully into the black morning sky, signaling the launch of imaginary missiles. The radio blared as referees called out the missile targets, bearings, and ranges.
The mock battle raged. The sky, the sea, the white sand beaches of the key glowed red as wave after wave of red flares arched across the sky. It was over in less than two minutes.

It took the referees three hours on the radio to score the attack. As soon as the attack had begun, O'Toole returned to his bridge chair and his silence. The crew was being served breakfast, but Flannery stayed on the bridge to hear the results. He knew what the results would be; he just wanted to see how O'Toole would handle it. Every man aboard was walking on air except O'Toole.

Finally ready and with clipboard in hand, the *Wainwright*'s referee motioned to Flannery and approached O'Toole to give his report. "Commodore, I apologize for the delay. Admiral Timmons is upset."

"I'd be upset if I let myself get butt-kicked like that. Get on with it," O'Toole snapped.

Flannery was relieved to see O'Toole back in form.

"We gave Force Blue every benefit of the doubt. You see—"

"The results?" O'Toole prompted.

The referee shifted his feet and began reading from his clipboard. "*Forrestal* took eleven direct hits from the opening salvo. Status; heavily damaged and out of action."

"Not sunk? Eleven direct hits and not sunk?" O'Toole bellowed. "Are you familiar with the explosive impact of just one missile? Are you familiar with the amount of ordnance the *Forrestal* carries? Do you know how small the probability is that all eleven direct hits missed her magazines?"

"I know, but Admiral Timmons—"

"Hang the admiral. The rest of the ships?"

"All sunk or sinking," the referee said in relief.

"What's the status of my squadron?" O'Toole asked.

"No damage. Force Blue didn't get off a single shot," the referee began. "Commodore, if I may, I'd like to congratulate you and your men. This is the finest coordinated attack I've ever seen. All the referees are in agreement. The attack was brilliant, simply outstanding."

O'Toole jumped from his chair. "Outstanding. You call that outstanding? How many missiles were fired at the *Forrestal*?"

"Twelve."

"So one missed?"

"Yes, but—"

"But nothing," O'Toole bellowed. "And if it hadn't missed, maybe you would have judged the *Forrestal* to be sunk. Twelve out of twelve would be outstanding. At best, I'd call this attack adequate."

Something snapped in Flannery's mind. *Adequate?* That was the kindest thing he'd ever heard O'Toole say.

"Commodore, is that a compliment?"

"Why . . . no . . . It's a statement of fact. You met your objective.

Your performance was adequate," O'Toole said with a huff.

All eyes of the bridge crew were on him, and he could hear the phone talkers providing a whispered play-by-play to the rest of the ship. He couldn't believe it; O'Toole was backpedaling. This was a once-in-a-lifetime opportunity, and he wasn't going to let O'Toole off the hook.

"We busted our buns to get down here at flank speed in heavy seas. The cooks are still cleaning the food off the overhead. Then, in the dark, without radar, without radio, in darkened ship condition, we navigate in here blind across a maze of reefs. In water you called a puddle! We hold our position in a spot that had less water than I could get in a sponge, then we launch a near-perfect attack and wipe out an overwhelming superior force. Everyone on this ship did an outstanding job. That, sir, has to rate better than adequate."

"Don't push it." O'Toole was growling. "Your tactics got a bit sloppy after the opening salvo."

"A bit sloppy? There were twenty-four ships angling and dangling at top speed back and forth across the same patch of ocean in the dark without navigation lights. It was worse than a church parking lot after services out there."

"All right. All right." O'Toole was forcing his speech, as if every word hurt him. "Your ship did a . . . a . . ." The words seemed stuck in his throat, then with an explosive force, they broke free. "A damned adequate job."

Flannery ignored the shrieks of joy behind him and shouted, "That, I'll take as a compliment, and I'm dammed proud of the crew."

Retreating to the bridge wing, O'Toole replied with a snort, "Me, too."

Flannery couldn't contain his exhilaration anymore. Satisfied O'Toole couldn't see him, he danced a little jig to the entertainment of the bridge crew. In the distance, he heard roaring cheers spring up from various parts of the ship. Flannery had never felt prouder of his ship or his crew and, more important, he was happy for them. He looked at O'Toole standing on the bridge wing, alone.

Flannery hurried to where O'Toole stood and said, "Thank you, Commodore."

"You have a damned fine crew." O'Toole was speaking in the same soft voice he'd used earlier. The gruffness was gone, replaced with soft admiration.

"You've done an exceptional job, and you should be proud."

O'Toole continued to stare at the horizon. Flannery searched for the right words. "Commodore, we did it because of you. It was your plan."

O'Toole cut him off. "I didn't do squat. It was your plan, remember?

I didn't say a word. Your crew, just like the crews of the other ships, did it. You did a good job with your crew. They did it without you, just like you did it without me."

O'Toole, changing the subject, said, "I just received orders, and a helo will be by shortly to pick me up. In the interim, I'm making you acting squadron commander."

O'Toole paused and pulled something from his pocket before continuing. "Sometimes good men get promoted to admiral, and their minds go to mush and they forget what's important. Someday, you'll make a damned fine admiral if you don't forget what you've learned and if you don't forget the men. To help you remember, I've got something for you."

O'Toole held out his fist and dropped two marble-sized bearings into Flannery's hand. Made of brass, they were cool and heavy in his hand. Baffled, Flannery asked, "What are they?"

"What every commander needs; brass balls."

§

```
REKEJET RCAEKEOKDY 847362-EIEIEI-RKEKLVBB.
ZCKEEEEE
R 27 1437Z NOV 71
FM    ADMIRAL TIMMONS  COMMANDER FORCE BLUE
TO    COMDESRON23  COMMANDER FORCE RED

SUBJ     GOLDEN LANCE
BT
CLASS    UNCLASS EFTO

1. GOLDEN LANCE HAS SEVERAL MORE DAYS TO RUN. FORCE
BLUE DESIRES TO REGAIN THEIR HONOR.

2. WOULD YOU CONSIDER BEST TWO OUT OF THREE.

BT
N0821
NNNN
```

§

```
REKEJET RCAEKEOKDY 847362-EIEIEI-RKEKLVBB.
ZCKEEEEE
R 27 1445Z NOV 71
FM    COMDESRON23  COMMANDER FORCE RED
TO        ADMIRAL TIMMONS  COMMANDER FORCE BLUE

SUBJ      GOLDEN LANCE
REF       Aⵁ YOUR Ø1 1437Z DEC 71
BT
CLASS  UNCLASS EFTO

1. IN REGARDS REF A  AGREED.

2. SEE YOU IN PANAMA.

3. TALLYHO.

4. BY COMMANDER JOHN FLANNERY  ACTING COMDESRON23.

BT
NØ821

NNNN
```

TRUTHS

December 1971, Fairfax, VA
Operation Marathon: Day 519

To Admiral Durham, it was Independence Day. At last he was forever free of Tufly the Terrible and Scalzo the Sadist. Grudgingly, Tufly had let him have visitors and do two hours' work a day for the past few days. He knew it tore her apart to see him happy like that, but there was nothing we could do; we had the doctor's permission. As a going-away present, he had presented Nurse Tufly with a bound copy of the Geneva Conventions and marked the pages related to treatment of prisoners of war.

His wife had converted the downstairs den into a temporary bedroom, where she could be close during the day and he could be close to his beloved books. The room was crowded with the bed, his small desk, and the reading chairs, which made it hard for him to get around with his cast. All in all, Durham was happy to be at home and to be permitted to work a few hours a day, even though the secure phone hadn't rung.

He hadn't heard from O'Toole or Beetham, and not knowing what was going on was driving him to distraction. It seemed as if the *Farnley* had dropped off the end of the earth. As Durham had it figured, O'Toole would be talking with Stoner today, so by tonight or tomorrow, he should have information. He knew something was wrong with the *Farnley*, and Javert's death kept haunting him. It was why he had gotten in the accident in the first place, and why he now had so much time to worry about it. He just wished he had the truth about what happened on the *Farnley*. He hoped someone would give him some information, anything; anything he could act on.

§

Pew had seen it coming and was more than prepared. At Elefsis, he'd seen Eickhoff walk out on extremely thin ice in an attempt to save Operation Marathon and his skin. As he suspected, the ice had broken under his feet, but Eickhoff didn't know that yet, and Pew wasn't about

Larry Laswell

to throw him a lifeline. Eickhoff was beyond saving.

After the final meeting on the *Farnley*, he'd accompanied Lee back to Naples, and Eickhoff had flown to Palma to catch up with the *America*. In Naples, he'd finished his report on Eickhoff's behavior and made copies of supporting documentation he'd carefully collected over the months. Since he didn't know when he would need it, or to whom he would have to deliver it, he'd left the addressee and date blank.

That information Commodore Stoner supplied himself without knowing it. Pew had seen Stoner's reaction to Eickhoff's board of inquiry and knew when the trouble started, Stoner would be the bellwether. So while Pew finished his report, he kept in touch with the DESRON 12 yeoman, a lonely sort of clerkish fellow he'd befriended.

Last night, the contact had paid off and told him Durham had sent O'Toole in to investigate. O'Toole had already talked with Stoner and was en route to Naples, probably to speak with Lee. Pew's contact had even supplied the arrival time for O'Toole's MAC flight.

Prepared, Pew was satisfied with the way events were unfolding, and since he had the weekend desk watch at the operations center, he wasn't even going to have to lose any free time. However, he did have to get up early to finish his report. When he got to his small cubicle office in the operations center, he removed the cotton ribbon from his typewriter and replaced it with the one he'd used to type the report so there would be no obvious difference in ink density on the type. He removed the report from the file, carefully registered it in the Underwood typewriter, and addressed it to Captain Patrick O'Toole, dating it the previous day.

Thirty minutes later, Pew was running across the cold rain-swept tarmac, chasing a taxiing C-130 cargo plane that had just landed. Despite the cold, he was sweating profusely from his exertion.

Pew, red-faced and panting heavily, came to a jarring halt about thirty feet behind the C-130 as the engines shut down. Still panting, Pew put his hat on and tried to straighten his uniform as best he could. With a loud, banging pop, the aft portion of the plane's underbelly separated from the tail section. Motors groaned, and the section slowly started to lower itself into a ramp like position.

The ramp was barely halfway down when a large red-haired officer dressed in a tropical khaki uniform climbed over the cargo pallets inside the plane and jumped to the ground.

O'Toole returned Pew's salute and walked directly up to him. Pew started to introduce himself, but the disgusted look on O'Toole's face made him freeze. He felt as if he was being inspected.

"Who the hell are you?"

Pew rocked back on his heels but caught his balance before

206

answering. "Lieutenant Charles Pew," Pew said proudly.

"I know that," O'Toole said, pointing at the name tag. "Don't waste my time telling me something I already know. Tell me something I don't know. Who the hell are you?"

"A . . . a . . . Sixth Fleet NATO Liaison Officer," Pew stammered.

"I know that, too," O'Toole said, disgusted. "Commodore Stoner told me all about a puppy dog bitch disguised as a navy lieutenant."

"Commodore Stoner?"

O'Toole softened his voice and said, "Of course. I'm sorry, Lieutenant, there's no way you could have known I met with Commodore Stoner yesterday, is there?"

Pew immediately recognized his mistake and corrected himself. "Yes, sir, I do know you spoke with Commodore Stoner yesterday, and that is why I'm here."

"So tell me who are you. What do you want?"

"Commodore, as you probably already know, I've been Admiral Eickhoff's aide for some time, and in good conscience, sir, I can't go on like this. I've been fighting the admiral on every detail for months. I'm sorry, but I must report what I know to higher authority. And a friend, the DESRON 12 Yeoman, said you'd be the one," Pew said, handing O'Toole the manila envelope containing his report.

"What's this?" O'Toole asked.

"My report, sir."

O'Toole opened the envelope far enough to read the address block and thumb through the pages. Looking at Pew, he said, "Lieutenant, I find it curious that you know my orders, know my travel arrangements, and are so willing to promptly betray your superior the second I arrive. How did you know what date to put on this report? How did you get this thirty-page report done in one day?"

This wasn't working the way Pew had expected. "But the information in the report is valuable. It has to be worth something," Pew said.

"To whom?"

"To the navy."

O'Toole snorted. He couldn't remember the last time he had truly lost his Irish temper. He couldn't help himself, but he kept his voice calm and soft. "Pew, I think I have your number, and I make it a point to avoid people like you. Please do both of us a favor and stay out of my sight. If I see you again, so help me, I'll have you court-martialed for impersonating an officer."

§

Lee braced himself against the damp, piercing wind blowing off the

207

Bay of Naples as he watched the empty liberty boat pull away from the quay wall. It was afternoon and the boats were running almost empty, but in another hour, the navy landing would be crowded with happy sailors coming ashore.

He was just about to jam his gloved hands deep into the pockets of his coat when he was startled by a deep voice coming from behind him.

"Excuse me. Mister Lee?"

Surprised to see a captain standing there, Lee turned and saluted.

"Yes, sir, I'm the landing officer. What can I do for you?"

The red-headed captain returned the salute and seemed equally startled as he looked down on the grinning young officer. "You're Lee?" he asked.

"Yes, sir."

"I'm sorry," O'Toole began. "From what I have heard about you, I thought you would be a lot taller. My name is O'Toole. I'd like to talk to you about the *Farnley*."

Lee's brow tightened, and his black eyes flashed at O'Toole.

"I'm sorry, Captain, I don't see what good that can do. I don't want to make a fuss or go outside of channels. You may not know, but I have a preliminary hearing next week on my request for a full court-martial. I just want to keep this clean."

O'Toole recognized the betrayed look in Lee's eyes and fought to maintain eye contact despite Lee's searing gaze. "I know. I just spent an hour listening to half of the Judge Advocate's office bitch about the case of heartburn you've given them. Not many junior officers have the guts to take on a fleet commander." O'Toole's voice contained a touch of admiration.

"I just want what's right," Lee replied.

"So I've guessed. Yesterday I was with Commodore Stoner, and he let me read copies of your engineering logs. They were interesting, to say the least. Tomorrow I'm taking the train to Genoa to meet the *Farnley*. I'd like to talk with you."

"I don't know what good it could do," Lee replied softly without altering his penetrating stare.

O'Toole could stand it no longer and looked away from Lee toward the harbor. With a sigh, he said, "I understand, and I don't blame you."

"Who are you, sir?" Lee asked.

O'Toole watched a blue and white fishing smack entering the harbor for a few seconds before answering, "I can't tell you, but I'm not connected with Admiral Eickhoff nor your court-martial proceedings."

The smack disappeared from sight, and O'Toole turned to look directly into Lee's eyes. "I already know a great deal about you. You're gutsy as well as unorthodox. You're resourceful. Some call that wrong. I call that Yankee ingenuity. I think you're a man of conviction, and from what I know now, you sound like a damn fine officer. You want what's right. I want the truth. In my book, that puts us on the same side. Where does that put us in your book?"

Lee's eyes probed O'Toole's face, then softened. His grin widened as he replied, "I think you already know the answer to that."

O'Toole smiled and tried to suppress a chuckle, then asked, "Where can we talk?"

"Over there out of the wind," Lee replied, pointing toward the white plywood shore patrol shack.

As both men walked toward the shelter, Lee said, "I just have one question, Captain."

"What's that?"

"Yankee ingenuity?"

THE GOD OF STORMS

November 1971, Tyrrhenian Sea
Operation Marathon: Day 522

Aboard the *Farnley*, Seaman Apprentice Michael Morrison had discovered why his new shipmates had been so kind and given him the lower bunk. The bunks were stacked five high, and two of the four men above him had gotten seasick last night. His great adventure had developed a few other kinks as well, like the kinks in his shoulders and legs. His small bunk wasn't made for his large, muscular frame, and he was now painfully aware why navy bunks were called racks.

He tried to work out the physical kinks while he balanced on the pitching deck trying to dress. That was tricky enough, but he also had to be careful not to elbow the shipmates dressing behind and on each side of him in the crowded compartment.

Morrison wasn't disappointed. His seafaring adventure had not let him down, and today was going to be another big day. The weather had been rough the past few days, but the way the ship was pounding, he could tell they were in a real storm. He could hear the pelting *shiishhh* of the water breaking over the decks, and everything was in a constant mixed motion of slow, graceful pitches and spasmodic, random lurches. It was his first storm, and since it was Sunday, he would have time to enjoy it.

Unfortunately, Morrison's stomach turned sour and felt as if it were trying to roll over in his gut. He decided to lie back down.

§

Meyers had been on the bridge for ten hours and hadn't slept for twenty. He turned his body diagonally in the captain's chair to wedge himself in firmly enough so he could sleep despite the storm.

The newness of command, the bad weather, and the night ops off the coast of Libya had exhausted him. Then having to deal with a badly demoralized crew had drained him emotionally. After the exercises were complete, the *Farnley* had sailed between Tunisia and Sicily and headed north for a two-day port visit in Genoa.

As soon as they entered the Tyrrhenian Sea, the weather went from bad to worse. The storm built constantly throughout the night, and at dawn the ship was rolling so badly, Meyers had ordered a westerly course to keep her bow into the seas. Just one-hundred miles east of Sardinia, he'd dropped the *Farnley*'s speed to five knots, so hopefully they wouldn't run out of ocean before they ran out of storm. It was still building, and he knew the best thing to do was to ride it out.

§

Biron saw the calm expression on Meyers' face and guessed he was napping. Biron hoped he was, but he could never tell with captains; they seemed to have transparent eyelids. Biron was impressed at how quickly and effectively Meyers had taken control of the *Farnley*. The metamorphosis from officer to captain had only taken a few days. Meyers was going to be one hell of a skipper.

Biron wondered what type of captain he would make. His new orders were as tempting as he feared they would be and included early promotion to lieutenant commander along with an assignment as commanding officer of a minesweeper. It was a small ship, but it was a command, and he would be called "Captain."

The orders had distressed Ann, and he could see she secretly hated the navy for its unscrupulous bribery. He also knew she was mad at him; he couldn't decide. He loved his family, and he loved the sea. The sea was his destiny, so how could he leave it? The love of his family was his most cherished gift. How could he choose between the two?

"What's the barometer doing?" Biron yelled over the pounding storm.

The quartermaster, hanging on the edge of the chart table, didn't look up. "Falling like a rock," he replied.

The bow mounted a huge roller, and the entire forward third of the *Farnley* became airborne off the back of the swell. Biron grabbed the gyro compass pedestal to brace himself as the bow started its graceful arching free fall into the trough. At the bottom, the downward force of the bow buried the forward third of the ship, submerging the entire forward deck.

The sky disappeared, and a menacing wall of gray water streaked with running white foam bore down on the bridge. Biron tightened his grip on the gyro compass. The *Farnley*'s forward motion drove the ship into the oncoming mountain. Within a second, the onrushing sea hit the forward superstructure like a roaring freight train. With a sickening shudder, the impact stole most of the *Farnley*'s forward motion, and the bridge windows went opaque with water. The buoyant hull started to rise, but not being able to overcome the weight of the swell, the entire hull flexed and bowed upward with the sickening groan of flexing metal.

The sea cleared the superstructure, and, lurching violently to starboard, the bow tore itself free of the sea, launching sheets of blistering white spay skyward to be caught by the sixty-knot wind and driven lashing into the bridge windows.

Biron looked at the compass heading. That last swell had pulled them twenty degrees off course. At five knots, they barely had rudder control, and he needed a bit more speed. Meyers was still asleep, but he would concur. "Indicate turns for seven knots," Biron called to the lee helmsman.

The deck pitched violently, and Biron looked at the bridge watch as each man grabbed a handhold to stay standing. He could see it in their eyes; they felt the same silent aching fear, the same dragging apprehension and realization that they were mortal men trespassing into an angry alien world. These were things unspoken, and every man knew that they were a breath away from death. Only skill, iron ship or not, kept the deadly sea at bay.

At times like these, the men became silent, and when they spoke, it was softly. All they wanted was to be alone with their thoughts of loved ones, hearth, home, safety, and dry land.

Biron looked at the row upon row of giant slate-gray swells coming toward them and tried to locate one that didn't line up with the others. There was a rogue swell out there somewhere. The swells had been running in sets of eight, with each set separated by a huge rogue swell coming from thirty to forty degrees to port.

Momentarily it had stopped raining, but in the distance, a new wall of low, smoke-black clouds like inverted black anvils marked the front of the next squall line. It's going to be a bad one, Biron thought.

§

Two hours later, Morrison decided lying down wasn't working anymore, so he got up to move around and retrieved the blue fishing jacket his mother had given him. The jacket was a perfect match for the standard blue uniform working jackets. His mother had turned every store in Santa Cruz upside down looking for it when she heard he was going to be stationed on a ship. She made him swear he would wear it, and since it was lightweight, comfortable, and buoyant, he assured her he would.

Morrison zipped the jacket and headed toward the mess decks. Moving around was helping, and he was feeling better already. The spirit of adventure was returning, and he wondered if he could find a spot where he could see the storm.

A few minutes later, he had his wish, and he snuck out on the main deck between swells just aft of the fair-weather bulkheads that shed most of the water from the waves. What he saw exceeded his wildest expectations. It was as if he were at the bottom of a huge canyon with greenish-gray roiling walls. Then suddenly, it was as if he were flying and all he could see was sky. The sight was too magnificent to describe. He ran to his locker and retrieved his Instamatic camera.

He waited inside the watertight door and listened to the ocean pound the ship and run off the decks while the ship plunged its way through two swells. Once certain that he knew the rhythm, he leapt out on deck and started snapping pictures. Sweeney had told him, "Never turn your back to the sea," but Morrison forgot and didn't see the approaching rogue swell.

Before Morrison knew what happened, he was submerged in a thundering, foaming churn of water. He was slammed against the side, then thrown upward. His head hit the overhang above him. He was stunned, but there was no pain. Helpless and tumbling wildly in the maelstrom, he lashed out in all directions, trying to grab onto something, anything. Upside down, he was thrown clear of the water and the ship. In the split second before he hit the water again, he sucked in a huge breath.

Morrison tried to understand what was happening. Somehow he understood the ship was above him. He felt the sea dragging him across the hard bottom of the ship. Only one thought came to his mind—*The screws.*

§

"Here you are, Captain. Made it fresh myself. Didn't spill a drop."

Meyers looked at the chubby bosun holding out a cup of coffee to him. "Thanks, Sweeney. I guess it pays to have a low center of gravity."

As Meyers took the cup from Sweeney, out of the corner of his eye, he saw the status board keeper go stiff and push the earpiece on his headset firmly against his ear.

Meyers was looking straight at him when he blurted, "Aft lookout reports man overboard. Starboard side. No. Port side. Wait. A wave washed him clean over the fantail."

Instantly, Meyers was on his feet. The suddenness of his movements spoke of urgency, but his voice was calm, slow, and rhythmic. "Which side? Port or starboard?" Meyers asked while throwing the binocular strap over his head.

"Port," the sailor replied.

"Sweeney, pass the word, then go to general quarters. Have the gunnery crews muster in after berthing. Bring us about, Mister Biron. Quartermaster, get our location to radio and send out a man overboard advisory," Meyers said while walking across the bridge. His voice sounded like he was ordering dinner in a restaurant.

Meyers undogged the bridge door, pushed the door open, and stepped onto the bridge wing. The door slammed shut behind him, but he could hear Sweeney's voice booming over the speakers, then the gonging of the general quarters klaxon. With his binoculars, he tried to scan the water aft, but he couldn't see the man in the confusing boiling sea.

A wave crashed over the bridge and threw him facedown onto the steel deck grating. Meyers grasped the grating with his fingers to keep from being washed away. When the water was gone, he was back to his feet searching for the man again. A voice yelled, "I've got him, Captain."

Meyers looked to see a signalman on the level above him pointing with one hand and clinging to the railing with the other. Meyers tried to follow the line indicated by the man's arm but couldn't find the man in the undulating seas, then he realized the ship hadn't changed course, and they were moving away from the man at two-hundred yards a minute. They were losing valuable time.

Sweeney swung the bridge door open and locked it into position. Meyers could clearly see the bridge now. Biron was hugging the gyro compass, his mouth agape and his eyes staring at the sea. The bridge crew had panicked, and men were yelling in disorganized frenzy.

Meyers stepped back on the bridge and headed for Biron.

"Man bears two-zero-five relative."

The quartermaster yelled, "At current water temperature survival time is six-zero minutes. In water time, two minutes."

"Engineering reports manned and ready."

"Man bears two-zero-zero relative."

"Plot has the man five-zero-zero yards astern."

"Break out the line guns, one aft, one on the signal bridge, and one here," Meyers said.

§

Biron watched wall after wall of water charging at him. He had to turn the ship, but timing was everything. One mistake, one minor miscalculation and they could capsize, and he would kill hundreds of men. He turned to look for Portalatin, but he wasn't there yet.

Biron swallowed, closed his eyes, and saw Ann and Sarah. Sarah's words echoed through his head. "Promise me you won't ever do anything that would kill people, please, Daddy. Promise me you won't get killed." The risks were too great. He had to wait until the time was exactly right to turn the ship.

"Mister Biron."

Biron turned to see the captain standing behind him. He was whispering, "I need you. If you wish, I can turn the ship for you, but that man out there needs your help."

In the back of his mind, Biron knew the storm was raging and men were yelling, but all he could hear was the captain's whispering voice. "Do you wish to turn the ship, or do you want me to talk you through it?"

"Captain, it's too dangerous."

"You're a damn good ship driver. That man, we, need you. Come on, I'll talk you through it. First, you need more rudder control. Bring the ship to all ahead flank."

Biron turned his head toward the lee helmsman and yelled, "All ahead flank." He realized he had to lean outward to see the lee helmsman, then it dawned on him. Meyers had positioned himself between him and the bridge crew. No one else could have seen or heard their conversation. It would just look like the captain was standing confidently behind his conning officer.

Biron swiveled his head so he could see the captain's face, and his confidence began to return. Meyers gave him a smiling wink. "I can handle this, Captain," Biron said.

"Helm ready, aye sir." It was Portalatin's voice.

Biron turned to acknowledge Portalatin, who as lay leader for Sunday service, was still in his dress blues.

Portalatin smiled, and Biron turned to the sea to take the measure of his adversary.

"Left full rudder. Port engine back full." Biron yelled, allowing his confidence to fill his voice.

Like a whip, Portalatin's arm lashed at the wheel.

The ship shuddered from the violent change of engine thrust and radical rudder command. Above the storm, he heard Meyers' soft, quiet voice again carrying its message clearly over the raging storm like a bell on Christmas night.

"Good to see we have the A-Team on the bridge. Belay the relative bearings to the man. I'll get that direct from the men on the signal bridge." Meyers sounded like he was ordering an after-dinner wine.

Biron tried to recall the procedures for storm rescue; he couldn't. He put it out of his mind; he had to get the ship turned around first.

The ship's bow swung sideways into a wall of water. The swell smashed the port side and blasted through the open bridge door, flooding the bridge and scattered men helter-skelter in its wake. The tidal wave subsided, and men scrambled back to their posts. The *Farnley* slid down

215

the back side of the swell, and wallowed dead in the trough when the next swell hit. Biron was about to yell that they weren't going to make it when Meyers yelled at him, "Steady on your rudder, and we'll squeak by this one."

The ship began its lifting rolling motion, heeling farther and farther over as she went. Biron watched the meter indicating the ship's roll swing past thirty, then forty degrees. It settled on the red line at forty-two, the point at which she would capsize. The ship stopped rolling. All motion stopped. For Biron, time stopped. He held his breath. The ship shuddered and trembled, trying to decide which way to go, then with a sliding, sinking motion, the *Farnley* started her slide down the back side of the swell and righted herself.

"Nice going, Biron," Meyers yelled from the bridge wing. "Next time, would you mind not cutting it so close?"

The bridge crew broke out in giddy laughter, and the men started breathing again.

The ship was swinging rapidly and was in danger of overshooting its turn. Biron steadied her on a reciprocal course and cut her speed. He made his way to the bridge wing and took a position beside the captain.

As both men scoured the horizon with their eyes trying to see the man, Biron said, "Captain, I don't know what the procedures are for a storm rescue. You have more experience. Maybe you should take it. The man doesn't have any chance in weather like this anyhow."

"No one has any experience at this," Meyers said casually. "There are no procedures. It's never been done before. The navy'll make us write the procedures after we get him back aboard."

Biron looked at his captain and knew somehow, someway, he was right. They would write the procedures, and they would get their shipmate back alive.

Biron looked at Meyers holding onto the rail, bracing himself against the storm, and sensed the magic; the captain's will, the crew's will, the captain's confidence, the crew's confidence were one, a powerful force committed without question against the deadly storm to save the life of a single man.

Sarah's words returned to Biron again. "Promise me you won't ever do anything that would kill people, please, Daddy." He finally understood. He understood Sarah would get her father back. He understood they would get their shipmate back.

"There he is. One-hundred yards to port." a voice yelled from the signal bridge. Simultaneously, the quartermaster announced calmly, "Sir, man in the water five minutes. Survival time remaining five-five minutes."

§

```
RTEEKYT RUKLKDTOTY 009682-EIEIEI-RAKDKESB.
ZNYEEEEE
R 05 0832Z DEC 71
FM     USS FARNLEY
TO         COMDESRON12
INFO       COMSIXTHFLT

SUBJ   MAN OVERBOARD
BT
CLASS  UNCLASS

UNIDENTIFIED MAN OVERBOARD 0827Z. SEA STATE EIGHT.
MAN IN SIGHT. RESCUE OPERATION UNDER WAY.

LAT 40 01 15 NORTH
LON 12 32 45 EAST

BT
N5867

NNNN
```

§

Chief Ross didn't need a window to see what was going on. They were trying to tear his engines apart, and by God, he was going to help them. It didn't matter; she could take anything they threw at her.

It had only taken the black gang two minutes to bring all four boilers to full power and another two to cross-connect the plant for full battle redundancy. When they threw the throttles wide open to answer the first flank bell, she was free of her mechanical harness, and her full seventy thousand horsepower exploded through the turbines.

The pitching motion of the sea became secondary. The sounds of the storm were drowned out. Every piece of machinery in the engine room roared in determined exertion. As the engine speed increased, the deafening howl increased, seemingly without limit. The engine room was electrified and trembled under the sudden release of power. Ross' thundering colossus had awakened, venting its fury through the turbines. The screws thrashed angrily at the sea.

The emergency back flank order on the port engine seemed as if it would tear the ship in two. Stucky had thrown the ahead throttle closed and opened the astern throttle while the shaft was still turning at over one hundred revolutions per minute. The deck heaved under the sudden reversal of power, and steam pipes the size of telephone poles flexed. The truck-sized turbine recoiled, sending shudders throughout the ship. The reduction gears screamed in ear-piercing, metal-tearing agony.

With the astern throttle half open, Stucky stopped, not knowing whether to close the valve or wait for the tremulous shaking to cease. "Jam it open, son. All the way. She can take it." Ross screamed.

The sudden change in the engine room had initially terrified Ross' young crew. Never before had they seen such power. Never before had they realized the fantastic power of the giant they tended. Yelling orders, Ross jumped up onto his bench and grabbed the main steam stop valve wheel to steady himself. He stood like a pillar, preventing collapse. Ross' crew drew strength from him, and he from them.

§

High above the storm on *America*'s flag bridge, Admiral Eickhoff was idling his way through some administrative message traffic when he was distracted by an aide who approached to hand him a message.

Eickhoff's stomach turned into a twisting painful knot. The *Farnley* seemed possessed by some sinister spirit bent upon his destruction, a spirit that made their captains go insane and commit suicide. Didn't Meyers know what his orders meant? After removing the unauthorized parts, the *Farnley* would never be able to survive a rescue attempt in treacherous sea conditions.

The *Farnley* would be lost with all hands. The board of inquiry would dig deep. Eickhoff knew he couldn't afford that. Everything would be open to investigation. He'd done many things the current aristocracy wouldn't understand, including his lie to Durham about safety and his orders to Meyers. Fear led to panic. His promotion was at risk, and the political leverage of Operation Marathon was slipping away. He couldn't afford to lose the *Farnley* now. He was so close. He had to stop Meyers.

§

```
RTEEKYT RUKLKDTOTY 009682-EIEIEI-RAKDKESB.
ZNYEEEEE
R 05 0845Z DEC 71
FM    COMSIXTHFLT
TO        USS FARNLEY

REF       A0 YOUR 05 0832Z DEC 71

SUBJ  MAN OVERBOARD
BT
CLASS  UNCLASS

SEA STATE INDICATED REF A INDICATES RESCUE
IMPOSSIBLE AND RISK TO SHIP SIGNIFICANT. DO NOT
REPEAT  DO NOT ATTEMPT RESCUE UNIDENTIFIED MAN
OVERBOARD 0827Z.

BT
N5957

NNNN
```

§

Buried in a torrent of water, Ensign Nat Hayes, helpless and on his back, tumbled across the deck like a leaf in the wind. He'd strapped himself into a safety harness used for working aloft and had tied a safety line to the back of the harness. With strong men holding the line in the aft deck house, he'd managed to rig two temporary safety lines on deck. They weren't much, but they were something to grab onto.

He'd been over the side three times already, but he wasn't counting. The men were keeping a tighter rein on the line now, and when the last wave decked him, they immediately began heaving him in. The water cleared from the deck, and Hayes scrambled to his feet. With the door locked open, the aft passageway was awash in six inches of water.

Another man was strapping on an identical harness. A phone talker had wedged himself into a corner, two more men wrestled a portable pump into position, and another thirty men sitting in the sloshing water, jammed shoulder to shoulder in the narrow passageway, coiled and uncoiled lines. If anyone else was going to be lost, the sea would have to pull all thirty men overboard with him.

"Bridge says we're coming down on the man now. Thirty feet to port," the phone talker yelled.

Hayes hadn't regained his bearings, but someone thrust a tethered life ring into his hands, and he turned to face the storm again. The ship jerked violently, throwing Hayes against the door combing and opening a gash above his left eye. Recoiling from the blow, Hayes fell backward on top of the line handlers. Hands came up, caught him, then pushed him back to his feet. Without a word, men paid line as Hayes made his way to the rail. Hayes caught sight of the man. It would be a long throw, and he would have to compensate for the wind. He would have to let the man pass his position, throw the ring as hard as he could, and hope the wind would blow it down on the man.

The man saw Hayes and raised one hand. Hayes thought he recognized Morrison, but he couldn't be sure. Covered with blood, the man's face was partially obscured by a large flap of skin hanging from his scalp. Hayes looked up the deck and gauged the foaming wall of water bearing down on him. The man slid past Hayes' position. He needed more time but wouldn't get it. Just before the wall of water hit him, Hayes let go of the railing and stood as straight as he could. Totally unprotected, he leaned over the railing and threw the life ring as hard as he could.

The wave threw Hayes against the deckhouse with such force, his organs and brain thudded in his body. Just as suddenly, it tore him away from the deckhouse and threw him toward the sea. A stanchion hit him in the gut, kicking all the air from his lungs. He somersaulted over the railing into the swirling water that sucked him deeper and deeper.

Thirty feet of rough half-inch hemp line tore through bleeding hands. Men screamed in agony, but no one let go. A chant went up. "Heave. Heave. Heave. Heave."

Stunned, Hayes fought to keep his mouth shut, but it was too late. Water caught in his lungs, and he coughed violently. Hayes felt the steady jerk on the line pulling him back to the surface. When his head broke water, Hayes coughed and frantically gasped for air. He twisted his head back and forth trying to find Morrison. The wind had blown the life ring almost forty feet past him.

§

"The man has been in the water one five-minutes. Survival time remaining: four-five minutes," the quartermaster yelled.

Biron had seen it. That was their third attempt to get close enough to Morrison to get a life ring to him. They finally got close enough to try, and the storm viciously denied success.

Biron knew the problems were enormous. He couldn't stop the ship or it would flounder in the seas. He'd tried coming at the man upwind and downwind. At slow speed, his rudder was useless.

If he got too close to Morrison, a wave could suck him under the ship and into the screws; too far away, and they couldn't reach him. "It's going to take blind luck to get him back, Captain. I have almost no rudder control at low speed in these seas," Biron yelled to Meyers.

"Screw the rudder; it's useless. Maneuver with the engines," Meyers yelled back.

"That's crazy, Captain, you'd have to use flank bells to have any hope at all."

"Then his only hope is for us to use flank bells, Biron. He's not giving up, and I'll be damned if we are," Meyers replied. "Take us around again, keeping him to port. This time let's see if we can keep her straight and let the wind blow us down on him."

Biron shouted engine orders while Meyers tried to find the man in the confusing gray sea.

"Captain, we just got a flash message from Sixth Fleet." Meyers turned to see the dry radioman standing beside him and took the clipboard with one hand while holding onto the rail with the other. Meyers looked at the message for several seconds.

"Any reply, Captain?" the radioman asked.

Meyers held the clipboard at arm's length until the wind caught it, then let go. It sailed out of sight before it hit the water.

"What was that?" Biron asked.

"Don't know. I lost the message." Then, to the waiting radioman, he said, "I don't have time for this now. Get another copy and bring it to me when this is over."

Smiling, the radioman replied, "Aye, sir."

"There he is off the starboard bow," a voice shouted from the signal bridge.

"Hard to starboard, Biron," Meyers yelled.

That attempt failed, as did the next.

§

Disgusted and mad at himself for taking a nap the previous afternoon, Durham gave up trying to fall back to sleep and switched on the TV, hoping he could find an early-morning news program. The secure phone rang. He picked it up halfway through the first ring.

"Sir, this is the watch officer. I have two messages on the *Farnley*, one she sent and the other sent to her from Sixth Fleet. I'm not sure they're important, but I thought you might want to know."

"Read them," Durham said, and by the time the man was done, Durham's mind had already formulated his response. He had for the moment forgotten his suspicion about the *Farnley*, but under no circumstances was he going to put up with what Eickhoff had done. No admiral, no one, was ever going to second-guess an on-scene commander; and no one, especially not an admiral in his navy, was going to tell a captain to abandon a crewman. It was against everything he'd ever learned and against everything he and his teachers stood for. *Not in my navy.*

There was nothing he could do for the *Farnley* crewman but pray; however, he could do something about Eickhoff.

Dispassionately, Durham asked, "Who's the next senior officer in the Mediterranean theater after Admiral Eickhoff?"

After a second, the response came. "A Captain Patrick O'Toole."

"Good," Durham began. "Patch me through to the senior duty officer in Naples."

When he was done, Durham hung up. *O'Toole will never forgive me.*

§

Ross had problems. The engines had taken more abuse in thirty minutes than they had taken in the previous thirty years. The engines were thrashing themselves to death, and leaks were springing up everywhere. Plumes of steam from pipe fittings strained past their breaking point filled the engine room with wet heat. Ross was playing a giant game of Chinese checkers ordering equipment isolated, fittings tightened, then equipment put back online.

Ross watched two men try to isolate the lube-oil pump. The work was difficult; they had to use both hands and were denied the luxury of hanging onto something solid. Their hands, already burned by steam or hot metal, were wrapped in rags; precious little protection against the hot fittings they were working on. The ship heaved hard to starboard. One man was thrown into the hot pump housing, the other thrown across the bilge like a toy. Both recovered and went back to work on the pump.

So far, Ross had counted eleven men injured or hurting in some way. They were all minor injuries, but Ross was concerned by the cumulative toll the injuries were taking. The toll would only get worse as physical fatigue slowly claimed his crew. He prayed they would get the man back soon.

§

"Man has been in the water three-five minutes. Survival time remaining: two-five minutes," the quartermaster yelled.

Meyers made his way across the bridge to the phone set near the captain's chair and put the phone to his ear. "Let me talk to Hayes," he said.

As Meyers stood talking with Hayes, his free arm bent back and forth at the elbow, indicating the ship's position as if Hayes could see it.

"Good, let's do it. It'll take us a few minutes to get in position. It's probably our last chance." Meyers concluded the conversation and headed back to the bridge wing to rejoin Biron.

"Man has been in the water four-zero minutes. Survival time remaining; two- zero minutes."

§

O'Toole fastened the leather buckle on his small weekender suitcase, then checked his small, boxish room at the BOQ to make sure he hadn't forgotten something. Before he left, he needed to stop by the operations center and send his preliminary report to Durham. There was no hurry since his train for Genoa wouldn't leave for another three hours and the taxi ride to the train station would only take thirty minutes. Still, O'Toole wanted the extra time; the combination of jet lag and lack of sleep had slowed him to about half speed.

He had read reams of paper over the last few days, but none were as interesting as Pew's report. He knew Pew's report, although well crafted, was little more than a cover-your-ass piece, but it provided inside background and supporting documents that pulled all the other pieces together.

Pew was another problem altogether. O'Toole had run into two officers like Pew before and had them both transferred to assignments where they couldn't hurt anybody. One he sent to a five-man communications station on the arctic circle, the other to the Mechanicsburg, PA supply depot, where he spent the remainder of his tour inventorying toilet paper and undergarments for enlisted WAVES, but Pew, being assigned to Sixth Fleet, wasn't his problem.

Tomorrow when he talked with Ross and Meyers in Genoa, his investigation would be complete. No matter what happened, he was sure Durham would make Eickhoff answer a long list of questions Eickhoff would have great difficulty answering, but O'Toole knew that wasn't his job. He just collected the facts. Durham would be the judge.

O'Toole reached the door when the phone rang. He thought for a second, then stepped back into the room and answered.

"Captain O'Toole?" O'Toole immediately recognized Pew's voice.

"Yes?" O'Toole let the displeasure of hearing from Pew fill his voice and was rewarded by a long, silent pause.

"Sir," Pew said finally, "this is Lieutenant Pew, the watch officer. We got an urgent call for you from Admiral Durham. He wants you to see some urgent message traffic we have on the *Farnley* and then call him back. I have a driver on the way to pick you up."

§

Fatigue was creeping in. Ross could see it. His men were moving slower. Heavy labor and heat didn't go together well, but they weren't giving up.

The throttlemen had the hardest time; constantly spinning the heavy throttle wheels open and closed quickly turned their arms to rubber. He'd taken a position between the throttles and was rotating throttlemen every few minutes, trying to keep them fresh.

Stucky, his young freckled face edged in grim determination and without its boyish glow, was back on the throttles again. "How much longer is this going to go on, Chief?" Stucky yelled so Ross could hear him.

"I think we're just starting. Seems we got a captain who didn't bother to read the book," Ross screamed back.

"What book?" Stucky asked, throwing the astern valve open.

Ross held the rail tight to steady him against the throbbing protest of the turbines.

"The one that says you can't charge hell with only a bucket of ice water," Ross yelled as he turned to see how the other throttleman was doing.

§

They were coming about again and were in the trough. A mountainous wave crashed down on the *Farnley* and bent her like a plastic comb. A man running down the main passageway above the engine room watched the ship flex until he couldn't see the far end of the three-foot-wide corridor. In one violent convulsion, the *Farnley* heeled over and snapped back like a spring to her normal position.

§

Ross' feet became airborne, but his tight grip on the railing kept him from flying across the deck. He looked down at the lower level. All of the men had been knocked off their feet. He turned back toward Stucky, but he'd disappeared. No one was manning the throttle.

§

Ensign Nat Hayes was ready. He'd stripped to his underwear and lashed himself back into the safety harness. Next he had put on two inflatable life jackets. The first one he put on normally, the outer one he put on backwards. In addition to the two deflated life jackets, he had three pieces of short, loose line tied to his harness. The shortest piece was only a foot long, and tied to its end was a spring-loaded snap hook.

With his eyes riveted on Morrison, he stood shivering on the deck. A man carefully coiled Hayes' safety line on his lap so it wouldn't get tangled in the sloshing water.

Hayes could see and hear the towering wave plummeting down on him. He was still too far away from Morrison. He wanted to wait another ten or fifteen seconds, but he couldn't. He dove headfirst over the side and into the torrentuous mountain of water.

A wall of water poured through the door into the deckhouse. Oblivious to the water, the man nearest the door concentrated on the line so it wouldn't get tangled. Three other men leaned into the onslaught and held him so he wouldn't be knocked over.

When Hayes came back to the surface, all he could see were mountains of moving, angry water. He spun around looking for the *Farnley*. She was gone.

§

"Get the stokes stretcher down here on the double." Ross yelled, tearing his shirt off.

Kneeling in the bilge next to Stucky, he carefully felt the arms and chest of the unconscious man. Satisfied no bones were broken, he lifted Stucky's head and pressed his shirt against the large gash across the back of Stucky's head.

"Hurry up. Get the corpsman down here." Ross yelled. Ross knew it was a miracle Stucky was still alive. The wave had thrown Stucky under the gauge board, and he'd fallen over twenty feet into the bilges. Ross couldn't remember how he'd gotten into the bilge.

Stucky opened his eyes and blinked for a second, then closed them. Ross grabbed the front of Stucky's shirt and shook him, yelling. "Son, Stucky, damn it, son, stay awake."

Stucky's eyes blinked open, and he tried to smile.

"That's it, son. Fight it. You gotta stay awake. You're a fighter, you can do it. You've gotta survive." Ross screamed.

Ross kept yelling at Stucky to stay awake while three other men placed him in the wire-mesh, form-fitting stretcher and strapped him in.

The men lifted the stretcher, and Ross stood. A sharp, jagged pain stabbed at his right ankle, and searing pain shot up the calf of his leg. The pain took Ross' breath away, and he collapsed onto the bloodstained, gleaming white bilge.

§

Startled by the sharp clap of plastic on plastic, Pew jumped and examined the phone until the ringing subsided from the phone's equally startled bells. O'Toole had slammed the phone back down on the cradle with such force, Pew couldn't believe the phone hadn't cracked like an egg.

O'Toole spun away from the counter in the communications center and scowled at the ceiling. "Balls."

Pew had listened intently to O'Toole's half of his conversation with Admiral Durham. O'Toole, who had done most of the talking, started with an amazingly accurate summary of Eickhoff's handling of the *Farnley*. Pew hadn't been able to discern a single word of opinion or judgment in O'Toole's brief summary. Then the conversation changed.

O'Toole became agitated and yelled, "No," and "Damn it, Ron," into the phone several times, then concluded with a "Yes, sir," before trying to demolish the phone.

The conversation had been strange and nothing like what Pew had expected. He guessed that sooner or later it would be over for Admiral Eickhoff, but he didn't know when or why. What really troubled him was that he had no idea of where he stood.

"What do we do next, sir?" Pew asked.

"We? I'm going to the *America*. You get me a helicopter ASAP and a secure radio link to the *America*'s captain."

"Why?" Pew asked, hoping O'Toole would let him know what was afoot.

"'Cause, damn it, when you're in command, you command."

§

Hayes was disoriented in the heavy seas. He'd frantically spun around several times, tangling himself in the safety line trying to find either the *Farnley* or Morrison, but ever-moving mountains of water blocked his view. Without a reference point, he didn't know which way to swim to find Morrison. He knew he would have to think this out.

From his water-level vantage point, the *Farnley* would only be visible for a few seconds at a time as she rose and fell from peak to trough. Spinning around was counterproductive.

Carefully, he untangled the safety line, turned in the direction he thought the *Farnley* would be, and waited. Staying steady in the heavy seas was almost impossible. His body was shoved up, down, forward, and backward as the sea tossed him about. After what seemed an eternity, he heard a sickening sucking sound behind him.

Hayes turned and watched the port side of the *Farnley*'s airborne stern, her half-exposed screws chopping at the surface, fall back into the sea not ten feet from him.

§

Meyers and Biron caught a glimpse of Hayes as the surge of water from the falling stern threw him clear of the ship. "He's lost it. He can't tell where he is," Biron yelled.

Meyers thought for a second, then grabbed Sweeney's arm. "Get me a line gun, then stand by the ship's whistle." Then to Biron he said, "Hold your position. You're sliding past them."

§

Biron knew it. He was in a box. With Hayes in the water, he couldn't go around again. If he stopped his forward motion, he would lose control; he had to keep the bow into the sea. The only option was unthinkable, impossible; ships weren't designed for it, especially not in these seas. Backing down was madness.

"Man in the water five-five minutes. Survival time remaining five minutes.

"All back flank," he ordered.

§

Meyers took the shotgun-like line gun from Sweeney, checked the throwing ball and the large metal rod attached to it. Satisfied, he inserted the rod into the barrel and checked that the line was safely coiled on deck. Shouldering the gun, he guessed the windage and readjusted his aim when he got a glimpse of Morrison. With his peripheral vision, he watched for Hayes; the men couldn't be more than forty feet apart. When the men were abeam, he shouted, "Lay on the whistle, Sweeney."

Meyers held his aim steady, then in the split second both men were visible, pulled the trigger.

§

Hayes had to get to Morrison quick. He was shivering and he sensed he was losing muscle control. Hypothermia was setting in. *How do I do this?* Occasionally, he caught a glimpse of the *Farnley*, but he hadn't been able to locate Morrison. He heard a deep-throated sound barely audible over the wind to his right and turned to see what it was. In an instant, the *Farnley* appeared, there was a white puff of smoke from the bridge wing, and a thin red line streaked through the air toward him. He watched the wind curve the line and drive the large white throwing ball into the sea. He realized they weren't shooting at him; they were pointing. He kicked with his legs and began swimming as hard as he could toward the line.

After swimming what he thought was twenty feet, Hayes came up for air. On the peak of one of the swells, he saw a head and started swimming uphill toward it. When he came up for air again, he was on top of the swell and Morrison was in the valley. In a frantic effort, Hayes plunged his head back into the sea and swam downhill as fast as he could. He tuned his senses to the motion of the sea. When the sea was lifting him, rather than swim uphill, he rested. At the crest, he spotted Morrison and plunged ahead, tearing at the sea with his arms.

Each time he tried to swim faster, but his strength was diminishing and his arms were growing heavy. Spray lashed at his face when he came up for air. Water filled his mouth and caught in his lungs. He fought the urge to cough and kept forcing his arms through the sea.

He hit something. It was Morrison's shoulder. Hayes lifted his head and spun the fighting man toward him. Morrison had a large gash across his forehead and was still bleeding. Arms thrashing, Morrison kept fighting the sea and Hayes.

Hayes screamed at him, "Hey, the food isn't that bad." Hayes felt foolish for saying that, but it had the desired effect. He saw a faint glimmer of recognition in Morrison's unfocused eyes.

Morrison coughed weakly and said something that Hayes couldn't hear, then Morrison reached for him like a baby and passively submitted to Hayes' care.

Hayes clamped the limp body to him with one arm and rolled over onto his back, sending both men under the surface. With the other hand, he snapped the eye hook over Morrison's belt. Satisfied the sea couldn't separate them, he twisted their bodies upright. Hayes pulled the outer life jacket over his head and placed it over Morrison. After snapping the loose straps around Morrison's chest, he yanked the lanyards that automatically inflated both their vests.

There was a tug on the safety line pulling him through the sea, but he ignored it. With the two remaining lines, he lashed their bodies together. With the last knot secure, he looked back at Morrison's flaccid face. "We got you now," Hayes said, wondering if Morrison heard him.

Hayes wrapped his arms around Morrison, hugging him tightly in a wrestler's grip. He had no idea where the *Farnley* was, but the reassuring steady tug, tug, tug of the safety line told him they were safe. The sea couldn't have him. He was one of them. They had him now.

§

```
RTEEKYT RUEKLEJCXY 158254-EIEIEI-RAMNDESB.
SNEERER
R 05 0942Z DEC 71
FM    USS FARNLEY
TO       COMDESRON12
INFO     COMSIXTHFLT

REF      A⓪ MY 05 0832Z DEC 71
SUBJ     SIT REP MAN OVERBOARD
BT
CLASS UNCLASS

MAN OVERBOARD REF A. IDENTIFIED AS F.A. MORRISON
MICHAEL M. USN ⓪689 24 5862⓪  RESCUED 0925Z.

SAME NAMED MAN CONDITION CRITICAL  HYPOTHERMIA
SEVERE LACERATIONS HEAD  LEFT SHOULDER  LEFT LEG.
SKULL FRACTURE PROBABLE. EMERGENCY SURGERY UNDER WAY
BY SHIP'S CORPSMAN.

INJURIES MMCM ROSS  JAMES  A. USN ⓪291 48 2398⓪
BROKEN ANKLE. MM3 STUCKY  ROBERT  C. USN ⓪868 37
9677⓪ CONCUSSION  SEVERE HEAD LACERATION. NUMEROUS
OTHER MINOR INJURIES. FULL EXTENT UNKNOWN. WILL
ADVISE.

PROCEEDING CAGLIARI. REQUEST MEDICAL EVAC AND
ASSISTANCE NEUROSURGEON.

WILL ADVISE ETA.

LAT 40 01 15 NORTH
LON 12 32 45 EAST
COURSE 272
SPEED 7

BT
N4586
```

§

The *America*'s captain was on the radio with O'Toole for less than two minutes, and now he had two hours of work to do in addition to making preparations for receiving a helicopter on a damnable day like today. It wasn't until after he notified flight operations that he made the connection.

He'd briefly met O'Toole years ago, and the stories he had heard painted O'Toole as a man with a blunt bow and a deep draft who cut a wide, straight wake. The conversation with O'Toole gave no clue where he was headed, but it was clear he was coming aboard the *America* at flank speed.

He was waiting for O'Toole on the rain-swept flight deck. As soon as O'Toole stepped from the helicopter, it was a chase to keep up with him.

Upon reaching flag quarters, O'Toole blew past the first marine guard. The second almost got run over as he tried to intervene. O'Toole

Larry Laswell

stopped and said, "Better get a security detail up here on the double. You're going to need reinforcements," before bolting through the door and charging Admiral Eickhoff's desk.

Admiral Eickhoff's face went blank at the sight of O'Toole. "What—" he blurted.

"Three things," O'Toole began, leaning over Eickhoff's desk so they were at equal eye level. "First, I just pulled the *Farnley* out of Operation Marathon."

Eickhoff jumped to his feet. "You can't do that. She's assigned to Sixth Fleet. You don't have the authority."

"Don't insult my intelligence, and don't make me repeat myself. Second, Admiral Durham wants you back in Washington within forty-eight hours. I think he wants to talk to you over a long green table with no coffee cups or ashtrays at your end."

Eickhoff didn't seem to hear O'Toole's last words due to the commotion caused by five marines dressed in battle fatigues storming through the door, M-16s at the ready.

"What is the meaning of this outrage?" Eickhoff screamed.

"Tell your men to stand at ease," O'Toole said to the lieutenant leading the squad.

O'Toole continued without interruption. "Three, there's a chopper leaving in fifteen minutes. I want your ass off my flagship. Start packing. Be on it."

Eickhoff took several deep breaths that seemed to deepen the redness in his face. He started to speak, then stopped. After a second, he looked quizzically at O'Toole. "Your flagship?"

O'Toole nodded.

"You can't do that. You're only a captain. You're overstepping your bounds, O'Toole. You'll pay."

"Yes he can, and no he isn't," came a voice near the door. The Sixth Fleet chief of staff pushed his way through the line of marines.

Turning to his former chief of staff, Eickhoff asked, "What in the hell's going on here?"

The officer, while trying to contain a smile, casually tossed the messages onto the desk and said, "We just got the orders from the CNO. O'Toole has been appointed to the temporary rank of rear admiral, and he's to relieve you immediately."

Eickhoff rocked back on his heels and stepped back from the desk a bit. "You . . . you and Durham plotted this to get me. It won't work because I have friends on Capitol Hill who will make mincemeat out of you two."

"You're wasting time, Admiral," O'Toole began. "If you don't get

230

packing, so help me, I'll stuff you into a duffel, label it third class M-A-L-E, and ship your butt home. Or maybe I should make you swim back like you wanted that boy on the *Farnley* to do."

"You may have been promoted to rear admiral, but I still have seniority. You can't order me around."

"Excuse me, Admiral Eickhoff," the chief of staff said while pointing to messages on the desk, "but there are three messages sent one minute apart. The first appoints O'Toole to rear admiral, the second relieves you of command, and the third promotes Rear Admiral O'Toole to vice admiral. He outranks you, sir." The chief-of-staff was smiling.

"What?" O'Toole bellowed, snatching the message forms. "I could've handled this."

The chief of staff addressed O'Toole. "Welcome to Sixth Fleet, Admiral. Congratulations, congratulations, and congratulations."

O'Toole looked at the chief-of-staff for a long second, then turned a complete three-sixty to take in the entire quarters complex. With a look of dismay, O'Toole turned toward his chief-of-staff and said, "Please don't call me admiral. It's only temporary." Then to the marine officer he said, "Are you familiar with the regulations regarding the handling of senior officers as prisoners?"

"Yes, sir."

"Then ignore them. I want him," O'Toole said, pointing at Eickhoff, "on the chopper when it leaves. I don't care how. Stuff him into a fart sack, carry him, put him in irons, whatever it takes. Do you understand?"

"Yes, sir."

O'Toole motioned toward the door and ushered everyone out except Eickhoff and the marines. Just as O'Toole was about to shut the door behind him, Eickhoff screamed at the marines to leave. O'Toole paused and watched the marines snap to attention.

The officer stepped forward and addressed Eickhoff. "It will take us two minutes to get to the flight deck, Admiral. You have twelve minutes left. Do you need assistance packing?"

O'Toole clicked the door shut and said, "Damned adequate lot, those marines."

§

```
RTEJJYT RKJKKEWOTY 0458567-IEIEI-RKJJCESB.
ZYYEEEEE
R 05 1015Z DEC 71
FM    COMSIXTHFLT
TO        USS FARNLEY
REF       A⦵ YOUR 05 0932Z DEC 71

SUBJ  WELL DONE

BT

CLASS  UNCLASS

CAN DO MEDICAL ASSISTANCE REQUESTED REF A. MOVEMENT
CAGLIARI APPROVED.

ADVISE MEN OF FARNLEY MY DEEPEST ADMIRATION THEIR
MOST ADEQUATE PERFORMANCE.

MY PRAYERS ARE WITH YOU. WISH I WAS ABOARD. GOD'S
SPEED. O'TOOLE.

BT
N4761

NNNN
```

EAGLE OF THE SEA

December 1971, Tyrrhenian Sea, 132 miles East-northeast of Cagliari, Sardinia
Operation Marathon: Day 522

With the ship still at general quarters, Biron had brought the bow back into the sea, and she was proceeding toward Sardinia at seven knots. It was the smoothest ride they could give the corpsman who was trying to stitch up Morrison's wounds. Morrison had lost a lot of blood, and thirty blood donors were lined up outside the wardroom.

On the bridge, everything was soaked, and men were wet and cold, but pride had pushed broad smiles out through the shivers. Replacements would be up shortly to give the bridge crew a chance to warm up and change into dry clothes. Biron knew the crew thought the battle was won, but it was only half over.

He'd looked at the charts. Their situation was hopeless. They were dead center between Naples, Rome, Cagliari, Obia, and Palermo. With the heavy seas, there was no way they could make any port by nightfall, and entering any port at night, or attempting a helicopter rescue, would be suicide in these seas. He couldn't figure out why Meyers chose Cagliari as their port. The harbor entrance was treacherous even in good weather. Perhaps the storm would blow over by dawn. He hoped Morrison could hold on that long.

Dry, fresh replacements for the bridge crew were straggling onto the bridge when Meyers stormed back through the door and yelled at Biron, "Bring us to twenty-five knots, course two-six-zero."

Biron looked at the fierce storm and in disbelief said, "Captain, she can't take it at that speed. These seas will break her apart."

Meyers, looking at Biron, said in a calm voice, "The corpsman says we have to get Morrison into surgery in no less than twelve hours. We only have six hours of daylight left, and we have to be in Cagliari by then. The storm is coming from the west. If we hug the shore, we should be able to stay in the lee of the land; then we can make some time. Besides they built our lady at Bath Iron Works. Back then they built

233

ships that were more like floating tanks. Your speed is twenty-five knots, Mister Biron."

§

Like it or not, O'Toole resigned himself to being an admiral temporarily and turned his efforts to fulfilling the responsibilities he'd been given. He returned to the Naples air base and set up a temporary office. His desk was cluttered with intelligence reports, political evaluations, ship schedules, and background information. As he scanned the material, he listened to Pew babble on about all the problems he was having lining up aircraft and finding a neurosurgeon. Pew was now his problem; not a totally unpleasant thought.

In the stack of paper, O'Toole had run across a routine administrative message from CINCLANTFLT advising ships returning to Norfolk of the scheduled sewer repair. Major sections of the base would be inaccessible. *Pee-yoo.* There was no time like the present.

"Pew," O'Toole began in a friendly voice, "I believe the navy should use the talents of its men to full advantage, and I think you're being underutilized. You seem like a man who is good at making connections, a man who would be good at cleaning up little stinks. I also think you're a man of ultimate discretion who would work well underground to help clean up little messes that admirals might make. Is that a fair assessment?"

"Well, that depends on what you have in mind."

"Can't tell you much, don't really know much about it, but the position is on the staff of CINCLANTFLT. It's an underground operation, and if you do a good job, every senior officer in Norfolk will be beholden to you."

"A fixer? Clean thing ups, make the right connections, and make sure everything is smoothed over? Reporting to CINCLANTFLT?" Pew asked.

"Exactly," O'Toole smiled, then continued, "If you want the job, I'll make a few calls, and I'm sure it's yours."

Pew nodded, obviously not believing his luck.

"Good. I'll make the arrangements," O'Toole said, widening his grin. "You'll have orders within the week."

The next order of business was Lee. "Speaking of orders, find Mr. Lee and get him in here. I'm cutting him new orders and transferring him back to the *Farnley.*

§

Biron had thought it would be headlong suicide, like the charge of the

234

Light Brigade. With unimaginable ferocity, the sea threw volley upon volley of waves at them, but with bone-crunching determination, the *Farnley* kept charging through the seas. It seemed the bow was airborne most of the time. Each wave she hit exploded with a teeth-jarring thud, then she would charge forward into the next one. It was impossible to see what was going on. The windows were constantly covered with a wave or spray. His only guide was the radar that showed the Sardinia coast twenty miles ahead.

Meyers was standing nearby, hanging onto the steel dogs that secured the door. Sitting down was impossible. Every loose object on the bridge had been removed because they became missiles as soon as they had reached twenty-five knots. There was nothing Biron could do but hang on and try not to bite his tongue off.

For now, Biron knew he was just along for the ride. Everything was up to Portalatin's skill and long, muscular arms. As he watched Portalatin whip the wheel from side to side, he remembered that Portalatin's skill as a helmsman was partly an acquired skill and partly a gift. Few men had the physique to do what he was doing.

Biron knew he had gifts as well; gifts for leadership and gifts for ship handling. It was strange, but somehow he'd been given the gift to understand ships, currents, wind, thrust, and maneuver to a depth and extent few others had. What others worked at and studied for years was intuitive to him. It was easy, he did it well, and he loved doing it, but the gift misled him, or maybe he misled himself, or perhaps the poetry of the sea seduced him; now he understood that a gift does not make a calling.

Captains were men called to greatness. These were men you could trust your life to, men you would fight and die for because these were men willing to die for you and for what they believed.

Initially he couldn't find the courage to turn the ship because of the danger, not for himself but for the safety of Sarah's father. He'd promised her. She was more important to him than anything else. He knew that now, and he knew he didn't have the gift to become captain and would never be able to make split-second, life-and-death decisions the office demanded. Sarah was his gift, and she would get her father back full time.

Biron checked the radar screen. They were fifteen miles from the coast and perhaps thirteen to calm water.

The spray covering the windows went dark, then black. The ship shuddered. In mid-thrust through a wave, all forward motion stopped. It felt as if the *Farnley* had run into a solid wall. The impact threw Biron over the top of the radar set. The bridge windows exploded inward with a thunderclap. Thousands of gallons of water shot through the openings, flooding the bridge.

Stunned, Biron picked himself up. Standing in almost two feet of water, he checked himself over. To his amazement, he wasn't hurt. The other men were up and wading back to their posts. Meyers still clung to the bridge door. "Captain, we have to slow down," Biron pleaded.

"We're already wet; just a few more minutes," Meyers said to Biron, then to Sweeney, "Tell the cooks to break out the battle rations for the crew. We'll be in calm water shortly."

§

The camouflaged DC-3, her engines idling, waited on the tarmac at the Naples NATO air base. Lieutenant Pew took a position directly behind O'Toole and Lee as they waited for the F-15A Air Force Eagle taxiing toward them. The fighter's canopy slid open, and the craft came to a stop. When the two Pratt & Whitney engines shut down, the pilot saw O'Toole, smiled, and gave him a happy salute. The pilot looked over his shoulder at the man riding in the backseat and said something to him. The pilot looked back at O'Toole and laughed, pointing to the backseat with his thumb.

Slowly the figure in the backseat emerged and climbed out of the plane. Once on the ground, a pale middle-aged man, unaccustomed to traveling at Mach 2.5, gingerly stepped away from the craft as if he were afraid the ground would betray him and not be there when he lowered his foot. Dressed in white shorts and white pullover shirt, the man was comfortably dressed for an afternoon of indoor tennis. In his left hand he held a tennis racket and a barf bag.

When Pew saw the man, his jaw dropped, and he retreated toward the waiting DC-3. O'Toole's face showed no emotion as the jet's engines roared back to life and the jet taxied away, leaving its pale, bewildered passenger behind.

The would-be tennis player walked up to O'Toole, and as he began to extend his hand in welcome, O'Toole asked, "Who are you?"

The tennis player shook O'Toole's hand and replied, "Why, I'm the doctor you asked for."

The softness returned to O'Toole's voice. "I know that, but who are you?"

The tennis player tried to hold his left-hand cargo a bit lower so it wouldn't be so obvious. "Colonel Groomer, NATO Hospital, Wiesbaden. I'm sorry about my appearance. I was just starting a match when this helicopter—"

"Surgeon?" O'Toole queried.

"I'm chief of surgery at Wiesbaden," Groomer offered.

"Neurosurgeon?"

"Yes, that's my specialty."

O'Toole smiled. "That's adequate. Let's go."

§

As soon as they were in the lee of the Sardinia coast, Meyers had turned the *Farnley* south toward Cagliari. They had rung up flank speed and told the engine room to make best speed. With the bridge windows out, the rain and cold wind reached every corner of the bridge and quickly numbed the limbs of the bridge crew.

After he was sure that the bridge crew had been given a chance to warm up and change into dry clothes, he went below and did the same. By the time he'd returned to the bridge, Sweeney had found a towel and dried off his captain's chair. Someone else had a hot cup of coffee waiting for him. These small tokens of approbation embarrassed Meyers, but he accepted them graciously.

It felt good to sit again. The ship was riding better now in the calmer seas. The seas were choppy, but there was no swell. The ship's ride reminded him of the time when, as a boy, he had sat on top of a lopsided washing machine during the spin cycle. The rough ride came only partly from the sea but mostly from the sheer force of the *Farnley*'s engines.

He couldn't believe what the *Farnley* had been through. She was a great ship, and he was proud of the crew. He was afraid that the violent maneuvering they did during the rescue would have torn her guts out. Ross had done one hell of a job.

Meyers thought that if Morrison owed his life to anyone, he owed it to Lee. The old *Farnley* would never have held up. He had to talk to Stoner about that and the ten unanswered letters he'd sent demanding action on past-due parts requisitions.

§

Biron stood shoulder to shoulder with the quartermaster examining the Cagliari harbor chart. Getting through the breakwater was going to be hell. They would have to make a one-eighty turn to enter the narrow and twisted breakwater, then execute an S-turn to enter the harbor. If they went in too fast, they would never make the turns. Too slow and they would lose rudder control and be blown into the breakwater.

Any conning officer who could maneuver their ship into Cagliari under these conditions would become a legend to the crew. A crew's *esprit de corps* centered on the skill of their captain. Biron knew he could bring the ship in, but he didn't deserve this victory lap. This legend belonged to his captain.

§

Ross had refused to leave his engine room, so the corpsman splinted his ankle and offered painkillers, which Ross refused. For the past several hours, he'd clung to his white bench and waited for this moment. He ignored the pain in his ankle; his ship and his men needed him.

The *Farnley* was running wide open and making forty-two knots. He watched his men move about the cavernous engine room in their blue uniforms against the blinding white background. The throttles were full open, her reins released.

She was his thoroughbred in full thunderous gallop, a sound he hadn't heard in almost thirty years. The cavernous engine room trembled from the white-hot steam exploding through the turbines. The sound filled the deck, his bench, the air, and his chest. The sound, the noise, the raw power possessed everything, and everything shook from the roar so deep that it couldn't be heard, only felt.

The men communicated with hand signals and raised their hands in a triumphant circular motion. Ross was proud of them. They had come through an experience most men could never imagine. Someday his men would tell their story to their wide-eyed children gathered at their feet. The children would listen, sharing a moment of greatness, and make it their own. They would know the *Farnley* was a great ship. That's the way it should be. *This is screaming steaming.*

§

Meyers cursed himself for sitting down. His tired muscles had relaxed as his nerves unwound. His body felt like it weighed a ton, and he had to fight just to stay awake. He tried to remember the last time he slept. He couldn't.

Every time he turned around, Sweeney would be there, belly hanging out, to hand him another cup of coffee. He gladly accepted the hot coffee not only for the caffeine and warmth but for the fluid. Every muscle in his body hurt, and every movement brought a sharp, painful muscle spasm. He was also extremely thirsty and guessed he'd become dehydrated.

The sea was a dark gray, and the choppy waves were trimmed with white foam. The sky was a featureless, uniform smear of gray. In the evening shadows, he could see a few white buildings along the coast dulled by the relentless gray of the day. However, his eyes were fixed on a low black line between the sky and sea jutting from the shore. It was the seawall at Cagliari.

In a few hours, he'd be able to sleep. All he had to do was get the ship to the pier first. The Cagliari harbor entrance was tricky, and with the current conditions, it would take some bold maneuvering. Biron could handle it and deserved the opportunity to try.

"Captain?"

Meyers turned, expecting to see Sweeney holding another mug of coffee. It was Biron.

"Yes?" Meyers replied.

"Do you want to take her in, Captain?" Biron asked.

The way Biron said it, it wasn't a question, but a request. Meyers was too tired and his muscles ached, but as he started to decline, he realized everyone on the bridge was looking at him. He'd never experienced a situation like this. Every face radiated pride, confidence, and hope. Every eye was on him, pleading, imploring him to say yes. He accepted their command, and his fatigue dissolved as he jumped out of his chair.

Without a word from him, Biron yelled to the bridge watch, "The captain has the con," and the age-old ritual began.

Meyers called out to his men, "This is the Captain. I have the con."

The quartermaster scribbled in his log and yelled, "The log shows the Captain has the con."

"Captain, my head is two-eight-zero," Portalatin called out.

"More coffee, Captain?" Sweeney asked.

§

O'Toole stood near the edge of the windy pier in the protected Cagliari harbor next to Lee. A half mile from where he stood, huge rollers pounded the seawall. As each swell hit the riprap wall, hundred-foot-high sheets of water like giant hands shot into the air, trying to claw their way into the safe harbor.

In the semidarkness, O'Toole strained his eyes for a glimpse of the *Farnley* as she approached from the east. As her bow emerged from behind the high bluff, he shouted to the other men huddled in the ambulance and the half-dozen Italian pier workers.

Pew ran up to O'Toole and offered him a set of binoculars. "Don't need 'em. I can see."

The *Farnley* cut through the seawall opening and swung toward the pier. After a second, Pew blurted, "My God, Admiral, she has to be doing twenty knots. You can't do that. She's coming too fast."

"Fifteen knots, and who says?" O'Toole corrected.

The doctor and the corpsman from Naples joined O'Toole.

Despite the bad light, O'Toole's sharp eyes scanned the *Farnley* as she bore directly down on their position. He could only imagine what she'd been through. The gun mount sat askew on the forward deck. Except for the anchor chains, the fo'c'scle had been swept completely clean. All the railings and stanchions were gone. Torn metal mounting pads on the superstructure showed where the storage lockers had been. The pounding seas had stripped most of the paint away from her bow and superstructure. All the bridge windows were gone, and the railings around the signal bridge had been bent back like twigs. Her signal flags held by taut, springy lines snapped back and forth in the wind.

From nowhere, a dozen men appeared on her forward deck and ran back and forth, laying out mooring lines. The activity prompted Pew to put the binoculars to his eyes. After a second, he said in disgust, "Admiral, she's a rusty wreck. It's going to take a lot of work to square her away."

O'Toole's chest swelled to the point he thought his shirt buttons were going to pop. "You're wrong Lieutenant, she's magnificent," O'Toole replied.

A strange mix of nostalgia and grief tempered his pride. Many years ago, she had been his first command, and he had been her first skipper. He had seen her carry battle scars much deeper than those he saw now, but today no courageous young men had perished on her sacred decks; thankfully, there was no 'Butcher Bill' to pay. Generations of sailors had guarded her honor and cherished her legacy. Her spirit and the steel of her crew had not changed since before the battle of Mujatto Gulf. Right here, right now, O'Toole could imagine no greater honor than the chance to walk her decks again.

"I think I've finally got my rusty barge," O'Toole said, smiling. "I'm shifting my flag to the *Farnley*."

Pew looked stunned. "If I may speak freely, sir," Pew began, remembering not to say the A-word, "I don't think that's wise. She's a disgrace to the fleet. Just look at her."

O'Toole didn't move but responded, "The only thing that would disgrace the fleet is not honoring her with the flag."

Pew persisted. "But she's small, cramped, and old. You wouldn't be comfortable. There wouldn't be room for your staff. It's unheard of. An old destroyer as fleet flagship. You're putting Admiral Durham in a difficult position."

"Exactly," smiled O'Toole. "It's my fleet, and she's my flagship. Anyhow, Durham promised me it's only temporary. By the way, Pew, you won't be inconvenienced at all. I'm sending you back with the surgeon and the injured. It wouldn't be safe for you aboard the *Farnley*."

The *Farnley*'s bow was aimed directly at the spot where O'Toole stood and still showed no sign of slowing down. O'Toole fell silent and listened as the wind carried the robust baritone rumble of her engines to his ears.

Pew and the ambulance drivers started to back away from the edge of the pier. The *Farnley* still kept coming. After a few backward steps, the men turned and jogged back to the ambulance. O'Toole came to attention and took one step forward so his toes just hung over the edge of the pier.

The *Farnley* was close now, and O'Toole looked at the cluster of men standing on the starboard bridge wing. None of the men wore hats, and all were dressed in olive-drab foul weather jackets. Instantly, he located the one he was looking for; a blind man could see it. O'Toole watched his man. The man's head moved slightly, and all other men on the bridge wing reacted. The rumble of the engines paused for a second with an airy whooshing sound, then resumed in a guttural growl as the engines backed down with authority.

The translucent smoke from her stacks shot straight into the air and seemed unaffected by the wind. The ship slowed rapidly, and the bow swung smartly to port. With the ship parallel to the pier, the man O'Toole had been watching moved his head again, and the engines stopped. Line handlers threw lines the last five feet to the pier. O'Toole saluted the *Farnley,* her crew and man on the bridge. He didn't have to ask who the man was; he was a singular man the crew called— Captain.

§

Stucky had been awake through most of it. The DC-3 was gaining altitude, and the doctor had gone forward to radio instructions to Naples. Chief Ross was in a fold-down canvas bunk above him, snoring like an asthmatic boiler. The corpsman from Naples checked Morrison's pulse again.

Stucky was groggy, and there was a sharp, burning pain across the back of his head. They hadn't let him walk to the ambulance or the plane, and treated him like he was really hurt or something. The doctor said he would have to stay in Naples for a few days' observation, so he got comfortable under the covers of his stretcher and submitted quietly to the indignity of being carried off his ship. Next to the tight bandage wrapped around his head, he disliked being taken off the *Farnley* most.

When they loaded Ross into the ambulance at the pier, Stucky was shocked. Not knowing Ross was injured, he asked the corpsman what happened. The corpsman simply replied, "Broke his ankle somehow. Couldn't get him to leave the engine room, so the doctor gave him a shot for the pain. Actually, he gave him enough Demerol to KO an elephant. He'll be in the hospital with a cast on his leg before he wakes up."

Stucky began laughing, but each laugh brought with it a heavy, pounding pain in the back of his head. He swallowed his laughter.

The corpsman finished checking Morrison's pulse and wrote

something on a clipboard. "Is he going to be all right?" Stucky asked.

"He's in pretty bad shape now," the corpsman began as he checked the white bandage that encircled Morrison's head, "but the doctor said if we can get him into surgery in the next two hours, he'll be good as new in a couple of months."

Satisfied Morrison was okay, the corpsman turned to Stucky and asked, "What the heck happened to you guys? Your ship's a wreck. Looks like you've been through World War Three."

Stucky's arm slid off of his chest, slipped down to his side, and grasped the gift Ross had given him. It was Stucky's prize possession.

Holding Ross' old, battered screwdriver tight, Stucky tried to put his thoughts together as he spoke.

"The *Farnley*'s a fighter . . ."

"We never gave up . . ."

"We had to get Morrison back . . ."

"Ya see, that's the deal."

ENDNOTE

In 1974, the men of the USS *William M. Wood* (DD-715) completed the first heavy-storm rescue of a man overboard in naval history. The rescue and medical evacuation to Cagliari depicted in the last two chapters are a fictional dramatization of that event.

Captain John B. Castano had the con and maneuvered the ship with only flank engine orders. Lt. Richard P. Fiske was the rescue swimmer.

On the *Wood*, you could spin the main steam stop valve open or closed with a single finger. She was a great ship, every inch a fighter, and her crew never gave up.

That was the deal.

The End

To My Readers

Thank you for reading *The Marathon Watch*. I hope you enjoyed it and will recommend it to your friends. As a self-published author, it is tough going up against the big publishing houses. Independent authors, like myself, must rely on reviews to spread the word about our books. I would be grateful if you would take a few minutes and leave a review on Amazon or another book site of your choice. Click here to leave a review on Amazon.

Don't be afraid to write me because I enjoy meeting my readers and sharing ideas. You can also stay in touch with me on Facebook, Twitter, and LinkedIn or go to my website, LarryLaswell.com. I have four novels in the pipeline, and the easiest way to learn about my new novels is to subscribe to my mailing list or RSS feed on my blog. I always run prerelease specials that only my fans know about.

Now that you've finished *The Marathon Watch*, you may enjoy the first installment of humorous series titled *A Ship-Load of Sea Stories & 1 Fairy Tale*. Just turn the page to read an excerpt.

Watch for the next book in the Marathon Series, *Vow to the Fallen* due out in August of 2015.

Thank you again, and good reading.

Larry Laswell

I enjoy interaction with my fans so don't hesitate to contact me.
Website: http://LarryLaswell.com
Facebook: http://bit.ly/larryfacebook
Twitter: @larrylaswell
LinkedIn: http://bit.ly/LarryLinkedIn
Amazon: http://bit.ly/LarryAnazon
Mailing List Sign-up: http://bit.ly/LarrysEmailPage

I always gives his fans a special deal on new books, so sign-up here for email notifications.

Seaman Recruit Cockroach

Excerpted from A Ship-Load of Sea Stories & 1 Fairy Tale by Larry Laswell.

Anyone who has been aboard a ship at sea knows the navy runs on coffee. But that is only partly true because if the navy ran out of paper, I believe ships would be stranded at sea, and the bureaucracy would grind to a halt. In boot camp, paperwork became the bane of my existence until I realized if you fed the paper monster the right paperwork, good things would happen.

Boot camp had its trials and tribulations, but overall, I got off light. When my company was formed, I was appointed the company yeoman and given a new name, Yo Yo. This excused me from some manual labor, but to compensate I had to spend long hours filling out sick chits, rosters, and other paperwork in triplicate. There was always more paperwork, and it always had to be in triplicate.

Sick chits were for men who needed to go to the sick bay. They are similar to hall passes that gave individuals permission to travel to and from sick bay. Company rosters listing the status of all company personnel and their location had to be typed daily. Each morning at formation, it was my duty to present the roster to the inspecting officer.

On the morning of the Charlie Cockroach incident, my company had formed to await inspection. Three men going to sick bay stood to the side with their required ditty bags and sick chits. A ditty bag is a small muslin bag filled with toilet articles and a change of skivvies. As usual, I presented my roster and informed the inspecting officer the barracks were ready for inspection.

After inspection, the inspecting officer approached me. "Yo Yo, you have some problems. We found a dead cockroach in the shower. We see no cockroach listed on your company roster. The cockroach was out of uniform and needed a shave. Being dead, he was obviously sick, but we found neither a sick chit for him nor his ditty bag. Furthermore, said cockroach was not in formation but in the barracks at the time of inspection, which is against regulations. Finally, you reported the barracks was ready for inspection, and it wasn't. That's a total of nine infractions, which is unacceptable. What do you have to say for yourself?"

Things couldn't get much worse. Bravery was needed to stare down this enemy. "Sir, there are no cockroaches assigned to our company."

"Are you saying your company security is so lax anyone can just wander into your shower room?" the officer asked.

Things had just gotten worse.

"No, sir."

"Then what are you saying?"

I had forgotten about the mutually exclusive relationship between the navy and logic. It occurred to me we were being framed, which was illogical, but this was the navy, which made it perfectly logical. With total disregard for the lessons already learned, I lawyered up. Why I did this remains a mystery to this day.

"May I have the body of the deceased?" I asked.

"Why?"

"Uh . . . for identification," I said.

"No, you may not. He escaped custody and is now AWOL."

"But you said he was dead."

"I didn't say that," he said.

"Yes, you did."

"Are you calling me a liar?"

"No, sir. I must have misunderstood. I will submit a correct roster tomorrow."

That day the entire company searched for hours trying to find a cockroach, any cockroach. Late that night, we found one, gently killed it, created a ditty bag for it, and scotch tapped its corpse to the front of the ditty bag. I then added Seaman Recruit Charley Cockroach to the company roster. Each morning thereafter, I made out a sick chit for Charley and placed him, his ditty bag, and sick chit next to the side of the formation.

About two weeks later, a guy named Squirrel went over the fence. An extensive amount of paperwork was required to report a missing man, and I listed him on the company roster as being AWOL. For three days, nothing happened. On the fourth day, I received official instructions, in triplicate, to drop Squirrel from the company roster. That was good—one less line to type on the roster. The man had disappeared, the paperwork was in order, and the paper monster was happy.

A week later, Charley went AWOL. I duly completed the paperwork in triplicate and changed Charley's status. True to form, four days later I received official instructions to drop Charley from the company roster. The paper monster was happy, and Charley was never heard from again.

Fed properly, the paper monster can be your friend.

ABOUT THE AUTHOR

Larry Laswell served in the US Navy for eight years. In navy parlance, he was a mustang, someone who rose from the enlisted ranks to receive an officer's commission. While enlisted, he was assigned to the USS John Marshall SSBN-611 (Gold Crew). After earning his commission, he served as main engines officer aboard the USS Intrepid CV-11. His last assignment was as a submarine warfare officer aboard the USS William M. Wood DD-715 while she was home ported in Elefsis, Greece.

In addition to writing, Larry, a retired CEO, fills his spare time with woodworking and furniture design. He continues to work on The Marathon Watch series, an upcoming science fiction series titled The Ethosians, and an anthology of over eighty humorous sea stories titled A Ship-load of Sea Stories & 1 Fairy Tale.

The next Marathon novel, *Vows to the Fallen* will be released in August of 2015.

Larry enjoys interaction with his fans so don't hesitate to contact him.

Website:	http://LarryLaswell.com
Facebook:	http://bit.ly/larryfacebook
Twitter:	@larrylaswell
LinkedIn:	http://bit.ly/LarryLinkedIn
Amazon:	http://bit.ly/LarryOnAmazon
Email Sign-up:	http://bit.ly/LarrysEmailPage

Larry always gives his fans a special deal on new books, so sign-up here for email notifications.

LEADERSHIP DISCUSSION GUIDE

1. In the chapter titled "Straits of Messina," Meyers, the executive officer, intercedes and commits an act of mutiny.
   a. Was his action justified, and why?
   b. Meyers and the captain had a professional difference of opinion about maneuvering the ship, yet Meyers usurped the captain's authority and acted on his opinion. What principles should someone use to determine what action to take when:
      i. Neither individual can be absolutely certain of the outcome of their intended action?
      ii. It requires disobeying an order?
2. In the chapter "Bastards," what did you learn about the leadership aboard the *Farnley*?
3. In the chapter "New Men," after Mr. Lee's initial tour of the engine and boiler rooms, what leadership traits did Mr. Lee display?
   a. How did Mr. Lee set the tone for his relationship with Ross?
      i. Did Mr. Lee act too early?
      ii. What do you think led Mr. Lee to take action?
      iii. After the tour, what do you think Mr. Lee's assessment was of Ross, and how did he arrive at that assessment?
      iv. From Mr. Lee's perspective, what were the key leadership issues he could positively identify?
      v. What information might have been missing that could have altered Mr. Lee's assessment?
4. Name the leadership errors in Ross's behaviors, words, and actions at the time of Mr. Lee's arrival?

5. How would you describe the relationship between Mr. Lee and Ross up until the time of the collision? What leadership behaviors did Mr. Lee exhibit, and why?
6. Name the leadership traits shown in the opening scene of "Operation Steel Henge"?
7. List the negative leadership behaviors and thoughts of Admiral Eickhoff, and explain why they are wrong.
8. After the collision, what core leadership value triggered Mr. Lee's reaction?
9. Did Mr. Lee murder Elmo, or was it an accident?
   a. If you believe Mr. Lee murdered Elmo, what was his primary motivation for doing so?
   b. If you think it was an accident,
10. What was Elmo's funeral really about?
11. Was Mr. Lee justified in ordering Ross to make parts? If so, why?
12. What led up to Meyers' final decision to take action on Javert?
   a. How did he resolve the dilemma between honor and duty? Which one won?
   b. What is the most important leadership behavior, or belief in Meyers' decision to take action on Javert?
13. After the collision, how would you describe Lee's leadership style? What positive things did he do, and what other things could he have done?
14. What leadership traits did Chief Barnes exhibit, and why were they important to Ross?
15. What key leadership behaviors did Ross exhibit between the collision and the man overboard?
   a. How do they show his growth?
   b. Was Ross justified in misappropriating the maple syrup?
16. When Admiral Eickhoff ordered Meyers to remove the unauthorized parts:
   a. How did Meyers handle it?
   b. Was he justified in handling it that way?
   c. Was Ross's response justified?
   d. For both Ross and Meyers, what do their actions tell us about leadership?

17. When the man went overboard:
    a. How did Meyers save Biron the conning officer? What does that tell us about his leadership style?
    b. Was Meyers justified in risking the ship to save the man overboard?
        i. If so, why and on what grounds?
        ii. How does this relate to leadership, and is it important?
        iii. What would have been the consequences if they had left the man to drown?
    c. From your sense of the novel, why did the crew willingly work to rescue the man overboard? Where did this come from, and what does it tell us about our innate sense of leadership and duty?
18. How was Captain O'Toole a leader, a teacher, and a hard ass?
    a. Are these three things related?
    b. What tools did he use to lead?
    c. What was the basic foundation for everything O'Toole did in his role as a leader?
    d. Why was O'Toole's leadership foundation so critical and what other leadership traits flowed from that?
    e. Why was Captain Flannery so elated when O'Toole said his ship was adequate?
        i. What made that so special?
        ii. How did O'Toole make is special?
19. Why did O'Toole make the Farnley his flagship?
20. How would you assess Admiral Durham's Leadership, and why?
21. What part did the following play in the leadership shown in *The Marathon Watch*?
    a. Duty
    b. Honor
    c. Loyalty
    d. Tradition
22. Review your answers to question 21, and explain their leadership implications.

Made in the USA
San Bernardino, CA
11 May 2015